TRIASSIC

BY
JULIAN MICHAEL CARVER

SEVERED PRESS
HOBART TASMANIA

TRIASSIC

Copyright © 2020 Julian Michael Carver
Copyright © 2020 by Severed Press

WWW.SEVEREDPRESS.COM

ISBN: 978-1-922323-58-3

To my beautiful wife, Cloey.
Thank you for supporting all of my writing endeavors and my love
of creature science fiction and horror stories.

PROLOGUE

3271 A.D.

At first, there was only darkness.

Then, in the quiet corners of the universe, an orange light slowly emerged from the distance. The rays bounced off rocky malformations and planetary debris as the first ship appeared. Behind the flagship, other cruisers began to materialize, fading slowly into focus against the dark backdrop of space.

White and orange-colored armor plating lined the exterior of the star ships, protecting important communication junctions and fuel ejectors. Beams of tungsten light shot out from their beveled fronts, illuminating the uneasy journey ahead.

The carriers were Federation transport vessels, having fled from Earth to find a new sustainable planet to colonize. On board the ships were among the last survivors of the human race. Earth had become completely unlivable and polluted in recent years. If the toxic air wasn't enough, strikes from nuclear bombs had caused the Earth's tectonic plates to break asunder, threatening to rip apart the planet's core.

The nuclear engagements of the past had been consolidated into one historical period, now known simply as the Old War. It was a tumultuous conflict hundreds of years ago that brought the world's superpowers of America, Russia, and China to utter destruction. With the annihilation of the greater countries, the ripple effect proved catastrophic for the smaller regions of the world. One by one, the governments and regimes toppled like dominoes, sending civilizations into turmoil. The economies and stock markets collapsed, and the value of money disappeared – and with it, the civility of humankind.

After years of violent rioting, rapes and murders by bands of rogue armies, a small fraction of like-minded people came together underground in secrecy. Unbeknownst to the barbaric clans that pillaged on the surface, they devised a plan to escape the imminent death of the world.

Thus, the initiative known as the Federation had formed.

It was primarily a fail-safe plan with the sole purpose of getting away from Earth's pending destruction. In the earlier days, when the Federation was in its infancy, most of the staff involved were scientists and idealists. As time went on and Earth's dilapidated condition grew steadily worse, additional help was needed to expedite the departure process. Existing robots, or simply *bots,* were modified and recycled to take on additional tedious tasks, like transportation, construction, and computer maintenance of the starships. To make sure the raiding armies didn't interfere with the development of the vessels, an infantry was also formed, officially dubbed the "Federation Infantry." Soldiers were trained in various combat skills, like hand-to-hand fighting and proper usage of pulse weaponry, which was still a recent innovation at the time.

Over the years, the number of volunteers grew and grew, and more ships were created to accommodate the number of workers. When the fleet would depart, the entire work force would be going along with it. The Federation adopted a "leave-no-man-behind" mentality. When the departure date was announced, everyone in the organization was guaranteed a spot on-board.

Finally, after two generations and a hundred and fifty years of hard work and sweat equity, the development of the Federation starships was complete. After rigorous security testing, all systems were a go, and the vessels shot off out into space, leaving the gray wasteland shrinking behind them.

That departure happened three years ago.

Resources wouldn't hold out much longer. They had to find a safe haven – and quickly.

At the head of the convoy, the *Star Jumper* flagship opened the lower cargo hatch and deployed an unmanned scout ship to move ahead to survey the unknown terrain.

A few hours earlier, the fleet had stumbled into a dense asteroid belt, deep in a dark pocket of space. It had been a slow and dangerous journey through the obstacles, and the personnel on board *Star Jumper* were cautious about what may have caused it. Normally at this distance in the universe, asteroid fields usually gravitated towards a common concentric force. They couldn't help but wonder…

What was that force?

Any one of the spinning rocks could permanently cripple the starships. They had already lost ten carriers on their voyage away from Earth, which had rapidly depleted their resources. One of the doomed ships, *Infinite Eon*, had been carrying a good amount of food supplies, which were now floating somewhere in the unknown cosmos.

In the command bridge of *Star Jumper*, the tired skeleton crew struggled to adequately map out a safe trajectory through the danger zone. Their vision could only extend so far through the observation deck. The rocks were so dense and large, that the pilots had to be on constant alert as they guided the ship along.

As the personnel looked through the glass, the slender Federation T50 surveillance craft streaked past the bridge and glided by the approaching space rocks. With a mechanical accuracy, the drone folded out a pair of sleek outer wings and shot into the dark. In the wake, a bright golden contrail fizzled away as the T50's thrusters vanished gracefully around a boulder.

Admiral Steven Perry looked out on the treacherous course, puffing uneasily on his cigar.

Something doesn't seem quite right, he thought.

He was having that bad feeling again.

He hated feeling this way. A tall, older gentleman with a muscular build, Perry was a common sight in *Star Jumper's* gym, constantly trying to keep up his fitness and health, even now in his older years. Among his crew, he was treated with reverence and respect. No one questioned—or dared to second guess—his authority. Nine times out of ten, his quick thinking and direction saved lives.

"Display the feed from the scout ship," Perry said, blowing an impressive smoke ring.

"Aye, sir," said a young, male voice from a terminal station.

A glitching orange-tinted hologram display from the T50 began flickering over the bridge, hovering just above the computer workstations and bleeping network towers. The feed had produced nothing notable; several large rocks and some metal debris left over from previous ships that splintered apart long ago. The Federation fleet had maneuvered through dozens of similar cluttered regions just like this one. It was nothing that they hadn't seen before.

But even in the confidence of his crew's capabilities, the admiral felt uneasy.

Perry couldn't help but ponder the origin of the asteroid build up.

Maybe some type of star implosion, the admiral thought to himself. *This field seems larger than previous ones we've passed through...*

He huffed out another smoke ring.

We should have been through by now...

He twirled and fiddled with the top of his head hair. It was a bad habit that Perry picked up during his childhood, and he couldn't shake it when he was stressed. It also served as an unfortunate reminder that, in his years away in space, he was starting to go gray.

"Nothing. Nothing at all... Switch off the feed."

"Aye, sir."

As the hologram began to dim, something in the center of the digital projection caught Perry's eye. Or rather, the lack of something.

The lack of stars, he thought.

"Wait, switch it back on! Upscale camera four to the forefront, please. As big as you can make it!"

"Aye, sir."

The hologram brightened back to life. The bottom right screen, labeled "Front View," was selected and quickly consumed the frame, forcing the other cameras to minimize along the bottom. As the T50 scout ship flew on ahead, the feed caught a hidden danger waiting just ahead of *Star Jumper's* flight path.

At first, the object was difficult to make out in the hologram imaging, but it soon consumed the entire frame as the light dissipated around the rippling edges. It was a vortex in space.

A black hole.

A monstrous one!

Several ominous gasps erupted from the bridge. Below, Perry saw the petrified faces of the crew as they looked up in fear from behind their glowing operation monitors. Their eyes were burning with fright. Many of the younger faces had turned white like ghosts.

No one spoke.

How did we miss this?

Black holes were often the end of starships and could swallow entire fleets with ease. During their trek, they had been fortunate enough not to encounter one – until now.

Perry cast his cigar onto the metal catwalk below and hurriedly stamped out the embers.

I'll light another one if we survive this, he promised himself.

"Contact the other cruisers! They'll need to turn hard! Tell them – hard right turns! Or left. Left's fine too – I don't care! Just tell them to use the evasive maneuver! Damn, it's coming up fast!"

Several "Aye, sirs" followed, and the crew on the bridge began relaying communication codes to the other Federation carrier ships.

The twirling black mouth was approaching rapidly.

It was now in plain view, appearing larger through the observation deck windows than it had on the drone's simulated imagery.

The hologram feed from the T50 began glitching as the unmanned drone got lodged in the immortal pull of the death trap. The feed began to convulse violently, and the camera flickered on and off, causing abnormalities to appear within the virtual image. High-pitched, disrupting static blared out of the speakers throughout the room. Any attempts of salvaging the scout ship now would be futile. With a final flash, the feed flicked off as the darkness enveloped the T50 drone, sealing its unknown fate behind the evil, swirling portal. The hologram above went black.

"Switch that shit off!"

"Yes, sir!"

"How long do we have?" Perry could feel his voice faltering with fright.

"About two minutes, sir! Sorry, re-calculating! That's less than two minutes, sir!"

Perry's heart felt as if it would burst through his uniform. He gripped the railing ahead, looking into the eye of the dark tornado that was advancing steadily towards them.

We need to break off – fast!

"Pull up hard!" he yelled.

As the distress calls continued buzzing and chirping around him, Perry shot a look down at the radar screen on his dashboard console. Small ship icons behind *Star Jumper* began to break off from the central convoy, turning hard in various directions. Indicator highlights predicted their paths on the screen, calculating their probability of survival.

Tumultuous alarm bells began to sound off in the room as *Star Jumper* began its vertical climb. Golden emergency lights danced in the corners and cast abstract, taunting shadows along the metal ceiling, adding more chaos and confusion to the dire situation.

Come on, you hunk-of-junk! Faster!

The black hole had grown to fill the majority of the observation deck.

It was directly ahead of the ship, swallowing up asteroids that dared tease the lips of the eager mouth. The flying rocks offered no resistance before spiraling away, forever under the dark veil of the cyclone.

BBRRRRRREEEEEEEP!

A warning indicator noise blared out. One ship began to turn red on Perry's radar scanner.

Lunar Envoy.

It was taking on severe damage.

It became clear to Perry what was happening. The ships were taking hits from the surrounding debris field as they fled in their trajectories from the black hole.

More ship icons on the screen began turning red as they swerved away from the primary path while being mercilessly sucked forward.

Lunar Envoy turned completely red on the monitor, and small damage indicator messages began tracing around the base of the ship's locator icon. As a crimson color filled the vessel's silhouette, a sudden sonic vibration sent shock waves past *Star Jumper*. The bridge tilted violently, and several of the standing crew members were thrown to the floor.

A message quickly began flashing in holographic static above the horrified observation deck.

Lunar Envoy down.

The ship and its crew were dead, scrubbed away in the asteroid field. The pounding continued.

Earth Emissary down.

Dammit!

The screen below looked grim. Perry could see the icons turning completely red as other ships failed to pierce through the dense space storm.

"How long till we're in the mouth?" he asked.

"One minute, sir," said a feeble voice from the back. "Now fifty-five seconds!"

Suddenly, all sorts of ship titles began to populate the overhead screen. They appeared so frequently that most were only visible on screen for a second before they switched to the next. The asteroid belt was eradicating Perry's fleet.

Solar Savior down.

Galactic Hero down.

The black hole was nearly on the bridge. Perry knew he had to act fast.

It's either certain death in there or probable death above in the asteroids...

"Pull up! Faster! All the way!"

"Aye!"

The *Star Jumper* dipped upward, lurching many of the personnel out of their chairs and knocking them back towards the rear wall of the bridge. Those who remained buckled in their seats held onto their workstations as the room dipped sharply upward. Perry buckled himself into his chair at the helm and watched in terror as the blackness approached.

Small space rocks began striking the glass of the observation deck, leaving spiderweb cracks at their points of impact. To his surprise, and to the surprise of the staff, the glass was holding up remarkably well against the rocky pummeling.

The other ships weren't so lucky.

From the corner of his eye, Perry could see the names still populating rapidly on the hologram. He realized that the majority of his fleet was now gone – most of what may be left of humanity.

The pull was growing stronger. *Star Jumper* was nearly vertical.

"Thirty seconds, Admiral!"

"Activate rear thrusters! Full-speed. All the way up! Grab onto something!"

It's now or never...

He prayed for a safe, quick trip through the uncertain asteroid shower.

"Aye!"

The ship launched upward as the objects beyond the glass blurred from debris streaking the bridge. Industrial booming noises followed as more space rocks pelted against the ship. The black hole began to disappear slowly from below the windows. So far, they were avoiding the larger asteroids and colliding with less harmful, tiny ones.

Above, the rocky waves began to thin and the space beyond became suddenly clear.

Thank God. We're gonna make it!

The pull of the portal suddenly dissipated, and *Star Jumper* leveled off just above the debris field.

Perry, leaning forward against the support rail, relaxed.

They were safe.

A thunderous applause filled the bridge as the crew rose to their feet and regained their positions. Amid the cheering, Perry stood up and gave a congratulatory wave to the staff. They returned with grateful salutes. After brief smiles and 'good-jobs', he was back to business.

"All right... Damage reports! Who do we have left?" His firm, authoritative tone returned.

The room grew suddenly quiet.

A solemn, female voice replied.

"Hardly anyone, sir. We have *Comet* and *Wayfarer*. I think *Universe* just pulled through, but she's heavily damaged, according to the systems report I'm getting."

Perry paused.

"Three other ships, besides us... That's all that's left?"

"Aye, sir."

Just three?

"You're telling me there are no Federation ships remaining below the asteroid belt?"

"I'm sorry, sir. There's nothing on the system." A few other voices agreed and confirmed the empty radar scan.

Four ships... Four ships total to save the human race and find a new home...

Perry didn't like those odds.

The admiral frowned and surveyed the observation glass. The damage was obvious but salvageable. Small asteroid fragments remained stuck in the cracks, but graciously did not cause any severe damage that would compromise the bridge.

Perry eased back, lighting up another cigar.

Their fleet had been depleted from twenty ships to four in the short span of several terrifying minutes.

"Okay. Tell the remaining ships to pull up, regroup, and send in damage reports. Get us out of this place! We're still dangerously close to that hole. After we're clear, we'll regroup and figure out what supplies and inventory we've lost..."

And the lives we've lost...

With a sigh, he collapsed back in his chair and began to puff on the cigar.

He knew a pounding headache was about to start.

Dead. They're all dead.

Star Jumper surged forward once again, with *Comet*, *Wayfarer*, and *Universe* following close behind. The fleet passed over the top of the black hole with ease and continued into the emptiness of the space ahead, quickly shrinking into the starry distance.

#

Below the fleet, still remaining in the asteroid belt, one last Federation ship drove slowly towards the black hole.

Supernova – the ship that brought up the rear of the fleet.

During their entry into the asteroid field, a large space rock left a damaging crater on top of the ship's command bridge. The impact did not implode the bridge, but it did strike an unprotected power component on the roof above the observation deck. Interior computers and terminal ports inside the bridge were fried, and the personnel piloting the ship were killed instantly during the resulting electrical blasts. As a result, all the doors to the bridge sealed themselves automatically – a safety protocol in case of an oxygen leak.

Due to the incident, which had occurred almost a half-hour earlier, the *Supernova* had been out of contact with the main fleet during the discovery of the black hole. Despite the damage, the ship had remained on radar screens of the neighboring vessels until recently, as if no accident had occurred.

Outside *Supernova's* command bridge, infantry squads tried desperately to breach the blast doors. There were only a few select soldiers on duty, and most were confused and panicking. The majority of the military units were still stuck in hyper-sleep chambers, which automatically locked after the electrical incident.

No one had heard from *Supernova's* bridge since the impact, leaving the remaining crew to assume the worst had occurred.

Through the hallway windows, soldiers and crew could see the other Federation ships breaking off from the main course.

Something had gone horribly wrong.

Detonators were placed on the security doors, but despite the powerful blasts, the panels remained closed and intact, keeping the bridge entombed behind them. As a squad of soldiers sent out to find one of the bots that could open the doors and free the remaining colonists trapped in sleeper pods, a darkness fell over the windows of the hallway.

Orange emergency lights clicked on as the primary lighting grid deactivated.

The ship moved slowly on as a wispy whirlwind of black surrounded the front exterior, swallowing the ship's bridge. As the remaining vessels of the fleet disappeared above the asteroid belt, the forgotten *Supernova* passed through the black hole, guided by the remnants of the other Federation ships that collapsed only moments before.

The lights in the hallway came back to life, but reverted to darkness a moment later.

The squad of soldiers besieging the bridge doors could see nothing. Seconds passed in silent horror, and the ship was lost forever behind the black hole.

I

I'm alive.

In the quiet ruins of the *Supernova*, a sleeper pod battery pack flicked off after centuries of operation, finally succumbing to the exotic world that consumed the hull.

The protective glass of the sleeper pod had fogged over. The outer edges of the compartment were caked with a filthy green substance where the window met with the metal chamber base. Above, the battery status indicators were off – the capsule life support systems had failed. Behind the windshield, the hallway was hidden by a thick layer of soot and fungal spores.

Where the hell is everyone? Corporal Severine Solens thought as she fought off the grogginess of prolonged hyper-sleep. The failure of the battery forced the air circulation to cease, waking her from the artificial coma. The remaining oxygen would only last so long. She had to get out – fast.

The pod doors, sitting on a layer of mossy buildup that hugged the hall floor, struggled to open. Using her feet, Severine finally nudged the hatch open. She was amazed by the lush scene outside.

Jungle had spread throughout most of the ship's interior. Weeds popped up through the floor at regular intervals where the marble tile had withered away. Rays of dim sunlight spilled through the hull above where the ceiling had caved in, revealing an array of plant life hugging the once spotless passageway. There was no artificial lighting or static voice from Central Command or *Star Jumper* bellowing down from the loud speakers.

All was quiet and still.

Severine struggled to get her safety harness off. Her body was numb and rigid from lying still for so long. After saying a thankful prayer that the oxygen respirator battery had lasted as long as it did, she managed to unlatch the harness mechanism by her waist and shoulders.

Gravity took care of the rest.

Oh!

She wasn't prepared for the ship's crooked position.

As her belt came loose, Severine fell forward out of the chamber and threw her hands up to brace her fall. As she landed on the warm ground several feet below, she realized that everything was slanted, as if the ship was lying diagonal on a seesaw.

She looked down. Through the blotches of mold that latched onto the floor, she could make out her appearance on the reflective tile fragments. Severine smiled, realizing she had hardly aged at all.

Well, there's a shred of good news!

As she struggled to gain her footing by using her hyper-sleep pod door for leverage, she shot a glance down the silent passageway.

Many of the other sleeper chambers were damaged or in ruin. Glass shards from the pod windows were scattered on the ground, hidden in shrubs. The skeletal remains of other Federation members stood frozen in time, trapped in their harnesses. Hideous sinister teeth greeted her with crooked smiles. Their clothes were tattered and stunk of rotten plant matter. A few of the occupants looked mangled and were missing limbs. Severine guessed that animals might have gotten to them. Many of the pods had small trees sprouting through the interior. Several of the others were ajar, revealing no occupants inside.

Maybe there were other survivors?

She stretched out, trying to loosen her limbs. Her body yearned for nourishment.

As her vision focused and she could begin to see more clearly, Severine stepped clumsily down the passage and continued leaning on the pod shells for support. Orange Federation emblems painted on the wall were covered in a green film, obscured by vines. Several other images were there too: ship layout plans, announcement boards, and directions to the nearest stairwell or elevator bays. Cobwebs wrapped the edges of the hallway where the walls met the ceiling. Many overhead lights were broken or missing. She dared not to disturb the wires that hung freely from above. If the pods still had some juice left, so could the cables and exposed circuitry.

What happened to the Supernova?

How long have I been here?

Where is everyone?

Severine rubbed her forehead, fighting off a tiring headache. She struggled to remember her life before entering her sleeper pod, but she could only piece together certain elements, like the names of some of her comrades, brief flashes of life back on Earth, and Federation Infantry combat tactics. Years locked in hyper-sleep could be detrimental to one's mental state, causing severe memory lapses and increased fatigue. Severine knew she was experiencing all the symptoms first-hand.

SSHEEEEEEEEEAAA!!!

A hissing noise interrupted her weary thoughts.

Hyper-sleep pod doors!

She spun around.

Another sleeper chamber opened from a bend down the hall, spilling a male crew member out onto the moss-cushioned surface.

The batteries for his pod were probably charged at the same time as mine...

The man braced himself as his palms absorbed the fall.

He's alive! Thank God!

In the fading light from his capsule above, she could tell by his shoulder insignia that he was an officer from the 9th Division, who looked to be in his early forties. The amber shield crest on his collar indicated he was a lieutenant. In her clouded mental state, Severine was surprised she recognized him.

Julius was his name, or Jordan – something of the sort. He was hailed for his excellent marksmanship with a pulse rifle. She remembered seeing him in the mess hall last week – if it was last week. It might as well have been a hundred years ago since the *Supernova* had been in orbit. Thankfully, she knew she wasn't alone anymore. It was great to see a familiar face.

Julius... Julius Lexand! Yes! That's definitely his name...

"Julius?" she asked. "Is that you?"

The man turned wearily over to her, before turning to cough at the ground.

"Yeah. It's Julius. And you're...Severine? Corporal Severine Solens." He coughed harshly, patting his chest.

Severine nodded as Julius rose to his feet, using the door of his chamber for support. He was a tall, muscular man, dressed in a white sleeper suit, which was regulation for all Federation units who entered hyper-sleep. The garb was spotless and unstained, decorated with many achievement medals and certifications. He stood out against the contrast of the archaic room.

"Jeez. What the hell happened here, Solens?"

"Crash, by the looks of it," Severine replied, trying not to make it sound so obvious. "Who knows how long ago, but by the looks of the crew, we've been here a long time. Maybe a hundred years. Maybe more."

The words seemed strange to say.

"Damn. Let's check all these chambers. Maybe we can save another life!"

The two scanned the hallway, walking carefully to avoid the glass shards. Debris and fragments lined the edges. Behind the glass, they found only zombified cadavers sealed inside their metal tombs for hundreds of years. The interior lights of the capsules were completely off, save for a few that flickered randomly.

Their oxygen supply probably cut off, she thought.

The pair reached the end of the pod bay and found no trace of living personnel.

"What could have happened?" Severine asked. "Surely there must be others? They must be looking for us!"

The officer shook his head firmly.

"The search would have ended a long time ago," Julius replied. "We've been written off as dead. I'd be surprised if anyone knows we're here."

"Do you remember anything?" she asked. "Anything at all?"

The lieutenant shook his head. "I was in hyper-sleep when it all went down."

"Why didn't the bots open our pods?"

"Could be that most of the crew, including the bots, died during the impact. Who knows... Hey, open that hatch there!"

Severine turned around.

Behind her was a small panel on the wall with a Federation skull symbol painted on the exterior. She heaved down the lever, jolting open the compartment. Wisps of pressurized air seeped out, revealing an XR-90 pulse rife and an X2-20 pulse pistol planted firmly inside their original support braces. These firearms were stashed regularly throughout the ship in case of mutiny or a problem with the armory.

The weapons were clean and unused.

"We better grab them! Which one do you want?"

Severine handed Julius the XR-90. The gun felt awkward under her tired palms.

"I'm not very good with that thing. They're too clunky! I'll take the 20!" Severine picked up the pulse pistol, examined it, and held it up confidently.

"Good choice. I like the 90 myself. I hope these still work..."

"They do! Look." Severine pointed to the bottom of her pistol. A small orange light blinked slowly at the base of the grip. The weapon chamber had preserved the battery life and, more importantly, the energy of the pulse rounds.

"So, what's our first move?"

"We should go to the command bridge," Julius replied. "See if it's still intact. From there, we can send a distress rescue call, provided that the bridge is at least partially operational. I'm not too optimistic on that... There should be an emergency signal emitter there. Hopefully Central Command gets a hold of us and gets our asses out of here – wherever *here* is."

Severine nodded, letting Julius assume the lead.

As they left the sleeping chamber crypt, the terrain inside the walkways became increasingly untamed and tropical. Wide leaves dropped down from gashes in the bulkhead, forcing the sunlight to cast green translucent shadows along the floors. There was a layer of murky liquid under their feet. A thin stream of water seeped steadily out from one of the overhead vents, emptying into a puddle as it ran down the wall.

Severine deduced that the ship wreckage might be resting on a marshy bog or rained out region of the forest. By the glow of her pistol utility light, she could spy small, strange fish swimming between the pools in little, watery inlets. At their approach, they scattered into burrows that were etched out long ago in the ship's walls. Outside, she could hear the cries of animals far away, howling under the cover of the wet canopy. Severine thought they sounded like primates.

I just hope they're friendly.

Julius turned. "Let's stop in here," he said, casting his rifle light over an entrance concealed behind some vines.

When it failed to open, he kicked powerfully into the middle, sending the door tumbling down with a powerful echo.

It was a locker room.

In the center, a small tree had started to grow, dropping rotten fruit onto the floor. The thought had crossed her mind to eat one of the fruits, but her opinion changed after she caught a whiff of their pungent aroma.

"Ahhhhh!" she cried, covering her nose.

The toxic smell knocked her back, making Julius chuckle.

Surely poisonous.

One by one, they rummaged through the lockers, finding mostly useless junk. They quickly recovered two infantry armor suits and threw them on over their sleeping garbs. Severine remembered how heavy they seemed as the gear closed in around her. The suits were mainly gray, with orange trim around the shoulders, belt, knees, and feet. As she latched the suit around her, a subtle light shined out from the golden belt clasp, indicating that the suits were drawing power from somewhere inside the *Supernova.*

This place must still have some juice left...

A sharp rusty clang rang out behind them.

Shit! She turned quickly.

Julius turned and aimed the 90 at the direction of the sound. In the corner of the room, a set of lockers sat horizontal over the ground. Suddenly, the unit began to shake and cling together. The hollow noise continued to ring when the corner of the lockers rattled against the floor.

Something was moving underneath, fighting hard to free itself from the trap.

Severine looked down the sights of her X2-20, anticipating an animal to lurch out and strike them, but lowered the weapon when a familiar series of bleeps came out from the rubble.

It was a Federation bot, no doubt.

The poor thing is stuck!

The pair rushed over, lifting the lockers off the trapped machine.

The robot was a small unit from the logistics department, as identified by the golden hypercube logo on the bot's shoulder plate. The outer body plating remained dented and bruised from the weight of the lockers. One of his eye sockets had a thin layer of muck on the rim. By the looks of the robot, he had been there for many years, and had probably been temporarily deactivated when the rubble trapped it during the crash. However, the shelter provided by the lockers led to the machine's remarkable preservation.

"How is he still working?" Julius asked.

"This little guy must have gotten stuck when the ship went down. When we came in and started rooting around, maybe something in the room shifted, causing his sensors to jump back to life. What's your name, little fella?"

The machine tilted its cube-like head in Severine's direction.

"JDY-093. Codename: Jordy." His voice sounded happy and appreciative.

He sure is a cute little thing!

Severine wiped off the dust from the shoulder plates. Jordy's golden LED eyes brightened the room. For the most part, he seemed very well-intact. The bots from logistics were usually built less sturdily than those from the infantry – this one was lucky.

Logistics bots such as Jordy were responsible for the overall upkeep and organization of Federation vessels. They maintained storage rooms, kept inventory in the culinary pantries, knew where to store the food properly, and even performed janitorial services when necessary. Unique from the other bots, the logistics department was known for creating units with humor and greater personality. They had the best computer-learning capabilities of the Federation. Their only drawbacks – flimsy external plating and a fragile battery compartment.

"Jordy?"

"Yes, Corporal?"

"Jordy, how long has your internal computer been deactivated for? Can you tell us?"

The robot flickered his eyes. He began searching his computer for answers. "Last logged data entry was January 27, 3271 A.D. My current date reads June 05, 3542 A.D."

"Thank you, Jordy."

No wonder the ship looks like shit!

"We've been down here for almost three hundred years," Julius said, lowering his rifle in anguish. He slumped back against a set of lockers and looked up at the tree. The sunlight from the hole above cast a glow across his solemn face. He hadn't taken the news well.

"I'm sorry. This message must come as quite a shock." The robot's voice sounded muted, probably from years of plant growth inside his interior parts. As he rose to his feet, Jordy fumbled slightly, before gripping Severine's shoulder to regain balance. "These feet aren't what they used to be!"

"Can you tell us if there's anyone else alive on the ship?"

The bot's lights dimmed as his computer processed her question. "My data tells me that no Federation suit signals remain nearby, but my sensors are only good for a hundred feet at the most. We should head for the bridge and see what we find."

"Right. Julius?"

"Yeah. Let's go," the lieutenant muttered, still processing the heavy news.

He must be in shock...

They exited the locker room and continued down the crumbling corridor. Jordy led the way, using his eyes to light up the halls. His metal legs clinked and quivered as if held together by loose screws. Severine could see small lichens sprouting on his back. The time spent in squalor had taken a toll on the robot.

A good twenty minutes passed before the machine spoke again.

"Here we are," Jordy's digital voice announced.

In front of the trio were a pair of large blast doors that remained sealed. The doors themselves had the same green hue as the rest of the ship, which told Severine that they probably hadn't been opened since the crash, three hundred years earlier. Around the sides, dozens of black streaks violently shot out in all directions, causing minor indentations. To Severine, they looked like blast mark impressions. The smears painted a picture of the ship's frantic last minutes in space.

They tried to use detonators to blow them open, and it didn't work...

Two large F logos stared back at them on each door, under the marred bomb impressions, the Federation fleet symbol.

"Any chance you can open them?" Severine asked.

"Let me see..." Jordy walked over to the control panel near the wall. The cover tilted and fell off as the bot attempted to hack into the pad. After he fumbled with the wiring, to their surprise, a few sparks popped out.

"The detonators thankfully didn't harm the access panel. Here we go! This should do it!" Jordy exclaimed.

A faint *hummmmm* started behind the wall.

The doors lurched apart in opposite directions but stopped in their tracks with an abrupt jolt after opening only a few inches.

"Maybe we can pry them the rest of the way. Good job, Jordy!"

"Thank you, Corporal." The robot's eyes blinked with gratitude.

Severine and Julius approached the doors and grabbed hold of the edges through the gap, forcing them open. They were heavy and cold – electric power had long since stopped flowing. It took all their strength to push the panels open the rest of the way.

So heavy! Severine could feel herself starting to sweat.

As they slid back into the walls, large desks and computer hardware fell through, landing in the hallway. Severine and Julius jumped as the parts crashed onto the hall floor and broke apart.

"What's all this?"

"A barrier," Julius replied. "Someone tried to barricade the doors shut..."

They tried to seal us in?

Jordy stepped inside the entrance, leading the way with his glowing eyes.

The command bridge was in utter ruin and had undergone a tremendous greenhouse effect. The glass windows of the observation deck had shattered, giving way to the rainforest behind them. Most of the terminals were in pieces and disconnected, covered in animal fecal matter that left a terrible stench in the room.

That's horrendous! Severine covered her nose.

She started to explore the rubble, looking for anything that they could salvage for supplies. She turned white as she came around one of the moldy terminal desks.

A lonely skeleton lay slumped against one of the mossy support beams. The skull was nearly split in half. The once pristine crew uniform had been torn apart, with the remnants scattered below the waist. Feet away from the cadaver's right hand was another X2-20 pistol. The gun was dirty and cracked, and the light was off on the grip.

Damn! It's out.

From the other side of the room, she could hear Julius cursing at the lack of working equipment. Nothing was salvageable. He cursed silently to himself. "Well, I guess that's the end of our call-for-help plan," Julius said. "Did you find anything over there? Anything we can use?"

She shook her head.

"Nothing over here! I'll keep checking..."

They continued rooting through the debris, looking inside desk drawers and under dusty tables. Most of what they found served no purpose: old Federation telecom links, several articles of torn clothing, rusty keyboards, and faulty equipment that hadn't seen the light of day for many lifetimes.

Junk! All of it.

Severine frowned. "That's a no, Lieutenant."

"Well, no reason to sugar-coat this. We're pretty much screwed here." Julius set his rifle down and stood behind a terminal desk, hoping to see the orange Federation symbol fade onto the monitor. He tried to enter his code into the computer, but the screen remained lifeless and black. The bridge was non-operational.

"Jordy, any chance you can start one of these?" he asked.

"Negative, Lieutenant. These machines are down for good. This room wasn't as well-preserved from the elements as our quadrant was. Frankly, I'd consider us lucky to be alive!"

WHRRRR! WHRRRRR!

As the bot spoke, a bright red light flashed on and off from his chest plate and emitted a series of high frequency beeps. Jordy fell backwards over one of the chairs, frightened by the body speakers. As he got up, he deactivated the whine and looked onward past the glass fragments of the observation deck to the mysterious forest that lay just beyond the ship frame.

"Jordy! What was that?"

"My radar, sir! Lifeforms nearby!"

"Lifeforms?"

"Yes, sir! Non-human! And they're approaching rapidly!"

II

"Lifeforms? Are they Federation units?"

"No, Corporal. I don't detect any Federation personnel or robotic signals nearby. These frequencies are something different – they don't match anything logged in my database."

A faint noise began to rustle among the trees of the forest that engulfed the front of the command bridge. It sounded like the scampering of a group of small animals. The sounds tore quickly through the undergrowth, signaling their imminent approach towards the colonists.

Whatever they are – they're fast!

"Safety off, Corporal. We don't know what's about to pop through! I'll fire first if they're hostile. Conserve your ammunition." It made sense. Julius had ninety shots in his rifle – her pistol only had twenty.

Severine nodded, taking cover behind a damaged terminal station. Julius stepped forward and maintained his defense behind the desk, aiming his 90 ahead at the knotted tree trunks. Jordy deactivated his lights and crouched down next to the lieutenant, cradling his head between his arms in a sort of odd fetal position, as if preparing for a chaotic firefight.

Typical logistics bot! Severine laughed as she flicked the safety off on her pistol. *Whatever's about to pop through, they had better fall back! Our pulse blasts will rip them apart! If the impact doesn't end them, the ricochet will!*

The scurrying noise grew louder. Whatever it was rustled up leaves and earth in its wake.

A reptilian call emerged from the thicket, echoing through the bridge. Before too long, the ferns and shrubs began to shake. At first, only a few plants moved, but soon many were dancing wildly just beyond the bridge. Suddenly the plant thrashing stopped and the jungle was calm again.

What are they?!

"Steady, soldier," Julius said. "Wait! Here they come!"

After a moment of silence, a small bipedal animal popped out of the greenery, landing on the overgrown floor of the observation deck. It arrived just yards away from Julius' position, searching the ruins with a graceful move of the head.

"Sev...you seein' this?"

"Yeah, what is it?"

"A lizard, I think..."

The creature contorted its long neck to a funny, upward angle, facing the degraded ceiling. With a funny gurgling of the throat, it let out a heavy reverberating growl.

Severine couldn't believe her eyes. The lizard was remarkable.

The animal bounced forward with dainty buoyancy. It was a small, green reptile with a skinny snout and a long tail that waved about wildly. Yellow, abstract splotches ran down the back of its neck and gradually faded away along the tail. The sharp, black claws on the creature's feet rasped against the cold floor, causing Severine to squint at the horrible screeching.

Ugly, guttural cries yelled out from the lizard's throat that sounded comparable to a whining cat. Through the foggy air, Severine could see the black eyes looking for something as the reptile sniffed curiously. The green nostrils shrank and expanded rapidly as it searched for a scent.

It was hungry.

Judging by the claws, the thing has to be carnivorous!

Thankfully, it hadn't spotted them – yet.

"Hold your fire. What do you make of it? I've never seen anything like it." His voice was low, as if not to disturb the green visitor as it continued its advance through the bridge.

"Me either. It's unlike anything the Federation had stowed away in the animal departments."

"The Federation had nothing like this," Julius confirmed. "Of that, I'm sure."

The reptile lurched forward, distracted by an insect that buzzed through the warm air. During the ferocious attack, Severine noticed rows of razor-sharp, killing teeth between the chomps. After a few short bites, it caught the bug. With a gulp, the insect was gone, perishing behind the scaly neck.

"The thing's gotta be four feet long," Julius said. "Clearly some kind of carnivore."

Definitely – and very intelligent.

"Sort of reminds me of a dinosaur," Severine said.

"That's funny, Corporal," Julius laughed. "It does look like one. Certainly something in the reptile family."

But dinosaurs were extinct. The fossils they left behind had spawned awe and wonder for centuries, but no living specimens were ever seen by humans back on Earth, despite several ghost stories and superstitious urban legends. This had to be something else.

Maybe some kind of rare, mutated lizard?

The creature started to cautiously approach Julius' position. The sunlight bathed down on the reptile, which led Severine to assume that its vision was partially blinded – an event that kept the colonists' positions concealed.

It landed with a primordial shriek on an old Federation counter, forcing the table legs to wobble uneasily upon impact. The creature seemed weightless, but landed with forceful strength. After it investigated the countertop, the beast froze.

Did it spot us?

The black eyes narrowed on Julius, and the lizard let out a menacing growl.

Yep, it spotted us!

"Uhm... Lieutenant?"

"Wait." He held up a hand, telling her to hold her position but not to discharge her weapon.

It's hunting us...

Julius lowered his hand slowly, while keeping his rifle aimed at the lizard. The creature turned its head towards the ruined ceiling and let out another horrid cry. No sooner had the call stopped before more growls erupted from behind the trees. The lizard was a scout, sending a hunting report back to the pack.

Landing on the glass shards on the floor, several more lizards weaved out of the ferns.

"Lieutenant?"

"Jordy, can you blink your lights at them? Scare them off?"

"I can try..." came a computerized, nervous voice from under the table.

The robot wearily regained his posture, popped up beside Julius, and turned his metal head toward the pack. His eyes flickered on, pulsating out varying levels of brightness. The spotlights lit up the animals as they hopped up beside their leader, revealing their brilliant, bumpy scales. At first, they seemed annoyed by the flashing, but soon adjusted to the light and resumed their treacherous advance. Altogether, there were five of them in the room.

In the trees behind the pack, more fronds began to shake. Yellow-spotted patterns streaked by, concealed behind the vegetation. Severine could hear additional claws scrapping against the dirt. More carnivores would soon be arriving.

Who knows how many are in there.

"All right, Sev, you win," Julius said as the jungle came to life. "I've seen enough!"

He pressed the trigger on his pulse rifle. After all these years, thankfully, it still worked.

VRRRRRR!

An orange pulse blast fired from the barrel and flew at the lizards. It only took a fraction of a second before the golden bolt struck the center monster, leaving a sparking crater in its abdomen. The blast seared into the green scales, and the creature yelped in agony as it fell from the desk. The round was so powerfully charged that it erupted the monitor behind the lizard, causing the hardware to explode on impact. As the dead creature hit the ground, the other reptiles hopped off the counter and retreated quickly to the tall grass of the wilderness. Soon the plants no longer shook, and the reptiles were gone.

Severine lowered her pistol with a grateful breath.

That was too close.

Julius approached the carcass and signaled them over. The lieutenant set the body of the monster on an empty table, brushing off the old keyboard and hardware parts to make room. In the morning sunlight, they studied the beast carefully, unsure of what they were looking at.

"Well, Jordy, what do you think we've got here?"

"Beats me, sir," the bot answered. Severine could tell the robot was getting more comfortable with them by his slang usage. Jordy brightened his eyes and studied the specimen closely.

The lizard was dead – no doubt about it. The black, hateful eyes were glazed over, staring outward past its captors that probed and prodded at the body. The reptile's hands were equipped with sharply curved, killing claws that looked comparable to the talons on the little toes. Organs and blood poured slowly out from the fresh wound made by the XR-90, which still shined with a subtle, residual glow.

"Sure is a cute thing, isn't it?" Severine commented.

Julius laughed. "Cute? Those things were ready to rip off my face! They were studying us – looking for weaknesses. I bet there were twenty more of them waiting in the trees." He nodded towards the silent forest. "All the more reason to get the hell out of here! Any thoughts?"

"Well, this place is no good. None of these machines will start. I didn't see any functional weapons. How about the mainframe room? The emitter may still be working. If there's any chance left for a distress call, that would be it!"

The bot referred to the solar signal emitter, an emergency communication tower built inside the ship's mainframe room.

That's our best chance!

The emitter was a powerful device that could charge an emergency call through reflective dish panels that lined the top of the *Supernova*. They had been installed on every major Federation colonist ship as a safety precaution in case of an electrical failure. It was a useless device, as far as communication whilst in space, but was built to relay coordinates in the event that the ship crashed near a sun. The sunlight of this new world might have kept the device running all these years.

"It's worth a shot!" Severine said.

That would explain why some elements of the ship are still drawing power!

"Right! The emergency emitter! Jordy, can we get to it?"

"Not if the blast doors are shut," the bot replied. "If they're closed, there's virtually no hope left of getting in – not without the proper key-card. And we would need at least a level five card. Those cards were only given to select officers, and usually on a confidential basis. I haven't seen any around. Not even in the skeletal remains."

He's right, Severine thought. *Only a few upper-level officers could get in there... and they're all dead or devoured by the lizards...*

"Well, let's hope they're still open," Julius said.

They picked up their weapons and headed to the far end of the room, towards another dark hallway that fed deeper into the ship's base. As their footsteps faded away, the command bridge was once more silent under the tall, invasive trees. In the high grasses beyond the wreckage, many angry black eyes waited quietly, watching as the colonists disappeared into the darkness.

#

"You don't think those lizards are lurking in here, do you, sir?" Jordy asked as they walked slowly along, checking their corners.

"I doubt it, little buddy. Those things are probably scared of this place." Julius had a reassuring, powerful voice that could make anyone feel safe. Severine hadn't spoken with him before the crash but remembered him well in basic training and their advanced individual training. He was muscular and one of the taller men on board the vessel. He was a confident and exceptional soldier for the Federation and very good-looking – that was her favorite thing about him.

Although, that's not such an amazing feat these days. All the soldiers left on board are crow feed by now!

She struggled to remember her fellow comrades. Despite the fogginess of hyper-sleep, several faces were still fresh in her mind, although their personalities and voices were somewhat hazy.

She could remember a man named Marcus Davenport, a disciplined sergeant in the infantry. There was also Collins, a female soldier. Severine couldn't place her first name. Evie Declaudio worked as a repair technician. Steven Brandstadter was another man in the infantry. Manuel Lazarre worked in logistics support. A final, vague face of an officer entered her mind. A face marred with wrinkles and some skin deformities. She thought his name might have been Tom.

Or was it Throm?

She suddenly found herself struggling to recall more names. *Supernova* was a massive ship, and with thousands of human and robotic personnel on board, it was easy to misplace a name. Severine decided to cut herself some slack.

There was another good-looking man who she remembered meeting on a few occasions. Brett. His name was Brett – of that she was certain. When his name faded into her memory, her heart felt suddenly funny, and she didn't know why. She tried to shrug it off, but the emotion wouldn't go away. Was it romance – that which was considered taboo among the infantry? Suddenly the feeling was gone, dying off before she could remember anything further of their relationship. Unfortunately, now Brett was probably a repulsive corpse, rotting somewhere in the interior of the colossal ruins.

And I've barely aged at all. Still 32 and a knock-out!

"They're all dead," Severine commented as they passed another grave of blackened, mummified remains that lay decaying in ashes on the ground.

"These ones probably died in the crash," Julius replied. His voice was trying to sound hopeful. "Look! They're all burned to a crisp."

"I didn't mean them," Severine said. "The others – our families and relatives on the other ships! All of them. They've been dead for a long time, Julius. The thought just crossed my mind now." She found herself sounding emotional. She hated that about herself. It made her feel vulnerable, and after she completed Federation basic combat training, she treated it as a weakness.

"Try not to dwell on it," Julius replied. "I need you to be on point down here. If any of those green lizards jump out, I'm counting on you to watch my back!"

He shot her a friendly smile.

Severine nodded, knowing the lieutenant was right. She pushed down the sad thoughts of isolation, resuming her inner warrior mentality.

Can't think about the past. They're counting on me.

"I thought you said the lizards wouldn't be in the ship," the bot called out, angrily.

Julius laughed. "They won't be, little buddy!"

An old map diagram appeared to their left, mounted on the wall.

"Let me look at this schematic. Memory is starting to fog up again. Three hundred years in a sleeper pod will do that to you – *sheesh*, this place is a maze!"

The illustration had withered and was hard to see through the smudged, reinforced glass that remained at the forefront. It would have been helpful if some sunlight filtered through, but this part of the ship had nearly no damage done to the sides. Most light came from their weapons or Jordy's illuminated body parts.

Julius squinted at the diagram.

"Jordy, shine some light on this, will you?"

The bot stepped forward and blinked both eyes, enhancing the lumens to the brightest level that he could muster.

The lieutenant studied the map under Jordy's new lighting. "Okay. Perfect! The mainframe room is literally right around this corner."

At the end of the hall, they made a sharp, right turn and were faced with an unpleasant sight. The titanium doors were shut, revealing the pair of faded Federation F logos. Surprisingly, one of the overhead utility lights remained shining over the door frame.

"Damn!"

Julius lowered his rifle, defeated.

"I'm sorry, sir," said the bot. "That is unfortunate!"

Severine approached the doors. To their right were a set of dark, tinted windows. Although they seemed completely glossed over, she approached and tried to stare through them, cupping her hands in front of her head as she leaned into the glass.

To her surprise, she could see the room inside.

The mainframe room was completely secure and untouched by time. There were no trees or vines growing from the walls, or technician carcasses decaying on the floor. The lights were still on, shading the pristine equipment with a delicate, sepia glow. A few workstation chairs were overturned – that looked to be the largest extent of the damage. In the center of the room was a tall device with a translucent shaft that disappeared through the ceiling. Inside the glass cylinder, the golden gears spun energetically as if the crash never took place.

The solar signal emitter! It's intact!

"Julius! I can see the emitter – and it's operational!"

He ran up beside her, cupped his hands, and looked inside.

"That's it! That's our hope, right in there! Jordy, how do we get in?"

The bot frowned. "As I've said, sir, the doors are locked. I'm afraid it's impossible to get inside."

"What about a detonator? There must be some around! We could blast the door open!"

"No, sir. The detonators will not work on the door. It has been built to withstand anything the Federation has created. Even if you could blast inside, it's likely the explosions would damage the emitter."

It's right there! Our way out of this place is right there, behind those doors!

Severine watched as the gears spun beautifully in the glass spire, eagerly waiting for someone to activate the terminal and send out the distress call to the fleet.

"Could we find a key-card off one of the bodies and use it to gain access?"

"Wishful thinking," the bot answered. "Remember, you need a level five. Good luck finding one of those. They were only given to a select few. And sadly, they kept the recipients confidential."

Julius turned, defeated and out of options.

"We can't sit here and sulk over this," he said. "What's done is done. That thing in there may not even work properly – how should we know? It's been spinning now for how long? A few hundred years?"

"What should we do now?" Severine asked.

"Only one thing to do. Head for the cargo bay and hope that there is at least one operational vehicle, and drive into the jungle. Maybe we will find something of use in the wilderness. Food and shelter should be our immediate priority – and more importantly, gathering fresh water. Not that murky shit flowing through the hallways, but refreshing river water. I'm parched! We won't survive long without it. Maybe afterwards, we can double back here and look for a key-card. Unless anyone has any better ideas?"

"It's your call, Lieutenant," Severine replied.

"Not anymore," Julius said with a smile. "We're equals now, Sev. You too, Jordy! Ranks are no longer needed. As far as I'm concerned, you two are just as much in charge as I am. No amount of Federation training prepared me for this. I'm officially relinquishing my position of authority and suggesting that we decide together what we do from now on. Are you both on board with that?"

Severine smiled, shaking her head. Jordy did the same.

"Terrific!" he said. "Now, how about that cargo bay?"

"The cargo bay," Severine confirmed. "That's my vote!"

"How about you, Jord?"

"Cargo bay," the bot answered, smiling at the nickname.

"Then cargo bay, here we come!"

III

The glow from Julius' XR-90 led the way down the stairwell, deeper into the shadowy corners of the *Supernova*. Ahead, a thick layer of frosted glass enclosed one wall from top to bottom. The view once looked out on the beautiful stars. Now it was caked with fermented, green slime and shredded plant matter, hiding the blurry forms of swaying trees. A bead of cloudy water droplets fell slowly from above, splattering in a pool far below where the stairs met the lowest level. Severine remembered a time when she trekked up and down the stairs while the ship was in orbit. This had been one of the primary stairwells used during times when the elevators were deactivated to conserve precious energy. It was a fleeting memory, as most of her recent thoughts were – one of the many problematic side-effects of hyper-sleep.

The rusted railings were broken in many areas, often missing the entire support rail. Severine chose her steps carefully, knowing that the structure was corroded and unstable. A few of the landings were fractured by debris that had fallen down during the crash. Whatever happened, it had been catastrophic and quick.

"Watch your step, team!" Julius said. "Big hole coming up on the next landing."

She gripped the brown rail tightly with her free hand, hoping not to scratch herself on the corrosion. The stairs didn't seem reliable. The support beams shook lightly with each step, making the colonists choose their moves wisely. As she listened closely, Severine thought she could hear screws winding loose in the reinforced girders.

I give these stairs another week – two, at the most, she thought.

"Here comes another," Jordy beeped, clamping his metal fingers down on the guardrail.

He was bringing up the rear, moving slowly behind the two humans. Severine guessed he was feeling safer, now that he wasn't shoving between them for protection. The bots manufactured by the logistics department were programmed to be afraid easily. This was done so the machines displayed a more human reaction to danger – an upgrade that made it easy to command them.

"These stairs should be Federation approved by the FCE; that's the Federation Corps of Engineers." The bot was trying to sound confident.

"Looks like the Corps spent too much time on the stairs and not enough time reinforcing the ship," Julius replied, laughing as he brushed past some vines that blocked another landing platform. The stairwell was so overgrown that they had to pause intermittently to clear the brush.

"They didn't account for an accident of this magnitude, I agree," the bot commented as his skinny little legs quivered down the steps.

"What're your thoughts on the *Supernova*, Jordy?" Severine asked. "An incident in space?"

"It certainly seems that way, Corporal. My data readings indicate that the ship underwent a sudden amount of damage at the time of my last data log, and, as you remember, that occurred nearly three hundred years ago! What happened next, we will never know – thanks, in part, to the locker incident! My database would have been able to tell us more if I wasn't trapped and deactivated. But then again, the incident enabled terrific battery conservation for all these years! Otherwise, I wouldn't be here lecturing you now!"

The bot roared to life, laughing mechanically at his own joke.

Ha-ha, Severine thought. The bot's sense of humor was dry, but she figured that was part of his charm.

"Stick with the logistics, buddy!" she laughed back.

"Possibly a mutiny?" Julius guessed.

"I ruled mutiny out," the robot answered. "No call-to-arms orders were sent out. And so far, I haven't seen any pulse residue on the walls indicating a firefight."

"Give it your best guess then," Severine said.

"Based on what we've encountered, it looks like the ship entered through a violent chasm in space – maybe something to the effect of an asteroid field. I've noticed several groups of odd-looking rocks wedged in the ship, and I'm fairly certain that they're asteroid remnants. That's not my only thought – here's another idea. When the *Supernova* crashed here, it struck a mountain, collecting the debris from an avalanche after the initial impact. During the crash, the rocks from the hills ripped the hull apart. However, I'm leaning more towards the first scenario – an asteroid field."

"So, your theory is such," Severine started. "We were cruising in deep space with the rest of the Federation ships. Sometime during our hyper-sleep, we encountered an asteroid belt. We couldn't make it through the field, and the ship sustained a great amount of damage – unable to continue. And then, what? Somehow, we ended up back on, say, Earth? Or a planet very similar to what Earth used to be like before the Old War?"

"Could be, Corporal. Could be…"

"Just call me Severine, Jordy. Ranks don't matter anymore, remember? We're equals!" She tried to sound cheerful, even in the dire situation.

The bot nodded.

"As you wish!" the digital voice replied, followed by an acknowledging blink of the illuminated eyes. "But there is one obvious problem with the Earth theory. The problem is that, by now, Earth should be completely unlivable. When the Federation ships pulled out, the time left on Earth was running out. It was desolate and wasteful – plagued by rival clans and abominations mutated from the nuclear winters. Yet life here is flourishing, populating in abundance. The climate seems to be arid, tropical, or subtropical. As we saw, life here has adapted well! No, my friends, I don't believe this is Earth. There are too many odd variables. I'm certain that we're somewhere else!"

"It doesn't add up," Julius said. "We get shot down by the asteroids and are fortunate enough to end up here? On a green planet with breathable air? Hell, I keep forgetting we aren't wearing protective oxygen masks!"

Severine had forgotten all about the Federation respirators. They were breaking protocol for not wearing them. If the air in this new world had been toxic, she would have suffocated when her sleeper pod oxygen tank had failed. But from what she had seen of the ship so far, there weren't any respirators around to spare.

24

"There's a missing piece to the puzzle, of that I'm sure," the bot confirmed.

"And what of the other Federation ships? *Star Jumper? Wayfarer?* And the others."

"What about them? Did they meet the same fate that *Supernova* did? It's possible that they crashed here too, after whatever happened in space. We may stumble across their wreckage when we head out into the jungle. But that raises yet another question – and a more unsettling one. If they did crash here with us, they must have landed nearby. And if that's true, why haven't they come looking for us?"

So many unanswered questions...

"The ship could be hidden! Tucked away under the canopy somewhere," Severine suggested. "Or, maybe they crashed on the other side of the planet."

"Hidden yes, but for three hundred years? Doubtful. If they were here – or alive – they would have found us by now..."

The bot had a point. Federation rescue parties would have long passed by and rooted through the jungle, with drone ships or T50s leading the search party. With all their radar equipment and communication protocols, the *Supernova* would have been found quickly, especially if the solar signal emitter was still in operation.

Finally, Severine thought.

At long last, they came to the bottom of the dank stairwell.

The floor was buried under a foot of murky green water that bubbled from unknown air pockets. From the glow of their utility lights, Severine could see strange amphibians swimming away into the green, fading away under the ripples. They looked like overgrown salamanders with bulbous heads, but also reminded her of lizards. Severine carefully avoided squashing them as she stepped into the small pond. Despite being a hardened soldier, she had a love for all living things, as long as they didn't try to eat her.

Jordy stepped around the water slowly, being careful not to touch any of his external components to the liquid. Water was problematic for robots to begin with, but if he got any in his internal battery compartment, it would prove fatal.

There was a wide utility shelf around the stairs just big enough for him to walk on until he reunited with the others on the other side of the pool. After climbing an additional step into another hallway, they were clear of the waterlogged portion.

The corridor was dark, for the most part, except for the rays shining from sunlight that leaked through the door windows ahead. Above the frame, a moldy sign spelled out: **Cargo Bay 2 – Entry 3 – Level 1.**

Looks like the cargo bay didn't escape the carnage either.

The doors were partially sealed, although open enough for a small child to easily pass through.

Someone probably tried to pry them apart shortly after the crash.

The Federation F logos were partially obscured from view as the doors remained half-sunken between the wall and the hallway. Hot air caused a low-lying fog to form at the foot of the inviting gap. Beyond the barrier, they could hear more taunting cries of animals roaming in the jungle.

"Hang back here, buddy," Julius told the bot. "We'll clear this room! The cargo bay is big enough to fit plenty of those lizards inside. I'm sorry... I know you're just dying to see them again!"

"You said the lizards were too scared to hide down here!" said a panicked computer voice.

"Yes, I know I did. Now here's the truth – they could be anywhere. Sorry, buddy! Hang out here and we'll circle back for you once we know the room is safe."

"*Uhhhhhhh*...all right," Jordy whined. "Please be fast! I'll be all alone here, after all!"

He's such a character, Severine thought. The cowardice and intelligence of the machine impressed her. She couldn't remember other robots having such personality – even the ones programmed by logistics.

The bot sighed and leaned onto the outer wall as Severine and Julius approached the cargo bay doors. Using all their weight for leverage, they managed to pry the entrance open, sending wisps of jungle mist filtering through. Weapons drawn, they entered the massive chamber as the sunlight overtook them.

Damn! It's almost wiped away...

The cargo bay was arguably equal to or in even more severe of a condition than the command bridge. After the ship's initial crash landing, many of the walls buckled in, giving way to a massive landslide that broke through the room. After many decades, the avalanche formed a lush hillside of jungle fronds and reeds that invaded the concrete floor.

The entire ship is falling apart!

The roof was barely held together. Severine took note of the crisscross pattern of the overhead exposed rafters. The lack of structure made it easy for more sunlight to flood through. The same canopy of vines that they encountered in the stairs had consumed the roof, bursting in through the air ducts. The plants drooped downwards like a saggy, old rope net, blanketing much of the ruins under their green tarp. The jungle below made it difficult to see clearly.

And the worst part: No vehicles!

Not a single one! Not even a T20 Speeder Transport!

"Shit. They're all gone, Julius!"

We can't catch a break...

"Maybe not. Do you see how thick this place is? We may be in luck and not even know it! I bet you that we'll find something buried down in the plants. Time for a closer look." He turned and slowly made his way to an ancient mangled set of utility stairs that descended to the parking area.

Once they stepped foot on the floor of the cargo bay, Severine found it more cumbersome to see through the mist. She placed the time of day at early to mid-morning, based on the color of the light and placement of the sun.

The ground was spongy. The moss felt like a cushion when she stepped on it. The concrete floor was only visible in sparse areas. For the most part, dirt and weeds had blanketed the majority of the bay, hiding the traces of life prior to the crash.

Still no vehicles...

"The crew probably snagged them shortly after the crash," Julius commented.

"If the vehicles remained in the bay. It's possible that they could have dropped out when we fell from the sky or when we crashed. They could be anywhere along the flight path!"

"The place looks safe to me," Julius stated, lowering the 90.

"Jordy," she yelled. "All clear, pal!"

A timid, mechanical voice called back, "Coming!" Jordy's frail form entered the chamber, walking down to the bay, creaking as he went.

Around them, buried in the old roots and thick shrubbery, were fragments left from the vehicles. Most of the pieces were severely deformed and bent with age. A few were in decent condition and could potentially be useful, but Severine had no idea what the parts belonged to. There were also old Federation chairs, mechanic tools like wrenches and hammers, broken ladder steps, useless pulse weaponry, and even traces of discarded Federation-issued armor.

And lizard tracks!

Severine turned pale when she saw them, weaving through the morning fog around her feet.

The footprints formed several intersecting pathways and figure-eight shapes, crossing over one another before hiding under the weeds. The sizes of these prints were comparable in scale to the feet of the green lizards that stalked them on the bridge.

Those things have been down here all right, but not for some time. The tracks look old!

"Oh my..." said a scared robot voice.

"Relax, buddy. They haven't been here for a while. Looks like they just passed through a few times, found the place boring, and decided the cargo bay wasn't worth their time. No food. They're hungry little things!"

"Any tracks from the vehicles?" Severine asked, crouching to study the deformed ground. "I can't find any prints from the land cruisers. Or any indication that they were here."

"Not seeing anything yet, Sev," Julius answered. "Just the lizard marks."

"What about back there?" Jordy asked, pointing with his metal index finger.

They spun around.

At the rear of the dismal ruins stood a closed hangar bay door. It looked like a quaint storage area for cargo gear and supplies. The walls and depth were about the size of a smaller transport vessel. Other than a patch of vines that climbed up the left wall, it looked like the best kept secret of the cargo bay.

"There could be a ship in there," Jordy stated. "Or maybe some supplies."

Or food! Food would be terrific right now!

"It looks sealed shut," Severine commented as they approached the front.

Their bodies parted the fog as they walked towards the large hangar door. Julius hopped up on the ledge and looked for a way inside, tugging vainly on the old, corroded levers. After pacing on the entrance platform, he gave up.

"It's stuck!" he confirmed. "Federation Titanium. We'll never get through these..."

"Unless... Jordy? Can you do your logistics-magic on this door like you did back at the bridge? We would be forever grateful!" Severine smiled at the bot.

"Well, if we can locate the panel, I could see if my old codes will be good down here. Does anyone see it? Wait – here it is! Jeez! I can't tell if it's still good or not..."

The bot found the access panel, completely covered by a thorny, invasive plant. They hadn't taken notice of it at first – it looked like a strange exotic tree lying casually to their right. Jordy brushed aside the ivy and typed methodically on the old, dusty buttons. As he pressed down, the numbers lit up at his touch.

It still works!

"Wa-la!" he exclaimed.

With a miraculous loud *hummmmmm*, the doors slid upwards into the ceiling of the storage compartment, hitting off the roof with a hollow *baannng*. Another layer of mist rolled out onto the room, followed by a stale smell – the smell of a chamber unopened for centuries.

"Bingo! We may have hit the jackpot!" said Julius. "It looks operational!"

At the edge of the room sat a Federation T80 armored transport rover. They were commonly referred to by Federation soldiers as T80s, or FATRs for short.

It's beautiful, Severine thought.

"I'm surprised no one grabbed it after the crash!" she exclaimed.

"The majority of the bots were probably fried during the impact and rendered useless! Logistics bots, like Jordy here, usually had access to these kinds of compartments, and could easily keep track of the clearance codes in their internal databases. Without a bot, I bet getting in here would be problematic – impossible even!"

The vehicle was tall and formidable. From the bottom treads to the armored roof, the FATR was easily twenty feet in height. With the XP-300 twin pulse cannons on the roof, the rover could barely fit into the storage room. Severine could tell the cannons were never fired, evident by the lack of pulse residue on the barrels. The orange-tinted glass of the cockpit was nearly crystal clear, except for a small dusty coating that had started to form. Radio antennas and communication equipment stood triumphantly over the cockpit. White, titanium armor plating jutted out from the sides of the vehicle's edges. The jungle outside had failed to penetrate the interior, freezing the FATR in its glory years.

"This must have been a spare rover. They probably put it here as a last resort, and after the *Supernova* crashed, they either forgot about it or couldn't get it out! Good job, Jord! We couldn't have opened it without you!"

"Thank you, Julius!" the bot replied, reveling in the praise.

"I always wanted to ride in one of these," said Severine. "In my basic combat training, from what I remember, they focused my unit heavily on reinforcement tactics – I hardly had any vehicle lessons!"

"Well, now you'll get your chance!"

"What makes you think we can get inside?"

"I've driven these things around plenty of times. Funny little fact: most times, I drove them around in this very cargo bay! See that little green light there under the cockpit? That means there's a good chance it's unlocked and likely still has juice! Those Federation lithium batteries can last forever, as long as they're properly maintained."

"What are we waiting for?" Jordy said. "Let's open her up!"

IV

The colonists walked around the side of the FATR, admiring the powerful vehicle. As they walked around the titanium plating, hidden security lights on the upper armor clamped on and guided their approach. The treads of the rover were polished and pristine, lined with rows of sharp metallic cleats several inches in length. Complex rotation pulleys, gears, and sprockets behind the tracks were interwoven with beautiful craftsmanship. Severine guessed that many bots and humans endured quite a few hours in the factories to build these durable monsters.

The entrance greeted them at the rear of the vehicle, sealed off by chrome security doors. Nonetheless, a tiny green light hovered over them, indicating that the doors could be opened without a key-card.

Beside the hatch, a strange access console system sat flush against the trim. There were no buttons, key-card slots, or a display monitor to view the user input.

Severine looked at Julius.

"Well, you're the pilot!" she laughed. "I don't know how to decipher that thing!" She had never opened any of the vehicle hatches for the Federation, especially for the rovers, and this one had her stumped.

Julius smiled as he walked up to the access port.

"Simple! It's a retina scan. From my memory, I believe this is one of the newer models. The older units required a keypad entry. Normally, only the pilot or co-pilot had code access. Now, after passing a simple battle-operations test, they give your eye a neon scan, and your data becomes available in the system. Once they had your scan in the database, you'd be able to open most of the Federation vehicles. I passed with flying colors – and on my first try, too!"

"You wanna quit bragging and open the damn thing!" Severine said, leering at him.

He smirked, leaning forward. "Hang on. This should work..."

Vrrrrr....

The access panel opened.

A small, black orb protruded out from the door frame, supported by a nimble extendable arm. Julius leaned into the sphere as a green scanning light descended over his face. After it lapped back up, the light flicked off, and the orb retreated neatly back into the compartment.

Then the doors jeered apart, granting their entry into the rover.

"Here we go!"

Severine followed Julius into the chamber. Jordy closed the blast doors behind him, sealing the group safely inside the vehicle. A peace closed in around them as the panels slid back behind their walls, blocking off the unknown world.

Severine shivered.

The inside of the FATR was cool, in contrast to the daunting heat they experienced in this new, tropical environment. A single red utility light rained down from above, casting sharp shadows on the industrial objects throughout the room. To their front sat parallel rows of infantry trooper seats, including another back-to-back row at the center. Behind the exterior seats were more military lockers, most of which remained closed. Severine saw that a few were empty through the front mesh of the doors, but most were crammed full of foreign items:

books, papers, scrolls, vials, beakers, and articles of clothing. Normally, the lockers would be carrying only military gear.

Someone must have hoarded that stuff in here – someone who had the balls to risk Federation demerits for tampering with infantry property.

"Refreshing to know at least something still has life in the ship," Severine commented, running her hand down the edge of a locker.

"These things were built to act as a force-multiplier for the infantry," Julius explained. "You could sit thirty-some soldiers in here, and when those doors opened, they'd storm out and quickly populate the battle field under protection from the rover's armor. The FATR units were made to be durable transport vehicles with many defense capabilities, like the XP-300 we saw on the roof. I doubt this one has ever been field-tested – it's like new!"

"Any chance to call for help in here?" she asked.

"My sensors tell me no, Sev," Jordy replied. "These machines only have short-range communication capabilities, but we may find some other useful items."

"He's right," Julius confirmed. "No long range comm systems in FATR vehicles. Just short range. The room ahead should lead up to a communication chamber, then to the cockpit. Sev, pull down on that hatch release on the frame, will you?"

She smiled. Severine was getting accustomed to her new nickname. Her pleasant smile faded as the door to the next room jarred opened and she came face to face with the glowing end of an X2-20 pistol, aimed precisely between her eyes.

Whoa! Her heart stopped.

Severine couldn't move.

The hostile stowaway was a Federation pilot bot. The intelligent machine was nearly six feet tall and built with a strength that could rival Julius in a one-on-one match. These bots were manufactured for a primary purpose: manning any and all types of infantry vehicles into uneasy terrain under direct command from the bridge or Central Command. They were hailed for their loyalty and devotion to duty. The bot's external radar dials were all switched off. Had they been active, Jordy's internal computer would have detected the pilot when they entered the vehicle.

His software components must be outdated or compromised for him to draw a 20 on a human corporal.

"Drop your pistol, Pilot," Julius' voice boomed behind Severine. "You're aiming your sights at Federation survivors!"

"Negative. Your order does not compute."

The voice was stern with digital precision.

Severine kept her hands raised as she stared into her captor's yellow eyes. The pilot's plating looked faded, as if he had been tinkering around in the rover since the time of the crash, awaiting orders that would never come.

He's been here since the ship went down, Severine thought.

Her theory made sense.

A bot could last years in the vehicle by plugging itself into the FATR's internal power computer. Its software components surely hadn't recently been updated. If the machine thought that Central Command was down, it could be acting out a mutiny-defense protocol as a scare-tactic for trespassers.

"The bridge is down," Severine said uneasily. "No active orders will be sent! If you're waiting for an officer to authorize our arrival, it won't be transmitted."

The bot stared blankly at her. The metal of the pilot's forearm creaked as it gripped down on the gun. Silver support cords and exposed banding stretched under the chest armor.

This bot is built stronger than Jordy. Although this guy wasn't under a locker unit for three centuries!

"What is your operating number, soldier?"

Julius was careful not to lower his rifle at the captor. The bot's trigger sensors could be activated easily from sudden movements.

"Operating Number: DDY-392. Codename: Daddy. Orders are to guard this vehicle until a superior human officer arrives. Do you have the authorization code?"

"Daddy, your operating orders are invalid. There has been an accident with the ship. All Federation orders are currently obsolete and unnecessary. Lower the weapon and let us pass!"

"Negative. Your order does not compute. Please exit the rover and return to your assigned positions on board the *Supernova*. If you fail to comply, I will send word to the admiral and have you all reassigned and presented with demerits!"

His orders are obsolete.

"Maybe we should do what he says, Julius," Severine asked, still staring into the barrel of the pulse pistol. She could see golden particles gathering on the generator inside, forming a deadly charge.

Daddy, like all pilot bots, was trained side-by-side by Federation human soldiers and their special forces counterparts. Their strong artificial intelligence programmed them for rapid learning. They were lethal with any pulse weapon and hard to compete with in marksmanship due to their auto lock-on capabilities. Normally they acted as pilots and cannon operators for transport units, but if called, they could be deployed as a reserve combat force.

The bot slowly lowered his pointer finger down on the trigger.

Surely he won't fire...

Severine contemplated reaching for her weapon and gunning down the bot. If she was fast enough, she could put a well-timed pulse blast between the eyes as she dropped back. But that maneuver would risk putting Julius and Jordy in the way of Daddy's return fire. And the bot was very smart. For all she knew, he could pick her off as she fell back, and then dispatch her friends with ease. She would be dead before she hit the ground.

Daddy flicked his wrist, motioning back towards the direction of the rear doors.

"Come on, let's move...*duuuhhawwwwwww*!"

The bot let out a robotic shriek.

The pistol wobbled uneasily in the pilot's hand, dropped from the palm, and landed on the ground below in a heart-pounding series of metal clangs. Much to everyone's relief, the weapon failed to discharge.

Severine glanced up.

Their captor suddenly began to twist and convulse in an absurd fit, causing his eyes to pop back and fold violently into slots in his head.

Duhawwwww–hawwww!

The bot's voice was garbled with computerized static.

The metal fingers began searching for the pistol, but eventually gave up and snapped parallel to the hips at an infantry attention stance. The dance looked as if the robot was undergoing some sort of epileptic spell that a human may encounter.

Daddy was being reprogrammed.

But how?

Jordy!

Of course, Jordy! That little bot has come in handy more than once on this trip!

She turned around to find Julius staring bewildered at their computerized friend, who was also doing the same ritualistic shuffle. On his mossy skullcap, a small antenna had extended out, producing a nasty squeal.

Logistics bots had the unique ability to override orders under situations where direct authority was compromised or not immediately available. Of course, this advantage had not come without its share of drawbacks. Scientists on board the starships had worked strenuously for hours making sure these modifications would not cause a revolt inside the artificial intelligence chips. They found quickly that the logistical units would challenge authority – peacefully, of course. So the Federation technicians made it easy on themselves. All logistics bots moving forward would only be authorized to use the reprogramming feature – dubbed *Feature L-391* – in times of intense peril for the ship. This was accomplished by reprogramming most of their bot-to-bot language learning. The order was tentatively titled "Order 391: Emergency Override Control." The command had gone into effect three years earlier.

"That's a neat little trick!" Julius commented, watching the two machines face off in their mechanical dance-off.

"We're fortunate to have found him when we did," Severine replied. "He's already been very helpful!"

Vrrrrrr....CHHHH!

The static ceased.

The two robots halted their movements and froze in their tracks. Jordy was the first to shake the spell. He activated his eyelids that brightened up the room as he resurrected himself back to life.

"Sorry about that," he told them. "Had to be done! Pilot bots don't back down easily. They're very stubborn." "I see that," Severine replied. "What did you do to him?"

"Just had to factory reset a few of his expired applications," Jordy replied. "Also had to clear his order database. It's a completely harmless process, but on the outside, it must look very painful." The bot laughed. "He should be coming back online now."

Daddy's restart was strenuously slow but proved to be more fluid. With the sound of his power restarting inside, the shoulder plates began to writhe and swivel. Eyelid panels extended back out on the helmet exterior, this time glowing with a peaceful, submissive green. With his pistol lying discarded on the floor out of his clutches, the bot already appeared more docile.

"System reboot complete," Daddy said, in a voice devoid of personality – a commonality among pilot bots. "All orders reset! What are your orders, Lieutenant?"

"Are the rover's internal systems in working order, capable enough to transport us out of here? The vehicle treads, weapons, and so forth?"

"Yes, Lieutenant. I've kept this machine in tip-top shape! All systems should be operational and are standing by for your immediate command."

"Excellent, Pilot! Head to the cockpit and turn her on."

"Yes, sir," said the dull, drone-like voice.

Daddy walked away briskly, jumping into a pilot chair in the cockpit straight ahead. He pressed some buttons on the control mechanism and swirled around in his seat to command more components nearest him on the wall.

With a loud roar, the FATR sparked to life. The inside vibrated powerfully during the engine start-up. Overhead lights changed from a muted red to a sterile white. Several of the titanium panels on the side folded up into slots in the walls, giving way to orange-tinted windows that looked out to the storage room. To their delight, a functioning bathroom rotated out of the wall, complete with a working toilet and compact shower stall.

Severine couldn't help but smile at the new luxuries.

It works!

She walked through the doorway, arriving in the middle room where Daddy had ambushed her. The chamber was built to send communication codes but was now converted to a storage bunker. Federation-stamped, battery-charged crates marked with nutritious symbols and identification tags lined the walls. The boxes were stacked as high as the ceiling, webbed in by utility straps that fastened the supplies against bracing handles. Intersecting cables hung down like snakes that plugged into the crates, supplementing residual energy from the rover. Behind the boxes stood shelving stands filled with old Earth literature, such as scientific books and scholarly documents. The room looked as if someone had been preparing for the end – or perhaps, a fresh start.

They sure picked a good spot to do it!

"Sev, you seeing this?" Julius said, walking happily through the doorway. "We're set for a while! There's enough supplies here to last a few months, provided the FATR battery holds up."

The food symbols stared pleasantly back at them from the deep freeze containers. The icons indicated the crates were full of foods left over from Earth; bananas, cherries, apples, oranges, carrots, blueberries, beef, chicken, turkey, potatoes, and many others.

Amazing! Here all this time, preserved in deep-freeze.

"They should all be edible," Jordy informed them as he stepped into the room. "Those freezing crates can hold out as long as the rover keeps them cool. You just might have to thaw them out for consumption."

Julius pressed a switch on one of the crates, lifted the lid off, and produced two metal water canisters. With a quick shake, he heard the sloshing of fluid inside and cracked open the lid. After a refreshing gulp, he swigged down the rest of the beverage.

"Fresh water! And thankfully, not frozen like the others. Just what we need right now – catch!"

He tossed another canister to Severine, who plucked it out of the air and engulfed the water like she had put in a hard day's work. The taste was serene and refreshing. The trek through the toasty heat of the *Supernova's* ruins made her appreciate the drink.

Food. Water. Shelter. All three in one spot!

"I vote we stay here," Severine said, content with their situation.

"Hold on everyone," Jordy said, blinking his eyes in new found confusion. "This is very bizarre! My sensors tell me that there is a third Federation human signal coming from this room. Surprisingly, I couldn't pick up the frequency before! There must be a lot of data flowing through here. My computer is taking longer than usual to process body signals. All I see are crates. Does anyone see anything?"

As they looked around, Severine caught an odd object in the corner of her eye.

"There!" she pointed.

Nestled quietly under columns of deep-freeze boxes was a stowaway hyper-sleep chamber glowing peacefully in an artificially-induced slumber. Unlike the pods back in the ruins, this compartment was powered on and humming with a gentle lull. Status holograms on the sides indicated it was functioning in immaculate condition. Thin wisps of air puffed out from bottom vent grates on the capsule's chrome edges. The glass on the upper surface was meticulously cleaned and cared for. Severine assumed that Daddy was responsible for the pod's impeccable performance.

The capsule was tilted horizontally. Sideways hyper-sleep was typically a no-no for Federation employees. She guessed that this was done to save space in the rover and as a support structure to hold additional deep-freeze boxes.

"Another *Supernova* survivor!" The face and identity of the passenger was blocked by the crates that stacked on top of the glass.

"Help me get these crates off," Julius said.

One by one they cleared the cubes off the glass shield, revealing the passenger beneath.

Below them lay a Caucasian man in his late forties, with funny glasses and disheveled hair. For a man trapped in a fishbowl for a few lifetimes, he looked very healthy. The eyelids were glazed shut, crusted over by brown mucus that formed over the years. Around the mouth was the spider-like Federation breathing apparatus, connected to oxygen tubes that fed back to the interior frame. The man's chest huffed quickly under his technician lab coat, causing the pens and pocket devices on his breast to rise and fall in a seamless loop. Other utensils had fallen out during his time in hyper-sleep, lying below the man on the pod's backing.

The name on the pocket read: **Francis Paluch – Federation Level 2 Robotics Technician**.

He's one of the scientists! Maybe he has a key-card!

"Opening now – mind yourself."

Julius released the door latch. The glass shield slowly rose from the pod and rotated backwards, stopping as it struck the FATR's wall. As the pod mist fogged the room, Francis' eyes opened wide as he took a strenuously deep breath. With a gasp, he yanked off his oxygen mask and stepped out of the chamber before struggling to find a sense of balance.

"Whoa there, fella!" Julius reached in and tried to help the technician. "Let the pod effects wear off first..."

"Thanks... I think," Francis said between coughs. He tumbled to the floor and let out a series of deep breaths, fogging the spotless ground below his lips. He swatted the crusty material from his eyes furiously to reclaim his sight.

"Jeez! I can barely catch a proper breath. Been cooped up in there for a while, huh? Few days? Sorry about the stock piles, Lieutenant. We didn't know what was going on, so Daddy and I brought some down here to hold out!"

"It's been more than a few days, Mr. Paluch," Julius said.

"Really?" Paluch replied, followed by more quick coughs. "How long then – a few weeks?"

"Try three hundred years!" Severine replied. "Almost, anyway."

She found it hard to hear her own words. The whole notion of a three-hundred-year time gap sounded ridiculous – the tales of pure fiction.

"Yeah, I'll believe that hogwash! You guys are busting my balls. I'm in trouble now for moving in here, right? This is the infantry way of screwing around with me. Well, I'm not buying that crap! Besides, Daddy and I planned to have all this shit back before anyone noticed, when and if things cooled down on the ship."

Paluch stood up, finally controlling his breathing, and cleaned his smudgy glasses with a handkerchief that he produced from the lab coat.

"This is no joke," she replied. "Tell him, Jordy."

"The last logged time in my data recorder was January 27, 3271 A.D. When we checked recently, my time indicator read June 05, 3542 A.D. It's been almost three hundred years from the last logged point of entry. You've been stuck down here in the capsule ever since! Just like we were stuck back in one of the pod quadrants."

"Julius and I were lucky enough to have long-lasting batteries on our hyper-sleep pods," Severine told him. "Everyone else wasn't so lucky. We just made it out of there moments ago, and you're the only survivor we've found so far!"

"Ha. All lies...cute story though."

He sure is cocky...

Severine could feel herself tensing up. His mere existence was already starting to annoy her. She wondered if they could put him back into the sleeper pod.

"Maybe you should have a look out the front window," Julius recommended, gesturing to where Daddy was sitting in the next room.

"Fine, whatever that proves!" the scientist replied.

Francis walked into the cockpit and squinted through the glass pane. The colonists followed and looked out past the hangar door frame at the green jungle that stretched in all directions.

"What the hell! Did we land somewhere? Wow, sure looks like a royal mess down here!"

"We crashed!" Severine replied.

"Ha-ha, yeah. You can cut it out now – I get it! Sorry for stealing some food during the crazy apocalyptic event. Won't make that mistake again."

"You still don't see it," Julius said. His voice was stern. "The ship's buried under those trees. See the rubble in the plants? You're staring at what's left of the *Supernova*. We're parked in the ruins of Cargo Bay 2."

That comment plus the visual was enough to convince him. Paluch turned white, quickly realizing the truth.

The *Supernova* was completely destroyed.

Through the cockpit, the group looked down at the long, obsolete computers and discarded equipment that lay besieged by the undergrowth and harsh humidity. Francis' wavering eyes turned left at the rubble. He fixated on the mangled utility stairs that still clung loyally to the crumbling interior wall.

"Whoa! Okay…yeah, this is bad," he muttered.

V

"Well, why the hell didn't you wake me up?" Francis yelled at Daddy, who was still sitting at the driver's seat, staring hypnotically towards the forested ruins ahead. Pilot bots were programmed to remain cool under intense human scrutiny, and the scientist was hyperventilating.

"I've been trapped behind that damn capsule for three hundred years! Meanwhile, the outside world has left us behind!"

"I'm sorry, sir. But I must insist – my actions were under your direct command! Your orders were the following..." Daddy's speakers emitted a garbled voice recording of Francis Paluch. The vocals blared clearly from the bot's chest speakers, despite being captured centuries earlier. The scientist's whiny nasal voice was instantly recognizable in the static.

"Listen! These things can withstand a good bit of force. I've heard the battery life on FATR vehicles are still unsurpassed! None of us know what's going on up there! We could very well be going down. The hyper-sleep pod's probably the safest place, so I'll hold up in there.

Don't let me out unless the power fails! If we make it through this and they come for me, they'll probably be pissed. I'm sure I'll have my hands full with demerits. I'll give them a bullshit explanation so they don't nail me for cowardice. I'll talk myself out of it, as usual. What are they gonna do – kick me out? We're in space!

No. No, you won't be in any trouble – you're operating under my own personal orders, remember? You're my bot now. No, no. You'll be fine! If they come, just auto-program a mutiny response protocol, and say you had to hold this position. Yes! Now please, do as you're told and seal me in!

But keep an eye on the battery! If it fails and you put those deep-freezes over the glass, the door won't open, and I'll die in here!"

The audio recording ended with the shutting of the hyper-sleep pod door, muting the scientist's voice behind the glass. Daddy switched off the message and retracted the speaker components back into his chest plate.

"Those were your orders, sir."

Francis, sitting down in the co-pilot seat, fumed with frustration towards his former servant. The scientist knew he was defeated, and by his own words.

How humiliating, Severine thought.

After a labored grunt, he nodded in agreement, making peace with the situation.

"You're forgiven," he said bluntly. "What's done is done. Those were my orders you were acting on, after all! I can't fault you for that. I'm alive, and I'm grateful. Good job, soldier."

Orders are orders. Paluch should apologize to the bot.

Severine kept her insights to herself. She knew that Daddy wouldn't demand forgiveness. Pilot bots weren't programmed to be emotional, and certainly didn't hold any grudges.

The bot nodded, gave a courtesy salute, and rotated again towards the indigenous path beyond the protective glass. The machine's previous order from Julius had attained his upmost importance, so he pushed Paluch's nagging further down on his priority list.

Now that Julius, a lieutenant in the Federation infantry, had arrived, the bot no longer recognized Paluch as the man-in-charge. In Daddy's mind, Julius was now the highest-ranking officer, and as such had attained command of the rover. His hands awaited the lieutenant's orders at the helm of the vehicle, anticipating their excursion into the lush world.

"I hate to break up this little reunion here," Severine started, "but you don't happen to have a key-card on you?"

"Key-card?" the scientist asked.

"Yeah! A level 5 clearance key-card."

Paluch shook his head. "No. Those are pretty rare. Why?"

Dammit!

"The solar signal emitter is still operational in the ship's mainframe room. The doors are locked, but the system is working at full capacity. A level 5 key-card can get us through so we can signal for help! I know it's a long shot, but it's all we have at the moment."

"So, why not slap a detonator on the door and blow your way through?"

"Can't," Jordy interrupted. "The doors are impenetrable. It doesn't matter how many explosives we put on them. Think about it! The mainframe room survived a crash landing! It's built with a titanium barrier around all sides. If the doors still work after that severe of an impact, they shouldn't have a problem withstanding our detonator blasts. Not to mention, we don't have any detonators."

Paluch leaned back uneasily in his chair, nervously scratching at his scraggly beard and massaging his neck. He was still processing the perilous demise of the ship and their remarkable survival three hundred years later.

Severine could sense his questions still bubbling to the surface.

"Any idea where we are?" Paluch blurted out.

"We don't know. Do we, Jordy?"

"No idea, Sev. It could be any of the millions of undiscovered planets! As you know, I don't believe this is Earth, but it does remind me of our former home in many ways."

"I can tell you with a hundred percent certainty it isn't Earth," Paluch replied sharply, shifting in his seat. "By now, Earth is a crumbling space rock. It was toxic and unlivable when the Federation left, and at this time it would be impossible to reverse the damage done by the Old War."

The Old War.

The war that ripped apart the Earth in a massive nuclear conflict involving the planet's rival superpowers. It happened before Severine's life. She was forced to grow up in the ruined cities – in the carnage that the past left behind. Billions of lives were lost in the nuclear fallout. The destruction of the planet eventually resulted in the forming of the Federation. When she first stumbled onto the organization, she was enthralled by the idea of escape. She enlisted immediately in the security force, later renamed the Federation Infantry, earning her way off the barren rock and a second chance at life.

"From what I see here, this planet is thriving," Paluch continued. "It's magnificent to see all these plants in the wild, and not in artificial *Star Jumper* garden chambers. How is the air quality outside? Breathable?"

"Completely breathable," Julius responded. "No need for respirators."

"Yeah, about that. Do you have any idea how dangerous that is?" Paluch cut in. "We haven't set foot on this planet before. The oxygen might seem breathable, but it's quite possible that there are unseen toxins in the air – toxins that haven't yet been identified in previous research. Our lungs might not be able to detect any anomalies. We'll know soon enough when or if you start experiencing side effects."

Paluch might be getting a one-way ticket out of here, Severine thought. The scientist was really starting to wear on her. They had enough to worry about other than mythical air toxins. All it would take was one incident to piss Julius off and the scientist would be on thin ice.

"I think we'll be good," Julius said gruffly, instantly silencing the technician. "If we'd found respirators, we would've used them. Given the circumstances, we didn't have that luxury."

Julius doesn't like this guy challenging his authority, Severine thought. *Not sure if I'm on board with it either…*

"So, if we can't find the key-card we need, what are we doing here?" she asked, thinking of the mission and their survival. "What's the next move? Do we head out into the jungle? We have enough power! My vote: drive the vehicle into the jungle and scout the area for possible crash survivors. We're safe as long as we're in here!"

"Just what I was thinking, Sev," Julius replied. "This baby's got enough power to keep us going steady for a few weeks – maybe more! The way I see it, that's the only option worth our interest at this point. Staying here is, in my mind, completely off the table. The ship's infrastructure is deteriorating from the inside out! Any one of the walls could fall and permanently damage our rover. I'm going to be optimistic here and say I think we'll find help, possibly even rescue. At first, I wasn't so sure, but after we found Mr. Scientist here, it may just be possible."

Paluch smirked. "Mr. Scientist. Good one…"

It certainly suits him. If it aggravates him, I'm for it!

He wasn't amused by his trendy new nickname.

"We should map out a few miles around the perimeter of the wreckage. There may be other ship pieces that broke off – pieces that demand exploration. We'll have to keep an eye open for any key-cards. And watch out for lizards."

The scientist looked up eagerly.

"Lizards?" he asked curiously.

"Yeah. We ran into a large pack of them in the command bridge."

"Tell me more about them." Paluch's unfriendly demeanor suddenly faded away, replaced by a childhood fascination for the animals.

"What about them?" Severine replied, taken aback by his sudden change in tone.

"Well, tell me more about them. These must have been *some* lizards. Sounds like they really got the jump on you guys! How many were there? What were they like?"

"Well," she began, "I haven't seen anything comparable to them in my life. Not on Earth, and not back in the Federation animal departments. There were probably dozens of them stalking us, but we couldn't tell for sure. The bridge was too dense with plants. But we could hear them coming! Fortunately, only five came out to investigate – any more and we might not have made it out alive. Julius had to shoot one! If we waited any longer, they would've attacked. And I found it odd that they walked on two legs, not four."

"The damn things were hunting us," Julius added.

"Two-legs?" the scientist asked. "Like a theropod?"

A ther-a-what?

"What?" Severine had never heard that term before.

Theropod.

"Never mind. I forget I'm speaking science jargon. You probably shouldn't have fired. Scaring them off may ruin our chances of studying the animals further."

"We had no choice," Julius said. "They'd have swarmed us!"

"Well, even so. The only lizard I've heard of that walks on two legs like that would be a basilisk lizard, found back on Earth. If I recall, there may be a few in *Star Jumper's* animal department, but don't quote me on that. Now, how big would you say they were?"

This guy must really be into man-eating reptiles.

"Pretty big! Probably about this long." Severine spread her arms apart, trying to accurately provide a measurement from memory. "Three, maybe four feet at most. They had long tails and narrow heads. Bright green in color, with yellow spots. And razor-sharp claws!"

He looked up thoughtfully, trying to find a logical explanation for the phenomena the colonists had discovered. "Well, they were bipedal. Very large. Clearly pack hunters. Interesting! I'm not quite sure how to classify them yet. I'll have to root through some documents I've stored away in the lockers. Normally it's easy for me! Being a scientist, I'm a connoisseur of all things involving biology."

Julius gave Severine a quick eye roll. Severine assumed since they had out-muscled him, he was trying to prove his prowess in scientific ways.

"Most of the books I've brought on board are of scholarly origin. I bet I'll be able to identify the species pretty fast and find out what we're up against! Any chance we can go and recover the specimen? What's your name again, man?"

"It's Julius," the lieutenant answered. "And not a chance! It's a long walk back up there without the elevators working, and not a climb I'd be willing to make in this heat. If we encounter another pack of those things, we'll waste more ammunition. And we can't afford that."

"Right. Well, Julius. I'm Francis Paluch, level 2 scientist for the *Supernova*. Admirer and lover of all things in nature. What you and..."

He was at a loss for words, fumbling on her name.

"It's Severine..."

"Right! Thank you. What you and Severine discovered here might be a new species, unseen before by human eyes. I wish you wouldn't have shot it, but I suppose now at least I'll be able to get a better look. It's imperative that I get up there to correctly identify the specimen, if it can be identified, and bring a sample back to the rover for proper preservation. We'll have to set aside room in one of the deep-freezes, but it'll be worth it!"

"We're not going back up there, Francis. It's too dangerous. Severine and I can't guarantee your safety. I'd forget about it, because the answer is no."

"He's right," Jordy interjected. "Very unsafe! And lots of debris."

"No one asked you," Paluch said.

Jordy narrowed his eyes, sending a computerized glare at the scientist. Severine realized the technician thought of himself as superior to the bots.

"Julius, I'm sorry I have to do this," Paluch started, "but I'm relieving you of command. Daddy, we're taking control of this rover!"

The pilot bot turned, blinking yellow cautionary lights at the invalid command.

"Negative. Your order does not compute," recited the bot.

"Daddy, lock all doors," Julius ordered, ignoring the scientist. "Prepare to roll out! We're going to see what's out there."

"Yes, Lieutenant."

As Daddy switched a lever by his side, a driving mechanism extended forward. The bot's lights turned back to green at the lieutenant's command. Daddy gripped the wheel with one hand before offering a courtesy salute to Julius. His reprogramming had erased all previous orders given by Paluch.

"At ease, soldier."

"What have you done to him?" Paluch asked. "It took weeks to program that level of servitude!"

"He's following new orders now," Jordy replied. "Technically, he is following one of the most important orders for Federation bots. Order 399. The order from Central Command states as follows: 'In times of war, loss of power, or depletion of infantry troops, all remaining bots are to answer only to human-officer counterparts.' I reprogrammed him myself through Order 391!"

"You did *whaaaat?*" He was furious.

"It had to happen," Severine added. "His orders were outdated. And he was waving that gun in my face like a maniac! I could've been killed! Your programming was shoddy at best, Mr. Paluch. Sorry to say."

"He was long overdue for an update," Jordy added.

"You don't have a problem with it, do you, Daddy?" Severine asked.

"No, Corporal." Daddy remained static in the chair, still staring out onto the crumbling ruins.

"Good," Julius said, finalizing the argument. "So why don't you sit back, relax, and let us try to get you out of here. Hell, go read one of your science books! Try to find out what the lizards are. Make yourself useful and stay out of our way."

Paluch, grumbling to himself, was about to offer another argument, but instead stood up and walked dramatically out of the room. He activated the far door in the FATR, took a seat against one of the lockers, and slouched begrudgingly as the motorized panel closed behind him.

"Sure is a friendly guy, isn't he?" Julius commented sarcastically.

"I'd certainly have dated him," Severine joked.

"Don't do that to yourself," Jordy said. "Then you would be settling!"

She laughed at the machine's quick wit.

"Thanks, Jordy."

The bot has a sense of humor, that's for sure!

Julius approached the front. "Let's take a seat. It could be a bumpy ride."

He fell down in the co-pilot chair next to Daddy as hologram pop-up options materialized to the front.

"Severine, could you retrieve Daddy's pistol back there on the floor? I don't know this Paluch well enough to trust him yet – just as a safety precaution. He's a little loony."

"Good idea," she said with a firm nod. She was thinking the same thing herself.

She returned with the pistol, putting it in a spare safety compartment behind her cockpit seat, and closed the hatch. With a click, the gun was out of harm's way.

"Technically speaking, scientists aren't authorized to carry a firearm anyway," Jordy affirmed. "He would be breaking Federation protocol."

"I don't think he cares about protocol," Severine said. "Look at all the rules he's broken already!"

VREEEE-VREEEE! A computerized tone started from the rover.

"What's that?" Jordy asked.

"My mapping projection has completed," the pilot answered.

As Daddy prepared to send the FATR rumbling out of the storage shed, he pressed a dashboard button–and a hologram dissolved into the windshield. As it shrunk back into the projector port, another image started, this time in the center of the room in a three-dimensional cube. The new virtual image expanded to fill the cockpit.

"This is incredible!" Severine said, staring into the light show.

Laid out before them was a geometric scan of the terrain around the *Supernova.* The readout information that typed away estimated a geographic radius of thirty miles, spanning in all directions. Around the ship, black and white rendered mountains and forests started to spring up in cyberspace. A river comprised of tiny blue particles curved by just north of their position, and a shallow sea rose to the east. Clouds and weather patterns circulated over the map, sweeping into the image cube from one angle and exiting through the other side. Secure paths were illuminated by white light particles that indicated where the FATR could travel safely. Occasionally, flickers of red and orange would radiate throughout the map, hidden under the forests.

"What are those?" Severine asked, pointing at the crimson radiating lights.

"Thermal signals," Daddy replied. "Lifeforms."

"Humans?"

"Not sure," Julius said. "They're hard to see."

The map had a hard time pinpointing them under the thick tree canopy, making their exact locations unknown. Usually they would only appear as a momentary blip before vanishing again under the virtual glitching branches. None of the heat signals were identifiable.

More damn animals probably. Hopefully something other than the lizards...anything but those!

"Well done, Pilot!" Julius congratulated. "Not sure how you activated this feature, but this will make our passage a lot easier! I've ridden in these many times, but never saw this. Needless to say, I'm very impressed!"

"Thank you, sir," Daddy replied.

A particle stream appeared and chased its own tail at the indicated position of the rover in a grassy area that must have been the computer's representation of Cargo Bay 2.

Hello, what's this?

Severine followed a trio of glitching arrows pointing to the northeast. Twenty-some miles away, on the upper right corner of the holographic cube, was a dome-like object embedded in the earth. The obstacle protruded out from the dirt like an ancient metal shrine. Severine was shocked that she hadn't noticed it earlier.

A digital data tab began to relay information over the strange object's location.

Classification: Federation E5 Escape Pod
Name: Mudskipper
Status: Downed/Damaged
Crew: N/A
Vehicle ID: 20492.129
Carrier: Supernova
Miles: 23.5 Northeast
Type: Short Range Signal/Location ID
Strength: Weak/Dying

An escape pod from the ship!

"It looks like that wreck still has power! Someone may have survived!"

"Daddy, can you get us there?" Julius asked.

"Yes, Lieutenant. Hold on! The journey could be rough."

VI

The FATR rattled passionately as the dusty exterior treads began to clink together and roll forward. The titanium panels that formed the outer protective shell folded farther out in defense positions. Roofing fixtures dropped down and were replaced with communication ports that populated the top. The XP-300 twin canons leveled forward towards the front side, parallel to the rover's driving direction. Through the orange windows of the cockpit, Severine could see the fog parting as the vehicle drove out from the storage room.

This is going to be fun!

"Which path shall we take, sir?" Daddy asked, referring to the multiple luminescent trails that dotted the holographic landscape. Several roads led to the *Mudskipper*, but most passed through unpredictable, rough terrain.

Julius studied the imagery.

"Let's go with Path-choice B, Pilot," he said finally. "That looks to be the most promising, don't you agree?"

"Yes, sir. A wise choice!"

Path-choice B appeared to be the safest route. It would take them through the jungle, then over a series of grassy hills that lay in the shadow of a mountainous ridge before passing the sea to the east. No immediate debris blocked their route, save for the immediate jungle region that stood to become mincemeat under the FATR's riveted underbelly.

With a clink, Julius pushed the levers forward and the vehicle lurched ahead with a powerful, mechanized groan.

Whoa! Severine felt herself lift out of her seat as the vehicle began moving.

"Oh, my!" Jordy yelled, grasping his armrests to stabilize himself in a comedic death grip.

The frame of the storage compartment moved towards them and shrank smoothly above the cockpit. Then the FATR rotated forward, dropping several feet below as the machine met with a brief impact as it struck the weed-covered concrete.

CLINNNKKKKKK!

The impact meant nothing to the rover. It picked itself back up and continued churning ahead, kicking up earth beneath the dark, motorized treads. Industrial noises and squealing commenced as the back half of the vehicle exited the storage shed and slipped down to the ground.

With a loud, heavy *brrrrrrrrrrrm,* they were in the cargo bay again.

Behind her in the next chamber, Severine could hear the deep-freeze containers swaying behind their rope harnesses as they plowed through the ruins.

"This thing's a tank!" Julius said.

"It's terrific!" Severine commented. "At least one thing's gone our way so far!"

She glanced out the right window, observing the awesome power of the machine. The treads slid by her gaze as they dropped forward and continued to randomize the ground. Old Federation debris buckled under the weight of the oncoming titan. In the wake of the vehicle's immense base, the dirt broke apart, exposing the fragmented concrete floor of the forgotten *Supernova* Cargo Bay 2.

Daddy operated the steering wheel, turning to avoid objects he deemed potentially too large for the rover to handle. Julius maintained two levers on the adjacent side at the co-pilot position. When Severine asked Jordy what they were, he told her they were most likely controllers for the tread pressure or overall speed.

"I'm glad you guys know how to work this thing," Severine admitted, smiling.

This vehicle has changed our luck entirely!

"Ten intense weeks of officer candidate school," Julius replied. "It was a nightmare, but I'm now convinced it's paying itself off. The hyper-sleep made me forget some details about FATR operations, but I know enough to get us moving."

"Where would you like to proceed, sir?" the pilot asked. "I'm seeing trees all around the rubble with no perfect way to find a point of entry to Path-choice B."

"Aim for those trees there!" Julius pointed. "Just make sure not to hit any of those old support beams. They're the only thing left keeping the roof up. We don't want anything to break off and damage our outer shell."

"Yes, sir. I'll be careful," confirmed the digital voice.

"Check this out," Julius said as he thumbed down two buttons on the co-pilot levers.

Above their heads, a massive folding mechanism fell gracefully in front of the rover. Equipped with menacing metal blades, the contraption landed a few feet from the ground. With the push of a button on Julius' lever, it jolted to life, spinning violently with an intimidating whine.

"We'll just have to make our own road!" Julius smiled, softly pushing his controls ahead.

The FATR reached the edge of the rubble where the concrete floor fragments gave way to green ferns that bordered the outlying jungle.

WWHHEERRRRRLLLLLLLLLL!

The metal teeth from the rover jaws ate away at the first unfortunate tree they encountered. The mossy trunk split neatly in half and transformed into tiny sawdust particles under the ferocious blades. As the tree became dust, Severine thought she could smell fresh lumber through the glass pane.

Incredible!

"Isn't that nifty?" Julius asked as more trees continued to fall into the blades. "These were a relatively new upgrade, last I checked. They dubbed it the 'Carnivore' attachment."

"We'll be there in no time!"

"You bet!"

Soon they were out of the ruins and into the unknown shroud of the morning jungle. Thick vegetation began to slap into the windshield, leaving wet dew marks along the glass. The greenery obscured their view, exposing only a few feet of jungle at a time. As the leaves fell past, fresh new ones would appear and take their place.

Under the warm glow of the sunlight, the dawn in the jungle was docile and beautiful. The rays from the sun pierced through the canopy and cast streaks of light over the trails. Many of the trees under the shade were surreal, splitting apart at the top with two separate, bristle-like branches. Other trees swirled upward in many crossing trunks. Bushes along the ground hugged together in spiral bundles.

What is this place?

Severine was mesmerized by the dreamlike landscape.

As the FATR continued along, the vegetation continued to grow more hectic. Julius extended a small, digital periscope over their heads, hoping for a more beneficial perspective, but the hologram display was virtually identical to the windshield view. The morning fog, which hovered above like a restless ghost, wasn't helpful either.

"I'm going to decrease our speed," Julius said. "I don't want to run over any sharp wreckage pieces that the Carnivore might miss. They could be buried nearby for miles, anywhere along the path. And we'll have no reaction time."

"Yes, sir," Daddy replied. "Go at a comfortable pace."

Severine took notice of the leaf shapes as they glided past. There were many similar shapes that she recognized as plants that the Federation had been transporting. But still, there were subtle differences. They were more untamed, and somehow, looked more primitive.

Ferns.

Lots of ferns! And strange stem plants.

The leaves were of various shades and sizes. Some were barely the size of her palm, but many of the larger flora were long and fan-shaped. What began as soft ferns suddenly gave way to slender, overhanging palm fronds.

The forest here was thick and abundant. Severine realized it may take longer to arrive at the *Mudskipper* crash site than they previously anticipated.

A cold chill blew over her spine as she felt a familiar presence behind her. The scientist had returned quietly to the cockpit, observing the landscape behind the glass. Julius frowned from the co-pilot seat after he saw the ominous figure standing in the reflection.

Here we go again...

Only this time, the scientist was silent – happy, even.

He was focused intently on the world ahead, watching as the rover pushed further into the botanical hedges. His right hand shot up and padded its way to his lab coat breast pocket, retrieving a pen and crumpled notepad. On the paper, he began to reproduce a crude rendition of the passing plants as best he could. When he finished admiring his work, Paluch passed the paper to Severine.

"Is that close?" he asked.

She squinted at the doodle.

What the hell is this?

"Yeah, pretty close," she lied.

The drawing was horrendous.

"Thanks. Drawing is a second hobby of mine." He pushed his sagging glasses back up his nose. "No hard feelings about earlier? Sometimes I can get a little carried away. You too, Julius, I'm sorry! You're in charge! Wow, these plant specimens are terrific!" He quickly changed the subject and snatched the notepad back from Severine and continued to sketch the wild environment. As he began to doodle away, she contemplated accepting his half-assed apology.

"Well, don't get any ideas to get out for a closer look," Julius replied. "These doors stay sealed. The answer is still a firm *no*."

"That's fine," Paluch replied. "We'll need to clear the crap off the treads eventually. I'll sneak a quick peek then." He smiled.

"We'll see," Julius replied with a sarcastic, weak laugh.

"Sorry," Paluch replied. "I can't help myself here! These plants are unlike anything I've seen before, and they're all over the place!"

"What makes you find them so interesting?" Severine asked.

"As an observer and aficionado of science and biology, I'm always on the lookout for new species. The plants we're seeing here are either very rare or remain undiscovered before by mankind. Some of these types, if harvested, could be edible or may even help cure illnesses – well, maybe. I could be getting ahead of myself! In addition to my botanical interests, I also dabble in the studies of history, archaeology, and paleontology. And this world we've happened upon looks like all three combined!"

"What do you mean?" Jordy asked. "You think there could be older civilizations out there?"

"Something like that, robot. I think we'll know soon enough! I've already deduced that this place is a very special biome in the scientific sense. See these ferns here on the upper right? I'm not entirely sure, and I'll have to double check some books in my study, but they look a lot like *lepidopteris ferns* to me. More specifically, they may be *Lepidopteris stormbergensis*. They existed once on Earth and have been long thought to be extinct. Yet they're here, thriving in abundance!"

"Looks like normal ferns to me," Julius said.

Severine laughed.

The two conflicting personalities would certainly make this trip interesting.

"Yes, to the untrained eye, they do look exceptionally similar. And you could be right. I would have to see them later and study them closely to draw a more accurate conclusion."

The FATR continued carving its trail through the forest. Tree ferns continued to topple in the wake of the spinning sears.

In the tropical heat, Severine could make out small bursts of insects as they fled from their positions among the leaves. Most were small, but a few were bloated and fat. One splattered into the windshield in a failed attempt to flee the chaos. Paluch flipped a page in his sketchpad and started fresh, this time drawing the grasshopper that lay smeared across the glass.

"Very interesting! Insects are flourishing here too! It'd be nice if it wasn't blown to shit over the glass and I could draw with better representation."

He pressed his notebook against the window for support and completed the sketch. Severine peeked over his shoulder. The drawing resembled nothing like the subject matter.

"You're really into this stuff, huh?" Severine said, trying to come off as friendly.

"Indeed, I am. See you folks later! I have more research to do. I hope I stashed the right books away. Maybe I can correctly identify these finds." Paluch did a goofy salute and walked away from the cockpit before once again disappearing back into the next room. Once away, he began rummaging through his personal library crammed inside the lockers.

Julius shot Severine a gloomy look, causing her to let a laugh slip out.

He isn't taking kindly to our house guest.

"Not sure what to make of him yet," he smirked. "And the salute? Was that mocking the infantry? I ought to toss his sorry little lab coat ass overboard."

"I think he may be coming around," she replied. "We need to make sure he always has something to study. Or draw!"

The lieutenant smiled.

"Well, he better stay out of my way!"

As they crashed through another wall of tree ferns, the rover flew suddenly into a trail hidden in the forest. Julius pressed another set of buttons on his lever controls and extended the Carnivore back over the roof. As the device lifted over the glass, they looked out on a grassy, overgrown path that ran through the jungle, slinking away in both directions.

"Daddy, do you think we can follow this road up to the escape pod?"

"It appears that way, Lieutenant," Daddy replied. "This will eventually lead right out to the open floodplains and take us around the swampland to the east. Safer to travel, and easier on the FATR. Once we're on the flats, it won't take much longer to reach the *Mudskipper*."

"Right then. Let's go right and follow the trail."

"Yes, sir!"

The rover turned and started up the grassy pathway. The trail was wide enough on both sides for the machine to fit quite comfortably. Tree ferns and stem plants lined the side while low-lying shrubs sprouted up throughout most of the road's center. On the ground, Severine noticed no more traces of *Supernova* debris. She assumed they must have already driven a mile or two inland from the wreckage.

"Some kind of old service road?" Severine asked.

"Or a hunting trail. Maybe animal made?" Jordy said.

"Just don't call Mr. Artist out here," Julius remarked. "He'll want to set up an easel."

"What do you think about what Paluch was saying?" Severine questioned.

"About what?"

"This place. The plants."

"Isn't it obvious?" Jordy interrupted. "I retract my previous remarks. Based on all I've been seeing, I'm fairly confident now that we're back on Earth."

"Well, that's a complete one-eighty-degree change of opinion," Julius joked.

"Earth is gone," Severine replied. "What makes you think we're on Earth?"

"A few reasons," Jordy started. "For one, we can't be certain that Earth is destroyed. When the colonist ships left, we abandoned the world in a state of disarray. The oceans were rising. The continents were shrinking. The radiation from the Old War would have wiped out mankind if we stayed. But, perhaps in our years in space, the planet flourished in our absence, returning to grace. We know that during space travel, time goes at a different rate. It's possible that we were away longer than our clocks read. The Federation assumed that Earth was gone, but maybe our old home was given a second chance when we left – that's my first reason."

"And what's the next reason?"

"Well, next would be the plants. As our studious, annoying friend has pointed out, these plants were at one time living on Earth. I don't see it likely that these exact same plants are on another planet. And the organisms we've seen thus far – the insects and the lizards. They're very Earth-like, too. My belief now is that we're back on planet Earth."

"That's reaching pretty far, little buddy," Julius replied. "All these plants have grown back and healed Earth in that brief amount of time that the Federation pulled out? I doubt it!"

"Well, I must admit, I'm not a scientist, like Francis. I'm strictly logistics. If we aren't back on Earth, it is certainly a comparable planet in many ways. We could even be stuck in a parallel universe."

Or this is all a dream, Severine thought.

She felt the topic was becoming very surreal.

A hologram suddenly blinked on above the dashboard in front of Daddy. Glowing thermal dots clustered ahead of their location on a radar scan. The pilot studied the map briefly before waving it back down into the console port.

"What is it?"

"I recommend we decrease our speed, sir," Daddy suggested. "The thermal scans are picking up several lifeforms directly ahead on the trail."

"Are they humans? Any Federation signals?"

"Not sure, Lieutenant. But they don't appear to be."

"Right, I'll decrease speed. Take us in. I'm actually curious as to what they are."

"Yes, sir."

More lizards? Or something worse...

The idea of more animals nearby both enthralled and terrified the group. If not for the protection of the FATR, Severine doubted they would be investigating the heat signals.

"How far away are they?" Jordy asked.

"We're coming up on them now," Daddy replied. "Just over this next hill..."

The group huddled close to the front to get a decent view. The rover slowly drove up the path before reaching the top of the small mound in the road. Small, beeping noises started to emit from the console and a warning radar light had become active.

They must be right over that ridge!

And indeed, they were.

What kind of odd animals are these?

The rover halted as a strange beast waddled in front of the right tread and scooted off into the greenery.

"Whoa! All stop," said Julius, jerking the levers back sharply before locking them into place.

The FATR stopped at the hilltop, looking down over the path ahead.

Several yards from the rover's treads, a group of the strange lumbering creatures gathered under the long shade of the tree ferns. They grazed intently on the shrubbery and roughage that combed through the trail, oblivious to their human spectators. More of the beasts wandered clumsily along the sides of the path near the jungle brush. They were unlike any animal Severine could recall from the Federation database.

There's gotta be at least fifty of them! She looked eagerly through the glass, interested by their fat torsos and bumbling movements.

"What the hell are they?" Julius asked, leaning forward.

"They look like big, funny cats," Jordy replied.

Severine thought the bot's comparison was probably the most accurate description the four of them could come up with. And yet, the animals looked nothing like cats.

The field beasts had fat tummies and meaty heads with strong, broad jaws. The mouths snapped open and closed as their teeth munched down their morning meals. Adults of the group were brown in color, while the juveniles had a creamy, mocha tone with spots lining their backs and dotting their small, wiggling tails. Severine took note of the maternal nature of the herbivores. The calves were packed tightly behind a defensive phalanx built by the adults. Most of the young were herded like cattle towards the center of the path, kept away from the edge of the jungle. The largest animal was nearly six feet in length, sunbathing on a rock as it kept a careful eye on the FATR.

"Amazing!" Severine exclaimed. She couldn't take her eyes off them.

"Why aren't they running?" Julius asked. "Surely they can see us. We're right on top of them!"

"They must not perceive the FATR as a threat," Jordy replied. "They probably don't know what to think of it. Maybe they assume it's just another plant-eater."

"Let's open the hatch and take a look," Severine suggested. "They're blocking the trail. After we check them out, we can shy them away and continue to the escape pod."

She found it difficult to suppress the obvious enthusiasm in her voice. When she saw that the animals were only plant-eaters, she wanted nothing more than to run down and observe them.

"Well, let's think about this," Julius started. "They could still be dangerous. And there may be other animals in the jungle that we're not seeing. The radar can only depict so much under the trees. The green lizards could be around…"

"Oh, Julius. Look at them. They're harmless!" Severine replied.

"I agree with Sev," Jordy said. "Running over them would make for some unpleasant tread-cleaning later. And firing the XP-300 would waste precious pulse blasts. It makes sense that we go out and coax them away."

"*Hollyyyyyyyyyyy* crap!" A voice spoke behind them.

Francis Paluch had returned once again. He stood frozen in his lab coat, staring wide-eyed at the grassland animals dispersed through the glass. His animal-discovery look was much more dramatic and aghast than his plant-notepad-sketching face.

"Please, Julius. You must let me out! Let us out, I mean. Severine, what do you think? Help me out here, kid."

Great…make me the decision-maker.

Thankfully, Julius knew he was outnumbered and consented. Everyone wanted to go out and see the unique animals, even the robots.

"All right. Stick together. Let's try to be quick about it, okay? No reason to sit around and gawk at them. Daddy, open the rear door and park the treads. We have a herd to move!"

As the group departed the FATR cockpit, another radar hologram popped up on the dashboard, unseen by the departing crew. As the image static flickered and settled, a second group of red thermal imaging dots appeared just south of their position. The shapes were moving slowly through the jungle, following the destructive path the rover had carved out just minutes earlier. As they grew closer, they began to fan out and encircle the human position, anticipating a showdown with the colonists.

They were being followed.

VII

Maybe he really is a good artist, Severine thought as she stood overheated in the morning humidity, fanning herself with her hands.

She craved the refreshing air from the rover's air-conditioned vents, but the outside world was too interesting and demanded exploration, even in the exhausting heat.

They had been loitering around the forest path for a little over ten minutes, each with their own varying agendas. Julius and Daddy vainly sought to scare off the animal herd at the front of the vehicle, where a large number of the species had congregated. At first, Jordy tried to assist, but decided he was getting in the way, and instead attempted to dislodge debris trapped in the rover's treads.

Severine resolved to use her utility light from her X2-20 to deter the creatures away from the left treads and managed to scare off some calves. As they begrudgingly dispersed, their places were retaken by bulkier, more stubborn adults. That's when she spotted Paluch, who sat near the edge of the tree line, parked contently on a Federation fold-out observation chair for a front row seat.

His wrist flicked away diligently as he sketched the grazing herd, this time on a larger notepad binder with a sharp pencil. When she came up beside him, she took note of the new drawing. This rendition had a greater level of detail than his first doodles, with special attention to form, depth, and shading. His focus was a cluster of the animals on the edge of the trail, migrating slowly towards the leafy jungle barrier. In the frame, he managed to capture both the adults and the juveniles of the species, despite their fluctuating positions.

"Looks good! You nailed them," she complimented him.

A lot better than your first drawings...

"Thanks," he replied. "I don't want to spend too much time on the art. I'm going to go in soon for a closer look, before Julius succeeds in actually scaring them away."

"Any idea what they might be? I don't remember any similar animals on the *Supernova*."

When their ship had been in orbit, she had made a point to visit the animals on board often. The division had been headed mainly by logistics bots and scientists, like Paluch. The Federation carried many species of animals in one of the supply docks that they rehabilitated into a sort of zoo, featuring dogs, cats, reptiles, aquatic species like amphibians and fish, and many others. The primary goal was to bring the fauna to a new, breathable planet and introduce them into the wild to flourish again.

Severine wondered what happened to the captive animals after the ship crashed.

They're all probably dead now. Rotting away in their cages or floating forever in the nothingness of space...

"Well, it's all very interesting, Severine," Paluch said. "Let's start with some of these plants here. These foot-long ferns are a plant called *Sphenopteris*. I remember it well from my botanical notes. It's an ancient plant species from

Earth, long since extinct – remarkable! When I first saw it out here, I did a double-take!"

Severine nodded, trying to feign interest in the fern.

"And again, more extinct plants over here! Look at that small, palm-looking bush. It's *Pachypteris*! Also thought to be extinct! They had a large distribution in the Mesozoic, ranging from Brazil to Russia!"

Paluch continued to churn out facts about the strange plants and their relation to the old countries of Earth. Soon she grew bored of his botanical lectures and decided to expedite the process.

"Yes, they're very interesting. But they're plants, Paluch – tell me about the animals!"

"Well, I have a few guesses – in other words, they could be a slew of things. I don't want to reveal my thoughts until I can be more certain. Let's just say if these animals are what I think they are, then we've just made a breakthrough discovery! And it also means, unfortunately, that we might be in for some very big trouble ahead."

Trouble?

"No need to worry yet, though," Paluch said, quickly changing the subject. "I don't know for sure what they are. Just have a hunch, is all."

You're not going to elaborate further on what trouble means? She waited and soon assumed the answer was no. Instead, Paluch chose to keep her hanging in an agonizing suspense. She was about to confront him for an answer when Julius' voice called out and interrupted her thoughts.

"Hey, Sev!" he yelled. "Hey, come check this out! Found something you should see."

Julius was standing near the edge of the trail, pushing aside leaves that blocked the jungle. She walked over to him, passing carefully among the peaceful animals, who paid her little attention. At her approach, for the most part, they simply lifted their heads and gave a welcoming snort before resuming their leafy breakfast.

"Look what I found staring back at me," Julius said, pointing to an overgrown, grassy patch at the jungle's edge. She crouched down to spread apart the golden stems and was greeted by a gruesome, frightening sight.

"Jeez, Julius!"

What happened here?

Hiding in the untamed weeds and lichens was an ancient Federation infantry suit. The chest plate was lying face up, revealing years of damage done by rain erosion and insect habitation. The Federation logo was almost unrecognizable from the battering of elements. What should have been a vibrant, orange-striped insignia was now a muted tan, faded from excessive sunlight exposure. As she leaned in closer, Severine could make out a trace of red smeared across the breastplate.

It's definitely blood, she confirmed, noticing bone fragments under the armor, buried in brush and mud.

A pair of sharp gashes ran the length of the neck to the waist, shredding some of the nylon fibers, leaving the plating scuffed, and exposing the metal backing underneath. Whoever had been unfortunate enough to wear this suit had been met with a grisly, violent end many years before.

"There were other survivors," Julius said as he stood behind her, examining the discovery.

"It would seem that way," she replied. "But from how long ago? This may be a suit from a soldier who survived the initial crash when the ship went down. Or maybe someone that left hyper-sleep much earlier than we did."

"By the fading colors, I'd say this one's from the original crash date – three hundred years ago. Just look at how corroded the outer plating is! I couldn't even tell you the rank! The stripe is all screwed up. A sergeant, maybe?"

The long rips in the suit stared grimly back at them. The width of the seams were almost two inches wide. It looked like someone stabbed the suit with a large spike, tilted it sideways, and pulled it straight down to the victim's abdomen.

"Knife wound?" she guessed.

"Hardly," Julius replied. "It was an animal attack. There may be bigger lizards in the area than we previously thought. Look at the width of those claw impressions. Something big did this..."

"It would have to be a pretty big lizard!" Severine replied.

"At least as big as us – maybe even a hair larger."

The thought of bigger carnivores prowling nearby made her shudder. She stood back up and looked no more at the armor outfit that lay taunting them at their feet. She backed up, letting the large leaves once again rise up, hiding the grave in shadows.

At their front, a chilly morning breeze swept through the trees, sending the fronds and stems moving in the wind, which provoked some of the adults to stir and glance around defensively. Something downwind made them alert, thus interrupting their morning meal.

"We need to get these animals off the path," Julius said urgently, detecting something was amiss.

Severine gave a firm nod.

And get the hell out of here...

#

Further attempts to clear the herd from the forest path resulted in continued, aggravated failure. The curious beasts were far more interested in their food than obeying the colonists. Several anxious juveniles barked as Severine approached, trying to shoo her away. The parents, in response, let out a cautionary growl and shuffled in front of their young. Julius, Daddy and Jordy tried to force the animals away by screaming and hollering, but the herd remained steadfast and held their ground.

Paluch gravitated over to one of the isolated adults. At the foot of the beast, the scientist collected specimens in a transparent vial for preservation and further study. His hairy subject was shedding small fur samples that the technician scooped up eagerly with a thin pair of tweezers. Severine winced as he gathered a soggy stool sample and put it delicately into a sealed canister, smiling at his find.

"Think I should make him get off his ass and help?" Julius asked.

"No, keep him over there. He'll just get in the way," she laughed.

Probably better if these two stay separated...

She presumed by now that their relationship with Paluch would be odd at best. Scientists in the Federation could easily become enamored with their work and were usually found holed up in their rooms, deep in study. They rarely fraternized with the other Federation divisions, especially the infantry. Now, thrown together in this tropical world, she debated to herself how their relationship with the scientist could improve.

"Any more ideas on how to clear these pesky things?"

"Well, can the FATR make some kind of noise?" Severine asked.

"Yes, Corporal," Daddy replied walking over. "It has a digital horn at the wheel."

Of course! A horn. Why hadn't I thought of that before?

"It's pretty loud," Julius said. "But it just might work! Daddy, why don't you go up there and give it a shot. Moving the animals by hand doesn't seem to be working."

"Yes, Lieutenant."

The bot walked away and disappeared behind the FATR. His robotic silhouette soon appeared in the cockpit above their heads and he gave a cautionary wave of his hand, indicating they should cover their ears. Once they cupped their hands over their heads, the bot activated an unseen button below the dashboard.

BRRRRRRRRRRRRR!

A loud vibration fired out of the machine's front side, reverberating through the road with a powerful echo that dispersed in the jungle. The force of the sound was so great it shook many of the leaves and fronds with a delicate wave. The animals closest to the machine jumped back and scampered away, but the majority of the herd remained rooted in their tracks.

"Hit it again!" Julius yelled.

BRRRRRRRRRRRRRR!

A duplicate horn call blurted out from the FATR, evoking the same result.

"They must be hard of hearing," Julius shrugged. "Or too stupid to fear it."

"Hey, stop doing that!" Paluch yelled, racing over to the group. "Ringing that thing is a death wish! Do you want to alert all the predators nearby that we're here? You should consult me before you make those executive decisions?"

"Easy, buddy!" Julius said in a masculine tone. "They aren't moving. We need to clear them by any means necessary and proceed with our mission."

"This is a delicate ecosystem here, Lieutenant," the scientist replied. "Any unexpected changes or fluctuations in the biome could be met with catastrophe. Do you want your lizard creatures to show up again? Blowing that horn will alert any predators in the area that we're here."

"Sit the hell down and go collect your specimens!" Julius replied. "Leave the decision-making to us. You're really starting to piss me off, Paluch! You don't want to get on my bad side." His tone was harsh, and an angry brow had formed on his forehead.

"Lieutenant, might I make a suggestion?" Daddy asked, stepping behind Julius.

"What is it, Pilot?"

"You have nearly a full magazine in your XR-90. A few warning shots might make the animals retreat."

"Yes, I was looking to that as a last resort," Julius said. "We're low on rounds and trying to save ammunition for emergencies. But the more we sit here, I'm starting to see no further options." Julius grabbed his weapon that remained strapped tightly across his back and aimed it in the direction of the herd.

"Why can't we just go through the jungle, like you were doing?" Paluch asked.

"If I can avoid doing that anymore, I will," Julius replied. "Visibility is low, making the journey risky. If we run over unseen crash fragments, we'll risk damaging the treads! Now shut up and let me do this!"

"Step back, Mr. Paluch," Severine said. "This will just take a second, and then we'll be on our way."

"Julius, I'm begging you! If you fire that weapon, our relationship with these animals will be forever scarred. We won't be able to learn anything more from them. We've already ruined our chances of studying the green lizards – don't do the same here! Please! They'll fear us…"

"So? Find another herd!"

Oh…shit!

Paluch produced Daddy's X2-20 pistol and leveled it at Julius.

He must have waited until we were all distracted outside and then went back into the cockpit to steal it back!

Severine snapped out her X2 pistol and aimed it at Paluch's head, confused and alarmed at the sudden turn of events. At only a few feet away, her round would be lethal, but so would Paluch's blast into Julius. It was a delicate situation, and she had to be careful and rely on what she could remember from combat training.

"Mr. Paluch, listen to me. You need to set your weapon down immediately," she said, trying to appear calm but stern.

Severine knew if he squeezed the trigger, she would have no choice but to put him down. It became clear to her that the scientist was very radical about preserving this new world and would go to extreme, radical lengths to prove his points.

"Francis. If you pull that trigger, there's no going back – Severine will kill you."

Thick beads of sweat began to drip from the technician's forehead as his weapon shook in his clammy hands. Severine realized that the scientist probably hadn't fired an X2 before, or any firearm for that matter. He held the weapon wrong and his firing stance was amateurish. If he discharged the weapon, the technician would be knocked to his back and would most likely miss his intended target.

He's nervous, Severine thought, watching his hands shake. *He didn't think this through…*

Beyond the scientist, she could see Jordy frozen in his tracks at the corner of the FATR. He was unsure of what to do and remained motionless, leaving the humans to fight it out alone. Severine saw his lights blinking on and off with silent radar alarms, but Severine shook them off.

"D-daddy," Paluch said with a nervous stutter. "Get that weapon from Julius."

"Negative. That would be breaking the chain of command."

The scientist grumbled. "I programmed you," was all he could manage to say, knowing his defeat was imminent.

Julius turned calmly, aiming the XR-90 at Paluch. The lieutenant's finger slowly lowered and grazed the rifle trigger.

"Your move," Julius said confidently, knowing the scientist was outnumbered and outgunned. "You kill me, and Sev kills you."

He breathed a heavy sigh of failure, knowing his only option was to surrender. Paluch had gravely underestimated the soldiers' loyalty to one another, and incorrectly assumed Daddy would remain loyal after a system upgrade. Slowly, Paluch lowered the pistol until it remained at his hip. Severine snatched the gun away when it was aimed at the ground.

He groaned as he felt the weapon removed from his hand.

"Sorry," he muttered feebly. "I don't know wha-a-a-*aauughh*!"

"*Aughhhh!*" Severine shrieked, lowering her pistol.

What happened next was surreal and so fast that Severine jumped back at the quick flash of green that streaked past her.

Out of the corner of her eye, she saw the slender forms coming. The first arrived with such an incredible speed and ferocity, Severine failed to fire. The warning lights from Jordy's armor suddenly made perfect sense.

The green lizards!

The pack had found them.

Bursting through the grass, the first reptile pounced on Paluch's back, sending him face first into the wet, trampled ground. He let out a shriek as the carnivore clamped down on his left shoulder and dug in with its devious, slashing claws. Behind Paluch, Severine could see more green shapes quickly bursting through the ferns, snaking quickly towards their position at the center of the trail. Beside the FATR, she could see Jordy's radar alarm lights continuing to pulsate.

What...the...

Severine was speechless. Her eyes were locked, and her feet wouldn't move. The hungry pack would be on them soon. The rover doors were far enough away that they would never make it without a fight. Below her, Paluch's defenseless cries of anguish continued to ring out as the rabid lizard bit down through his flesh.

"Get it off! Get it off!" he cried as the monster shredded his lab coat.

What is this terrible world? she thought.

As the realization of death shrouded over her, Severine's basic combat training re-established itself, and she came back to reality. She breathed softly and raised her X2. Her targets snaked by quickly and would be a challenge to hit, as they maneuvered with agility through the herbivores that moaned in turmoil. She had only twenty shots before her weapon would be rendered useless – twenty chances for survival.

Please let this work...

Given the recent turn of events, she decided staying inside the FATR didn't seem so bad after all.

VIII

"Get it off!" Paluch yelled, clenching the earth as he squirmed in agony.

Severine knew her first move would be saving his life. Paluch was a scientist, and as such was a civilian in the Federation. The infantry had a strict code about civilians – take care of them first and worry about your fellow soldiers after.

Paluch's screams were muffled as the weight of the lizard forced his face into the earth. The reptile finished gnawing on the shoulder blade and began scooting up the technician's back, preparing to land a killing bite on his exposed neck.

Vrrrrrrooommm!

A blast from Severine's X2-20 pulse pistol sent the lizard flipping to the earth, landing on its side with a powerful flop. The bolt struck the scaly head, leaving a glowing crater right behind the carnivore's eye. The monster convulsed and hissed as it died, foaming blood at the quivering mouth. With a strong flick of the tail, the lizard was dead, leaving behind a scornfully cold gaze.

19 shots left...

She knew they had to conserve ammunition, making a mental note to choose her next targets more carefully.

All hell had broken loose on the path and surrounding wilderness. The herbivores were fleeing into the jungle, terrified and confused by the carnivore ambush. Several adults stayed behind to fight off their opponents and defend their young. The lizards weren't phased by the bravery of the adults and easily hopped on top of their backs to force them to the grass. Poor, whining cries rang out as the creatures collapsed under the weight of the lizards that slashed wildly at their heads. Many of the timid juveniles were encircled and ripped apart. As more of the herbivores lay dead or retreating, the focus of the green monsters gradually turned to the humans.

One of the vile things began trotting briskly towards the colonists. Several others of the pack took notice and started to advance, spurred on by the bravery of their leader.

They're relentless!

Severine knew if they didn't break through, they would be ripped apart. Her hands clutched tightly on her X2 grip, grateful that she had something to defend herself with.

"Get up!" Severine yelled, pulling Paluch to his shaky feet. The scientist was yelling profanities and clasping the shoulder wound, his face covered in wet clumps of grass. He stunk of animal piss, and his glasses were bent in a crooked angle. One of the lenses had cracked.

"I think it broke my bone!" he cried, clenching his teeth in agony. "The damn dinosaur broke my bone!"

Dinosaur?

VRRR! VRRR! VRRR!

Quick bursts of the XR-90 rang out from behind and whizzed past her head. The beams struck several reptiles that approached, causing them to jump back in fright of the deadly blasts. Julius had set his rifle to burst-mode, a move usually reserved for high-intense war-time situations for Federation soldiers. The lieutenant was certainly on top of things.

Good thinking, she thought.

"Thanks!" Severine called out to him.

Julius nodded in acknowledgment, prepping the weapon for another barrage. The XR-90 had a terrifying sound when fired, followed by a mean echo.

Pulse blasts from Julius' weapon began sailing in all directions. Severine tackled Paluch back to the ground for cover as some of the blasts sailed past her. The scientist grunted as her body fell on top of him, sending his face once again into the damp shrubs.

As she closed her eyes and hoped none of the pulse shards would hit her, Severine heard the patter of reptile feet scurrying past, before slumping over with yelps of pain. When she looked up, she was thankful that one of the blasts took down the lead reptile, causing the creature's followers to break off and fall back to the tree line.

Severine tossed the extra X2-20 pistol to Daddy, who ran over and helped her up with his strong, robotic arms.

"Head for the FATR, Corporal," the bot's digital voice replied. "I'll provide cover!"

The pilot switched the safety off his weapon and began sending concentrated blasts back at the brazen adversaries. Between X2-20 and the XR-90, the colonists had created a window of time for a narrow escape. But they would have to hurry – the window wouldn't be open for long.

"Come on!"

Severine pulled the terrified scientist back to his feet and pushed him towards the side of the FATR while stepping cautiously over a dead adult lizard. "Stay against the side! They can't get at you from the back. That's it – keep against the treads!"

He nodded with uncertainty and headed back to the rover, his knees shaking with fear. Severine followed closely behind, keeping a reassuring hand on his back as he jogged ahead. She fired two more blasts, sending a pair of approaching lizards spiraling into the mulch.

That was too close!

"Move faster!" she yelled.

Hateful eyes stared out at them from behind the dead herbivores, snaking their way towards the humans and the rover. Every now and then, a green snout would pop up from the obstacles and snap its reptilian jaws before sinking down for cover.

As she pushed Paluch along the FATR, Severine shot a look back, worried about her comrades who lingered behind as a diversion.

Another clan of lizards had begun to enter the road from the rear. Ten green forms moved silently out from the bushes, unseen by the lieutenant and the pilot.

They're flanking us! The resilience of the reptiles amazed her.

"Julius – to your rear!" she yelled. "Six o'clock!"

VRRR! VRRR! VRRR!

Julius spun around just in time, sending several more pulse blasts firing in the new direction, thus dispersing the lizards and killing a few in the middle.

Severine found Jordy shaking near the back of the rover. She shook the bot out from his mechanical stupor and pushed him forcefully along the titanium plating. She continued herding the two civilians towards the rear access hatch.

It's gonna be close!

She was sweating now, wiping her brow as the harsh sounds of gnashing jaws filled the valley. Her heart was beating fast under the armor and she was drenched in sweat. Severine wanted to yank the whole suit off, but knew the alternative would be worse if one of the lizards caught her.

The monsters had grown tired of their herbivore meals. She could see their black eyes following her position around the vehicle. They let out aggressive hunting calls as they jumped off their vanquished foes and closed in. Soon they formed a small wave that threatened to trap them against the FATR.

Finally!

They reached the rear hatch and found the door open.

"Okay you two, get insi –"

The sudden flash of green streaked by.

A reptile body slammed into Paluch, this time catching him at his front. The lizard was a younger member of the species, two feet in length. Nonetheless, the creature was lethal, tearing wildly with its little front claws. The scientist was caught off guard and failed to shield himself from the merciless attack. As the agile reptile tore into his face, the technician collapsed to the ground, blood flowing out from between his defending fingers as his hands tried to push the attacker off.

"*Holy sssshhhhhhh – ittttt!*" he shrieked between feral screams.

His cries of terror stopped as Severine dispatched the creature with a burning kill-shot to the head. She bent down to examine the wounds as Julius and Daddy caught up with them, scaring away the rest of the monsters with another few rounds from the 90.

"Get on board!" Julius yelled. "Is he dead?"

"No, I got to it in time," she replied. "Francis? Can you hear me?"

Severine moved the scientist's hands away, grimacing at what stared back.

Paluch had lost his right eye. The claw marks left a series of bloody scrapes from the forehead down to the right cheek, sending gushes of red dripping onto the frilled lab coat. What was left of the eye looked like a deflated grape and had broken off into the grass. Severine thought she heard Paluch wishing silently that he wanted to go home between terrified, exhausted sobs.

"Dammit, Sev!" Julius cried. "His eye! It's gone!"

She nodded. "I think he's in shock!"

"Well, pull him on board – more are coming!"

And he was right.

Shit!

A new wave of the green carnivores converged on the rear doors several feet away. Julius pushed Jordy inside while Daddy helped him defend the hatch.

With all her strength, Severine pulled Paluch backwards, sheathing her weapon into her utility belt holster. As she pulled him from under his armpits through the door, she could see his free hand blindly start to reach for something.

No, please. That's disgusting... Surely, he doesn't want it!

The scientist felt along the ground until his hand clenched on the neck of the lizard carcass that maimed him only seconds earlier. His grip was strong, and with a powerful heave, he pulled the corpse with him as Severine yanked him strenuously into the FATR. After the scientist was inside, she dashed back outside, grabbed Paluch's glasses that lay bent on the earth, and jumped back through the opening.

Julius fired off another few bursts as Daddy shut the entrance, sealing the colonists safely inside. On the other side of the hatch, the lizards threw themselves repeatedly at the closed door, trying desperately to force their way inside. Short groans of pain could be heard as their bodies ricocheted off the FATR's door and skidded across the hard ground.

Thud! Thud! Thud!

Safe, at last!

Severine let out an exhausted breath before slumping back on an infantry deployment chair and cracking open a water canister for a drink.

"Do you think they'll give up?" Julius asked.

"Doubt it," Paluch said, in between mournful tears. "They want us dead! They've probably been tailing us since we left the ship!" He kept his hands clenched against his face, trying to stop the bleeding that squirted out onto his collar.

Severine tried hard not to visualize the pain he was going through. With cords of bloody organs slinking out from where his eye had been, he looked like absolute hell.

Thhhuuddddd!

Behind the door, the ceaseless barrage of the jungle carnivores raged on.

They're not giving up... Severine could feel herself reaching for her X2. *We're not out of the woods yet.*

"It should hold," Julius replied.

"It will most likely hold," Daddy corrected him. "The constant pounding, however, may damage the door components, which may lead to further electrical failures throughout the rover. My recommendation is to find a way out of this quickly, Lieutenant."

"Right, let's go to the cockpit and check out the road!"

"Jordy, can you patch him up?" Severine asked.

"Should be able to," the bot answered, studying the scientist's wounds. "I saw a medical crate in the next room. There should be some first-aid kits."

"Great! Make it happen – fast! Oh, and he'll need these!" She handed him the glasses.

She followed Julius and Daddy to the cockpit, leaving Jordy, Paluch, and the dead lizard in the rear chamber. Even in his frail, wounded state, the scientist was infatuated with the dead creature. He held his head wound firmly but had already begun to study the specimen with his free hand under a magnifying glass.

Severine looked out of the windshield as Julius and Daddy resumed their positions.

The road ahead was a scene of her darkest fears. Near the edges of the trail, the herbivore bodies had piled up as the lizards devoured them. Amid the carnage, the green, slithering shapes filled most of the open spaces between the carcasses. Severine quickly counted at least fifty of them at the vehicle's front.

Hissss!!!!

"*Aaghhh!*" She screamed as one of the reptiles leaped at the windshield and bounced off the glass, falling back to the ground with a regretful yelp.

They can jump that high?

As the impact from the first monster hit the ground, several others took notice of the cockpit and began hopping up, chomping at the humans.

"Daddy, try the horn!"

"Yes, sir."

The deafening blast rang out again and amplified through the interior floors of the FATR. The carnivores nearest to the rover withdrew briefly from the sudden sound, but resumed their attack once the blaring ceased.

They have us surrounded, and they know it!

"Again!"

"Yes, sir."

The lizards jumped up angrily, gnashing their teeth at the colonists protected behind the windshield. One reptile clawed at the glass, leaving a small indentation before gravity pulled it back below the dashboard.

"Damn! I think it's just pissing them off – what else have we got?"

"We have the XP-300 canons, but it won't aim low enough to hit the targets. We could do an electrical strike," the bot replied. "I wouldn't recommend this option. It will draw a lot of power from the internal battery and may take a few days to recharge."

"I think we're gonna have to do it – we're out of options..."

"Yes, sir! Here we go."

The bot punched in a shortcut on the blinking console keypad, causing the radar screen to fade up once again. Around the base of the rover icon, Severine saw thermal signals enclosing on the FATR exterior, bouncing violently off the armor. Holographic circles locked onto the lizards from an aerial view, tracing their movements and calculating their dimensions and body mass. Although many were dead from the skirmish outside, Severine saw there were still a hundred of them congregating around the vehicle – a massive pack!

They really do want us dead!

Behind the radar screen, a blast radius icon popped up and fanned out, displaying where the electric strike would cause the most damage. According to the warning indicators, everything within ten meters of the rover would perish in the blast.

"Looks good to me," Julius said. "Fry them!"

"Yes, sir."

Daddy leaned forward, pushing a holographic lightning bolt button on the upper left corner of the radar screen.

VRRRROOOMMMM!!!

A quick flash jolted out from the rover, sending dancing lightning bolts shooting along the grassy trail before burrowing into the soil. Below the windshield, the reptiles dispersed as the volts shook into them. A few were lucky to hop away, but Severine noted that many thermal body signals on the radar display were twitching or lying still.

Aftershocks in the ground reached the farther lizards who were fortunate to stay beyond the blast radius. The wattage wasn't at a lethal level when it hit them, but it was enough to scare them back into the jungle. The carnivores fled from the road, leaving only their mangled victims behind as they darted back into the ferns. The pounding on the rover stopped, and the wilderness was silent once again.

Severine looked at the empty radar screen, giving Julius a commemorative pat on the shoulder.

"No hostiles remaining in the area, Lieutenant," Daddy said. "I think the blast took out the majority of their pack."

It's over, Severine thought, finally relaxing as her heart rate returned to normal.

"That was way too close out there," Julius replied. "I don't think any one of us could've been ready for that! They came out of nowhere!"

"And they could still be nearby," Severine said. She had no intention of going back out to explore the jungle, no matter what beautiful animals they would encounter.

"Is the road passable?" Julius asked. "I'd hate to have to go back into the trees…"

"Most of the animals are on the sides of the road," Daddy replied. "I think we'll be safe to continue without damaging the treads. Shall we commence with our mission?"

"Let's go," Julius said, sliding his hands once more over the driving levers.

"I'll go check on the scientist," Severine said, preparing to leave.

Julius grabbed her arm firmly as she rose out of her seat, causing her to turn. "Watch yourself back there. He drew a weapon on us!"

"I know – I'll be careful. He's practically harmless now…"

"He still has one eye, doesn't he? He's capable of anything. After he's patched up, I recommend containing him in the rear chamber. He won't be able to try anything if he's locked up. Eventually, I'd like a word with him. We need to be sure he doesn't do anything stupid like that again."

"I agree."

Severine headed to the rear door. In her mind, she assumed the scientist's aggressive stance on the road was a bluff to prevent any harm to the animals, but it was impossible to be certain.

She recalled the scientist's apology after he drew his gun on Julius, and it had sounded heartfelt, coming from a man in deep regret. She knew the lieutenant heard his apology too, although his macho demeanor might prevent him from accepting it. Either way, she hoped Paluch meant it sincerely, for his sake. Another slip up, and they'd have to leave him behind.

Something else refused to leave her thoughts – a word Paluch used after the first creature trounced him.

Dinosaur? she thought. *Yes, that was it.*

He referred to the green lizard as a dinosaur.

IX

Severine stepped through the rear chamber.

When the door opened, she found Paluch bending over the deceased lizard with his magnifying glass, wincing as Jordy bandaged the scientist's head in gauze after treating him with anti-bacterial wipes and lotion. The scientist had a makeshift laboratory set up and positioned the lizard over a white laboratory cloth near a flimsy, cordless lamp. He leaned over the carcass, setting the magnifying glass down often to sketch the specimen with his free hand. Except for some subtle moaning, Paluch seemed to forget all about his injuries. He was so lost in his work he didn't even hear the door veer open.

The man just lost an eye and he's more concerned about a dead lizard!

"This is the best I can do," the bot told him, finishing the bandage. "Just don't apply too much pressure – it may aggravate and reopen the wounds."

Paluch winced. "Could you not bind my head so tightly?"

"You're lucky I don't suffocate you for what you did!" Jordy reprimanded him. "You drew a gun on us – and you could've killed the lieutenant!"

"I wasn't going to kill him," Paluch retorted. "I could never kill anyone! But I couldn't let him disrupt the ecosystem any more than we already had. Shooing them off the road was one thing but gunning them down is another! Those animals are incredibly rare. Who knows when or if we'll run into them again."

"I believe Julius was trying to scare the herd, not harm them," Severine said, announcing her presence as she leaned against one of the deployment chairs.

Paluch jumped at the sound of her approach, but relaxed when he realized it wasn't Julius.

"Oh, it's you! Sorry about what happened back there…" He set down his utensils and turned sharply in his chair, almost knocking over his lamp in the process.

"I can never take back what happened out there," Paluch started, in what seemed to be the beginning of a heartfelt apology. "I acted on my feelings and wanted to preserve our relationship with those creatures. If I hadn't gotten involved in your affairs, my damn eye might still be intact! Most of all, I probably would've seen the little bastards coming! My decision to draw the gun was ill-advised, but I assure you, it was meant only as a scare-tactic to prove my point, and nothing more. I realize this might have scarred my relationship with you and Julius and understand my actions may demote me within our group. Thank you for saving my life, by the way."

She glared at him, processing the apology.

"Am I to be exiled?" he finally asked.

We'll see.

Severine studied him and found no trace of deception. She liked to fancy herself as a mind-reader and could often determine when people were lying or being manipulative. The only bad trait she sensed in Paluch was his foolishness.

"Julius and I haven't talked about that yet," she replied. "As of right now, you're being quarantined in here until we come up with something. I would recommend, however, obeying everything we tell you to do, when we tell you to do it."

He gave a firm nod, gently padding the gauze over his eye.

"What if I have to go to the bathroom?"

"Then Jordy will let you into the middle compartment to use the stall. After that, you'll go right back in here. No questions asked – understood?"

"Yes, I understand. Where are you taking us?"

"What?"

"The FATR. Where are you driving it to?"

"Not that it's any of your concern, Mr. Paluch, but we're taking the rover to a signal Daddy picked up on a radar scan. Apparently, there are reasons to believe an escape pod crashed nearby that may be beneficial to us. That's all I'll be telling you right now. Until then, hold your hand over your wound and keep applying pressure over it, and pray Julius doesn't decide to kick your ass out! I guarantee, one more trick like that and you'll be in the jungle, running from the lizards."

"Coelophysis, actually," he replied, with a corrective tone.

"What?"

"Never mind; you're right. I'll behave."

"What are coelophysis?" Severine pressed him. "Are they dinosaurs?"

"Dinosaurs?" He was trying to sound dumb.

"Yeah, dinosaurs. I heard you call them that right after the first one slashed you. You said that the *dinosaur* bit you..."

#

Severine couldn't help but scowl as she crossed back through the entrance, locking the hatch behind her.

What an irritating man – and he couldn't be more stupid! Drawing a gun on a Federation officer... If this wasn't an every-man-counts situation, he'd be in the woods scratching two sticks together! And what the hell is coelophysis, or whatever it's called?

Most of all, Severine found it irritating that Paluch refused to truthfully answer her question, implying that he misspoke when he referred to the lizard as a 'dinosaur.' For now, her curiosity would have to remain unanswered, despite her head spinning as she tried to come up with answers.

Dinosaurs.

It couldn't be... she thought. The word sounded ridiculous – impossible even.

"I'm surprised you saved his life after what he did," Jordy said. "If the lizard would've hung on for a few more seconds – well – Paluch probably wouldn't be here, gracing us with his winning personality. Quick thinking, Sev! I congratulate you! You're one hell of a soldier!"

"Thanks, little guy!" Severine replied, patting the bot on the head. "All of us were caught off guard! If they hadn't sacked Paluch first, who knows? None of us might be here. Well, maybe you and Daddy. We're still unsure if the lizards have a craving for metal parts!"

The bot gave an electronic giggle.

"One thing still haunts me though," she started. "And I didn't want to ask him, because he's really pissed me off after all this, so I'm trying to keep my conversations with him to a minimal. But what did Paluch mean when he said they 'wanted us dead'? And that they've been following us since the crash site?"

The robot paused and thought, wobbling back and forth as the rover barreled over the uneven terrain below.

"Well, I suppose he's implying that they're the same group of animals we encountered back on the command bridge. We only saw a handful of them, but by the looks of how things were going, there may have been dozens more that stayed hidden. I think during this last fight, we caught the brunt of the pack and probably wiped out most of them with the electric blast."

"So they decided to follow us all the way here? After getting their asses handed to them on the bridge and running with their tails between their legs?"

"That's funny, Sev," Jordy laughed. "I, for one, don't try to understand the minds of these primitive animals. They have hunting habits and behavioral patterns that no one from the Federation, or the world for that matter, has encountered before. We can only deduce that they're incredibly violent and are willing to stalk their prey for considerable distances."

"Do you think they're still hunting us now?" she asked.

"It is a possibility, given what we've learned of them so far..."

Great...

Their conversation was cut short by a deafening thunderclap that rang out above the ceiling. Tiny pelting noises began to strike the FATR on the roof, dissipating with small splashes. Soon the pitter-patter commenced all around them on the exterior of the vehicle.

Rain!

"Sounds like a pretty big storm," Severine stated, trying to talk over the loud sloshing.

"Maybe we should check on the cockpit," Jordy suggested.

#

"Shit, this is a mess!" Julius grumbled as waves of rainwater cascaded down the windshield.

"It is very undesirable, sir," Daddy agreed, turning the wheel to avoid a boulder in the road.

Severine walked into the FATR cockpit, staring out into the tumultuous wilderness. The peaceful rays of the morning light had faded away and were replaced by overcast, gloomy skies. The trees on the edges of the trail shook with great tenacity and began to strike the sides of the rover, leaving wet streaks along the metal plating. Puddles began to consume the low points in the road. And the worst part: The thick layer of rain had prevented a clear line of sight.

"I'm happy we found this game trail," said Julius as a distant bolt of lightning brightened the cockpit. "This would be a very bad situation if we were still plowing through the jungle. I mean, it's like a solid wall of water! Thankfully, we still have the radar to guide us."

"Just as long as our green friends stay away," Severine joked.

"Speaking about friends," Julius turned, "how is that poor excuse for a scientist doing? Does he understand that he's in a world of shit?"

"Yeah, I made it very clear of where he stands in the food chain," Severine replied. "There shouldn't be any future problems – not that I can see."

"Good! I was debating on leaving his ass at the next available stop. But I'm hoping he may yet prove useful. Does he regret his actions?"

"It sounds like it – he definitely regrets losing his eye!"

"What made him pull that gun?" Julius asked, with no shred of sympathy for the scientist's injuries.

"Impulse," she answered. "It sounded like he wanted to prove a point with no real intention of pulling the trigger. Basically, he was trying to ruffle your feathers to save the animals."

Julius turned and shot her a funny look, doubting her theory.

"Hey, I didn't say it was a good way to make his point," she laughed.

"It was the worst way to make a point," he replied with a smile. "His stance was all wrong anyway. With a trigger hand like that, he probably would have hit one of his beloved animals, missing me entirely. And I was just trying to scare them off. Hell, I wouldn't waste a round on a plant-eater – you know that."

Another thunderclap boomed through the sky, sending streaks of thin lightning through the clouds above the canopy. The pounding of the rain continued to flood the forest road. Streams of water were running down the branches and plant limbs, splattering as the drops struck the unearthed root systems below. Muddy clumps of earth flung past them from both sides as the treads rolled by the cockpit, tearing apart the saturated ground.

We picked a good time to get back inside!

"Lieutenant, it looks like we may be coming out of the path," Daddy informed them.

"Don't tell me we're coming to the end? Not into more trees!"

"No, sir. Looks like the floodplain or a field. I can't tell from the radar, sir. But the terrain should be more open, with fewer obstacles."

And at once, the pilot's words were spoken into reality.

The front of the vehicle crashed through the overhanging palm branches, sending the FATR into an expansive plain. Directly ahead was a nearly level stretch of vast grasslands that eventually gave way to a tall barrier of mountains to the north. Far away, a sea materialized in the east, lying low on the plains. Here they were able to decipher a greater sense of depth without obstruction from the canopy.

"By the looks of it, it appears 'floodplain' was the correct term," Jordy said, taking a seat.

The region collected a large portion of rain, probably created by poor drainage and fewer tree roots to soak up the rising water. The grass was tall and untamed. The tips of the golden blades came a fourth of the way up the height of the FATR before clumping into brown seed pods. They parted with ease as the rover rolled through into the heavy downpour.

Humidity and the change of weather forced a thick fog to materialize ahead, but even with the mist and rain, getting out of the thick vegetation made it all worthwhile.

Severine noted that the ground wasn't level after all, but sloped steadily towards the east until the land transitioned into the waves of the approaching sea several miles ahead. Before the large lake was a stretch of land dabbled with many rippling pools, indicating the region was frequently given over to marshes.

"How long do we have until we reach the escape pod?" Jordy asked impatiently.

"We have traveled about a third of the way there," Daddy said. "*Mudskipper* is still very far."

"The trek will go faster now that we can see better," Julius added. "The fog bank might be an issue, but I'll take it over that crowded jungle any day!"

"And what if we get to the pod and don't find anything?" Jordy laughed.

"Jordy! Why would you say that?" Severine asked. "Have faith!"

"Oops – sorry! Still getting used to human-humor."

"Well, that's what we humans call 'not a good time' for that kind of joke," she smirked.

"Believe me, Jordy, we're gonna find something there," Julius said. "This trip won't be in vain – I won't let it! Who knows how long *Mudskipper's* signal will last? We need to investigate while we can. And in here, we have all the food and water we could ask for. What else are we going to do to kill the time?" He laughed.

"Daddy – watch out for the boulder!" Severine interrupted.

"I don't think that's a boulder, Sev," Jordy said, standing up and peering through the watery shield that distorted their view.

To the left of the windshield, far away from the FATR's immediate path, a large brown object began to fade up in the mist. The dark surface was uneven and coarse, covered in subtle dimples and imperfections. From their angle it resembled a sunken meteorite, rising above the gold grass.

It's another animal, Severine noticed. *This one's dead!*

The torso of the massive creature came rapidly into view as they tumbled through the floodplain. The neck and head of the victim were gone, and what remained was a dark mess of rotting organs and tangled flesh. Bones and fractured ligaments popped through wounds that had dried out days earlier. Insects and maggot-like parasites plagued the gaps and had devoured most of the skin, rendering the original version of the animal unrecognizable.

Whatever it had been – it was massive.

"Thirty-feet," Julius guessed at the size. "Thirty-feet at least!"

What could have done that? Severine thought, as an uncertain chill climbed up her back.

On top of the giant carcass, three other animals pecked at the bloody flesh. They resembled the herbivores from the jungle trail, but were black and white in color, hairier, and clearly carnivorous. The scavengers reminded Severine of giant rats, chattering away as they nibbled at the kill. They looked sinister and aggressive, but she guessed they weren't the cause of the larger animal's demise.

They're too little... Something bigger brought that beast down...

As the vehicle rode by, the center animal growled at the rover, determined to defend its food, before turning downward to continue devouring the savory snack.

Fog soon overtook the animals from behind and the massacre was once again out of view, vanishing into the bleak world.

"I'm glad we're all in agreement about getting out of here," Severine said. "The excitement's worn off!"

We've spent enough time here. Time to go home...

Julius nodded.

"Escape is the one and only priority," he reassured her.

#

Just out of radar range at the edge of the jungle, the coelophysis pack stopped, refusing to follow the colonists any further. As they watched the FATR slipping away into the fog, they shrieked mournfully, depressed that their prey had escaped once again.

The bog was a treacherous place, especially during the rainy seasons. The green dinosaurs dared not venture out in the wide expanse of the swamps, fearful of what may be lurking behind the tall grass.

The alpha male, a taller dinosaur with a large pair of yellow rings around its neck, stepped out through the wet leaves onto the swampland. Thick raindrops bounced off the snout as the leader studied the floodplain, eyes locked on the departing vehicle. Finally, it let out a deep, commanding bark from the expanding throat, signaling a retreat.

Answering with prehistoric yelps, the pack turned back to the jungle, splashing into the soaked foliage. With a final look out onto the prairie, the leader followed, its scaly tail disappearing into the shrubbery hedge.

High above to the north, the mountains cast a powerful shadow down over the low-lying trees. On the other side of their steep peaks was yet another forbidden region – a vast territory claimed by another, deadlier species of carnivore.

It was a swath of land the colonists would soon be forced to discover for themselves.

X

Storm clouds continued to pass over the floodplain, dumping unforgiving amounts of water onto the FATR as the trek continued towards *Mudskipper's* signal. The journey had now become a race to the northern hill slopes, where the ground had not yet submerged under the rising pools. The shallow sea seemed to jump ahead as tiny puddles soon evolved into impassable lakes that joined the great body of water. Runoff flew down the face of the cliffs, bouncing off the windshield, as they continued uphill.

I hope we can find a way back, Severine thought. The monsoon had quickly transformed the grassland into an underwater world. They would have to stay on the slopes to avoid the rising tides.

"Daddy, let's stop for a ten-minute break," Julius suggested. "My arm's getting sore."

"Yes, Lieutenant," Daddy said, deactivating the driving functions on the holographic pop-up menu. Julius lowered his steering mechanism forward, bringing the vehicle to a grinding halt.

"It gets tiring after a while," Julius said, stretching out in the co-pilot seat.

"I could take over if you want," Severine offered. "I think I could figure it out, if you give me a crash course!"

"Thanks, Sev. I'd appreciate it, but I think I'll be all right to get us there," he said chivalrously. "We're about halfway there – right, Daddy?"

"Affirmative, sir," the pilot replied.

Daddy pressed a hologram indicator on the console keyboard and the flickering topology of the radar grid faded up again, revealing the rover's coordinates at the map's center. To the southwest, the images of the *Supernova's* wreckage were now glitching and approaching the edge of the frame, shrinking away under the digital trees. At the right corner of the layout sat the escape pod crash site, now slightly closer to the middle and lying just beyond a gap in the hills. Around the *Mudskipper*, the map displayed various industrial shrapnel littered around the central dome.

Wreckage from when the pod crashed.

"We're getting there, sir," the bot confirmed. "Another two hours at most."

"Perfect! We should do a munitions check. I know my ammo has been cut by about half. Daddy, how's your X2?"

"It's out, sir."

"Damn. What about you, Sev?"

"16 shots left, I think. I tried to be conservative with the rounds during the attack. Only picked off the closer ones."

"Good thinking," Julius replied. "My 90 has about 35 shots left. You were more careful than I was."

"So about fifty rounds between the two of us?" Severine asked. "That's all we have?"

"Sounds about right," said Julius. "Fifty rounds to get us out of here."

They had only been awake in this world for a few hours, and already their ammunition had been depleted by more than half. Another ambush by the reptiles and they would be down to sharpening sticks into spears.

At least the FATR battery is holding up, Severine thought, looking at the status indicator bar.

"Daddy, are there any lifeforms nearby?" Severine asked. "Any lizards?"

"No lifeforms nearby, Corporal," the bot responded, scanning briefly over the hologram map. There didn't appear to be any thermal imaging around the rover's glowing concentric circles.

That's a relief!

Outside the windshield, Severine could tell the FATR was under a large cliff face, hidden in shadow. The stone ceiling was held up by natural rocky columns that had weathered out during the past centuries. The shelter seemed like a great place to fortify. It was at the top of the plains, provided shelter from the rain, and lent a wide view of anything approaching for miles.

I hope that mountain holds up, she thought, realizing that if the columns collapsed, they would be sealed inside the rover forever.

"Excuse me," called an apologetic voice buzzing through the FATR loudspeaker. Severine jumped, unaware that the rover had an intercom system installed. Paluch's tone sounded sincere, even masked with glitching radio static.

"Just what we need right now," Jordy commented sarcastically.

"I was hoping the dead lizard would keep him busy," Julius grunted. "What does he want?"

"Maybe he wants to make peace with you," Severine suggested.

"Excuse me," said Paluch. *"Is this speaker working?"* His voice was far more annoying when converted into muffled radio airwaves.

"The man won't quit," Julius said. "I'm still debating on leaving him here and making for the *Mudskipper* ourselves! Might make the trip go smoother, huh? Do you think the Federation would give me demerits for that?"

He smirked.

"Yes Julius, it probably wouldn't be a wise move!" Severine laughed.

"He wouldn't last ten minutes," Jordy joked.

"I, again, apologize for the events that unfolded back in the woods. Keep me back here as long as you see fit; but through my notes, drawings and recent findings, I've arrived at some pertinent information that may concern us all! Regardless of how much of an ass you think I am, it's something you'll want to hear."

Julius looked at the loudspeaker above the dashboard, turning back to Severine as if expecting some advice. She shrugged, unsure of what the scientist wanted to discuss or how to proceed.

The intercom bleeped again.

"Again, you may want to hear this. Hello? Hello?"

#

"Okay, Julius, let me start by offering my personal apology for the error in my judgment. I've already given my spiel to Severine, but it's mainly you I should apologize to. You must believe me! All I wanted was to eliminate all probability of you harming this fascinating ecosystem. My motives were right—and I still stand by them—but my method was wrong! I won't question your command again, and you have my word on that."

Under the overhead dim lighting, the two soldiers loomed over Paluch in his makeshift, jailed-off room. His chamber looked like a civilian child's room in the *Supernova*. There were papers, books, and toy-like science contraptions scattered everywhere. From the time Severine left him to when they returned, Francis had left his chamber a mess in his willingness to study and research his findings.

The scientist knelt before Julius, begging with his hands clasped together. The lieutenant, on the other hand, looked ready to deck Paluch across the jaw.

The gauze bandaging was now soaked with blood, but through the medicine that Jordy administered, it appeared he was in little pain. The eye that remained was peaceful and teary-eyed at the chance of forgiveness...and at the prospect of avoiding exile.

He must really think he's getting kicked off, Severine thought. *Well, as long as it keeps him scared, maybe he'll start wising up!*

"You realize how close we came to shooting you?" Julius replied angrily. "Your actions are commonly referred to in the infantry as 'insubordination' or even 'mutiny'! As for forgiveness, I'll give you one more chance – just one! You'll remain back here until I feel comfortable letting you into the inner rooms. If you pull another stunt like that, we're giving you the boot! It's as simple as that, get it?"

"That's very fair," he admitted. "Thank you, Julius."

"Now, explain yourself! Why did you do that?"

"I had to prevent you from inflicting harm on those creatures. We have a rare opportunity to study and learn more about them and how they operate. All we know about exaeretodon could be multiplied a hundred-fold if we don't interfere immensely with their lifestyle. Firing on them may have forever fractured our chances! Not that it matters much now..."

"Exaeretod-*what*?" Severine asked.

There's another scientific term again...

"Exaeretodon: a herbivore from the late Triassic period," Paluch answered.

"You're losing us," Julius said.

"I'm sorry, let me double back a little." Paluch got up from his knees and walked over to his seat next to the reptilian carcass he had been examining.

"It's all quite excessive, but I'll attempt to paraphrase with a few pithy punchlines."

"Go on," Severine said, anticipating some juicy information.

He paused dramatically before he went on.

"Well, let's begin, shall we? The incident in space..."

The soldiers nodded impatiently.

"We know an atrocious act was inflicted on the *Supernova* while in transit amongst other colonist ships. I believe, from what we've observed from the wreckage, it's fair to wager that asteroids were involved in this catastrophe. I will admit, this next part is pure speculation! During the time of the event, I was raiding supplies in this ship's interior in case the worst happened, which it did. A cowardly act, but one that I don't regret! I never saw the catastrophe, or the sequence of events that led up to it. All I remember, frankly, is hearing the alarm bells go off! It must have been the asteroids! Federation ships have been downed before from asteroids, as you two may recall."

The Meteor Traverse. The Cosmic Wave.

The names of fallen star ships drifted by in Severine's mind as they listened to Paluch. The ships were lost shortly after the flight from Earth and were the first two vessels to perish in the quest for a new world. Both were struck down in wild asteroid fields and thousands of lives were lost when the interior hulls split apart.

"Continue…" Julius said, unimpressed.

"My guess is something probably took out the bridge or one of the Central Command ports on the upper levels. After the grueling beating the ship took, many crew members would have been killed instantly in the chaos! Electric failures undoubtedly followed, causing countless bots to malfunction or short circuit! Lastly, numerous hyper-sleep chambers would have remained empty. If the battery packs inside didn't hold up, the passengers in the pods wouldn't have lasted very long. You know this because you both came from them. It's the only explanation that addresses how we're all here and having this conversation. Are you with me so far?"

They nodded.

"Yeah. We know all this – now get to the meat of it!" Julius had grown impatient.

"With the pods sealed and half the crew trying to stay alive or find new ways of sending a communication link to *Star Jumper*, *Supernova* was a ticking time-bomb. It was only a matter of time before it went down! But instead of burning up somewhere in the asteroid belt, somehow, the five of us were given a second chance! And years later, we awoke on a breathable planet! One that we've been on before, and one that our ancestors knew before it became dilapidated!"

"Where?" Julius asked. "Where are you talking about?"

"You can't be serious?" Severine said, picking up on his reference.

It can't be…

"Yes," Paluch replied. "Surely, it can't be, but it is! This is planet Earth!"

The scientist's powerful words filled the room, and a smile cracked across his satisfied face, as if he just solved a large physics equation.

Julius' mouth sagged to an irritated scowl.

"That's bullshit, Paluch. Earth's dead – long dead! That's no secret. The Old War ripped it apart! The atmosphere collapsed, and the people left there are long dead."

"Right you are, Julius!" Francis smiled, trying to mend his relationship with the lieutenant. "But as our current situation tells us, the facts of Earth—no matter how compelling or true they may be—matter not! The Old War, among the others throughout history, have not yet happened! That's right, I said it! I apologize for my remarks earlier when I disregarded the Earth theory. Now, I have enough evidence to prove that we're indeed in Earth's prehistoric past!"

"So, we probably won't encounter more humans?" Severine asked.

"Don't count on it," Paluch replied. "But there may be hope with this E5 *Mudskipper* pod you're going after! Perhaps we find another group of castaways holed up there. But the whole thing could be a wild goose chase. The impact happened so long ago! I don't want to dampen anyone's spirits, but my thoughts on the matter are grim. I believe the E5 crash site survivors are dead."

"What makes you think we're in the past?" Julius said. Severine could tell he was beginning to warm up to Paluch's ideas, despite how ludicrous they sounded. In a morbid way, the scientist's abstract tale was starting to make sense.

"Because I've found all the answers here – in this!"

The scientist grabbed a dusty old book, published long ago. The bindings were failing and the jacket stitching was ready to tear off. Some of the pages were slipping out. Beautifully drawn, fantastic dinosaurs in strange, exotic environments populated the cover.

Severine could make out the title.

TRIASSIC DINOSAURS, ARCHOSAURS, AND OTHER PREHISTORIC BEASTS
- THE COMPLETE COMPENDIUM -

"The Triassic?" Julius said. "What is that?"

"An ancient time period from the Mesozoic era," Paluch replied. "The Mesozoic was a long stretch of time in Earth's prehistory, and the Triassic served as the dawn of the Mesozoic. Depending on what you go by, the general notion in science is that the period began about two hundred and fifty million years ago. Some religious groups dispute this, implying that the creatures of the Triassic are only a few thousand years old – perhaps even ten-thousand. Whatever your preferences are, I can safely conclude that these animals, like the ones we encountered in the jungle, haven't been around for a long, long time."

"And you think we're in this time period?" Severine asked. "The Triassic?"

"Yes," he nodded. "Yes, I do."

"Why is that?"

"Several reasons. One: There are no humans other than us…at least, not yet! Two: The flora! I snipped off several plant specimens when we exited the rover back on the road. I found traces of *sagenopteris*, an extinct fern, *ginkgoites*, *chiropteris,* and many other Triassic stem-like vegetation. My third exciting, and terrifying, reason: The bulky quadrupeds on the jungle road. *Exaeretodon* is their name! These cynodonts have been extinct since the Triassic period. They are herbivorous, and now we can safely assume they're docile. However, for the natural order of life to continue, there must be a form of population control to balance the biome. Therefore, we have our predators!"

"The green lizards," Julius answered, pointing to the reptile carcass.

"*Coelophysis* is their scientific name," Paluch said. "They're fast, nimble hunters with sharp, little claws and an unforgiving bite. Now, we know they travel in huge packs and aren't to be trifled with! Apparently, whatever you did back at the bridge must have pissed them off enough to pursue us through the jungle. My guess is when you killed their buddy, they experienced a primordial crisis, and now feel the need to purge us from the area. Vengeful little creatures, as we've now learned. Myself, especially!"

He gestured to his missing eye behind the gauze wrapping.

"When we encountered them on the road, the pack obviously didn't intend for us to survive. Hell, they nearly got me, but thanks to Sev, I made it out!

Dinosaur behavior has never been documented or observed, so I'm all very new at this! Exciting stuff, isn't it?"

Dinosaurs! He finally admitted it...

Severine could feel herself smiling.

"You're joking!" Julius barked. "They're just over-sized, irritable lizards!"

"Sadly, Julius, they aren't! They're dinosaurs from the Late Triassic. Probably during the Carnian stage, based on what I've found so far. There is a fossil skeleton image from this old book excerpt, plus a little blurb about the research done on this animal. And here is an artist's rendition – a quite beautiful one, at that!"

Paluch held up a torn sheet of paper that was lying next to his magnifying glass.

"As you can see, the drawing is severely distorted from the actual dinosaur, as we know now."

"Well, I still say they're lizards," Julius argued, after studying the ancient illustration.

"For the sake of argument, let's assume for a second, that I'm right," Paluch continued. "I'm ninety-nine percent sure I am, given the presence of exaeretodon herds we've found that existed during the same time as coelophysis. Call them whatever you want! "Lizards" surely seems appropriate. Minus the feathering, they could pass for lizards on two legs. Sort of like how the basilisk lizard walked back on Earth. But if I'm right, regardless of whatever you call them, the coelophysis pack could be the least of our worries."

Julius frowned.

"And what's the worst?"

"Well, I'm not quite certain yet. Triassic history really isn't my thing. I preferred to dabble in other time periods, like the Carboniferous – dubbed the "Age of Insects." During the remainder of our trip, I'll continue to research, and hopefully my findings will ready us for whatever comes our way! I'm making a habit to thumb through the *carnivore* section especially, so we know what we're getting into. I've already narrowed down our position to a rare lush location somewhere in ancient South America, known then as Gondwanaland."

Paluch seemed proud of his findings.

Julius sighed. Severine was unsure of his feelings on the subject. Talk of dinosaurs and ancient worlds wasn't something she thought the lieutenant would care to understand.

"Apology accepted," Julius said finally, ending the subject. "Don't be a dumbass next time, and I'll do my best to steer you clear of the lizards!"

In a series of heavy steps, Julius left the room, and headed back to his co-pilot chair with Daddy.

He must not believe Paluch's theory, she thought, after the lieutenant refused to lump the creatures into the 'dinosaur' category.

"Do you believe me?" Paluch asked.

Severine walked towards the exit, turning back at the question.

"I can't believe I'm saying this, but honestly, I do," Severine replied. "It's all too convenient to be an accident. Keep looking in your book! Maybe you can try and convince him again later."

She walked through the archway and sealed him inside to continue his punishment, hoping that he would keep searching for answers in his isolation.

#

Paluch smiled at another chance at redemption and flipped happily through the pages of his book, identifying more creatures.

As he studied the documents, many of the old pages flew out of the book.

"Dammit!" he yelled.

The mess made him pause and reorganize himself. Paluch had always been serious about creating a clean work space for study, despite the hectic laboratory he had made in his frenzied excitement.

His fingers closed around the first fallen page as he began his cleanup, and a dark thought crossed over him as he looked down at the paleoart illustration.

It was a large, carnivorous dinosaur.

The human comparison scale suggested the creature could grow to great lengths, even fifteen to twenty feet, and was probably more lethal than coelophysis. The last nail in the coffin followed with his discovery of the location/environmental description near the bottom.

Fossilized specimens recovered in South America.

The artist depiction lingered off the page. The long razor teeth and killing claws haunted him. He padded his head wound softly, remembering the stinging sensation that had befallen him at the hands of the carnivores. If they ran into this bastard, the result would surely be much, much worse.

He scanned the name again.

Herrerasaurus

He shrugged off his imagination, flipping the page over and inserting it back into the book, resuming his research.

XI

Mudskipper's three-dimensional icon approached on the radar map.

"The E5 crash site is dead ahead, sir," Daddy stated, swirling through a series of location holograms that hovered over the windshield. "Just need to cross through that valley ahead and we should end up right on top of it."

"Watch out for dinosaurs," Julius said, with a hint of sarcasm.

The drive had continued for an hour and a half at a slow pace along the slopes. Clouded skies above remained black and ominous, thundering intermittently in the afternoon shower, as the floodplain continued to sink beneath the downpour. The lack of dinosaurs was frequently noted by Julius as they continued through the wilderness.

Paluch's coelophysis evidence had not been enough to convince the lieutenant, although he admitted to Severine privately that the two species did look similar. Julius was confident that the forest carnivores were none other than over-sized lizards, undocumented before by mankind.

When Severine asked him about the exaeretodon herd, he offered the same explanation.

"Undiscovered, primitive animals," was the uninterested reply.

To her, the exaeretodon and coelophysis were enough to persuade her that Paluch's Triassic theory was accurate. The wildlife, coupled with the plant evidence, was all she needed to hear. Severine was certain that somehow they had traveled back in time and returned to Earth. Now, they had to find a way out.

She asked Julius if he thought they were back on Earth. He said yes, stating that the departure of humans led to the planet's rapid recovery. These animals were side-effects of the new world, and any alleged dinosaur resemblances were purely coincidental.

Severine nodded in agreement, but still firmly believed the scientist's theory. She figured explaining her belief that they were in the Triassic might lead to ridicule from Julius, and she didn't know him well enough to defend her reasons. Keeping quiet was her best bet, and she hoped that eventually Julius would come around and acknowledge the truth.

"If Paluch is right, will there be other carnivorous dinosaurs waiting for us out there?" Jordy asked, sitting beside Severine in the rover cockpit. The bot hadn't stopped obsessing about the creatures since the attack, despite escaping the battle with zero injuries.

"That's something you'll have to ask him when he's done with his time-out," Severine said. Although Julius had forgiven the scientist, she had no idea how long he would vote for keeping him isolated. In this unpredictably new environment, he had suddenly become useful. His knowledge about prehistoric life was a great advantage.

"Well, when we get to the *Mudskipper*, I'm staying in the rover," the bot said.

"You can't, pal," Julius replied. "If there's any old doors, we may need your help to gain access. Out of everyone, you and Daddy are the safest. Those of us with meat on our bones must worry. Cheer up, pal! We won't let anything happen to you."

Through the cockpit, the gap in the hills to the north was quickly approaching. The vehicle began to descend from the base of the mountain slopes while Julius carefully kept an eye on the rising tides. The shallow sea continued to swell to the right. The rain flooded the fields, causing the grasslands to shrink and condense as the brown water of the bog overtook them. Soon the field ahead began to slip under the rising water.

Julius guided the rover slowly through the small wave, careful not to let the vehicle slip too deep. They could clearly see where the grasses dipped into the earth, learning that the flooding was only a few inches deep.

"The water won't be an issue?" Jordy asked.

"Not at this depth," Julius replied. "You worry too much, buddy!"

The way back to the Supernova will be hell if this continues, Severine thought.

At the rate the storm was going, the floodplain would soon be completely underwater. The FATR was a strong machine, but she doubted it could travel any deeper and function properly.

"The monsoon won't quit," she commented. "And those clouds don't look like they're letting up! At least we're almost there!"

"Wouldn't be surprised if it rained all day," Julius replied. "Those grasslands are going to be a bitch to cross when we double back! But it shouldn't be too bad if I go slow. I'm sure the rover will do fine."

"Are you sure?" she asked. "Maybe the radar can take us another route. Are there any other path options for the return trip, Daddy?"

"No immediate options, Corporal. There seems to be another forest to the north-west, on the other side of the mountains that we just passed through, but it looks to be overgrown there as well. If we go through there, we'll be driving blind, just like before. And *Mudskipper's* valley is only accessible through this path, so unfortunately, we won't be able to take the long way home."

"We'll go over other options when the time comes," Julius said. "My gut tells me we'll be fine coming back, as long as it doesn't get too deep. Hey – straight ahead! I can see the crash!"

As they crossed through the space between the hills and pulled themselves out of the shallow flooding, a large obelisk rose from the ground. From the distance, Severine saw that the pod was consumed with ivy and plant growth after years of remaining a permanent fixture in the Triassic landscape. The indent in the ground came to a low point near the center, where the *Mudskipper* loomed triumphantly, facing towards the sky like an ancient, onyx shrine.

The rover slowed as the treads cautiously advanced on the debris field. The ground was layered in thin, metal star ship fragments that speared through the dirt like crude swords, preventing their advance.

"Would you care for my recommendation, sir?" Daddy asked.

"Go ahead, Pilot," Julius replied.

"We should leave the rover here and scout the site on foot. The FATR could get stuck in the crater and the wreckage might add unwanted wear and tear to the treads. Those fragments look pretty sharp. But it's your call, sir."

"Well, let's think about this," Julius said. "Are there any lifeforms nearby?"

Daddy activated the virtual radar map, studying the 3D geometry that surrounded the vehicle icon. The glowing circles around the FATR didn't display any heat signals in the floodplains or in the debris field around the crash.

"None on the radar, sir."

"I can't see any out there through the windows, can you, Sev?"

"No, it's mostly level grassland up here," she replied. "I can see pretty well for maybe a mile or two, and nothing's around."

"Okay. Daddy, maybe you should stay here and man the vehicle. The rest of us will scout down to the pod. We'll bring Paluch with us and give him a chance to prove himself useful. Remember to conserve your ammunition. Dinosaurs or no dinosaurs – anything could be living down there! If anything's under the *Mudskipper*, the radar won't pick it up, so be on your guard."

#

As they approached the crash site, Severine remembered how big the E5 escape pods were as she found herself walking in the ship's shadow, which was practically a smaller colonist vessel itself.

The ruined transport towered before them, tangled in wild vines that latched onto the exterior like tentacles. After the impact in space, the vehicle must have lost control of the thrusters, made apparent by the cockpit rising to the highest point and now tilted towards the rainy afternoon sky. Words faded by the elements appeared twenty yards above them, stenciled on the pod's dented plating.

SUPERNOVA E5 POD
MUDSKIPPER
VEHICLE ID: 20492.129

The colonists weaved through the treacherous metal blades and rubble that descended towards the *Mudskipper* like a ring of teeth. Julius led them, tactically checking his corners around the ship fragments that could serve as hiding places for unseen predators.

Clearly, he doesn't trust Daddy's radar system.

Grabbing a rectangular piece of debris, Jordy held the shield above and blocked the rain, fearful of what the storm might do to his internal battery. The wind was violent, casting the shower in different directions, causing the bot to constantly adjust his safety barrier.

Paluch kept to the middle, staying close to Julius and his XR-90. They had to deter the scientist from lingering too long and studying the plant-life, consistently reminding him of the mission at hand. Severine held the rear, keeping a finger on the X2-20 trigger and an eye on the ruins.

They reached a rocky precipice that dropped down to the *Mudskipper*. The centuries old impact of the escape pod was so powerful, it deformed the ground around the hull, creating a steep funnel effect that imploded the earth.

I guess we'll have to jump, Severine thought, as they skidded down the ravine after Julius.

Confusion resumed after they dropped ten feet to the crater center, where the ground leveled off, and the ship exterior was only yards away.

"Shit! That was terrifying," Paluch said, dusting off his jacket and catching his breath.

"Pipe down," said Julius. "You're fine!"

"Do we just walk in?" Jordy asked, his voice shaking with fright.

"Looks that way, buddy," Julius replied.

The destroyed space craft looked ominous and ghostly. Crater marks a foot wide slid down the hull, exposing the dim interior and operating mechanisms. Black patches of charred metal populated several areas where the *Mudskipper* burned up in the atmosphere, just before the crash landing. In one of the upper windows, an ancient hand print stuck to the glass, leaving a haunting tale from the pod's final moments.

Oxygen leak, Severine thought. *If they weren't in hyper-sleep pods, they were screwed.*

Several yards ahead, a tear in the ship's side slashed downward until it disappeared underground, providing a narrow entrance to the inside. Space debris clung to the edges of the opening. An asteroid impact. Severine knew them well from the *Supernova's* ruins. Paluch confirmed the creation of the marks, pausing to study the gash.

"Watch yourself," Severine told the scientist. "Don't disturb them."

"Who – *whoa!*"

To their right, embedded into the ground, was a series of shallow graves, marked by crudely made twig crosses bound by twine. At the base of the wood, the ground was lumpy and uneven, indicating that the corpses were buried just beneath. There were about forty crosses all together.

"How many people can fit on an E5?" Paluch asked.

"Fifty-ish," Severine replied. "Maybe sixty if you crammed them in like sardines."

Most of the crew died...

But there was still hope.

Someone had to bury them!

"Stay close behind me," Julius told them. "I don't intend on any green lizards getting the jump on us while we're separated – I'm sorry, dinosaurs – eh, Paluch?"

The lieutenant laughed.

Paluch shot him an angry glare. Severine thought it was a good sign that Julius was finally starting to joke with the scientist. She took it as a symbol of peace, with a hint of poking fun.

Julius raised the 90 and started through to the hull, slowly leading them into the *Mudskipper.* Severine squinted while her eyes adjusted to the changing light exposure. They finally escaped the heavy downpour.

It was dark inside.

By the glow of Jordy's panels and the pulse weapon utility lights, they saw a room reminiscent of the *Supernova.*

Damaged deep-freeze crates lined the edges, thrown about randomly in the sudden crash. Hyper-sleep pods sat opened and abandoned, piled up neatly in one of the corners and drained of battery life. The floor was comprised of sand and dried mulch, spilling through the walls and forming small mounds that looked like anthills.

A stale smell lingered on the air, fighting to keep the tropical breeze at bay near the opening. The console panels and operating ports were lifeless, devoid of energy.

"Abandoned," Julius said. "With a little touch of 'creepy.'"

"I bet no one's lived here for a hundred years," Paluch commented. "I was right: The E5 survivors are long dead."

In the center of the damp room, a thin brown strand dangled through the air.

A rope?

It started in a squiggly coil on the ground and ascended through the air until it reached the cockpit high above in the ceiling. Severine followed the rope with her eye until she saw where it knotted around a column. To her surprise, the dashboard consoles glowed brightly behind the pilot's seat.

"Look!" She pointed. "Up there – light!"

The cockpit hummed to life. Holographic indicators rotated and blinked in front of the windshield, flickering with exhausted energy, but otherwise operational. Buttons lit up and radiated excitedly at their keyboards in front of the pilot seat.

"I guess we found where the signal was coming from," Julius said. "*Mudskipper* is still operational after all this time – but how?"

Suddenly a sharp voice from behind cut through the air. The intruder caught them all off guard. Severine felt her heart jump, expecting to turn and find the rabid coelophysis pack bursting through the opening, eager to shred them apart.

"Severine," boomed the strange voice. "Is that you?"

She spun around, aiming the 20 at the newcomer who had been observing the colonists all along from a darkened nook.

A nomad! And he knows my name.

An older man, who looked to be in his mid-fifties, stood in a shadowy nook. He was dressed in a gray shredded cloth, stained by years of grass and mud. His shoes looked familiar, but had been heavily modified with twigs, which held them together like cheap sandals. White hairs ran down his neck in an untamed beard. Slung across his right shoulder was a makeshift crossbow and quiver with at least six sharpened arrows at the ready. A rock dagger hugged his waist behind a belt. His arms were tanned and muscular, exposed from the lack of sleeves.

From beneath his scraggly demeanor, Severine briefly caught nostalgia.

Do I know you?

His voice sounded vaguely familiar.

She held her fire, realizing the man meant them no harm.

"How do you like my house?" the man laughed. "It's the best I could do. The dinos won't come in this area. Not enough food to sustain them, and the ground's too unpredictable with all the crash rubble. I've kept the cockpit communication signals charged by hand. That's a bitch to do, by the way. It takes about an hour and needs doing at least once every few days."

He's clearly Federation, she thought. *He has knowledge of our star ships.*

Severine was certain she knew the man, but couldn't put a name to the wrinkled face. She couldn't shake the thought that they had met before, many lifetimes ago on the *Supernova*. If not for her hyper-sleep memory lapses, she knew it would have clicked instantly.

"Who are you?" Julius asked finally.

The nomad smiled.

"Brett! Private Brett Ambrose. Don't you remember?"

Brett... Ambrose. Yes, of course!

"Yes! It's coming back to me! Brett. Yes, I do remember you!" She lowered her pistol and was relieved when Julius did the same, relaxing at the sight of another Federation soldier. Severine studied his eyes, trying to get a feel for the man – a man whom she had once known very well.

"Ambrose?" Julius asked. "Damn. You're older than me now, Private!"

"Thanks, Lieutenant," Brett laughed.

"What were you saying?" Jordy asked Paluch. "Oh, right. There wouldn't be any survivors?"

"It was just a guess!" Paluch retorted, glaring at the robot.

Severine smiled.

The bot could be a real ball-buster!

Brett Ambrose was a good-looking, thirty-year-old private in the Federation infantry, from what she remembered. But he wasn't thirty anymore. Behind the white beard and wrinkled brow, Brett was looking like an old man – an old man who had been stuck in this prehistoric bubble for a long time, trying desperately to escape, even if it meant climbing a tattered rope every so often to keep the cockpit operational.

Severine realized she was having that feeling again – the same feeling when she remembered Brett Ambrose on the *Supernova*. There was a vague flashback of romance and sensuality, one that she yearned to remember. There was another, more hazy memory too – a face hidden behind ice, trying to reach out to her...trying to pull her towards him. But pull her towards what? She didn't know.

"The monsoon isn't going to stop all day," Brett said. "Why don't you all make camp? *Mudskipper* is a great shelter from the rain. It won't flood down here – the soil above is well-drained. Unless you want to walk all the way back up that steep crater in the storm?"

A harsh wind blew violently behind them near the gash in the ship, slipping through the opening. Rain continued to pound the graveyard outside as the thick drops splattered over the dirt.

Damn, that's cold!

Severine shivered as the breeze nipped at her neck.

"Staying may not be such a bad idea," Julius said. "Daddy will be okay to man the rover. He'll probably enter sleep-mode. I, for one, don't feel like climbing all the way back up there in that storm. And it will be hell on Jordy's battery. Ambrose, can this place warm up any? I'm freezing my balls off down here!"

"Yes, sir," Brett replied with a gruff laugh. "I'll pull my makeshift curtains down and start a fire."

"Then we'll stay," Julius affirmed, setting down the 90 against the wall.

Brett smiled.
"We have a lot to catch up on..."

XII

Embers crackled and fizzled away as the inviting fire filled the interior of the *Mudskipper* with warmth. The residual smoke fed up the hull to the cockpit, filtering out through a hole in the cracked windows that served as a chimney.

Outside, the powerful monsoon continued to swell as the shower pinged off the exterior, beating like a drum on the metal. Brett placed a tarp cloth over the opening to block the wind from knocking any rogue drops into the fire pit. The ground absorbed the excess water well, sucking the runoff deep into the soil before puddles could form and turn their shelter into a sunken submarine. Above, the furious breeze howled through other small holes in the ship, sailing in under the dark midnight sky.

Although the *Mudskipper* shielded them from the elements, Severine missed the FATR. She pictured Daddy, alone in the cockpit, staring out at the rainy Triassic landscape but warmed from the rover's heating ducts. As she shivered inside a crude tunic garb that Brett gave her, she debated heading back to the vehicle. But the storm had grown worse and she would be drenched by the time she made it back.

It's best to wait it out until morning, she thought. *But damn, that rover's probably nice and toasty.*

Another factor that anchored her to the *Mudskipper*: venturing out into the dark...alone. The dinosaurs could be nocturnal, and with just one X2 pistol, she wouldn't last very long.

The colonists huddled around the flames, listening to Brett's sequence of events. His tale started almost three hundred years earlier when the *Supernova* was still in space.

"The command bridge was the first to go," Brett confirmed, rubbing his hands forward at the warmth of the fire. "I was on duty at the time. It was a direct impact from an asteroid, or so everyone thought. No one could get to the bridge, and believe me, we tried everything to breach the doors! Detonators. Pulse blasts. Those suckers wouldn't budge. By the time we decided to find a bot to open the doors, the ship dipped forward, threw everything off balance, and fried a lot of the computerized features. Electrical malfunctions followed, and I'm sure a lot of bots were killed. Then, darkness. Suddenly, we were in the atmosphere, sailing towards the planet's surface. Many of us made it to the last escape pod, *Mudskipper*, but others on duty weren't so lucky... That's when I jumped into a sleeper pod and tried to free up some space for more passengers."

"I figured it was some type of asteroid impact, followed by a communications failure," Paluch added, snacking on a savory treat that Brett had offered them before starting the fire.

"It's what happened all right. When my pod finally opened from battery failure, many years had passed. I found out the other passengers had died centuries earlier, probably in an oxygen leak, and I buried their bodies outside the entrance – you may have seen the small cemetery. Thankfully, the ship still had life, but just enough to sustain the cockpit and some minor components, like my sleeper pod, that shielded me from the crash impact and the oxygen leaks. Those pods are life-savers – I swear by them! I knew if I kept the signal going and people from the *Supernova* survived, they'd come find me! Sure glad that I've kept that ritual going all these years!"

"And how long has it been?" Severine asked. "How long have you been here, out of hyper-sleep?"

"Twenty-some years," Brett replied. "Twenty-three years and three months I believe, to be exact. Since my pod opened, I've tried my best to keep track of time."

"You've been out here for two decades?" Julius asked.

"Just about."

He's survived out here for twenty-three years! And we've almost exhausted all of our weapons and ammunition within one day...

"Do you have any workable weapons?" Severine asked. "Pulse weapons?"

"One D7 Detonator – that's it! I used up all the other weapons shortly after I came out of hyper-sleep. Those things are great, until they're all out of ammo... It took some experimentation, but eventually I fashioned this little beauty back here."

He gestured over his shoulder to the primitive crossbow.

"Nothing like having one of these!"

He was very proud of the contraption, grabbing the piece and handing it around the campfire. The bow was comprised mainly from wood, held together by tightly bound rope fragments and hardened mud. At the front of the shaft, a finely chiseled crosshairs sight made of withered rock looked out at Severine as she studied the crude weapon.

"I'm impressed," she said. "You're very resourceful!"

"It's something I had to learn on the fly," he replied. "And it works like a charm. There's a small herd of leaf-eating animals just north of here that make for easy targets and good food. I've lived mostly off their meat and fish from the river, just to the west. Adapt or starve – that's all there is to it! Or, if you're lucky, one of the dinos will pick you off, and it'll be quick and painless."

"What makes you think they're dinosaurs?" Julius asked. He remained skeptical of the Triassic Earth theory.

"Because that's what they are, Lieutenant," Brett replied, as if the answer was obvious. "They're dinosaurs – well, not all of them, but the meat-eaters certainly are! I've read enough books back on Earth when I was a kid to discern the difference. The carnivores I've seen so far are straight out of the old, ruined museums that remained after the Old War. I've been pretty close to the bastards to confirm that's what they are – closer than I'd have liked to be! Don't you remember the museums, Lieutenant?"

"I was never much of a museum-goer," Julius replied.

"I see you've had an experience with the dinos yourself, Mr. Paluch."

Francis raised his head at the sound of the question. The gauze of the wound glowed in the fiery heat, revealing the blood stain in the dimming orange light. He seemed to have forgotten about the eye wound altogether, but Severine couldn't bear the sight of it.

"If you'd like to call it that," the technician replied. "The damn thing still aches a little. Lost an eye, but came close to losing my life, if Severine here wasn't watching my back!"

"What got you?"

"Coelophysis – the green jungle dinosaurs. There's a large pack of them just outside the *Supernova*, about twenty miles west of here. My guess is that their nesting ground must be near the ship. They're very territorial!"

Brett winced, shaking his head in agreement.

"They're mean little shits, aren't they? And they can hold a grudge – I don't piss around with them! If you're within their territory, they'll track you down until they catch you. However, I've learned that they won't cross the southern marshes. I've figured they must be scared of the marshland – maybe something near the sea?"

"We first ran into them on the command bridge," Julius added. "We scared them off with my 90, and we thought that would be the last of them. Later on, some other plant-eaters blocked our road through the jungle. When we left the rover to shoo them away, the lizards attacked us again! And that's when that cute little memento happened..." He pointed to Paluch's wound on the scientist's bandaged face.

"You won't see those dinos past the plains," Brett confirmed. "Carnivores won't come near the *Mudskipper*. The ground is too sharp and unpredictable here with the pod debris, and I don't think there's enough prey up here to sustain them."

"What else should we know about?" Jordy asked. "You had to have seen other dinosaurs since you've been stuck up here."

Brett nodded.

"Most of them are peaceful and are easy to shy away when you approach them. The majority live in the more deciduous areas and keep off the floodplains. I've seen land ones, flying ones, even amphibious ones!"

"And what about the meat-eaters?" Julius asked.

"There is another pack – a fairly large one, although not as big as the coelophysis pack. But these dinosaurs are larger. Most of them are contained between the river and the mountain range to the south, in a large stretch of coniferous trees. There's a whole pack in those woods. Large, nasty ones too – man-eaters! Some are twenty feet in length and very fast! I only go up there periodically to hunt, but only when food is scarce and there's no other options."

"What do they look like?" Paluch asked.

"What? The carnivores?"

"Yes."

"Well, pretty big. As I've said, maybe twenty feet long, though some may be longer. I'd say they range from six to nine feet tall. Usually orange or dark brown in color, and sharp-ass teeth! I'm serious, like razor sharp! These things are vicious! There's one big mean one with a set of red stripes. I figure it must be the queen of the colony."

"Probably the alpha male, actually," Paluch corrected him. "I think I know the genus you're talking about. Does this drawing resemble the dinosaurs?"

Paluch handed over a torn sketch from his Triassic field manual.

"It's almost a mirror image, I'd say! How do you pronounce that?"

"Herrerasaurus – part of the herrersauridae family," Paluch replied. "Their fossils were first discovered by a man named Victorino Herrera in the 1950s, according to this book. They're some of the larger predatory dinosaurs from the late Triassic. One of the most effective hunters of the time period, and one of the oldest dinosaurs ever discovered. And yes, from what I've read, herrerasaurs are definitely among the superiors of the Carnian stage. Frankly, I'd rather meet the coelophysis pack again then run into one of those guys."

"Sort of looks like a T-rex," Julius commented. Severine couldn't help but smile, betting a tyrannosaurus was probably the only dinosaur the lieutenant had ever heard of.

"It's basically a much smaller version of a tyrannosaurus," Paluch stated. "Tyrannosaurs didn't come onto the playing field until years later, in the upper Cretaceous Period. Thankfully, we shouldn't be running into them any time soon!"

Julius examined the illustration closely.

Maybe it's finally starting to sink in, Severine thought, hoping the lieutenant was warming up to the dinosaur idea.

"And you're telling me these things are right in our backyard?" Severine asked.

"They're limited mostly to the other side of the mountains," Brett replied. "As long as you don't go into the conifer jungles, you'll be fine."

"Have you ever encountered any other humans?" Jordy asked. "Any other Federation survivors?"

"Nope – it's just me. It's always been just me."

"We've found traces that others may have survived," Severine said. "Open sleeper pods. Missing vehicles in the cargo bay. We even found a Federation infantry suit in the jungle. It looked like the dinosaurs picked him off."

"I'm sure there may have been other survivors, but they would've died off long ago, probably a few weeks after the impact. *Supernova* went down in the west jungle, right into the kill-zone of the coelophysis. I'll be honest, if you didn't have the FATR, I don't think we'd be here having this conversation. You would've never made it out onto the plains. Nothing personal, it's just how this place is – violent! Violent and unpredictable."

"Well, we're heading back there at first light," Julius said.

"You must have a death wish."

"Not exactly," Severine cut in. "The solar signal emitter in the mainframe room is operational! But the doors are jammed. We've been trying to find a way inside to call for help."

Brett leaned backwards in deep thought, taking in the news.

"I've suspected it all along. The hologram indicators on the *Mudskipper* suggested that *Supernova* still had some operational rooms. It only makes sense that the ship would be drawing power from the sun to survive. The solar signal emitter would be the ship's main backup power source if the bridge failed. Imagine how tempting it was for me to get back there and check for myself, especially after having found this off one of the cadavers…"

He pulled back his tattered collar, revealing a small laminated lanyard that hung around his neckline. The light from the embers made the object dazzle with significant beauty.

Could it be? It is!

It was a level 5 clearance key-card.

A large, orange number five was stenciled onto the middle of the dangling rectangle. Micro authorization printing lined the bottom, followed by a golden pristine strip for sliding access. The edges of the card were encased in thin copper trim.

Severine wasn't sure that she'd ever seen one in person. They were objects of great admiration and achievement among the upper ranks of the Federation – and very rare.

"Ambrose, let me see that!" the lieutenant said, reaching for the card.

Brett handed the key-card to Julius who looked admirably at the object, cradling it in his hands before confirming its authenticity.

It's an actual level 5! She couldn't believe it.

"You've had this card all this time and you never tried to activate the signal?"

"I've tried many times to get back to the *Supernova*," Brett replied. "The wilderness there is too unpredictable. The coelophysis packs populate like rabbits in those woods. I've been fortunate enough to escape every time, but the carnivores continually grow bolder. And I won't dare try the shortcut in the northern pass. The herrerasaurs are infinitely more terrifying – trust me..."

"I'll take your word for it," Severine said.

"My only hope was to keep *Mudskipper's* console active and hope someone would eventually see my short-range signals. The truth is...I've never made it back to the *Supernova* – not even close! Eventually I gave up trying, figuring the risk of being eaten alive outweighed the reward."

"Well, now it's all changed for the better," Severine said. "Come with us, Brett! We'll be safe in the rover. With the key-card in our back pocket, we'll all be getting out of here!"

A subtle look of uncertainty crossed Brett's face.

"I don't know," he said, taking the card back from Julius. "Staying clear of the jungles has kept me alive all this time. FATR rovers are great, until they fail out. What happens if the vehicle stalls?"

"Then we'll have to deal with it then," Julius said. "The bottom line is this: The signal emitter is still functioning, as of now. Every passing second is another chance for a tree or rock to fall on *Supernova's* roof and destroy the solar-charging panels. If that happens, the emitter will be rendered useless, and our one and only opportunity to return to the Federation will be vanquished forever. And I don't know about you, but I don't want to wait here to be some dino's meal."

Severine smiled. It was well-said, and he finally acknowledged the dinosaurs.

"It's true," Jordy said. "The signal could be cut short at any moment! I've searched my databases multiple times for another potential way of escape and signaling for rescue, but after the discovery of the bridge, the emitter is the only option left on the table."

"We would be honored if you will come with us," Severine said. "Plus, we need your key-card – and your good company, of course!"

He laughed, returning a loving grin under his old, gentle eyes.

"Thanks, Sev."

There it is again! That memory...

For a moment, she recalled the flashback of romance with the foreign stranger, back during the years of Federation military training. Perhaps she had met him more frequently than a few occasions. She knew they had been more than acquaintances, more than friends.

In the quiet of the crackling fire, she let her thoughts die and buried them deep down.

It was useless to dwell on a vague memory that she couldn't fully remember and wasn't prepared to ask him about in front of the others. Maybe if they lived long enough to enter the mainframe room and signal for help, she would question him about her memories, and see if he had them too – or could help her fill in the missing pieces.

"Well, you'll need someone there to watch your back and serve as a guide," he said. "My only demand is no-one leaves the FATR – not until we get back to the *Supernova*. If you hadn't discovered the rover, I wouldn't be agreeing to be going on this suicide mission – but you're right! This is our only chance. We'll leave at first light. Most of the carnivores are less active in the morning."

Julius smiled. "Sounds like a plan to me! I'm not a big fan of leaving the rover either."

"I'm eager to see my old home again," Brett said. "Maybe I'll even find an opportunity to use my detonator."

XIII

"Daddy, prepare to take us back to the *Supernova,*" Julius commanded, stepping into the cockpit. "I'd like to make it back there by mid-day. Take us back the same route we came. We should be able to follow the rover's path back, right up to the cargo bay."

"Yes, sir," the pilot said, rousing himself out of sleep-mode.

Daddy snapped to reality and started pressing buttons on the dashboard as situational holograms emerged, powering on the rover's engines and checking the indicators for status reports.

The colonists had just made it back to the vehicle as the rays of a new, golden sunrise began to brighten the valley. The prehistoric sun rose over the horizon to the east, bathing the beautiful Triassic landscape in a yellow tint. When she sun started to gleam out from over the mountains, the group spent about twenty minutes laboriously climbing out of the crater hole before they finally made it back to the FATR.

Vrrrrr!!!

Severine relaxed as the rear hatch sealed behind her, taking comfort inside the security of the armored transport.

I could go for a shower soon, Severine thought. The climb out from the *Mudskipper* and the humidity of early morning left her coated in sweat.

Julius resumed his place in the co-pilot chair, flipping through the useless, virtual update displays until he arrived at the driving menu. Severine, Jordy, and Brett assumed seats in the cockpit, and Paluch returned to the rear department.

Severine knew that Julius had forgiven the scientist for his stupidity back in the jungle, essentially ending his punishment and isolation. When she asked Paluch to join them up front, he responded by thanking her, but wished to continue his study of his coelophysis specimen, hoping to learn more of the animals in case they encountered them again.

I hope we don't, Severine thought as she sat down. *And I bet he does too...*

No one could find a reason to argue with him.

Let the scientist do his work – it may come in handy later...

"Ever ride in one of these?" Julius asked, turning back to Brett.

"I can remember a few times," Brett replied. "In vehicle training and advanced individual training operations – and of course, only in simulated environments. I see this one has an XP-300. Have you fired it yet?"

"No reason to," Julius said. "They don't aim low enough to hit anything that we would need to take out. However, we did deploy an electric strike – it worked beautifully!"

Brett laughed. "Yeah, the animals won't stand still for the 300 to do any good. The engineers probably had human warfare in mind when they developed them. They didn't figure that one day we'd be relying on them to survive dinosaur attacks!"

"Certainly not," Jordy chimed in.

"All right, team, let's get off this rock – what do you say?" Julius said.

Everyone nodded in agreement.

"Daddy, send her!"

"Yes, sir!"

With a loud *vrrrrrr,* the engine snapped to life, rattling the cockpit. Daddy pushed his levers ahead and the treads began rolling past, kicking up the wet ground near the rover. Julius rotated his driving shafts, spinning the FATR southward. *Mudskipper's* ruins started to disappear past the right windshield pane. The crater was soon out of view, and they continued the trek back to the floodplain.

Severine smiled, sitting back in her seat.

The mission, so far, had proved successful. They tracked down the short-range frequency of the E5 escape pod, rescued Federalist Brett Ambrose, and had now miraculously attained a level 5 key-card. The solar signal emitter was all but within their grasp, and rescue would surely follow.

We're getting out of here! Severine thought, watching the shrapnel and debris slide by on the grass below.

"What happens when we make it to the crash?" Brett asked. "We'll have to go in on foot to the mainframe room. If there's any coelophysis packs in the area, we'll be sitting ducks!"

"They don't go into the ruins," Julius told him. "At least not very far, anyway. I think the place scares them. They're very cautious about the ship."

"Or maybe there's something in the ship they don't like."

"Like what?"

"Just a guess, Sev," Brett replied. "Those dinos don't scare easy, except when they're up against the larger predators."

"We probably would've noticed larger predators when we were there," Julius replied confidently.

"*Supernova* is a big ship, Lieutenant. I doubt you covered all of it."

"*Whoa!*" Jordy yelled in a digital scream. "What's that ahead?"

"Flooding!" Brett observed. "The fields are gone!"

Julius pressed down hard on the levers, bringing the FATR to a grinding halt.

The monsoon had submerged the grasslands under a massive sea, stretching far up to the mountain slopes and to the tiny jungle trees at the other side. Rain had significantly extended the swamp in all directions. Grass blades popped out in sparse areas, indicating that the depth was still relatively shallow in certain points. In the morning wind, small waves blew across the surface before breaking up as they skated over the soggy coast. The way back to the *Supernova* suddenly seemed treacherous.

Shit! The path's gone...

"I didn't see it coming!" Julius said. "The water color looks about the same shade as the ground – it practically blends right in!"

Although the two shades were similar, Severine could see the difference clearly. The surface waved in the glint of the morning sunrise. Pockets of rippling bubbles shot up through the murky waters, slipping away in current. Large fish snaked by between the grass blades and reed stems. The tracks that the FATR had made the day before vanished into the water, hiding the path they carved out under the clouded surface.

"We can't cross this," Brett said.

"Damn right, we can't!" Severine replied. "There's no way to tell how deep it goes! The water's too diluted."

"That's actually incorrect," Daddy said. "Our virtual map displays topological terrain in the area around the rover. To access it, I'll just have to amplify the map closer to our location. This should also increase the hologram detailing – like this!"

He brushed through the digital map, landing on an 'enhance' function, and the virtual camera zoomed tighter to the rover's three-dimensional icon. By sacrificing the distance data of the map, the computer was able to process the closer geographical information more accurately. The ground became clear around them via the computerized display, calculating the depth.

"The rover will survive crossing through that?" Severine asked.

"It should, as long as we stick to the shallow parts," Julius said.

"In exchange, we will lose the long-distance radar," Daddy stated. "But we shouldn't need that feature right now."

"What if we double back?" Severine said. "Find a different route?"

"Won't happen," Brett answered. "The region around the *Mudskipper's* crash site is enclosed completely by mountains and rivers. That's another reason I held up in there all those years – it has great natural defenses! There won't be anywhere else for the rover to double back. This valley is the only way in and out..."

"Have you seen the swamps flooded like this before?" Jordy asked, his lights blinking at the question.

"Not this bad," he replied. "But it does happen now and again. This time of year is the rainy season, and flooding will occur more often. Might take a week or more to drain, if you want to wait it out – just to stay on the safe side."

"I vote that option," Severine said, raising her hand. "The emitter will still be there."

It's worth the wait to save the rover.

"You don't know that, Sev," Julius replied. "Even yesterday's storm could have done damage to the *Supernova*. Every passing second is another chance for something to destroy the device. Daddy, what do you think?"

"The trip in the water will be slow. But it should be doable as long as we stay in shallow water, as you've said. The mission should be safe if we proceed as planned, sir."

"That's good enough for me," Julius said. "Let's take her in slowly."

"Don't I get a vote?" Jordy asked.

"You just sit there and look cute," Julius replied, shooting the robot a warm smile. "I'll take good care of you, little buddy! We'll be through this marsh in no time. Okay, Daddio – take us in!"

"Aye, sir."

Severine frowned, offering up a silent prayer.

Jordy would surely have broken the tie in her favor. She contemplated further argument but decided against it. She wasn't the one driving, and out of everyone, she knew the least about FATR capabilities. But as the water began to inch closer, she couldn't help but think they were making a grave mistake.

The rover slowly moved towards the coast line as the soaked ground gave way under the massive transport gears. A *wooooooossshhh* of sloshing water overtook the treads as the machine eased into the swamp. Waves parted at their approach, welcoming them as the pool silently encircled on the vehicle.

Here we go...

Daddy's holographic mapping depicted their slow journey as he guided the transport gracefully along the shallow points. Little representative blips of virtual fish could be seen in the images, swimming curiously around the submerged treads before darting away as the cleats kicked up dirt clouds.

The height measure noted a current depth of one foot of water.

That's not so bad...

"Try not to take her any deeper than that," Severine suggested.

"You a little jumpy back there, Solens?" Julius laughed. "Relax, we'll be fine! Save your concern for our reunion with our green friends."

"I'm serious, Julius!" she continued. "What if the water gets under the base of the machine where all the gears and the electrical circuits are?"

Severine suddenly felt compelled to state her case, feeling guilty for second-guessing the lieutenant's decision.

"We'd have to be at a depth of ten feet or more for those kinds of problems to occur, and the most I plan on going is five feet, if the swamp even goes that far down. So far, it's not very deep."

Severine wasn't so sure. Already the measure indicator had increased by a few inches.

"Just be careful," she said, patting his shoulder.

"Yes, ma'am," he laughed. He didn't seem at all worried about the water.

The treads continued to kick up spouts of murky algae past the windshield as the colossal vehicle moved further into the filthy waters. The depth calculations ticked away as the rover's computers monitored the ground. Severine watched the gauges closely.

We're going down again...

The rover was now two feet deep.

"As long as we keep heading to the mountain slopes, the water level should start receding. Daddy, any estimated time of arrival at the slopes?"

"No current statistics, sir," Daddy replied. "This enhanced mapping display is using most of the computing power. Our reserve power was exhausted during the electric strike."

"Those fish look funny," Severine said as the tiny creatures slid quickly out of the rover's path in the map. Their fins protruded out like tall sails as they faded from the screen into the watery clouds.

"They don't look like anything back in our aquariums," Jordy commented, studying the hologram reception. "Much more primitive...Severine?"

The bot was whispering.

"Yes, Jordy?" she answered softly.

"Do you think the emitter will work?"

He blinked his light panels with a curious tilt of the head. She could sense the concern in his voice.

"It has to," she replied, trying to reassure him.

It has to...

Her thoughts on the plan to breach the mainframe doors had plagued her dreams, costing her most of her sleep. A variety of factors plagued the perfection of the plan. The journey back through the marsh. Their likelihood of encountering the coelophysis pack – or whatever else was out there in the jungle. The functionality of the mainframe doors. The capability of the solar signal emitter. The range the frequency could travel. The probability of contacting the Federation. And the final, most jarring factor: The hope that the Federation was still out there somewhere, alive and on a breathable planet.

The towering slopes rose high above them, shrouding what lay behind in mystery. The rising sun lit their peaks with splashes of gold, causing the rocky surfaces to shine like torchlight.

"The mornings are beautiful here," Brett said. "No cities or T50s flying overhead."

"We can leave you here if you want?" Julius joked, turning a lever.

"Who knows," Severine said. "When the rescue party arrives, they might want to cultivate this world and plant the Federation flag here."

"It could happen," Jordy said. "Just might take a few decades to push the invasive species out."

Notions of the Federation colonists overtaking this world hadn't been discussed yet, but Severine thought it seemed like a viable option if the Federation hadn't found another planet already. Settling in Earth's prehistoric past could change the course of history, and possibly for the better, now that they had knowledge of the planet's catastrophic future.

"Hey, what are these ovals?" Jordy asked, pointing at the glitching geometry.

The FATR had begun splitting strange pods that lay submerged in the bog. Upon impact, the ovals split apart, sending flattened shell fragments and organic material under the crushing treads.

Eggs...

"I think they're eggs," Severine said. "It's a nest."

WHEEEEEERRRRR!!!

The rover stopped with a dramatic lurch forward, sending massive waves splashing in all directions.

"*Whoa!*" Julius screamed. "Daddy, what's happening? We've stopped!"

"I'm working on it, sir. Checking the damage reports now. The machine is stu –!"

With a bright flash, a beam of electricity surged through the cockpit, dancing over the dashboard, leaving terrifying sparks in its destructive, unpredictable path. The console lights began to blink sporadically with failure warnings. Some had stopped blinking altogether, flickering one last time before shooting out of the hardware in little flames. The mapping hologram struggled to stay on, now emitting the image at about fifty percent transparency.

The battery's dying!

Violent aftershocks followed as the crew tumbled from their seats. Severine, Brett, and Jordy avoided a large part of the danger. Their seats were out of the blast radius. Julius suffered from a few of the volts as he struggled to hold onto the levers but regained his posture after the wave passed through.

Through her disoriented vision on the cockpit floor, she could see Julius reaching over to Daddy, who had taken the brunt of the shock.

The bot convulsed in his seat, fighting hard to recover his computerized functions. The panels on his armor performed their duties in a trance, accomplishing nothing as they folded in and out randomly from their positions.

"I'm alllll-rri, sir! Just a shh-kkkk..."

Daddy's stuttering voice indicated the bot was severely impacted from the blast.

Red warning messages began to populate the hologram map. Severine studied the status report.

The ground beneath the rover had collapsed and was slowly pulling the vehicle downwards. In the sudden drop of elevation, water splashed upward and fried the bottom electrical strips – just as she had been afraid of.

"What's happening?" Jordy asked, as Severine helped the bot to his feet.

"We're going down," Julius replied, frantically trying to revive Daddy. "It's a damn sinkhole!"

Shit!

Severine bit her tongue, resisting the urge to reprimand the lieutenant for his lousy decision-making, but figured he was already aware of his bad judgment. Bitching at him now wouldn't save the vehicle – or their lives.

"I'll pop out the upper hatch," Brett said, shouldering his crossbow and walking out from the room. "We can get out through the ceiling!"

"Get out?" Jordy asked.

"Yes," Brett replied. "We'll be underwater in minutes!"

"Minutes!" The robot was petrified – the water could ruin him.

"Sev, I'd start preparing to abandon ship! I'm going to make sure the roof's secure!"

"Okay," Severine replied, shaking off the feelings of sudden shock.

Brett ran into the communications room and began fiddling with a roof lever before releasing a hatch, letting sunlight flood into the chamber. A rope ladder fell to his feet and the soldier scrambled upward, out of view.

As she turned back to her companions, Severine managed to catch another object swimming nearby in the fading holographic imagery. When it came around one of the rear treads, she could accurately see the form of the creature before it vanished again in the murkiness.

Is that a crocodile?

The virtual reception began to fill with static and the feed struggled to retain the mapping data.

As it suddenly clicked off, Severine saw more crocodilians circling around the sinking treads as the water level continued its horrifying ascent.

And just like that, it's all gone to hell...

XIV

"Let mee ss-e if I can regain conntt—l," Daddy glitched. His dying fingers fumbled for the FATR controls, missing and pressing malfunctioned buttons.

"Daddy, override that order!" Julius yelled, trying to revive the pilot. "Daddy, can you hear me?"

The bot was stuck in a computerized limbo, ignoring the lieutenant's commands.

The surge probably fried his responsive/listening components, Severine thought, realizing that Daddy was unrecoverable and would soon shut down permanently, becoming the first casualty of their risky quest.

As the sounds of Julius yelling at the dying robot faded behind her, Severine ran into the communication room with Jordy right on her heels. Above, the ceiling hatch was still open, with Brett nowhere in sight. She expected to see him motioning up to them, instead of a blank sky.

Dammit. Where is he? Checking on the roof shouldn't be taking this long...
Cliccckkkk!!!

The white overhead lights switched to red alarms. Computerized warning sirens began to loop loudly throughout the room.

"Sev, look over there!" Jordy pointed.

A thin waterfall began to trickle out from a floor vent, starting a thin puddle in the far corner of the room. A second stream flowed out from another grate, collecting along the wall behind the deep-freeze crates. The ground beneath the vehicle began to give way, causing subtle tremors throughout the interior.

It's going down fast!

"Jordy, go through those boxes! Fill up some supply packs full of water and food – as full as you possibly can, okay?"

The bot looked fearfully at the water as it splashed through the chamber.

"Jordy!"

"Huh, yes – Sev... I'll do it..."

"Okay, do it fast! Thanks, Jord!"

Jordy shivered before giving her a slow nod, grabbing a Federation pack hanging on the wall. This event would surely cause internal damage to his computers, if he was lucky enough to survive.

If any of us are lucky to survive...Paluch!

She had forgotten all about the scientist.

Severine tried the door to the rear chamber, but the power outage impacted the locking mechanisms.

"Dammit!"

There isn't time for this!

She kicked it down, sending the door splashing onto the watery floor in the next room.

"What the hell's going on up there?" Paluch said, hopping up from his makeshift laboratory. "Did we spring a leak? Or is our bathroom plumbing screwed up?"

Water was swelling in this room too, bubbling up from all the air ducts. Several pens and science utensils were already floating in the brown pools, wrapped in algae.

"Are you blind?" Severine yelled. "We're going under – a sinkhole is dragging us down! The rover is suffering from an electrical spike – there's no stopping it! Grab whatever you find useful, including food, and get through the upper hatch as soon as possible!"

"Sinking? Are we in a lake?"

"Yes! Now do as you're told!"

Severine left him bewildered and confused as she ran back into the communication room. Jordy was fumbling with fruits, shoving them quickly into a pack. Beyond, she could see Julius trying to repair Daddy in the cockpit, wrestling him out of his driving posture. Behind the windshield, the water level crept up to the bottom of the glass, exposing the dark river beneath.

The rover is more than halfway underwater already!

Muddy dirt chunks began to surge through the vents, temporarily clogging before water forced through the grates and poured onto the floor. The room swayed backwards with a sudden tilt. Gravity lurched a few of the deep-freeze crates towards the rear. Severine could hear Paluch cursing in the back, scrambling to gather his valuables as his room dipped.

The ground is collapsing...

"Is this enough, Sev?" Jordy asked, showing her the contents of the supply packs.

"That's good! Grab two more waters and climb up the hatch!"

"Okay!"

"Wait – give me the packs! Your parts aren't strong enough to swim with those on."

"Swim?"

"Yes, Jordy. You may have to swim. You'll make it – I promise! Now get up the ladder! I need to get Julius."

Jordy nodded. "Please hurry, Sev!"

His chrome feet stepped onto the first ladder rung as the water flowed across the floor. Severine moved around him before running back to the cockpit.

Thankfully the glass is still holding.

"Daddy! Daddy, override all orders. Reset your functions! Can you hear me? Daddy!" The lieutenant rooted through a small mechanic chest that was stashed under the dashboard, but none of the tools could repair the pilot's fried circuits.

"Julius! Leave him – he's done for!"

"I can bring him back!" he yelled. "I've done this before in training. Just get the others out – we'll be along shortly."

Daddy stared blankly through the window, no longer communicating with the lieutenant. The bot's eyes had dimmed, a giveaway that his battery had failed.

"Julius! He's fried! He's not coming ba –"

Severine froze as a shadow passed over her face.

Behind the windshield, a massive crocodilian glided by in the waves. The head was monstrously large, adorned with rows of sharp, serrated teeth under its heavy jaws. The coloration of its scales were various shades of brown, from dark tan to light mocha. The eyes of the monster searched the cockpit but quickly averted their gaze.

He must not be able to see through the glass, she thought. *That's a relief...*

With a great flick of the tail, the beast propelled itself downward, vanishing into the cloudy haze.

"What the hell?"

"It's a saurosuchus," Paluch said, coming up behind her. He was all packed and ready to go, but was now distracted by the new creature.

"What's that?" Severine asked. "A glorified crocodile?"

"You could say that. It's a paracrocodylomorph from the late Triassic. They're massive carnivores that were first discovered in South America. Strong neck. Curved, serrated teeth. My God, they're beautiful! They must be defending their territory. Definitely not something we're equipped to deal with right now."

The overhead red light clicked off, and the console buttons let out one final flash. The only remaining light source came from the solar flare off the rippling waves that had now risen halfway up the windshield. If the glass broke, the cockpit would be flooded instantly.

"There's another one!" Severine pointed. "It's huge!"

Behind the brown swamp water, another saurosuchus swam towards the glass. This beast dwarfed the first creature, almost double in size. Paluch guessed an estimated length of twenty-five feet – a true apex predator of the late Triassic.

As the sauro swam towards the cockpit, Julius finally took notice, watching in horror as the prehistoric monster passed inches behind the glass. Bubbles surged out from the jagged mouth as the croc dove sharply under the windshield, out of view. With a fierce bat of the tail, it sent a wave splashing over the cockpit window.

"Shit! Severine, what is that thing?"

He's petrified...

"Hey!" Severine yelled, jerking his shoulder armor.

"Huh... Yeah?" Julius said, turning away from Daddy.

"Get the hell up the ladder! We're getting out!"

"Right..." He nodded, finally understanding the gravity of the situation.

The FATR was sinking fast, and if they didn't get out now, the flooding or the crocs would trap them at the bottom of the marshes.

Grabbing his XR-90 from a nearby shelf, Julius ran out of the cockpit. Paluch followed as they started to climb the ladder to the roof. The floor was now submerged under a foot of brown waves that sloshed around the flooded rooms. In the middle of the walls, more higher vents were now dripping with waterfalls.

Severine snatched up her X2-20 from her seat where she left it, casting a final look at Daddy's robotic corpse. The robotic face stared lifelessly out the windshield, watching as the swamp consumed the glass. The bot was done – the first, and hopefully last, casualty of their trek.

As she slipped out of the cockpit, another saurosuchus drifted by the glass, covering the room in shadow.

Paluch was waiting above her, holding out a courteous, outstretched arm from the hatch opening. Somewhere above on the roof, she could hear Julius' XR-90 going off and echoing throughout the floodplain.

The sauros! They're on the roof already!

"Come on – hurry up!" Paluch yelled. "It's a shit-show up here!"

She scrambled up the ladder as Paluch grasped her forearm, hauling her upward. She was surprised by his kindness, hoping it was there to stay.

The rooftop was a battleground.

Julius and Brett were using the various communication structures for defense against the saurosuchus herd. The monsters swam quickly around the base of the rover, forbidding the colonists to swim to shore. The water was almost seeping onto the roof ledge, inching up to the peak of the cockpit at the front.

Jordy struggled to deploy a small emergency watercraft, which Severine was surprised he remembered to grab amid the chaos. The boat was inflated and ready to go, but the bot refused to throw it out onto the surface, fearing an approaching sauro would devour it.

Their nests! We screwed up their nests! And now we pissed them off.

Although she doubted that their young would have survived the flooding from the day before, the pack was still intent on defending the nests. Now that the FATR had squashed a few of the eggs, the sauros felt the need to press an attack, determined to rip the colonists from the roof and death-roll them into the depths.

Three of the primordial titans lay lifeless on the roof, dispatched by Brett's knife or Julius' pulse rifle. Paluch walked beside a corpse, pulled in by his curiosity of the prehistoric beast. He began to examine the scales and teeth, careful not to slip his hand under the lifeless skull, fearing that the sauro might still be alive.

Severine kept her 20 aimed at the siege that roared around them, taking selective shots. Her pulse blasts hit their targets, sending the monsters croaking in pain as they dipped back under the surface.

The scientist placed a hand on the colossal animal's head, carefully examining the textured patterns, but careful not to touch the glowing residue from Julius' pulse blast.

"Incredible – they're enormous! This would explain why the coelophysis didn't follow us out of the forest. They knew these bastards would be waiting just beyond in the marshes! When the monsoon flooded the area, their territory expanded. And here we are, smack-dab in the middle of it!"

She found his comments interesting, but there wasn't time to dwell on his speculation. There were problems afoot and no time for scientific deductions. The FATR would soon be underwater, and when that happened, their defenses would be useless.

We need to get off this thing!

Her eyes darted around, searching for the safest, easiest exit. All around, the waves raged as the crocs circled the rover, creating a small whirlpool.

With a terrifying growl, a large saurosuchus snapped at the scientist, who fell backwards, screaming as his shoulder wound smacked off a utility box.

The enormous monster lumbered onto the roof. From the snout to the tip of the tail, Severine assumed an estimated length of twenty feet. Jagged claws protruded out from the four muscular legs as it trotted along towards the scientist.

"*Whoa!*" he cried, frantically backing up as the beast pursued him.

Paluch kicked against the snout, trying to force the sauro backwards. The beast was undeterred, charging forward with a final chomp. Severine couldn't get a clear shot – a telecom spire blocked the skirmish.

Dammit!

"Sev! Shoot the son of a bitch!"

VRRRRR!

A pulse blast from Julius fired out from the side, striking the monster in the head and scorching through the skull. With a helpless croak, it collapsed to the ground, knocking over the telecom spire and sending another burst of sparks showering over the roof.

"Close call," Julius said, helping Paluch to his feet.

"These waves aren't getting any smaller," Brett stated. "We can't toss the raft out – the crocs will tear it to bits!"

"How's your ammo?" Julius asked.

"I have ten shots left. You?"

"Twenty."

"She's going down fast," Paluch said, as the sea continued to rise around them.

The sauros continued to swirl around the FATR. Trails of water began to cross over the metal roof in the lower areas…it wouldn't be long now.

Severine looked to the nearest stretch of dry land.

The slopes of the mountains dipped down just to their right. The shore was close, but not close enough to swim to with the sauros hovering just below the current. Swamp water touched Severine's boot, dampening the heel.

We don't have much time…

"We could climb up the barrel," Paluch said, pointing to the tall turret. The XP-300 twin pulse cannons towered over them, eclipsing the morning sun.

"They're angled too high," Julius replied. "We'll just slide back down and be croc food."

"Can we shoot the canons?" Severine asked. "I don't know anything about these vehicles, but I remember learning about Federation turrets. In manufacturing, they usually installed manual access panels near the back of the stock. The noise might be enough to draw the crocs away – long enough for an escape. How many rounds does it have?"

"You're right!" Julius exclaimed. "Let's try it! It's our only card left to play. Should have a few hundred rounds. Just pray the pulse charge is still good!"

They ran back to the pulse cannons and studied the rear stock that connected to a raised swivel platform. With a clang, Julius kicked in the access panel and stared into the interwoven wires.

"Sev, you're a genius! Here's the manual firing mechanism!"

"Don't say that yet! We don't know if it'll work."

"Well let's find out! You had better cover your ears!"

The lieutenant's fingers fumbled through the wiring, joining the copper ends together. A spark sizzled out and whistled past his face as he frantically began shuffling cables around. Behind the hardware, a reverberation began to wind up.

BRRRNNNNNNNNNNNN!

It's still operational!

A tremendous blast rang out from the barrels and an orange laser bolt rocketed into the sky, causing the FATR to wobble in the bog. Several of the approaching crocodiles skirted backwards and tumbled into the water, fearful of the noise that rang out through the valley. The bolt sailed high into the atmosphere before being swallowed by the golden clouds.

"Can you set it up to keep firing?" Brett asked.

"Yeah, this ought to do it…"

BRRRRNNNNNN!

The sauros had vanished under the bog, buying the colonists a small window of time.

"It's all set! A blast will go off every ten seconds!"

"Now you can thank me!" Severine said.

"Thanks, Sev! Nice quick thinking! Well the XP-300 won't last forever. When it sinks, the blasting stops! We'll have that much time to paddle to shore. Toss her in, buddy!"

BRRRNNNNNNNNN!

With a gentle throw, Jordy cast the raft into the water beside the turret platform. By now, the entire roof was under an inch of water, leaving the gunner platform the last remaining dry patch.

"Get in!"

Brett jumped into the water, climbed onto the boat and cast a friendly hand to his companions that splashed in behind him. Jordy waited behind on the sinking platform.

"What about Daddy?" the bot asked.

"He's done, pal! Come on – we don't have much time!"

Julius grabbed the bot's arm and lugged him into the raft, before kicking off the gunner platform with his foot, sending the boat away from the vehicle. Brett passed around a set of oars as they began paddling away from their former sanctuary. Severine felt an icy chill climb her spine as a dark shadow passed below them, only to swim away at the sound of another charged particle blast from the XP-300.

BRRRNNNNN!

"They won't hurt us," Paluch proclaimed. "The cannon trick is working!"

"Don't stop rowing," Brett urged them. "And don't look down!"

Severine didn't turn around until they were far away, when she felt herself slipping under the shadows of the towering mountains. The XP-300 fired away against the Triassic backdrop, the rounds shrinking into the horizon. Slowly, the brown waters consumed the last of the barrel, as the weapon let out a final blast. Bubbles filled the gun as the cannons vanished, and the FATR was gone.

Severine checked her X2, making sure it still had juice for the uncertain journey on foot that awaited on the coast.

No more rover… and hardly any ammunition…

Their luck had completely changed.

#

On the other side of the swamp, in the jungles of the coelophysis, a pair of eyes watched the ship rowing to shore. With a wave of a hand, the human tried to contact the passengers. But the distance was miles away, making it hard to flag them down.

The boat was heading for the northern valley, just beyond the mountains. If he wanted to link up with them, he would have to pass through the coniferous jungle – the jungle of the herrerasaurs.

Her jungle...

The territory of Gretta.

XV

Gentle swamp waves rolled onto the shores of the mountain slopes before sinking into the pebbles that littered the ground. Occasionally, Severine would see bubbles rippling in the distance where the FATR sunk, but the sauros didn't bother to give chase to the coast. Instead, they encircled the area where the rover went down, diving through the waters to save their precious eggs that lay crushed beneath the treads. Somewhere under the water, Daddy's mechanical corpse remained, frozen in time at the dashboard, staring out into the brown.

Who knows how long the wreckage will keep them busy? she thought, checking the status of her X2 pistol. Although the beach was far away from the crocs, they were still within earshot, and she feared the monsters might eventually wander over.

Ten shots… Ten shots to last to the Supernova…

She would have to be very strict with her usage of the weapon. Julius had only twenty rounds left in his pulse rifle. Before long, Brett would be instructing them on how to make spears and crossbows – a skill that she wouldn't mind learning.

The colonists huddled at the edge of the bog, near the northwest passage that Brett claimed led to a lush, coniferous forest just beyond the rocky peaks. The flood, surrounding the shoreline, had isolated them from all other options. The terrain around them was wobbly and uneven, making traveling on foot along the cliffs arduously risky and painful.

To make matters worse, as they headed away from the FATR, the boat struck a rock, leaving a fatal tear in Jordy's inflatable raft. Passing back through the murky sea without a boat wasn't a popular option. The bot tossed the raft aside, letting it drift away in the current.

"Okay, it's confession time," Julius said, turning to Severine. "Sev, I'm sorry. You warned me about the FATR driving through the swamp, and I doubted your advice, thinking my way was the better option. And now we're marooned, without our rover, with limited ammunition and food, and no shelter. Next time, I'll take your advice more seriously."

She smiled as wide as she could, given the circumstances.

"Apology accepted, Lieutenant," she replied. "Thank you – just don't be an ass   next   time."
He laughed.

"Okay, let's do a damage report," Julius said, channeling his Federation infantry training. "What do we have? What did you all grab from the deep-freezes?"

Severine pulled out the pack that Jordy had crammed full of supplies. She let it fall off her shoulder, relieving herself momentarily of the weight, and unzipped the top.

"Looks like a few frozen apples. Some oranges. Eight water canisters – good thinking, Jordy! A few other medical items: gauze and antibacterial ointment. All useful."

Not sure how long this will last us...

"Very good," Julius said. "Paluch, what's in your pack?"

The scientist had been quiet since they paddled out from the flood. Dismayed at the loss of Daddy, his personal assistant and great friend from before *Supernova's* crash, he sat beside Severine and stared blankly at the horizon. Severine found it surprising that Paluch cared so much for the pilot bot. He didn't seem like the emotional type, at least not for robots and artificial intelligence.

"Hey, scientist," Julius snapped impatiently. "What have you got? We're counting on you!"

"Sorry," Paluch replied, coming back to reality. "I grabbed five waters and my Triassic identification book. I apologize – my pack wasn't that large." He held up a smaller satchel pack that looked stretched full of items.

"That's not a lot of food," Julius observed. "At least we'll have some fresh water."

"We can follow the valley here up into the jungle," Brett said. "If we head north for a few miles, we should eventually hit the river. There may be a lower spot in the cliffs that we can climb down and catch a few fish. I have a makeshift net."

He produced a scraggly net from his pack, littered with dried leaves and algae.

"Other than that, I have two water canteens, and arrows for my crossbow."

"That brings us to ammunition. Severine and I only have thirty rounds between the two of us. Sev, we have to save our shots and pick them carefully from here on out. The road ahead might be pretty dangerous. Mr. Ambrose, I seem to remember you saying the conifer jungle is a pretty rough neck of the woods."

"It wouldn't be my first choice," Brett replied ominously.

"If we make for the river to the north, crossing as quickly as we can through the forest, where will it lead us?"

"West. Eventually it turns northward, and from there it's a straight shot south to the *Supernova*. Either way, we'll want to get to the river as quickly as possible. At least from there, if we're in a bind from one of the dinos, we can jump down and let the current carry us away."

"Paluch, what can you tell us about the carnivorous dinosaurs in there?" Severine asked.

"Herrerasaurs. That's what we've identified them as, according to Brett's description and by comparing them to my field guide. They're very fast with razor-sharp killing teeth. That we know of, they seem to top out at twenty feet long, but some could be even larger. They weighed over six hundred pounds and are probably considerably more dangerous than the coelophysis packs!"

"Anything else we should know?" Julius asked.

"Well, frankly, Julius, there's not much known about them. They aren't as widely written about, unlike tyrannosaurs, and the other more well-known carnivores. One might conclude that herrerasaurids are ancestors to later carnivores of the Mesozoic, having existed much earlier than Tyrannosaurus Rex. If we go into that jungle, we're dealing with one of the big dinos of the Triassic period. We've already met the other."

He gestured to the swamps, indicating that the sauros were one of the larger carnivores that he knew of.

"Would these weapons be enough to take them down?" Julius asked.

"I wouldn't count on it," Brett said. "You may get lucky and tag a few, but they're fast and very shrewd! Honestly, I would recommend flight over fight, like climbing a tree. There's a good number of conifers in there for a height advantage. If that is the route we're going, which right now seems like the only route, keep an eye open! Dark Orange – that's what we need to watch out for. That's all you'll see of them when they attack."

"Is there anything we can do to deter them?" Severine asked. "Assuming that we will encounter them somewhere along the way?"

"Not sure, Sev. I haven't been around them long enough to memorize their hunting habits. I try to avoid the pine forest as much as possible."

"Any idea when the water will recede here?" Paluch asked.

"Not for a while. Monsoons are common here. It's possible if we wait, more rain will come, and we'll have to wait longer to move through the floodplain. And who knows if any crocs will come by in the meantime. They might want to bask in the sunlight here later."

"What if we stick to the shallows?" Paluch asked.

"I think it's best if we make for the trees," Brett said. "These crocs will make their way over here eventually...we shouldn't be here when they do. We're low on ammo already..."

"Technically speaking, they aren't crocodiles," Paluch started, "but saurosuchus, a crocodylomorph from the late Triassic. They're much larger and more agile, but you're right. Their territory has expanded, probably at least to the foot of the jungle, and now we've pissed them off! If they're anything like coelophysis, they'll want revenge!"

"You don't think they'll follow us in the jungle?" Julius asked.

"Doubt it," Paluch said. "Their territory probably ends at the mountain base, right here on these slopes."

"Jordy, can you do anything for the trip? Any internal mapping software?"

"I have a ba-asic inter-nal compass. Ot-ther than that, the besss—sst I can do is retrace our ste-e-eps." His voice was strenuous, fighting to get the words across.

"Jordy, what's wrong?"

"Sorry, Sev. Some water got into my core computer-ers. Battery levels will drain... I might have a day le-eft..."

What!

"Oh no!" was all she could mutter, but inside Severine was an emotional wreck.

In the quick escape from the FATR, either sometime in the rover, during the rooftop battle, or during the raft escape, the logistics bot must have taken in water. His lights dimmed gently as he spoke, and his head began to twitch slightly between words. The speakers on his chest produced muffled, stuttering noises with his garbled sentences. The battery was the bot's soul, and it was depleting rapidly.

Within a day the bot would die.

"I'm sorry, buddy," Julius said. "Jeez, this is my fault. Everyone can put this on me, one hundred percent! My decision to go through the swamp corrupted Daddy – now the swamp's gonna take our other bot too."

The lieutenant's voice was cracking. The situation was really starting to tear him up.

The pair had formed a strong bond in their two days stranded together – a bond Severine hadn't seen before between man and bot. She refused to let the others see the sadness that welled inside her, forcing it back down and trying to grasp her hardened, inner warrior.

He will be well missed. Dammit! Keep it together, Solens...

Severine hurriedly wiped a tear away before it ran too far down her cheek.

Training never prepared me for this...

"It's all-ll-right. We better ge-et moving. With my processor I sho-sh—uld be able to steer us in the r—i-ight direction, making use of my in-tern-nal compass. We can head north to the r-rrr-iver. Fro-om ther-. As Brett has sa-aid. We fol-low the river west. If I make it tha-at far, I should be able to-at-least point you in the ge-ener-al direc-tion of the crash."

"Save your breath, son," Julius told him, his voice trembling. "If we need you, we'll ask. Conserve as much battery life as you can, okay?"

Jordy nodded.

First Daddy, now Jordy too...

\#

Trudging up uneven rocky outcroppings and rugged cliffs, they climbed northward up the slope, towards the infamous valley entrance to the conifers. The pass was first referenced by Brett back at the *Mudskipper* and was now confirmed as the pine trees approached.

During the hike, Jordy had run several software scans and pinpointed the source of his pain – several ounces of swamp water had penetrated and now sloshed around in his primary processor, located behind his chest plate.

His battery, Severine confirmed with a hard gulp. *There's no stopping it...*

Julius asked if they could crack it open and spill the water out but realized they didn't have the proper tools or skills to perform that operation. Nonetheless, he made peace with the bot's approaching demise, and spent a great deal of the trek helping Jordy climb over the terrain. Guiding the bot up the hill added an hour of extra travel to the ascent, and by the time they reached the end of the rocks, the sun was directly above them in the sky.

Must be around noon, Severine thought, trying to keep her mind off the bot's declining condition.

"Shit," Paluch proclaimed. "We need to go in there?"

They stood at the summit of a tall hill that formed a ramp leading away from the swampy basin. Ahead, a powerful wall of conifer trees formed a dense needle barrier in their path. Beyond the great trunks, darkness commenced. The canopy of needles and fronds blocked out much of the sunlight, though Severine could see small, bright patches breaking through on the forest trails. Little animal paths ran criss-crossing under the branches, gradually dissolving in the distance.

"Unless you want to try our chances in the swamps," Julius began, "with a leaky raft that can't float?"

"And an injured robot," Severine added, patting Jordy softly on the head.

Paluch turned back, second guessing the descent back to the coast. In the distance, they could still make out the tiny forms of adult sauros, bewildered by the sunken FATR as they fought to free their dead hatchlings from the treads.

"What if we wait here for a day or two?" Paluch asked. "The waves may still recede…"

"Or they may continue to rise," Brett added. "How long can those solar signal emitters hold out for, anyway?"

"Forever," Severine replied. "As long as the proper conditions for its survival are maintained."

"What do you think, Sev?" Brett asked. "Let's hear your opinion."

"Yeah, Sev," Julius added. "What are you thinking? If you have a problem with this way, we can always try a different solution."

She appreciated the lieutenant's effort to include her, and Brett's suggestion for her thoughts.

"As much as I hate to say it," Severine started, "I think we should continue through this jungle and keep going. The crocs will be scoping the shore to dry off, and they may even wander all the way up here… Yeah, that does it for me! Let's get going and take our chances in the trees."

"If we keep going north to the river, using Jordy's compass, we should be fine," Brett assured them. "Just need to keep close and be vigilant. There's plenty of trees to climb if the shit hits the fan."

"What about Jordy?" Severine added. "He can barely run, let alone climb…"

"I'll be fin-ne, Sev," the dying bot answered. "I'm of no use sta-a-a-aying here. I vote we g-o-o."

"You sure?"

"Ye-es. What are w-w-e waiting for?"

In his declining stupor, the bot had grown bolder and more dedicated to the mission, eager to please and help the colonists in his final, waning hours.

He must be trying to emulate Daddy's loyalty, Severine thought, knowing the bot had made peace with his untimely situation.

"Okay, let's hit it!"

They began to walk toward the pine tree wall that populated in between the rocky landslides. Julius walked ahead, holding the 90 in front with a scouting stance, keeping the barrel up and ready to rattle off a few bursts. Brett walked alongside him with his crossbow lethally extended against his shoulder. To Severine's surprise, Paluch remained at Jordy's side, helping the bot walk. The machine's inevitable death had a profound impact on everyone, even the know-it-all Federation scientist.

He must miss Daddy…

"Hey, what is it?"

With a harsh rise of his forearm, Julius stopped at the base of the first conifer and knelt on the ground. The others gathered behind him to observe the reason for his sudden stop. Constructed from the excess rainwater that fell from an overhanging branch, a small, soggy patch of dirt lay at the foot of the trees. The roots failed to soak up the rain and left the ground bloated and easy to manipulate with foot impressions – and that's just what they were looking at.

"This can't be good," Severine remarked.

Pressed into the saturated mud was a four-toed animal footprint. The three primary toes stretched out in the front and pointed outward like a broad-leaf. The fourth hung towards the back, cocked arrogantly to the side. At the tips of the toes, triangular-like ends jutted out with sharp edges until they met with a fine-tipped, formidable spike. The entire impression was significantly larger than any human track.

It was clearly made from a bipedal, carnivorous dinosaur.

"Okay, Paluch," Julius said. "Check this out and give us your two-cents, will you?"

"Certainly, big fella," Paluch said, eager to prove his worth.

He ran up to the front and bent down, studying the track. With a grim nod, he looked back up at them.

"Herrerasaurus," he said. "An adult. The impression is maybe a day old, at most."

Severine felt another icy wind creep up her back.

Herrerasaurus...

The word made her shiver.

Behind the scientist, they looked through the dark, dense woodland that awaited their passage. Behind their innocent trunks and playful vines, Severine wondered what may be watching them, just beyond the thicket.

XVI

The branches of the conifers were still soaked with the rain from the day before. In the heat of the tropical afternoon, the humidity of the sun beat down on the canopy, spawning unbearable heat in the woodland. Insects and strange primitive pests hovered nearby and sucked down the dew drops off the pine needles. Along the ground, ferns and stem plants sat crooked in over-saturated soil among the tangled roots.

Bzzzz!

Severine swatted at a large dragonfly that veered past her eyes.

Damn. Missed!

The bug flew away into the leafy branches to her right, quickly out of swatting range.

They had been following an animal trail through the jungle for an hour, and so far, hadn't encountered any predatory dinosaurs – or any animals at all for that matter – other than the damn bugs.

In the mid-day heat, the jungle seemed empty. Far off in a distant location, an animal cry echoed through the trees. Severine thought it sounded like a bird, but she couldn't be certain. Her thoughts often were interrupted by her paranoia, as her eyes looked back and forth through the undergrowth, searching for that quick burst of dark-orange that hadn't come.

Herrerasaurs...

Apart from the lonely track back at the forest's edge, they hadn't caught any trace of the elusive, tyrannical monster. She hoped that their luck would hold out and they could traverse the entire forest back to the ship without encountering more predatory lifeforms.

She was bringing up the rear of the group, holding the X2 pistol in front like a shield, spinning backwards at every snap of a twig.

Ten shots...

That's how many chances of survival she'd have before she had to climb one of the trees. But by the looks of her surroundings, there were plenty of opportunities for an escape.

The conifer trees were plentiful. Their trunks abundantly encompassed the majority of the area, bordering the thin path on all sides. Occasionally, a tree fern would break up their pattern and add a tropical flare to the backdrop. She studied the branches as she went, looking for an easy way to scurry up in case they were ambushed.

Paluch was helping Jordy walk, but frequently would pause to look at the surroundings and try to guess what flora they encountered. He noted that most of the species were most likely a genus of *araucarians,* an ancient coniferous tree that resembled modern-day pines and flourished in various parts of Earth in the Mesozoic. He figured its exact species was *araucaria angustifolia*, based on his assumption that they were hiking somewhere in prehistoric Brazil.

Brett and Julius walked at the front, securing the path. Brett leaned down often to study the ground for signs of danger, such as additional tracks that may have doubled back, but had found none so far. Julius would cover him with the 90 as the private wearily searched along the earth for signs of danger.

"Hey," Severine called, "if you're getting dazed, we should take a rest. I don't want to get lost in here."

The heat was beginning to affect them. Getting lost in this jungle would be easy. The mulch paths intersected at regular junctions, snaking under decaying logs and through conifer patches. Sometimes, the little trails would split off into several smaller offshoots, weaving off in sporadic directions. Jordy's internal compass had come in handy to keep them on track, and it steadily led them north to the river.

"How far?" Paluch asked, fanning himself with his sweaty hand.

"Not sure," Brett replied, rising to his feet. "At this rate, maybe a mile – maybe two."

"Why can't you be certain?" the scientist insisted.

"Because it's hot as hell and I haven't been through here in a while," Brett answered angrily. "Remember, I try to avoid this region..."

"Then let's take a break," Severine said. "No need to carry on dehydrated and miserable."

"I was waiting for someone to suggest one," Julius said. "Sev, let's crack open one of the canisters and set up under that grove there! We'll have cover from all sides. Looks like the visibility is a little better over there too."

Trekking over to the grove of pine trees, they threw their supply packs down and drank the first water canister from Severine's supply pack. The fresh taste was honey to their throats, but Severine knew they had to use the water sparingly. Since the sinking of the rover, most of their supplies had perished, and they had only a few canisters to last them to the *Supernova*.

And when we make it there, what then?

Signaling the emitter wouldn't mean an instantaneous, glorious rescue. She knew there would have to be a waiting period. But the question was, for how long would they have to wait?

A week? A few months?

It was impossible to predict.

They would have to quickly find additional nutritional sources. The fruit would not last long, and it wasn't overly enjoyable to consume. The apples had the foul smell of food crammed in a deep-freeze for too long. Severine craved meat.

"This is awful," said Paluch, biting into one of the red fruits.

"Well, it's all we got," Julius replied. "Most of the food in that rover would have probably tasted the same – they've all been cooped up just as long."

"Well, that doesn't mean I have to like it," said the scientist.

"Hey, just a few bites!" Brett insisted. "It's not like we have a lot to go around."

"Yeah, yeah..."

Severine took her two bites and discarded the apple core on the mulch below. After they passed around an extra swig from the water canister, she put it back in the pack and closed the opening.

Should've eaten more food from the FATR when we had the chance.

She could hear her stomach growling in discontent.

"*Whoa*, get up – quick!" Julius called, snatching up his 90. Severine spun around, pointing her pistol in the direction Julius was looking.

A gray blob trotted innocently among the pines with a delicate grace. It ran with a speed that told Severine that it was probably a harmless herbivore. After a moment, three more gray blurs appeared to run behind the forerunner, following a few steps behind. They each ran on two nimble legs that kicked up like horses as they came down one of the mulch trails, slowly into view.

Red scales covered their heads, descending down their long necks that led to their plump bodies. Crimson stripes ran down their backs and gradually thinned out as they passed over the tip of the tail. With a brief snort, the leader paused twenty yards away from the colonists in the pine grove and looked up carefully. The rest of the pack stopped in their tracks, freezing in place.

More dinosaurs!

"Okay, Paluch," Julius said. "Tell me. What are we looking at here?"

The scientist quietly flipped open his Triassic field manual and glanced back at the gray dinosaurs, thumbing through the tattered pages. Finally, an illustration appeared that matched the creatures.

"Ah, here we go!" Paluch read, pointing to an illustration. "This one's a new one for me! Pisanosaurus – herbivores. Apparently, also from South America, which further backs up my theory that that's where we are. From the Carnian stage of the Triassic. Presumably, they're harmless."

The leading dinosaur looked over at them, yipped again, and munched at an overhanging pine branch before snapping it like a twig. The smaller animals of the group came near their leader and helped pull the branch down to devour it more easily. The dinosaurs didn't look much larger than four feet in length, hardly anywhere near the size of the tremendous saurosuchus pack from earlier.

"They won't try and ha-arm us?" Jordy stuttered.

"No," Brett replied. "I've seen these herds near the *Mudskipper*. They would come by often from the northern mountains – they make for good food!"

"You eat them?" Severine asked. She could feel herself starting to salivate.

The thought of savory meat sounds amazing right now!

"Yeah, no problem! We would just need to start a fire to cook them."

The large pisanosaur crunched down on another branch. Again, the others emulated his movements and jumped happily at the wood, helping pull it down to the earth. The smaller dinosaurs yelped happily as the adult lowered a sizable frond leaf down for them to munch on. From what Severine observed, the creatures didn't care much for the humans.

They must not see us as a threat, she thought. *Just like the exaeretodon.*

"Ambrose, can you pick off one of them with the crossbow?"

"Maybe," he answered. "There's a lot of trees in the foreground."

"Hey, maybe we sh–" Paluch started, but was silenced by Julius' hand. Severine knew the lieutenant wasn't ready for another debate on extinct ecosystems. Wisely this time, the scientist stayed quiet, offering no further rebuttal on the issue.

Brett crouched forward and prepared to pull back the crossbow string, sliding an arrow back to the rear of the stock, and clicked it into place.

Cliiiiiiiiiiiiiiickkk!

The front pisanosaur lifted its large head quickly over to the pine grove, narrowing a helpless gaze at the bowman. Before Brett could release the trigger, the creature moaned and bounced away behind the trees. The young followed close behind, hugging its hind quarters as they shrank away into the pines. Squeals and groans gradually faded away as they vanished back into the brush.

"Damn drawback string," Brett cursed. "I need to work on that. It's screwed me before!"

"Hey, let's follow them," Julius suggested. "They're headed the direction we need to go. North. Right, Jordy?"

"Cor-rr-rr-rect," replied the stuttering digital voice.

"Maybe we can snatch a few for a late lunch," he said. "And they'll lead us right to the river, if they keep going in that direction."

"Works for me," Severine said, tossing her pack over her shoulder.

"They're pretty fast," Brett added. "We'll need to be brisk. And don't forget to watch the trees! The carnivores are still out there! We've been lucky so far..."

They set out again into the forest, based on Brett's hunting expertise he had learned throughout his years in isolation. The journey was challenging at times. The dinosaurs ran through many overgrown portions of the wilderness, between crumbling logs and through clusters of thorny vines.

Suddenly a fowl stench hit them as they passed through a rocky valley.

"Shit, what is that?" Julius asked, cuffing his hands over his nostrils.

The answer quickly revealed itself.

Dino-shit!

On the path ahead, sitting atop the mulch layer, was a patch of fresh feces that had splattered across the wood chips. The pile coalesced around a central mound that was already besieged by an insect raid. Tiny bugs climbed into the moist poo, burying themselves into the sticky interior.

Gross!

"That's terrible!" Severine said, taking a step back.

It was a very strong aroma, made nauseating in the afternoon heat.

"Pretty fresh," Brett remarked. "We're very close!"

"Do you hear that?" Julius asked.

They stopped.

In the distance, through the rows of lumbering pines, a swelling sound began to rise through the trail. It broke and started consistently but failed to reach a climax. Small offshoots of the main sound broke off into splatters against stone barriers not far away in the jungle.

The river!

"Ambrose, are we there already?" Julius asked. "That was quick!"

"No, not even close! We must be at another water source somewhere in the woods. I haven't accurately mapped out this region. There could be other tributaries I haven't found."

Cries of the pisanosaur herd rang out through the trees and were soon greeted by others somewhere close by.

"There's more of them?" Julius asked.

"Many more," Paluch confirmed. "Look here!"

Rows of parallel tracks ran down a trampled embankment under their feet, running around a rocky slope before dropping off into a smaller hidden valley ahead. The tracks were certainly from the pisanosaurs. Severine noted the similarities of the toes and compared them mentally to what they saw at the grove. The tracks from the family of dinosaurs they had been following appeared to join up with a larger herd before the two groups merged and proceeded ahead.

"Looks like there may be a big herd around here," Severine suggested.

"They should be right through here, actually," Brett said, pulling aside a large fern frond. "There they are!"

Oh my!

As the plant passed from her view, Severine looked out at the clearing below. The forest had given way to a small passage that cut through the conifers, illuminated by the afternoon sun that beat down to the grassy basin. To the right of their position, a steep waterfall surged down into a lagoon that drained into a creek, carrying the overflow further into the greenery. Around the shrubs that bordered the serene pond, a bigger group of pisanosaurs licked up the water. Several of the alpha males stood guard at the edges on both sides of the tributary, looking out into the border of trees at the valley's ridge. Little juveniles played along the shallow shores, seeking approval from their parents that stood nearby, proudly.

"Well, now we know where we can fill up our canisters again," Julius said. "Drink up, team. Fresh water is no longer an issue!"

They unpacked quietly on the precipice of the short cliffs, drank more water from the canisters, and watched the dinosaurs frolic in the falls. The scene was a picturesque masterpiece from a moment in time long forgotten.

The pisanosaurs hadn't yet noticed the colonists from their position atop the cliffs. Brett made sure they stayed hidden behind the fern fronds out of the herd's direct view.

"It's magnificent," Julius said. "So many in one place!"

"An oasis," Brett added. "Hidden here right under our noses."

"They won't remain for long," Paluch said. "A stream like this running through the middle of the jungle is trouble waiting to happen. Predators will be here before long, including dinosaurs like Herrerasaurids."

There was that awful word again, Severine thought.

"Can you snipe one from here?" Julius asked. "Hell, there's so many of them. You could probably aim blind and pick off at least one!"

"Shouldn't be a problem," Brett answered. "I recommend we don't eat it here. Should probably take the body somewhere away from the water source. As much as I hate to say it, the scientist is right. The waterfall is sure to draw unwanted attenti –"

BRAAAAAWWWWWWWWLLLLLL!

Before he could finish his sentence, a powerful drone erupted from the trees, originating from somewhere to their left between the dinosaurs and the waterfall. Flying creatures sprang out from the canopy and took to the skies, making the branches shake and droop at their sudden plight. On the ground below, one of the pisanosaurs lifted its head and called out a horrendous groan to answer the unbearable, rising boom. Several others imitated the alpha male's defiance, tilting back their mouths and barking in agreement.

"Okay. What the hell was that?" Julius asked, reaching for his pulse rifle.

"Herrerasaurus?" Severine asked.

"Don't think so, Sev," Brett replied. "Something else. We need to hide! Whatever it is, it's close by... Let's move!"

The group jumped to their feet, frantically gathering their supply packs. Brett lent a helping hand to Severine. She felt their eyes lock, and again felt that trace of deep connection. For a moment, in the sudden fear that commenced around her, she felt safe once again.

XVII

BRAAAAWWWWWWLLLLL!

The second horn bellowed out through the waterfall basin, noticeably more powerful than the first, and considerably closer.

Below, Severine saw the pisanosaurs starting to falter and spin at the lagoon, unsure exactly of what the terrible call meant or where it was coming from. A final, deep honk from the alpha male was all it took to send the other adults snapping at their young, forcing them towards the adjacent trees. Their peace shattered and the bumbling herd tripped and fell over one another as they splashed back into the jungle.

As Severine turned to follow the others southward through the forest, another call rang out, cutting off their escape.

BRAAAWWLLLLL!

Shit! That's really close!

"It's all around us!" Julius yelled.

"What are we doing?" Paluch asked, spilling the contents of his pack and scrambling to put them back correctly into the unzipped opening. Confusion overtook the colonists. The horn caught them all by surprise.

"Hide!" Brett replied. "Come on – slide down!"

"What do you *mean* slide down?" Paluch asked again, giving a little attitude.

Slide doow–

The thoughts left her head as Severine unknowingly listened to Brett. Ground gave way under her feet at the edge of the plateau, sending her tumbling down to the oasis below. In the swirling blurs and agonizing impacts that followed, she could hear her companions rolling down after her. Upon impact with a rock, she felt a quick, excruciating flash of pain.

"*Shit!*" she screeched as her face skidded along the dirt.

Her right arm was dislocated, and it hurt like a bitch.

As she howled in pain, she felt her X2 pistol effortlessly leave her hand, discharging once into the earth. Where it landed, she didn't know. Behind her, the other colonists cried out as they were rewarded with their own individual wounds.

With a final *thumppp*, she landed face-first into the mud, letting out a quick wail that was muffled by the ground. Before she had a moment to process what happened, Brett pulled her up by her unharmed arm and forced her toward the pool.

"Come on," he muttered. "Behind the water! I think there's a cave!"

BRAWWWLLLLLLL!

Another riveting blare erupted through the thicket, sending more fliers from their roosts.

With a sudden splash, she fell again, this time at the base of the lagoon. Silence befell her momentarily as her head fell below water. She resurfaced, wiping clumps of wet hair out of her eyes before looking back at her comrades.

What...the...

There was no time to form a cohesive thought.

Brett was behind her, shoving her into the waterfall that instantly thundered around her head. With a gentle heave, Brett flung her back against the rocks of the hidden cave, just as Julius and Paluch hastily crashed in from behind the watery veil.

The cave only extended a few feet back behind the falls, but it was enough to accommodate them comfortably. The falling water was thick and wide, offering them invisibility from anything that loitered outside.

Severine coughed and spat up water on her armor suit.

This piece of crap is heavy. Augghh! My arm…

You okay, Sev?" Brett asked, coming over to check on her. There was a genuine concern in his tone. He knew she was hurt.

"Yeah, I think," she replied. "Thanks for helping me in here."

"Sorry I had to be so rough," Brett said. "I just know they're close by."

"It sounds like it," she replied, wincing. "Brett, my arm…it hurts like a mother! It's dislocated, I think."

Brett studied her shoulder through the gaps in her armor plating.

"Yeah, it's dislocated all right."

"Hang tight, Sev," Julius replied, breathing heavily from a mossy boulder beside her. "I'm banged up pretty bad, too! I'll reset your arm once whatever this is goes away." His head had sustained a severe gash across the brow, spilling blood over his eye. If they were back in space with the other colonist ships, a doctor would recommend that the lieutenant receive stitches.

Severine's shoulder pulsed in torturous pangs, but still something was wrong.

Someone was missing.

Jordy!

She peered out of the water, as best as she could through the distorted shower that raged to their front.

There he is!

The bot was still moving, struggling to walk. The fall from the cliff had banged him up just as bad, if not worse than the humans. Chunks of dirt hung between his alloy joints that made running impossible and walking twice as difficult. The lights on his plating blinked with internal damage reports.

He must be so scared!

With a painful step, the bot entered the pool and floated over to them, trying to keep his chest above water to prolong his imminent death. With each slow step, the bot grew closer to the falls, until Jordy stood a few feet away on the other side.

BRAWWWLLLLLL!

"Hang on, Jord!" Paluch called out as he emptied his pack, sending the contents scattering freely over the wet boulders.

Then he did something that Severine thought was very out-of-character for the scientist.

Springing through the water, Paluch threw the pack over the bot's head. The satchel sank down over Jordy's skinny figure, and the water rushed harmlessly over the pack's exterior. With a yank, the scientist pulled the bot through to the dark cave, gently sitting him on the rocks beside Julius.

Severine hugged the machine and began to pick the dirt clods from his metallic joints. Thankfully, the water didn't appear to cause the poor thing any further damage.

BRAWWWLLLLLLLLLLLL!

The sound was partially muted behind the waterfall but was nearly in the basin.

"Bo-o-oy am I gla-ad to se-e-e you..." uttered the glitching voice.

Severine smiled.

"You okay?" she asked.

"I've be-eee-en better. That fall was ro-uu-uuh—f..."

"Quiet," Brett said, peering through a gap in the water near the far side. "It's close... There! Up where we came from!"

The scene was hard to visualize from Severine's position in the cavern, but a blurry shape gradually materialized from behind the falling water, and it wasn't another dinosaur.

It was a man.

Severine wiped her eyes, trying to rationalize what she was seeing. At first, she thought it was a hallucination brought on by her shoulder wound. She wiped away a muddy drip that sloshed past her nose and checked again.

It was still a man.

A man?

The nearly nude human lifted his right arm and pulled out a crooked white instrument, before pressing it to his lips and blowing through the hollowed edge.

BRAWWWLLLL!

A native hunter... That's what we heard!

"Paluch, how do you explain this?" Julius asked, grunting as he pressed his hands down on his injured scalp.

"It's a scientific impossibility! Man didn't live during the Triassic – only dinosaurs, among other early primitive animals and lifeforms. This can't be real."

Only it was.

The primitive man hopped onto the cliff edge, catching himself with an expert grasp on a protruding boulder. Spears and hunting gear hung off a rope that wrapped around his back. Along his athletic, sweaty waist, a loincloth made of plant matter dangled between his toned legs.

He was young.

Early twenties, maybe even a teenager, Severine thought. *And what's he looking for?*

The man bent down, wrestling something out from a muddy crevice.

Oh, that's it... Terrific.

With an archaic chant, he picked up Severine's X2-20 and sniffed curiously at the chrome enamel that encompassed the barrel. He was infatuated with the gun and hopped around playfully at his discovery of the shiny treasure.

"Sev, he's got your gun," Julius observed.

"Thanks, I noticed," she moaned.

The damn thing's gonna get a nasty surprise if that finger falls on the trigger.

Severine found herself wondering if she remembered to switch the safety on. Thankfully, the humanoid stashed the firearm away in his makeshift bag, clamoring once more into the white horn.

BRAWLLLLLLLL!!!!!!!!

At the top of the cliff, feet away from the indigenous hunter, three more rugged men shuffled through the ferns, surveying the oasis. In their hands, they carried large torches, blazing with untamed fires that crackled loudly. Quivers crammed with arrows were strapped tightly across their backs, along with what appeared to be wooden longbows. They walked on the ground with leafy sandals bound tightly with burlap, or something similar. Red paint was smeared across their heads with a tribal-like, artistic quality.

"Shit. Julius, who are they?"

"Humans, I think. Very basic ones – ancient."

"There's no way," Paluch replied. "Not in Carnian of the late Triassic."

"More importantly, are they friendly?" Severine asked.

"I wouldn't count on it, Sev," the lieutenant answered. "I'm pretty sure that the red crap smeared on their faces is blood."

"Have you ever seen these people before?" she asked.

"Negative," Brett answered, just as perplexed as the others. "We've never crossed paths."

"Maybe we should attempt to contact them," Paluch suggested, quietly filling his pack up with the fallen supplies.

"No, sit still! Let's watch them..."

On the cliffs above, the first Neolithic man produced the metal treasure from his pack, holding it proudly above for the other hunters to see. With a harsh groan, he jumped up once more in a celebratory ritual dance, letting the sunlight flare off the firearm as he waved it towards his companions.

Severine was feeling uneasy.

Put that damn thing away!

"*Uuugghhh!*" cried the first hunter.

In a fit of jealousy, one of the newcomers rushed into the bragger, kicking him down the crumbling edge and sending him shrieking in terror as he fell. Severine clenched her teeth at the sound of brittle bones breaking as they hit rock, followed by frightened gasps and panic-induced breaths.

Instantly, the aggressors descended swiftly down the cliff, pouncing on their injured companion and pounding him mercilessly with their rock hammers.

Thwwaak! Thraaakkkk!

The attack was barely visible through the waterfall and boulders that bordered the pool.

A pair of hairy arms shot up and tried to fend off the deadly swings of the cave-tools. With a strong *craccckkkkk,* the bloodied hands fell, ending the horrifying skirmish.

The victor raised his precious prize triumphantly, keeping his hatchet raised at his bewildered subordinates, who chose not to pursue the object of power. Instead they retreated, cowering in fear.

BRAWWWLLLLLLLL!

Another sudden horn call erupted – this one from above the waterfall, somewhere out of view.

Sloshing down the slopes, ten more tribesmen appeared to the right of the falls, climbing swiftly down with spears and torches drawn. As the larger group approached, the victorious caveman pushed the X2 clumsily into his knapsack, whilst motioning to his cohorts to remain quiet. Gradually, the larger group converged with the first, surrounding them at the cliff base.

"You still want to go out and say hello?" Julius asked.

"I'm fine in here, actually," Paluch said, trying to mask his mortified tone.

From the center of the small army, a chieftain appeared. He was a head taller than the other members of the clan. On his head sat a small crown of sharp horns and teeth picked from dead animal remains. Other members parted as he approached the three lackeys, holding a sturdy spear in his right hand and a wooden shield adorned with blood in the other. He stopped at the base of the cliff, noticing the dead man lying at the foot of his murderers, who turned white at the shaman's ominous approach.

"I think they're screwed," Julius remarked under his breath.

The leader yelled something in an unknown, forgotten language, beating his chest once aggressively with his spear rod. His warriors quickly rushed the trio of defectors, who found themselves caught between their angry brethren and the ravine. The knapsack man – the one who claimed the hidden X2 – quickly tried to scale the cliff, only to be brought down by a thrown javelin that pierced him through the spine.

He let out a laborious breath and fell backwards, breaking the shaft apart before landing with a thud. Severine assumed his co-conspirators had met the same grisly fate, although she couldn't confirm it from her vantage point.

"Retribution for killing one of their own," Brett remarked.

The chieftain picked up the pack of his vanquished foe and threw it over to one of his servants, who caught it with enthusiasm before shouldering it.

There goes my gun, Severine thought.

Suddenly, a computerized flashing started beside her.

Jordy! No...

The bot's chest panel lights began flickering brightly – an unfortunate side-effect of his deteriorating condition. The automatic message served as a haunting reminder that his time was growing increasingly short.

To her horror, the glow from the light panels reflected out of the waterfall, amplified and morphed from behind the roaring curtain.

One of the warriors turned toward the falls, attracted by the beautiful light show and called out angrily. The rest of the tribe turned and raised their spears in defense.

"Our position's compromised!" Brett whispered harshly. "Cover his lights!"

"For-or-orgive me," Jordy said in a regretful voice.

"It's not your fault, pal," Julius said, trying to sound comforting.

Paluch threw the pack once again over the bot's core, instantly cutting off the brightening glow.

It's too late!

The Neolithic army slowly converged on the waterfall. A few of the warriors skirted around the sides, while several brazen men began to wade cautiously into the bubbling pool, raising their barbs at the falls. After they encircled the lagoon, they halted and awaited orders from their shaman.

"Okay," Julius said. "Twenty rounds…and they better count!"

He picked up the 90 and aimed it through the watery curtain at the human blurs that lingered just outside. "Should be able to hit them all and still have a few to spare – if they don't stick me first!"

"Save it," Brett told him. "I've got a better idea…"

The tribal leader waded into the pond, holding his spear tightly as he cautiously approached. Behind him, three bulky warriors followed, holding their bows or pikes in front, ready to die for their captain. Eager, hairy faces watched excitedly as their champion lifted his weapon and pressed the spear into the rapids.

As the sharpened tip began to disappear behind the waterfall, a chrome sphere came sailing out, splashing water after it crashed through. It landed into the pool just beyond the chieftain, causing him to turn and pursue the strange little dome.

"*Guhaawk!*" he barked.

Angrily, he fought off the suddenly disobedient hunters who dropped their weapons to race for the object. With a firm roar, the chieftain's will prevailed, and he proudly produced the object from the pool's floor.

As he held the sphere out for his army to gawk at, the release mechanism snapped inside the detonator, prompted by the shift of weight in the chieftain's hand.

Cliiick!

A brilliant blue flash fanned out from the sphere, instantly killing the native leader, who roared with fury as he was consumed by the vibrant aura. The orb expanded rapidly, slinging deadly, burning embers with lethal force into the hunters nearest the pool, blinding them first before melting through their flesh. Crying with fear, the three hunters that remained alive ran away, dropping their spears with fright as they hurried up the eroding cliffs and shimmied into the fern fronds above.

The blue embers were swatted down by the waterfall and failed to harm the colonists behind the watery shield.

Close call!

They emerged from the cave, stepping into the scene of the catastrophe. A fading blue crater dimmed at the base of the pool, which was now half-full due to the implosion. Bloody torsos and marred limbs bobbed about the bouncing waves as the lagoon started to refill. More cadavers lined the shore, gripping their disintegrated spear shafts with their charred, blackened hands.

"Good thinking, Ambrose," Julius congratulated. "Didn't even have to waste a round on those bastards!"

"I'm gonna miss that detonator," Brett remarked.

As they prepared to leave, Severine searched the bodies around the sandy coast, irritated that her pistol was taken by one of the fleeing savages.

Dammit.

#

The tribesmen ran.

Sprinting through the animal paths that weaved away from the waterfall, they dashed through the brush, unsure of what they had seen and fearful of what the strange globe had done. The orb had caused great destruction within the clan and murdered their brothers. Their mission was simple – get as far away from the falls, as fast as possible, and pray that they never meet another shiny sphere again.

They fled with such determination and fright that they failed to notice several orange dinosaurs spying from behind the nearby pines atop a small hill.

Cold, murderous eyes watched the hunters sprint past, but decided not to give chase, although it would have been an easy meal.

Instead, the herrerasaur pack turned towards the direction that the strange boom had come from just moments earlier and took off toward the sound of gushing water.

At the head of the pack, a massive herrerasaur shrieked with a terrifying prowess that echoed through their coniferous kingdom.

XVIII

Gently beeping and glowing with a sad crimson light, Jordy stumbled down the path, helped by Paluch and Severine as they scooted deeper into the jungle towards the river. In the distance, swelling sounds of rushing water gradually sailed along the late afternoon air. The river was drawing near.

It wouldn't be long before the bot's computer defense systems would fail under the constant sloshing of water that was trapped forever inside the battery compartment.

The fall down the cliffs had expedited the bot's fatal condition and shuffled around the internal components. When they took breaks, Severine attempted to free more muddy fragments from Jordy's joints. The machine tried to wave her away as they took a short rest under a large araucaria tree, a few hundred yards from the cliffs bordering the river Brett mentioned earlier.

"It's us-ss-sseless Sev. Just let them b-e-e…"

The damn machine's going to make us all tear up!

"Knock it off!" Severine returned sharply. "You're gonna be fine. Now, just let me clean you up."

As the words left her lips, she knew they could not be true.

The bot would surely die. The machine's labored, digital breaths and slow, fading lights indicated that life would leave him in a few short hours, probably by nightfall. Jordy had made peace with his condition, having felt accomplished that he had guided them to the river. From there, they could follow the current westward. Then it was a straight-shot to the south, back to *Supernova's* ruins.

Jordy's situation was depressive to everyone in the group, especially to Julius. Even Francis Paluch, who had started off frequently belittling the robot, was now sympathetic and regretful of the grave situation.

Severine herself found it hard to cope with the machine's slow passing, unsure of how to make it go more smoothly.

"Why don't you switch off to sleep-mode, buddy?" Julius suggested.

"Yeah," Francis Paluch added. "Save your strength. We're practically at the river."

"Goo-ood id-ee-a," said the bot, dimming its lights and slumping gently forward. Behind his chest plate, the gentle hum of automation fought hard to keep the reserve power on. After a short bleep, the bot lay still, resting peacefully under the shade of the overhanging conifer canopy.

"That was some spectacle back by the waterfall, huh," Paluch said, sipping from a canister before passing it around for others to consume. "Crazy-ass savages…"

"Yeah," Julius started. "About that…I thought you said that there were no humans in the Triassic? If indeed, this *is* the Triassic! I was starting to believe your theory. Now I'm not so sure…"

His tone was sarcastic, intent on provoking the scientist.

"There wasn't, imbecile," Paluch replied. "The Triassic should've predated mankind by many years. Millions, even! Dinosaurs, archosaurs, and primitive lifeforms inherited the surface of the Earth. But the fossil record doesn't indicate the presence of mankind until much later, long after these other creatures disappeared. From what we've seen so far, other than the primitive humans, I can lump everything accurately into the Triassic. More specifically, the Carnian of the late Triassic! Coelophysis. Saurosuchus. Exaeretodon. Pisanosaurs. All Triassic, from South America or Gondwana."

"Well, they're here, somewhere in these forests, and now we've probably pissed them off," Brett replied. "If we stay along the river, maybe we can avoid running into them until we reach the ship."

"How many do you think there are?" Severine asked.

"Based on what happened at the waterfall, I bet there's at least a hundred," Julius answered. "Maybe more. What we saw was nothing more than a hunting party. They were gathering food for their tribe, wherever that is. I'm praying it's nowhere close..."

"They were tracking us," Brett added.

"How do you know?"

"They were either stalking us or stalking the pisanosaur herd. They followed behind with a few hunters but sent the larger party ahead to intercept us at the falls. My guess is that they caught our tracks back at the forest's edge and were curious as to who made them. Our boot impressions must look strange compared to their bare footprints, or whatever goofy sandals they were wearing."

"Let's pray they tell their clan about the detonator blast," Julius laughed. "Maybe that will keep them off our backs long enough to reach the ship. All right, Sev, you ready to fix your little problem?"

Huh? Oh, my arm...

She could feel herself turning white, bashful of her wound.

"Honestly, not really," she replied. "But...do it. Do it before it gets any worse."

Her dislocated arm had been killing her since the moment she snapped it backwards during the cliff collapse. Although the pain was unbelievably unbearable, what bugged her more was the naked feeling she felt without her X2-20. Somewhere deep in the jungle, one of those bumbling idiots was running away with her firearm, and she yearned for it.

Despite her combat training, she felt helpless without a gun in the Triassic wilderness.

The lieutenant knelt beside her, carefully stepping around Jordy's unconscious form to avoid jolting the bot out from his precious sleep mode. His kind hands reached out and took her arm lightly. Severine winced at the touch and sat back, closing her eyes. Around her, she could hear Paluch and Brett turning away, trying not to see Julius' treatment.

"Let's see. I remember how to do this. Just trying to figure out the best way..."

"That doesn't sound very convincing," Severine shot back. "You know what you're doing, right?"

Julius laughed. "Yes, Sev – I do. Okay, here we go!"

"Do it!"

"I'm gonna count to three. On three, I'll reset it."

"Sure. Go!"

"One…"

I can do this. I just need to relax and—

CRACKKKKK!

She swore she heard a deafening drone or another detonator blast, but as the pain subsided, she realized it was the barbaric yelp that flew out of her mouth.

"SHIIIITTTTTT!" she screamed.

Julius had taken her by surprise, pulling her right arm straight ahead of her with the bulk of his weight before the time he had indicated. Severine figured he would try something like that, so she wasn't ready for the pain. During the procedure, she was ready to punch him, but after it ended, she was grateful for the lieutenant's methods.

With an amount of time that seemed like eternity (although it was probably a little more than a few seconds), the arm finally aligned correctly with the shoulder. The wind left her, and she collapsed backwards onto the ground, holding her hand in an attempt to calm herself.

"Jeez, Julius," she said, smiling that it was finally over. "I wanted you to relocate the damn thing, not break it again!"

The lieutenant smiled.

"You're welcome kid. I haven't done that in a while."

She regained feeling throughout her forearm, moving it about slowly, trying not to disturb the sore spot near her shoulder.

"Hey, let's make you a sling," Brett said. "Here!"

He ripped part of a tunic that he had tucked into his pack, weaved it around Severine's shoulder and tied a masterful knot around her wrist. Suddenly the soreness subsided greatly, and she rested her arm snugly in the sling.

Ahhh… That feels incredible!

"Thanks, Brett!" she said.

"No problem, Sev. Glad to see it works!"

His touch was gentle and caring.

Once again, just as she felt back in the *Mudskipper*, she encountered a twang of a former romance with Brett. Maybe it was just a fleeting thought, or a ping of appreciation initiated by her thankfulness. But it was there, nonetheless. A memory – a very hazy, blurry memory. She could see a younger, more boyish Brett Ambrose on board the *Supernova*. His face appeared in front of her, through a cold distortion. Again, she shrugged it off. It was useless now. It was in the past and couldn't be beneficial to their current situation. She repressed the feelings once again and let the soldier deep inside her take charge.

"Probably should take it easy for now, huh?" she asked.

"Definitely," Paluch chimed in.

"I'd give you some ice for it, if I had any," Brett told her.

She noted the sympathetic tone in his voice – a voice she never thought she'd hear again only a day earlier.

"That thing's going to be sore for a while," Paluch joked.

"Thanks, Francis," Severine laughed. "Not what I want to hear right now."

Above the pine canopy, the sun continued to descend toward the westward mountains, giving way to the evening hours. The haze from earlier began to melt away, replaced by a cool mist brought on by the river that swelled just through the trees. Clouds began to darken the jungle, but thankfully didn't unleash another torrential monsoon like the day before.

"Might be good to make camp for the night," Julius suggested. "We're close enough to the cliffs. If something happens, we can climb down. The dinosaurs won't be able to jump down after us, right?"

"Not easily," Paluch told him.

"The primitive humans may be another story," Severine added.

"They won't be back anytime soon," Brett assured her. "I'm confident that my detonator did its job and gave us a break from them."

"I'm all for stopping for the day, if it gives him a break." The lieutenant gestured to Jordy, whose digital breaths hummed in the artificially-induced slumber. "Maybe if he rests long enough, he can make it till morning. The heat could evaporate the water out of his battery."

"Julius," Severine said, shaking her head. "It won't…"

She knew the terrible truth all too well. When the bot awoke, it wouldn't be for long. Shattering the lieutenant's dreams of salvaging his robotic friend's life wasn't something she enjoyed doing. But in the Federation Infantry, she recalled being prepared for such an event, and memorizing the signs. Water inside the chest was the death sentence without the proper maintenance tool set.

"Yeah, okay…" he said, resting a soft hand on the bot's head. "Rest easy, little buddy."

Crack!

"Heads up," Brett whispered, snapping up his crossbow and commencing a shooter's stance.

"What now?" Julius asked, picking up the 90 and pointing the weapon toward the darkening trees. Severine hopped up to her feet, unsure of what was happening. Paluch was right behind her.

Jordy's metallic frozen form remained seated on the mulch-covered trail, unfazed by the noise.

"Yeah, what?" Severine asked. Something awful had gripped her, and she found that her legs were frozen with fright. But she already knew the answer. When that twig broke, Brett had seen something moving behind the shadowy pines.

"Ambrose! What is it, soldier?"

The private didn't answer, but instead stared hypnotically into the black. His eyes had found something in the dark.

What? What is it?

"Private! You better start elaborating." Julius was getting pissed. A hint of fear was in his tone.

"Look there," Brett pointed. "Down my sights – about twenty meters. To the immediate right of the mossy log that's stuck between the two pines. And don't make any quick movements. They've found us."

They?

Severine noted Brett's position and the direction the crossbow was pointed, and turned to the pines, trying to place the mysterious visitor. The forest had grown eerily dark in the past hour and seeing too far ahead had become a chore.

Eventually she found the log, seeing nothing immediately resembling danger.

"There's nothing there…"

"Like I said – at the immediate right. Look to the right, Sev."

Again, there's nothing th--oh. What the hell is that thing?

It was a wicked, toothy grin.

Hidden in the coming night, to the right of the rotten fallen tree, sat a pair of entrancing red eyes that locked magically with Severine's. They were small and hard to differentiate from the various specks of light that littered the woods, but when she saw them, Severine found that she couldn't look away.

She found this creature infinitely more horrifying than the coelophysis or the sauros. The eyes were powerful and dominant, wishing nothing more than to tear them all limb from limb.

Below the ghastly stare, two rows of serrated carnivorous teeth ran around a thick snout of a powerful, large head. The mouth spread open slightly, and the monster let out a terrible rumbling noise. Thin drool strands spilled out and slipped onto the mulch, slathering the trail below.

It's hungry.

"Uh, Paluch? Enlighten us on these, uh…" Julius fumbled for words.

"Right, hang on," replied the scientist. He flipped slowly through his book, careful not to turn the pages too suddenly or too loudly. Finally, he returned to the illustration that Severine remembered from the *Mudskipper's* campfire.

"It's a herrerasaur," he finally said, after a deep, whimpering breath. "And it's spotted us…"

As the sun briefly passed between a gap in the clouds, Severine couldn't help but notice the dark orange scales.

XIX

The herrerasaur blinked its menacing eyes in the diminishing sunlight, refusing to retreat from the spot behind the pines. With a heavy step it turned to the side, walking slowly behind the cover of a thick hedge of trunks. A heavy tail whipped around, smacking the needles off a high branch, sending them spiraling to the dirt. The dino had an arrogant saunter with each step, keeping both eyes fixed on the colonists.

"Damn," Brett whispered, aiming the crossbow. "It's back in cover..."

It's enormous!

Between the trunks, Severine could see the colossal carnivore lumbering behind the bark, appearing intermittently between the thin spaces of trees. Now walking from a sideways profile, the tremendous length of the dinosaur was evident. From the front to back, Severine guessed the monster easily exceeded twenty-five feet in length. Logs crunched under the weight of the reptilian footsteps as the tyrannical monster continued its dreaded orbit around the colonists.

"He's herding us," Paluch said. "We're in a kill-zone."

"Can you hit him?" Severine asked.

"I can try..."

Brett squeezed the trigger of the crossbow, releasing the drawback string that sent an arrow sailing into the brush. With a loud *thummmmmmmp*, the bolt struck a pine tree that sat defensively in front of the herrerasaur, narrowly missing the mark.

"It's using the trees as cover. The damn thing is smart!"

The fading sunset poked out from the cloud cover for a fleeting moment. In the glowing orange rays, streaks of dark red descended down the creature's scaly back, beginning with a crimson ring that formed a textured collar around the neck. The patterns were deceptively alluring.

"It's the leader," Brett observed.

"The alpha male..." Paluch replied in a panicked voice. "Can we make it to the river in time? Get down the cliffs?"

"Quick movements will draw it out," Brett replied. "Some of us might make it, but it's unlikely we all will. These assholes know how to run."

"*Whoa!*" Julius cried. "There's more of them!"

Deep, guttural rumblings caused the group to spin around. Another set of daunting eyes peered out at them behind a patch of dark palm fronds. The muscular chest puffed with a ravenous appetite as the eyes settled on the humans. With a quick bob of the massive head, the dinosaur vanished behind the ferns, shaking the leaves as it faded away into the black.

There's more!

Their situation had gone from bad to hostile.

More flashes of orange appeared frequently among the trunks, followed by angry groans and the crunching of bark. The carnivores appeared only for moments and then were gone, shrinking back into the dimmed foliage that bordered the trail.

"How many?" Paluch asked.

"How should I know?" Julius replied with a sharp whisper. "It's too dark! There could be a shit-ton!"

"Sounds like maybe ten or twelve," Severine assumed.

"They're surrounding us," Paluch observed, with a loud gulp. "Thwarting our escape!"

"Why aren't they attacking?"

"The 90," Julius replied. "They must have seen one of these in action before, probably by earlier *Supernova* crash survivors. Stay tightly together! We need eyes in every direction in case one of these things gets bold. Everyone – pick a different direction and keep your eyes alert! I can only face one way at a time."

He aimed the XR-90 toward the last known position of the alpha-male, although the current whereabouts of the malevolent behemoth remained to be seen. Brett kept the crossbow pointed in the other direction, where more orange shapes were slithering swiftly among the leaves. Severine and Paluch stood between the two-armed soldiers, facing in opposite directions, ready to raise the alarm.

Jordy's form lay still on the ground a few feet away, effectively out of the conflict.

Brett handed his rock knife to Severine.

"For what it's worth," he said, as she gratefully accepted the weapon. She gripped the handle and pointed the sharp blade outward in an infantry combative stance that she had learned in combat training.

Better than nothing, she thought. She could feel her heart racing again and found herself acutely aware of her surroundings.

Another growl slipped through the cool night wind. Severine could feel herself growing restless.

Come on! Just get it over with!

"How about a warning shot?" Brett suggested.

Julius nodded. "Here it goes…"

He pressed the trigger, sending a beautiful golden shard of light into the darkness. The pulse blast struck a young tree, splitting it from the center and creating a small explosion at the splintering seam. A young herrerasaur lurking behind let out a fearful yelp before jumping back to a farther spot in the foliage.

"They're afraid of the pulse blasts, but not enough to leave us alone."

"*Whoa!* Behind us – my direction!" Paluch shrieked.

Severine felt the ground beginning to shake.

THUMP! THUMP! THUMP!

Here we go!

With a powerful roar, one of the dinos stampeded towards them. The beast had stealthily moved up close to the colonists under the shroud of the trees and leaped from a hidden corner, charging the group. Severine turned, her face draining of color. They had no reaction time.

Watch out!

"Julius! Shoot him!" Paluch yelled.

The brutal jaws opened wide as the carnivore charged.

Julius turned to fire a round off, but the beast crashed into the lieutenant's midsection, throwing him off balance as he tumbled to the ground. Severine grabbed Paluch's pack from behind and pulled him roughly to the side, out of the herrera's reckless flight.

Before the monster could pounce on Julius, who struggled to pick up his discarded rifle, a crossbow bolt found its way into the creature's midsection. Howling with a hideous shriek, the animal cried in pain and ran away into the brush, whimpering as it went.

Severine relaxed, gripping down hard on her knife handle.

"It's gone!" Paluch observed.

"Nice shot, Ambrose."

Brett snapped another arrow on the drawstring as Julius picked up his rifle, and the humans returned to their circular defensive ring, awaiting another barrage. The orange blurs continued to swirl around in the trees, darting around too fast to snipe.

They're taunting us...

"The dinos are getting brazen," Julius said.

"It might be a good idea to start heading for the cliffs," Paluch suggested. He was shaking in fear.

"Trust me," Brett replied, "We'll never make it – it's now or never. This is our last stand. If I were you, I'd start thinking of finding a weapon. A rock – anything!"

Crrrkk!!!

Two branches ahead split apart violently.

"Here they come again!" Severine pointed.

Shiittttt!

Two orange giants burst through the leaves on opposite ends of the jungle, snapping their rabid jaws in a deadly duet. With an impressive jump, the first dinosaur flew through the air, claws extended at Severine. Shaking herself from her frozen state of shock, she felt her knees give out as she collapsed in a clumsy roll. Her opponent sailed above her, locking onto a new target.

Julius!

With a surprised yelp, the lieutenant dropped his rifle as the powerful jaws clamped over his armored shoulder plate, which saved him from a broken collarbone. The weapon fell and discharged once, striking the second oncoming dinosaur in the calf and sending the beast to the ground before it could reach the intended victim. It roared angrily as it crashed head-first into the mulch bed.

Thuddd!

It was a lucky shot.

Three more herrerasaurs took notice of the colonists' disorder and pushed through the branches. Brett fired two crossbow shots before turning and fleeing, pushing through the pines that blocked his escape. His flight attracted the oncoming carnivores, and they quickly changed course, pursuing him through the woods.

"Brett!" Severine yelled. "Wait!"

Her heart sank as he vanished into the brush. Their defense was shattered.

"He's trying to draw them off," Paluch muttered, crawling below her.

The scientist scurried over along the path and dove under a crumbling log, out of the immediate battle zone.

Severine turned over to Julius. She had to do something – it was her fault he was being mauled.

The lieutenant was pinned beneath the herrerasaur. Above him, the monster snapped furiously against his brutalized armor suit. He reached blindly for his rifle that sat just out of his reach. His chest plate and shoulder guard were dented and scratched.

"*Agghhh!*" she yelled maniacally.

Swinging her knife wildly, Severine hacked away at the dinosaur's hind quarters. As blood dripped out from the scales, the dinosaur cried angrily as the dagger became lodged in the red, throbbing flesh.

The attack was enough for Julius to rise to his feet, pushing his attacker away. The wounded herrera cried in agony as it fled down the trail.

As he reached for the 90, another pair of dinosaurs charged from the trees, forcing him to stumble in fright before regaining his balance, sprinting off in the direction Brett had disappeared down moments earlier. The rifle remained neglected on the ground.

He's going for the river...

"Sev, run! Get up a tree!" Those were his last words before he slipped away into the night.

Severine shivered. She was alone now, quickly pondering her next move. From her peripheral, she could see the orange shapes scurrying just beyond the path.

The XR-90! I have to get it.

She got up and ran over to the chrome weapon, now buried partially in mud from the skirmish. As her fingers spread apart to grab the handle, jaws clamped down on her left arm.

"*Augghhhh!*" she let out a mortified scream.

She cried in pain as the beast swung its muscular neck about, trying to break her remaining functional arm. Turning to face her adversary, she noted it was a younger carnivore, about half the size of the other adult species that were still rustling nearby.

At that moment, she was suddenly very thankful of her armor suit, which so far was holding up well against the savage attack.

But her arm beneath hurt and bruised painfully. The pressure was excruciatingly painful.

With her free hand, Severine attempted to batter down the juvenile attacker, but her forearm was still stuck behind Brett's sling. Panic overtook her as her knees buckled and the monster worked its way up her forearm to her exposed neckline. Her legs kicked furiously at the creature's abdomen as they wrestled over the path.

She was now flat on her back – exposed and helpless.

Above, the herrera stepped onto her chest. The dinosaur felt as if it weighed a thousand pounds. She felt its toe claws scratching over her breastplate. The chomping mouth snapped at her face, and she saw the rows of beautifully sharp teeth falling towards her, shining off the final rays of the sun.

Shit. This is it...

Suddenly, an awkward yell rang out, filling the path.

In a fit of bravery, Paluch rammed into the dinosaur's side from his hiding place. The impact was enough to scare the herrera off Severine's arm and send it fleeing back into the wild.

Thank God!

She couldn't believe what happened, even as the scientist helped her back up.

"Paluch, thank you!" she exclaimed, out of breath. She was taken aback by the technician's bravery, and now felt grateful to be alive. "That thing nearly had me..."

"Are you okay?" he asked.

"Yeah. The armor suit saved me."

"Well, we're not out of the woods yet... Let's get down to the clif –"

HSSHHHHH!

In a sudden flash of terror, the alpha male herrerasaur rose up behind Paluch, spread its frightening jaws, and crunched them down over the scientist's head. From inside the mouth, she could hear Paluch's muffled cries of terror. The attack was quick and brutal.

Under the lab coat, his arms flung spontaneously in panic but quickly flopped down to his waist as the tyrannical monster swerved his skull to the side. With a painfully sharp *cracckkkk*, the scientist's neck was broken, killing Paluch instantly.

No!!!

Severine felt her jaw drop at the awesome power of the dinosaur.

The giant lizard dropped the technician's body and fixed a hateful gaze at Severine, who decided not to wait for death.

She spun around and took off for the trees. In her frantic sprint to the closest trunk, she could hear the ground vibrating as the giant herrera was right at her heels. She could feel the beast's hot, terrible breath at her back. The breaking snap of Paluch's neck replayed on a loop through her mind.

Not me! Not me!

The jungle streaked past her.

Okay... Which one? Which one?

Her eyes searched hysterically for a tree – any tree – to climb. Several logical ones appeared instantly, but Severine wasn't thinking clearly. Panic set in, forcing her to keep running straight, which hindered her from grabbing any nearby branch.

"This one!" Severine said, finally breaking her trance. It was a tree with low-lying branches and easy accessibility.

Suddenly the ferns ahead parted, and an orange head was waiting just behind the dark bushes.

No! Please!!!

Another herrerasaur emerged ahead of her path, just feet beyond her means of safety. The monster raced towards her, ready to cut off her escape and seal her fate below the canopy. Rows of teeth greeted her as the giant jaws spread apart to embrace their meal.

"No!"

Severine shrieked as her foot struck a misplaced rock, and she flipped over herself as momentum pushed her forward. Above, the alpha male collided with its subordinate and the two titans fell into the earth before rolling off one another.

"Yes!"

Another brief window of opportunity had presented itself.

Grabbing hold of the first branch with her free hand, Severine threw herself up the side of the tree, climbing until she found herself out of reach from her antagonists lurking below.

Severine looked down as she fought to catch a stable breath and wasn't surprised to see the tormentors staring up at her with vile grins. Her chest pounded laboriously from behind her damaged armor suit, ceasing to relax as the dinosaurs bounded off the ground, trying to bite her foot.

You stay down there… she thought, holding out her hand as if to order them to halt their attack.

The large herrerasaur jumped high into the air, breaking off a branch several feet below Severine before falling back with a heavy *boom*.

Irritated growls and frustrated moans told her that their leader was furious that she had found refuge just a few feet out of their reach. Angrily, the beast jumped up again, scratching at the ancient trunk with a slashing claw.

Please, just leave me alone!

Again, the herrera fell back, missing Severine's branch.

The tyrant looked up once more and roared angrily, casting spiderweb spit patterns dripping down its gnarled lips. Severine could feel the evil in the dinosaur's eyes. She knew it wanted to taste her flesh.

The herrera turned its ugly head and yipped at the smaller dino, who answered with an abrupt groan. With a final scowl, the alpha male peered up at her one last time before running off into the jungle, towards the distant sound of the river.

He's going after Brett and Julius, she thought.

Below, her guard hadn't moved, and instead was laid down near the base of the trunk, coiling his body around the tree like a cobra.

"Dammit!"

You better go away! I'm not waiting here forever.

But she had no choice – she was trapped.

Her thoughts were interrupted by the sound of nearby sloshing and crunching. Through the drooping pine needles that hung below her spot in the tree, she noticed three orange blurs condensing on the path below. Tails shot up into the air as they began pecking and devouring a hidden victim in the dirt. Bloody organs and entrails flew up and plopped back down, splattering over the jungle trail.

She grimaced. The sounds were wickedly disturbing.

Oh no...

With an odd motion that hurled her forward, Severine threw up, shooting bile and fruit fragments to the ground below as she held her heaving chest, careful not to scoot her butt off the tree limb.

Paluch...

The herreras were feasting on his remains.

Above the treetops, the sun had given way to a full moon that lit up the distance and cast white light over the jungle. From up here, the landscape seemed serene and peaceful – a stark contrast to the horrific world that lay just under the araucaria branches.

Thoughts began to float by as she pieced together her options.

Key-card. Solar signal emitter. Escape. The others. Are they alive? Where is the Federation? And how the hell am I getting out of this tree?

XX

A slow hour had gone by as the moon continued its ascent over the starry sky. As the time passed, the sun had completely dissipated over the distant mountains and the golden rays no longer glowed around the peaks. In the time after the attack, the forest had grown peacefully quiet.

Most of the herrerasaur pack had moved on from their spot at Paluch's body. One hungry dinosaur remained, chowing away at the scientist's bloated corpse, now buried under dirt and fallen canopy leaves. Below, Severine's dinosaur guardian stayed planted at the base of the tree trunk, waiting patiently for her to make a false move and fall from her perch.

Not a chance, pal, she thought. *Maybe I can wait him out. Perhaps until he falls asleep.*

She shifted in the tree as best as she could with her primary arm still trapped in the sling. Her feet carefully rotated on the branch below. The turning of weight caused the wood to creak.

Oh...

She could hear the beast below shifting at the sound.

The herrera looked up in hungry anticipation, rising to its feet.

After Severine made herself comfortable again, the monster groaned and plopped back down on the forest floor, moaning impatiently in frustration.

"You might as well forget about it!" she yelled at the creature. "I'll wait up here until I'm dead!"

She wasn't sure, but she thought the beast might be getting tired, since it seemed to be preparing for a nap.

Severine studied the animal.

It was a large dinosaur, although not as large as the alpha male herrerasaur that she narrowly escaped from just hours earlier. For the most part, they reminded her of a smaller version of a tyrannosaurus that she recalled from old, withered books for children, left behind after the Old War had ravaged Earth. The herrerasaurs were primarily dark orange, just as Brett had described them, but with a few added shades of brown and speckles of red. Their heavy bodies were sturdier and more muscular than the coelophysis pack. A few of the larger specimens had black stripes that dotted their backs, ending at the tails. Several herreras had scars, which Severine assumed may be from territorial disputes or inner-pack battles for mating. All of them had insidiously red eyes that seemed to glow at night when they were most active.

They must be primarily nocturnal.

She found it interesting that these creatures exhibited more cautious and precise hunting patterns than the coelophysis and the saurosuchus. They valued their pack and waited patiently for the right time to strike, choosing the blanket of nightfall as an advantage.

Smart bastards!

And now, the humans were scattered. Paluch was dead. Brett and Julius were either dead or missing. She assumed they were far downstream.

At the very least, they're probably injured, Severine thought.

Paluch's body continued to be decimated behind the dark needles below. She watched in horror and disgust as the feast continued. In the meantime, the moon slipped out through the clouds, scattering hints of light over the forest floor. Slightly below the grisly scene, a small speck of silver glimmered in the moonlight. She recognized the object immediately.

The XR-90 pulse rifle!

The gun was still there, waiting for her under a leafy bush. During their rampage, the herrerasaurs had unknowingly kicked it closer to her pine tree. In the darkness, she could see the dim ammunition light glowing under the muddy ground.

It still has some rounds left!

She began to drum up a plan to rescue the firearm.

Two herrerasaurs. That's it…

First, she looked around in the trees. The forest was completely black, but as the moonlight popped in and out of the clouds, she noted that there were no additional herreras in the area. If she could get to the 90 in time, she could kill both Paluch's tormentor and her own.

She glanced down.

The dino was asleep, snoring contently at the base of the pine trunk.

So far, so good.

The carnivore at the trail shook its head as it yanked out one of Paluch's organs. Severine studied it for a while and realized that it probably didn't know she was in the tree.

If I'm lucky enough to grab it and survive, I'm making a break for the cliffs.

She looked around again as the moon lit up the forest.

Nothing.

No red eyes.

In the surrounding trees, no hidden foes were lying in wait – at least, not from what she could tell. As she had learned already, these carnivores were experts at deception and cloaked themselves in the darkness of the environment. After one final safety check, she confirmed her objective: Get the 90 at all costs or starve to death in the tree tops.

Every moment she waited was another opportunity for more herreras to show up, adding further difficulty to the reckless, suicidal escape plan.

I'm not going anywhere if I can't get this sling off.

Moving carefully to try not to disturb the slumbering dinosaur below, she moved her left hand over to the knot and slowly untied the makeshift sling. As the knot came undone, the cloth fell into her open hand and she carefully placed it on an extended branch. The soreness of her shoulder socket came flooding back to her, but she shrugged it off.

Okay. First step – complete.

A grumbling snore slipped out from the dinosaur. The herrera was still asleep.

Next step – climb down. Bonus step: survival.

Severine knew her humor would make it easier to proceed.

Easy does it, old girl.

Her foot dropped onto the branch directly below. To her surprise, the wood didn't creak or bend, and she could continue her journey in privacy.

Maybe I should climb down on the other side of the trunk.

Hugging the bark, Severine shimmied around the wood until she could only see the herrerasaur's tail that wrapped around the other side. She was thrilled to see that the dino still hadn't budged.

Hopefully he's a heavy sleeper. I guess there's no way of knowing for sure.

She dropped down to another branch, carefully letting her fingers curl around the bark.

Okay, this is easier.

The descent was less dramatic now that she couldn't see the dinosaur's head and rows of intimidating teeth waiting for her at the bottom.

Ahh! This arm is killing me!

Her shoulder ached with each demanding move. She made a mental note not to become sloppy as the ground drew near. For now, her luck was holding up, but one loud snap of a branch could ruin everything, and she would face a swift, vicious death.

I don't believe it...the big lug is still out cold!

The herrerasaur snored loudly. From her position on the tree, Severine could see a corner of the creature's body as the ribs appeared between breaths. One of the scrawny feet twitched and the claws rasped against the surface of a rock.

Just sleep tight for now. I'll be back for you.

She paused once more about seven feet from the ground, observing the massive tail that swayed unconsciously beneath. The forest was illuminated once more – again, no red eyes. Much of her fears came from the alpha male, who was still out there somewhere in the dark forest. She didn't want to meet him again.

Hopefully he's far away by now.

Holding a few of her breaths, Severine cringed as her left foot touched down on the mulch, just inches away from the thumping orange tail. Slowly, she let her entire foot lay flat on the ground and hoisted the rest of her body silently onto the soil. The anxiety of the night's events had given her a splitting headache.

The dinosaur remained asleep.

Good. Step three: Reach the rifle.

But the weapon was still far away, situated between the two carnivores.

Severine mentally began to consider her options.

Option 1: Sprint for the rifle and risk waking up the first dino, but get to the weapon quicker. Option 2: Walk slowly, knowing that at any moment, Paluch's dinosaur could spot her and alert his buddy, and the two would trap her in the middle. Or, Option 3: Screw the gun and head for the cliffs, unarmed...

All her ideas were both good and bad.

She settled for Option 2.

The approach to the 90 was tedious and nerve-wracking. Every step she took disturbed the twigs on the ground. She cursed quietly as her foot kicked a pebble, but relaxed when nothing changed.

She chose to approach the rifle from the left, following a small animal path that led behind the cover of a few araucaria trees – the same trail the herrerasaurs used during their shrewd ambush. Through a slit in the wood, she could see her enemy tasting Paluch's exposed chest cavity as it yanked out a rib bone, grinding down on the treat.

The munching of the scientist's brittle bones made her nauseous.

Choke on it, you son of a bitch...

Severine shot a look back to the woods. Her dinosaur remained knocked out where she'd left him.

The XR-90 sat a few meters away, lying dramatically under the moon's blue rays, just out of reach. She had to get closer. If she made a break for the rifle from her spot, the conscious dinosaur would beat her to it.

She went forward on hands and knees, crossing through a gap under a low branch. Ahead, a small slope fed into a ditch that was within a few steps of the 90. Brushing aside the shrubs that wiped by her face, Severine kept an eye ahead at the red pool that had formed on the trail. Fortunately, the dinosaur had its back turned and wasn't paying any attention to her direction.

Smells from Paluch's mutilated torso wafted over the ground, hitting her senses hard. She held her breath, forcing herself not to throw up a second time.

With a quiet roll, Severine landed in the ditch.

It's right there... I can get it if I run...

She turned back again to peek at her surroundings.

NO!

Her dinosaur was gone.

The orange herrera no longer waited under the tree and had vanished into the night. Around her, the ferns and branches began to rustle with a faint vibration as the awakened dino searched for her. It knew she had escaped. It was coming for her, and she had no idea from where.

Shit!

The race was on.

Leaping heroically, she shot out of the ditch, racing frantically towards the 90 as her legs and arms flung like limp noodles. Her vision narrowed as she ran out from the ditch, catching the first clear glimpse of Paluch since the trail ambush.

The scientist's face was missing, and an exposed, dented skull greeted her under layers of scraggly, clumpy hair. Her sudden movements caused his hungry dinosaur to turn and roar, intending to maul her.

Time was running out. Around her, Severine could hear the other one coming, stampeding towards her.

But from where?

It sounded like it was coming from all directions. She didn't care, and there was no time to look. It was do or die.

Finally, she made it to the rifle.

Diving onto the ground, she clasped her hands tightly around the 90. The feeling of the rifle gave her renewed comfort and power as she whipped the barrel upward at the darkness. The hungry dinosaur stepped off Paluch's body and whirled around with a quick foot pivot, hustling towards her with open jaws.

It didn't get very far.

"Die!" Severine yelled, squeezing the trigger when she had a clean shot.

The 90 kicked to life, lighting up the nearby trunks as an orange beam shook fiercely from the barrel. The blast zipped through the carnivore's snout and exited out of the back of the head. Dead on impact, the herrera let out a confused snarl as its soul left the body, collapsing a foot away from Severine.

One down!

Behind her, heavy footsteps pounded through the dirt, getting louder with each monstrous step.

Here comes number two...

THUD! THUD! THUD!

Severine swiveled back around, laying on her belly, and looked quickly down the sights. She felt her heart beating furiously again behind the armor. Finally, the target came into view.

There you are...

The orange streak surged towards her, zigzagging into the ditch. There was no time for accuracy.

She squeezed the trigger.

Missed!

The monster passed under the ditch, avoiding the pulse blast as it shot just past the snout. A second later, the herrerasaur appeared again, flying towards her as it rose from the trenches.

Sweat began to bead down her forehead.

Okay, how about now?

She pulled the trigger again.

Missed! Damn! No...

The pulse blast nicked the carnivore's neck, but the impact wasn't enough to bring down the dino.

Her hands trembled with fright.

She flicked the firing setting to burst mode, rattling off a few more shots. Gold lasers whizzed out of the chamber as the creature leaped above her head.

"No!"

Severine fell backwards as the beast landed on top of her, using the XR-90 as a shield. Terrifying, lashing teeth bit down on the rifle stock, threatening to slice off her exposed fingers that had a death grip on the weapon. She cried as the unbearable weight of the dinosaur compressed her armor suit, blinking as the monster's spittle drenched her eyes. Support braces shattered apart behind the plating, spearing into her skin beneath the chest plate.

"*Augghh!* Get off, you bitch!"

The 90 would soon be ripped from her hands and the rabid dinosaur would shred her face apart. A calm peace came over her as she accepted her situation, knowing that she was about to die.

Just let it be quick...

She closed her eyes.

WHERRRRR!!!

A powerful light show and siren blared out from under a nearby tree, causing the herrera to stop the attack.

"What?"

Jordy...he's still alive!

She had forgotten all about the bot.

The dinosaur hopped back in confusion as the bot stood slowly back on his weak legs. The sudden movements to his front must have unknowingly roused its sensors from sleep-mode. The lights were quick and random, typical for robots with dying batteries. The pulsating patterns were enough to make the remaining herrerasaur re-evaluate the situation.

Severine wasted no time spinning the rifle around to pop off another shot – this time with Federation accuracy.

Go to hell!

A *zingggggg* rang out of the front barrel, scorching through the dinosaur's skull. The red eyes glazed over with a funny look, and the beast was gone, slipping back into the ditch.

She let the gun drop as her heart rate slowed. All was normal again.

"Sev-v-v. Is that you-u-u?" asked the digital voice.

"Yeah, buddy, it's me." She rose to her feet, clinging tightly to her rifle and running over to the bot.

Jordy's lights had begun to fade. Scaring the dinosaur had used a great deal of the machine's internal reserve power.

"Wha-a-at happen-n-ed? Whe-e-e-ere is every-one?"

"Brett and Julius are missing. Paluch is dead..."

"Damn. How-w-w long d-o-o I have?"

"I don't know, pal. But I'll tell you what. I'm not going anywhere. I'm gonna stay here the whole time, okay? Just let me rig up a safety perimeter. If I can get a fire going, it may deter any other dinosaurs in the area from coming over."

"Oka-a-ay. I'll try to wa-a-atch your ba-a-ack."

"Thanks, Jord. It shouldn't take long."

She gave the robot a sweet pat on the head and searched the ground for Paluch's pack, stepping around the herrerasaur bodies. After shooting one last look at the moon tucked above the canopy, she gathered her thoughts, happy to be alive. Since the danger had passed, a sense of peace washed over her. Somewhere far away in the coniferous jungle, she knew her comrades were alive, looking up at the same, beautiful night sky.

Where are you two?

She smiled.

They better not make me come looking for them...

XXI

Snnapppp!

The herrera's jaws chomped tightly shut, barely missing his neck.

Entangled vegetation cut across his face as Private Brett Ambrose crashed through the jungle. The final rays of sunlight were quickly fading away as dark clouds began to blot out the day behind the horizon.

Behind him, the herrerasaurs growled and snarled as they pushed through thorny web that overtook the path.

The river sounded close, perhaps just through the next patch of oncoming greenery. Brett could hear the gurgling current sloshing over the rocks before sliding back into the waves. It sounded flooded and dangerous – he didn't care.

Jumping off the ledge was his only option.

I escaped once. I can do it again...

His enemies were undeterred by the forest obstacles, determined to pounce on his back and bring the soldier to the ground, tearing him apart in the shadowy landscape. Twice he had felt their fowl breath warming his neck, casting damp saliva over on his flesh.

I hope they made it out, he thought of the other colonists.

He prayed that his comrades wouldn't think of him as a coward for running. He knew his flight would draw a bulk of the herrerasaurs towards him, away from the others.

The crossbow bounced along his back as he bounded down the overgrown vineyard. Thoughts of shouldering the weapon and fighting were cast aside after he failed to determine how many dinosaurs were giving pursuit. He may be able to bring one down, but the remaining attackers would finish him off long before he could draw another arrow.

Snnapppp!

More snarling erupted behind him. The sounds of the claws clacked along on the earth as the dinos ripped through the bushes.

Brushing aside a patch of stem plants, Brett emerged onto the plateau. Ahead, amber rays of dying sunlight filtered through the cloud layer, spilling out onto the serene backdrop ahead. Vast floodplains appeared beyond the river, which gradually ramped up to the northern mountains far away. Below the steep ravine, the powerful river rushed past, empowered by a day of heavy rain showers.

No time to admire the view!

Before he could take in the breathtaking sights, Brett Ambrose was airborne.

Taking a running leap, his momentum propelled him over the edge seconds before the carnivores scurried onto the landing. As he fell, he could hear the shrieks of the herrerasaurs whining at his escape as they halted abruptly at the ledge.

Brown waves plowed past in the rippling current below Brett's feet as he fell through the air.

After a quick glance up, he saw his predators staring down at him from fifty feet above, helplessly watching as their dinner descended into the depths.

He looked down as his feet quickly broke into the water, submerging in the riptide.

Cold!

Temperatures plummeted under the river's bubbling surface. Visibility was low. Everything was brown and blurry. As he pushed back through the surface, he could feel his toes hit the river floor, but not long enough to stand and stabilize himself. His feet slipped on the rocks and the current forced him into the maelstrom.

Disoriented and fighting to stay above water, Brett found himself searching for something, anything, to grab onto. The river was wild and unpredictable, tossing Brett upside down in cyclones as it bobbed him above and below the surface. Water splashed at his face when he found an opportunity to surface again, causing violent coughing fits as waves crammed down his throat.

Good, they're not giving chase.

As the waves carried him away, he caught a final glimpse of the herrerasaurs looking down from above. They growled at him before giving up, trotting back into the hedges.

At least that's working in my favor!

The river swirled around a series of sharp bends. Brett crashed on a rock, tried quickly to grab anything he could, and was again pulled downstream. He could feel himself getting farther away from his companions – farther from Severine.

After twenty years in this backwards world, fate had thrown them back together.

But why? Just to taunt me before I drown to death?

In the murky nothingness that enveloped him, and with uncertainty of life or death, she wouldn't leave his thoughts. Years of hyper-sleep and loneliness blanked out much of his memory. But after he focused, Brett found he could remember a few things.

#

He first met Severine while stationed on the *Supernova*. Their eyes first locked during a routine lunch break in the infantry mess hall. They sat together and found that conversation flowed easily between them. She was infinitely more beautiful than any other woman on board the ship. Her higher position in the Federation was another quality that Brett found attractive. Severine was a corporal in the infantry and therefore outranked him.

In the years of solitude in space, their chance encounters grew rarer. Everyone on board had specific tasks, and although it was a time of peace, the infantry personnel were kept busy, constantly being put to work. In the colossal ship, running into the same face more than once a week was uncommon.

During an emergency fire drill, Brett encountered Severine once again, this time initiating the conversation. He tried to make himself appear more interesting than a simple private in the Federation, and from what he could remember, it worked.

The conversation led to a friendship, and later a romance.

But to his aggravating depression, what happened next – or the order of what happened next – remained a mystery. He could only remember a few, hazy details.

One in particular stuck out among the rest: The night they spent together.

It was an event considered taboo among unmarried infantry personnel. He wished he could remember more of it, but the hyper-sleep only permitted him a few brief seconds in time. The way her hair looked and felt between his fingers. The sweet, fruity scent she was wearing. The dim, sepia shading that the lighting cast over her smooth skin as they embraced, secretly, in his soldiers' quarters.

He yearned to piece together the gaps.

Other events that followed weren't linear in his mind, but he could pick out a few moments that he was able to salvage. The two of them had received a demerit for skipping drill once. They argued over whether or not they would find a redeemable planet to call home. And to his embarrassment, he remembered that Severine bested him once in a target competition – an event she didn't let him live down.

His final memory of Severine on the *Supernova* was a dreadful one, and one that he remembered all too well. He shuddered in the freezing waves as he recalled the vision.

A vision he refused to share with the others.

You coward!

Three hundred years ago, during the cataclysmic voyage through the populated asteroid belt, Brett abandoned his post to find her.

Many of the E5 escape pods had already deployed from the ship, sailing away to origins unknown. In the emptiness of the hull, he traversed the many maze-like corridors, frantically searching for Severine.

Eventually he found her, sealed away in a hyper-sleep pod in artificial slumber.

He scanned the halls for a logistics bot to open the pod to release her.

As the asteroids continued to batter the *Supernova*, he knew the ship was a lost cause. The outside, for some reason, was starting to turn black and searching for a bot was useless in the dark. The robots he came across were fried due to ensuing electrical failures.

Defeated, he stared helplessly at her from behind the pod glass, for a time that seemed like an eternity. There was nothing he could do. Severine was stuck behind the reinforced glass until her battery pack gave out. The other pods in the hall were also locked and headed towards the same fate.

For a moment, he saw her eyes open and rouse from sleep.

They settled on him, and she managed a faint smile. By the time he realized she had woken up and could've opened the pod door, she slipped away again into unconsciousness.

If he broke the glass, there was a good chance the shards would severely cut her. If the ship imploded suddenly, the pod exterior would sustain oxygen, keeping her alive. He pounded hard on the shield to wake her back up, but she was out again – this time for good.

His only hope was that her battery pack would fail and the doors would open, but they never did.

As the ship plunged forward, Brett knew he couldn't wait any longer.

Ashamed of his failure, he fled to the escape pod deck and found the *Mudskipper*, which happened to be the only pod left that hadn't ejected. When the pod was full, the crew on board activated the launch sequence and the E5 jettisoned out of the *Supernova*.

That was the last time he saw her. He thought their separation would be forever.

But now, he was given a second chance.

After they pieced together their blurry past, they could rebuild a future together. If he could just find a way back to the jungle!

Have to get back... Have to survive...

His journey down the rapids jolted him from his flashback.

A large wave threw him against a slippery, flat boulder that tilted outward, before spilling him back under the current. This time, Brett latched onto a sturdy vine that webbed down into the water. The vine ascended back up the cliff and disappeared over the high ledge into the greenery.

He grabbed it.

It may support me if I climb...shit!

Federation coloring drifted by.

Julius!

The lieutenant floated past, half sunken below the cold waves. In the fading light, Brett saw that his friend may be dead. He slipped along lifelessly, making no effort to keep his head above the tide. His eyes were closed.

"Lieutenant! Julius!"

With an expert dive, Brett let go of the vine and plunged back into the water after the static armor suit that flew downstream.

In the watery darkness, the faint lights from the armor flashed orange as the body rose and fell below the foamy surface. The current picked up, writhing and frothing when it came around coarse, submerged obstacles. The journey was getting dangerous.

Gotta be quick. Could lose him at any time!

With a wet slap, the private's hand curled out of the water and snagged Julius' arm. Brett took a firm hold of the officer and kicked back through the rapids, headed for the cliff base. The water smacked harshly into his face as he whipped wet hair away for better vision.

Behind the armor suit, the officer's limp form made it arduously difficult for him to swim.

Come on! Help me out here!

Another vine appeared, snaking along the surface a few feet away.

Yes! Give it here!

After his fingers clutched around the plant, Brett tugged at the vine, pulling his friend with him onto the sandy embankment at the edge of the ravine. High above, the jungle rose out of the overlook. He relaxed when he saw no herreras lurking at the peak.

The dinos must be far upstream by now...

The river had carried them a great distance away, but he wasn't sure exactly how far.

He heaved Julius against the rocks, keeping his face out of the rushing water that surged past them.

"Julius!" Brett yelled, smacking the lieutenant's face lightly.

The officer remained comatose. His eyes were closed, but his mouth remained slightly ajar, as if his last moments were spent screaming for his life. Brett checked him over for dinosaur wounds and bruising from the river rocks.

Thankfully, he was unharmed.

He took in water and needs resuscitating – fast.

He flipped Julius' head from side to side, shaking out any residual fluid that had collected in his mouth. Spreading his lips apart, he breathed through his throat as he pinched the officer's nostrils tightly shut. Brett had done this many years before in an emergency resuscitation class in infantry basic training, although he was now out of practice. When the lieutenant's eyes failed to open, Brett wasn't sure his method was working.

Julius remained lifeless.

Dammit. Come on!

Brett tried again, this time applying pressure to the lieutenant's chest with both hands as he continued to breathe into his mouth. The officer's head rolled effortlessly to the side, narrowly missing the rushing waves that washed along in the sand.

His armor suit... It's too thick! I need to take it off.

He pulled at the armor plating, found the latching mechanism behind the shoulders, and yanked the breastplate off the officer's front.

Here it goes…

Brett shoved into the chest with a final, forceful push, and Julius' eyes bulged open.

Yes!

The lieutenant sat up and spat out brown water onto the coast. Brett stepped behind him and patted his back, helping Julius work up more liquid and eject it safely.

"Jeez, Ambrose," started the gruff, water-logged voice. "If we were back with the Federation, I'd promote your ass ASAP. Good job!"

Brett laughed.

"Thank you, sir!"

The private was relieved the trick had worked. As Julius came to and regained his composure, Brett double checked that he had everything, relieved that he still had his crossbow, arrows, and the invaluable key-card.

"Fill me in here."

Julius pulled his half-submerged legs out of the waves and leaned back on the shore, grateful for a second chance at life.

"The dinosaurs stopped chasing us when we fell from the cliff – just like I knew they would. I'm guessing when you fell, you hit a rock that knocked you out cold! I just saw you floating by a minute ago and grabbed you."

"Any idea on the others? Solens? Paluch?"

"Alive – last I checked. But I can't be certain. It happened pretty fast..."

"Sev saved my life! One had me pinned. I think she stabbed it – or scared it off. Either way, her actions let me get away. We need to get up there and make sure they're okay."

She's one in a million, he thought.

"I couldn't agree more," Brett replied. "But we're losing the light. Are you comfortable making the climb in the dark?"

"Absolutely," Julius confirmed, studying the exotic surroundings.

In the confusion of the river escape, the moon had risen in the night sky, casting serene blue rays down on the river's wavy surface. Voluminous mists had begun to form over the water. Above the cliff top, stars winked over the tops of tree ferns and conifers, watching over the prehistoric jungle. The day had slipped by and gave way to a refreshing, cool evening.

"Do we climb up here?"

"I don't see any other option, it's either that or—what the hell? Be careful, Julius!"

The lieutenant paused, carefully withdrawing his step.

"What's this?" he asked.

"A grave, I think. A grave – of us! Federation survivors, throughout the years…"

On the other side of the sandy cove, a small stretch of rocky buildup had collected below the ravine. As the moon brightened the area, the light revealed a large concentration of skeletal human remains in various tattered Federation outfits, including infantry armor suits and withered lab coats. Crumbled fragments of XR-90s and X2-20s were littered among the corpses and clasped between the frail fingers. The bodies draped randomly over one another, forming an undead pile near the center.

"It's the crew…" Julius said. "There's got to be at least a few hundred bodies here!"

The skulls smiled out at them from their places among the rocks. The old teeth glowed under the blue light from the moon and stars. Most were old, but there were several recent cadavers, all at varying stages of decomposition. The stench of death glazed over the cove.

"Damn, why are they here?" Julius asked.

Brett searched for an answer but found none.

One of the closer colonists still had pale skin sagging through the sunken eye sockets.

It's as if they have been collecting here for centuries…

"They were thrown down from above – from the cliff. I'm surprised the current hasn't swept them away all these years…"

"Let's find a way back up," Julius urged him, trying to keep their minds off the tomb.

Brett chose to let his thoughts of Severine, and their distant past, go unmentioned. He hoped to reveal his memories to her once they reunited in private.

The two men walked carefully over their fallen comrades, trying not to disturb their final resting places, as they prepared to scale the treacherous ravine.

Hang on, Sev… I'm coming back!

XXII

Frrrrr!

Severine shoved the last paper down the sharpened twig, pushing it far enough so the wind wouldn't blow it away as the flames ignited.

That oughta do it...

Her dinosaur defensive perimeter was finally complete.

The makeshift twig torches crackled to life with bright, fiery auras. Severine had found Paluch's Triassic book in his discarded backpack, ripped out the old dried pages, and (with a burst of the XR-90) lit them ablaze. She collected the wood, bent the sticks into X-shapes, and stuck the tattered pages onto their ends after igniting them. To her surprise, the pages lasted a long time before she had to replace them. The entire event took no longer than twenty minutes.

Her theory so far had proven itself accurate. The dinosaurs feared the fire. This explained why the wild tribe they encountered earlier had carried torches.

She had set up a second perimeter farther out in the trees and spread sparsely apart. When the second fence didn't make her feel safer, she built a final, closer barrier that was more compact with fewer gaps.

She shoved the last twig post firmly in the ground, admiring her work.

The flames lit up the surrounding jungle more brightly than the moonlight, enabling her to see a good distance into the undergrowth.

When the first torches were lit, she was shocked to see a few slender heads staring back at her. They dispersed into the brush as the pyre grew more brilliant. She relaxed when she recognized them by their gentle, timid forms.

Pisanosaurs.

It must be the same herd from earlier, lingering nearby.

Severine had just finished relocating their encampment to a position closer to the cliffs. After a quick debate on what would be better, Jordy convinced her it would be more strategic if the ravine was at their backs. Severine didn't argue with the bot. She found it creepy to build her fortification next to Paluch, whose mangled remains still painted the forest floor.

They camped out on the plateau overlooking the moonlit valley far beyond. They were protected by the torch lights.

Sadly, she found no signs of Brett or Julius.

They're probably so far downstream by now, she thought.

"Should we g-g-g-oo-o- look for the-m-m-m-m?" Jordy asked, with an unstable twitch of the neck.

The bot's battery life was getting weaker by the minute. Severine could hear the water trickling around in his chest cavity when Jordy moved.

"No, it's too dark," she replied. "We don't know if those herrerasaurs are still around. If we leave the safety of the torches in the dark—well, let's just stay here."

It was a lie, but for the right reasons.

The bot was dying, and she felt compelled to stay by his side until the battery finally drained. Telling the truth would probably just depress him.

The behaviors and emotions of Federation robots were a hot topic of debate among colonists. Technicians and scientists were usually very shallow about their beliefs with robotics, spending days and months personally developing each unit before progressing to the next. The same was true for the infantry. Normally, bots were thought of as none other than servants or grunt workers, lacking all forms of human consciousness.

But Jordy was different than the rest.

By now, she was convinced Jordy had a soul, or at the very least, a beautifully programmed personality unlike all other robots.

"Wha-a-at do you th-i-n-k they-ll do?" he asked.

"If they're smart, they'll head for the ship. Looking for me will just waste more of their time. They know if I'm alive, I'll be going that way as well – if I don't get lost in the jungle first!"

"Yo-u-u-u don't th-i-i-i-nk they're de-a-d?"

"Absolutely not. In fact, I'm certain of it!"

She didn't want to entertain that thought. If they were dead, floating at the bottom of the river somewhere, that meant after the bot's batteries finally gave out, she would be the last one left – the sole survivor of the *Supernova*.

The thought freaked her out. She quickly tossed the idea aside.

They had to be alive.

They must be!

She hadn't found either bodies of the two soldiers on the plateau or the trail leading up to it, and she couldn't see Julius' glowing armor suit floating below in the dark river waves.

Severine sat across from Jordy in a center fire that she constructed, anticipating a wet, miserable evening. But the air wasn't anywhere near freezing, and actually felt refreshing after the humid afternoon. Small bugs hovered around the flames, perishing into the glow when they circled too close. Beyond, the fiery fences continued their endless task of maintaining light until the sun returned.

Still no sign of the herrerasaurs...

"Ho-o-ow long do I ha-a-ave n-ow?"

"Not sure, buddy," she replied. "But I'm gonna be here the whole time." She wasn't sure if her consolation would make the bot feel better, but without the required Federation tools, it was all she could do.

"Tha-a-anks, Se-e-v."

"What a cruel, upside-down world we've found," she said. "I'm convinced Paluch was right. Somehow, we've ended up back in the ancient days of Earth. I, for one, have outstayed my welcome, and I'm ready to get the hell out of here!"

She tried to distract the bot from his approaching demise, regardless of how obvious his situation was.

Poor thing. It has hardly any life left...

"He is ri-i-i-eee-ght. This mu-st be the Triassic period."

"You want to hear my theory?" she asked.

"I've no-o-o-thing bet-ter to do-o," the glitching tone replied, causing Severine to smile.

He still has some humor left in him!

"The missing piece still lies within the time-jump – our path backwards in Earth's history. Even Paluch wasn't completely certain what happened up there. Brett didn't know either. Honestly, I think we flew right into a time-continuum, or whatever the scientists call it."

"What's t-tha-t?"

She shrugged.

"I'm not really sure. It was never really explained to me. Maybe something like a portal, or a wormhole – I think that's what they call it. When the ship passed through whatever it was, we were thrown into another time, and somehow, luckily, ended up back on Earth, during a period that sounds like a fairytale. A period when life thrived – I never thought I'd see our old planet like this. All I've ever known was the ruins...the wars... What do you think of my idea?"

"Se-e-ems likely that wa-a-as th-e case, Sev. I've ne-ehhhh-ver known any way to-o successfully t-i-t-i-i-ime travel, but I suppose that w-orm-holes could be responsible."

"Hopefully other ships crossed through the portal and are floating nearby. It's been three-hundred years. They could've built settlements on the other side of the planet, for all I know. There's no way of telling until we activate that emitter."

"You-u-u mean wh-en you activate it," the bot corrected her.

Damn. She misspoke.

"Sorry, Jordy..." She realized the bot wouldn't be coming with her.

Jordy waved off her mistake.

"Thi-s new world isn't meant-t-t-t for robotics. Daddy pro-o-o-ved that to m-e-e."

The recent departure of Daddy was still fresh in her mind. She remembered the bot's valiant last stand in the FATR by sacrificing himself to bring them safely out of the swamp.

But despite the pilot's ultimate sacrifice, she wouldn't miss him like the way she would miss Jordy. Daddy was a programmed robotic soldier with limited quotations and automated features. Jordy, however, had infinite adaptive learning abilities, built-in humor, and was far more personable – more alive.

"Wha-a-a-t are you going to do if you're re-s-s-cued?"

The bot was trying to be polite and change the subject.

"Well, I'm never going on another star ship again," Severine laughed. "When they realize I've been alive all this time, if they've even kept records that far in the past, they should discharge me, and I'll move on with my life. Maybe find a home, start a family..."

Children and a life outside the infantry was a thought she usually brushed aside, given her prior lengthy commitment as a soldier. Throughout their experience in the Triassic, her views on the subject had changed. She had seen enough action for her lifetime and couldn't wait for the day that she didn't have to hold another pulse rifle. Although the X2s did feel great in her hands.

"Tha-at sounds ni-ice..." Jordy sounded genuine.

A colonized world on a livable planet was something of folklore, tucked somewhere behind the stars. Since the forming of the Federation, years after the carnage created from the Old War, the surviving members of humanity dreamed of the day they could step foot on dry land again. Civilization would be rebuilt in a new light, with special attention given to the natural balance of things, the survival of life, and most importantly, the human race.

"I ho-o-ope you'll fin-d that peace one d-a-y…"

Me too, if it exists, she thought.

Far away in the valley, a howl drifted out on the evening breeze. Severine turned to look, knowing that whatever loon made the sound was far out of eyesight, lying somewhere at the base of the ravine, masked in the night.

"You don't think the di-i-i-nosaurs will come b-a-a-ahhh-ak?" Even in the bot's depleting energy levels, he was still worried about the herrerasaurs.

"Not as long as these flames do the trick," Severine replied. She quietly thanked Paluch for bringing the book, although now it served a purpose other than reading.

"You-u- be careful, Sev. It's a s-c-ary world out here… No matter what the cost, promise me. Pr-o-omise me you-ll m-a-a-ake it to th-e signal emitter, and cal-l-l-l-l for he-l-l-lp. Ge-e-t out o-o-f here, for a-ll our sakes. Ge-et back home…"

Shit! That's right – the key-card!

She suddenly remembered her way into the mainframe room – the key-card – was currently missing in action, last seen with Brett. And if he was still in the river, it would be impossible to find him, or his precious card, until morning. She felt herself sweating and shifting uncomfortably at the thought of the lost card, buried underwater or inside a muddy river embankment.

Without that valuable little rectangle, heading back to the *Supernova* would be pointless.

That would be her new goal as soon as morning hit. She would begin to patrol the edges of the water below the ravine and try to find her friends. The mission depended on it.

Severine decided not to tell Jordy about the missing key-card, knowing that it may upset the bot in his final moments. In Jordy's mind, he still had hope for her, and found solace that she might be able to make it out.

"I promise. I'm getting out of here," she answered finally. "Thanks to you and the others."

"We-e-e- were a good te-eam…" the bot uttered.

"We were," Severine replied.

She smiled, giving a sympathetic nod as the bot's cooling fans began to wind down.

As they sat there, behind the blazing fence barriers, she found herself looking again at the stars. Somewhere within the twinkling spheres that webbed the night sky, she thought, maybe, that there was another colonized world waiting for her.

A world without dinosaurs.

Severine wanted desperately to stay awake and keep watch, but the events of the day before took a toll on her endurance. Blackness began to consume her, and her head gradually began to caress the soft frond leaves on the ground. Soon she was fast asleep, not caring what may be festering in the jungle as her exhausted mind switched off for the night.

Across the fire, Jordy kept watch for another hour, deploying his scanners into the foliage beyond Severine's fencing. Inside his chest panels, the water ate away at precious electrical wiring and circuit systems. A red light faded on behind his eye panels, and gradually dipped to black. Jordy died quietly in the cool evening, happy he had stayed alive long enough to keep watch.

His shape slumped forward with an odd jerk, and the bot was gone.

#

Phrrr! Phrrr! Phrrr!

Human feet pounded down the small cliff leading into the waterfall valley. The lagoon had formed a large circle from Brett's detonator blast hours earlier. Cool water rushed down tiny, residual streams generated by the plasma shards. Bloated corpses floated nearby, coating the water with a bloody hue.

This party was much larger than the first scouting group. Numbering almost thirty strong, young men, they had been skewering the woodlands, searching for the mysterious valley that supposedly housed the other scouting party. They received word from a handful of survivors that something remarkable had happened at the falls, and that it was possible the other warriors, including a shaman, had been obliterated during the event.

The informants spoke of a strange orb that broke apart on impact, disintegrating the clan in a deadly force field.

The leader bent down over the marred earth. Several specks of glowing blue pulse plasma still radiated on the rocks. He touched the stones carefully, trying not to make skin contact with the insidious blue goo.

He knew the power of the pulse weapons.

Warriors crowded behind the man, spying on what he discovered. Spear shafts clicked along the ground as they chattered excitedly to themselves, pondering their ruler's next move. The clamoring grew louder, and with a quick movement of the leader's arm, they were silent once again.

His eyes fixed on a patch of bent grass on the other side of the pool, leading to an animal trail that shrank away into the night.

A herd of pisanosaurs had crossed through recently, but behind their footprints came another trail. The tracks didn't seem predatory and were perhaps made by a herrerasaur or the much smaller panphagia. The leader knew these carnivorous dinosaurs were common tenants of the northern jungle and weren't the creators of the second trail.

The tribe crossed over to the other side of the lagoon. As the leader studied the new trail more closely, he instantly noticed several, recognizable features in the prints, and the answer presented itself.

Humans!

Humans had wiped out his scouting party. Humans from the ancient ship.

From his belt, he produced a primitive horn and gave a series of short calls. The crew raised their pikes in agreement, happy for another chance to battle. The intruders had to be punished, just like the others were punished years earlier – before their bodies were tossed down the river bank and left to decay under the unforgiving Triassic sun.

XXIII

Morning washed over the Triassic.

Finally.

The golden sun rose over Severine's head, shining a beam of light through the tree ferns that nearly blinded her. The familiar heat and annoying insect buzzing she recalled from yesterday resumed. The dragonflies returned, hovering around one of the extinguished torch posts.

Severine jumped up, quickly realizing she had fallen asleep in herrerasaur territory.

But the jungle was now soothingly quiet. The conifer trees swayed along in the morning breeze. Flying reptilian creatures glided above the treetops before shrinking away behind a vapor cloud. Below the cliffs, she heard water continue to roil and sway as it skirted into the rocky basin.

After rising to her feet, she discovered her entire body ached and felt numb after the hectic night she had endured. Her hair was in disarray, littered with twigs and leaves. Her armor suit was stained with muck. Paluch's dried blood was smeared across her breastplate in an artful spatter pattern. The chrome plating of the XR-90 was indented with carnivorous bite marks from the herrera. Severine was pleased to see that after all the damage, the operational light was still glowing.

That's a relief.

Wisps of swirly smoke billowed above the papers and seared sticks that comprised the defensive barrier and burned brightly just an hour earlier. Many of the fences were down, either by animal interaction, harsh winds, or simply by burning up and dissolving to a crisp. A few had toppled over in ashes along the grass.

There were no signs of the herreras. In the dawn of the jungle, their orange bodies would be easy to spot. Darkness was where they flourished. Severine looked around for the alpha-male, expecting the ferocious creature to rip through the branches and annihilate her.

More silence.

The caws of the overhead reptiles creaked as they passed over again, chasing one another through the araucaria trees. Severine relaxed and turned to celebrate with Jordy, only to get an unpleasant surprise.

Oh...

She froze, unsure how to react.

The robot was dead. The light panels had shut off and failed to blink back to life as she moved closer. She couldn't hear the therapeutic *hummmm* of his cooling fans or the chirping of his processor computers calculating background tasks. The metallic face was drooped to an unnatural side. Lifeless eyes stared out at the fire's ashes, watching the embers fizzle into the ground.

"Jordy?" she asked, waving a hand over the metal eyes.

Nothing.

"Hey, buddy, you there?"

Come on, pal.

The bot sat motionless under the swaying shadows of the pine trees. Severine half expected the machine to jump back to life, as if Jordy encountered an unseen miracle while she napped. Instead, one of the bot's knees pivoted in the soil, and the body fell into another awkward position.

He's dead.

"I'm sorry there wasn't more I could do."

Severine wished she had learned more about Federation AI and the skills needed to revive and maintain bots. Certifications for robot construction and development took years to achieve, and usually ended with aggravated failure and ejection from the program. Many who entered the robotics labs couldn't cope with the long hours. And there was the software side of the process. Severine knew that angle wasn't for her.

Goodbye, pal.

Her hand touched the bot's cold steel, and Severine knew Jordy wasn't coming back.

She had to move on and make use of the day. Grieving for the machine would have to wait until a later time – she had to get out of the jungle before nightfall, before the herreras returned. There were only a few pages left to burn for fire, and even less ammunition in the 90.

Severine sat down beside the dead robot, looking out into the trees and back down at her firearm, double checking once again that the light was shining.

Ahead, the wilderness loomed out, and with it, the sudden uncertainty of her future.

She was alone, and for the first time, she felt it.

The cliffs.

Brett and Julius.

The key-card.

The thoughts wouldn't stop.

Walking over to the gorge, she raised her rifle and carefully approached the edge of the grassy overlook. Flashbacks of her incident at the waterfall valley in the jungle mocked her as she slowly peered over the edge.

This one better not collapse...

The fall would probably kill her.

Below, the river was wide and deep. Waves broke apart at the edge of the cliff where a small shoreline had formed along the coasts. She looked up and down the river for her friends. Under the surface, her eyes played tricks on her as they scanned across some oddly shaped boulders that vaguely resembled Federation armor suits.

Damn! Nothing...

Severine scooped up her pack and gathered several more paper fragments that remained from Paluch's book, anticipating another lonely night in the woods.

Staying away from the treacherous gully, she started off towards the west, keenly monitoring the river below. Jordy's body and their encampment soon vanished behind the vegetation. Severine knew she wouldn't return to that location and wished quietly that the bot's spirit, if it had one, was in a better place.

The sounds of rushing water continued to swell as the river below gave way to rapids, snaking through the forest. The paths along the cliffs were bare and easy to maneuver. Animal droppings and dinosaur tracks were common along the matted grass. Life had crossed by here frequently to access the water source, only to retreat when they discovered the steep drop off.

Wooooshhh! Flap! Flap! Flap!

The flying reptiles continued to soar high above her. They were tan, funny little creatures that chirped and played tag with one another under the golden sun. During a few of their aerial dive bombs, they sailed just above her head, blowing her hair back.

Cawwawawwww!

She ducked and aimed the 90 at the flock, but before she could get a shot off, they were already out of range, flying into the vapor again.

They're just playing. My, the little things are quick!

She kept track of her steps in relation to her starting point from the jungle camp. When she estimated that she had walked about two miles inland, Severine took a respite on a mossy boulder, looking out over the majestic valley. Retrieving a water canister from the pack, she replenished her fluids and admired the view.

Phhhhrr! A wild noise snorted out from below.

A group of bipedal dinosaurs had gathered across the river and were lapping up the water on a coastal mound. The dinos, brown and speckled with random spots, huddled together for protection. Several of the younger ones were kept towards the center, much like the exaeretodon herd had done just before the coelophysis attack. As they submerged their heads into waves, Severine glanced up and down the waterway.

Still no signs of Julius or Brett.

Where the hell are you guys?

Severine kept looking down, thinking that one of the armor suits would come swishing around the bend. Instead, she only saw schools of primitive fish. The creatures splashed out in arc motions before diving back underwater.

Above, the sun continued its predetermined trek over the sky. By the position of the light, Severine guessed it was transitioning into late morning. She finished her water canister, placing it into her supply pack before pondering her next move.

There were three options – none of which sounded promising now.

Supernova. Follow the river. Or go out and try to survive forever in the Triassic until someone finds me. If someone finds me…

She decided to complete her first objective: Find her friends.

Without the damn key-card, continuing to follow the river looks to be the only option. Eventually, the two of them should appear…

She gave herself a bonus option of finding a way down to the river to fill up the water canisters.

Shrkk! Shrkk! Shrkk!

Something caused the ferns behind her to stir.

What was that?

She pivoted with the precision of a Federation soldier and aligned the 90 sight with her right eye. A glimpse of orange scurried through the trees, meters away behind the golden reed stems and swaying petals.

A herrerasaur!

She wasn't expecting them back so soon.

Her finger itched over the trigger, eager to press it back, but she was unsure how many rounds she had left. There weren't many. She would have to wait until her target was close.

As a backup plan, she planned to dive off the ledge and pray for the best in the rapids.

Come on already!

Sounds of furious sprinting commenced behind the brush, battering down the path. The footfalls were spread apart and easily audible.

Sounds like there's only one...

The form appeared again, this time with patches of white intermixed with the orange. As it ran by a bundle of dense vegetation, Severine second-guessed what the visitor was. The white and orange coloring had thrown her off. For a second, she saw a shimmer of light reflecting off the coating.

Was that a trace of metal?

The steps drew close. A branch split apart several meters away, and a human male tumbled out towards the plateau.

Whoa!

A man dressed in Federation armor pushed violently through the thicket, collapsing and clearly out of breath.

Severine relaxed when she saw it wasn't another herrerasaur.

But he is running from something...

The man was pale in color, breathing heavily as he gripped at his chest plate. His hair was disheveled and sweaty. Beads of perspiration dripped down the sides of his head past traces of facial stubble. At his side, an empty X2-20 rested firmly in his utility holster. The pistol grazed the rock as the man fell to his knees. When he heard the weapon touch stone, he grabbed it and cast it aside, confirming the absence of ammunition.

He must be fresh out of hyper-sleep!

She lowered her weapon.

The armor suit indicated a rank and position from the *Supernova*. He appeared to be in the infantry as well, with an insignia suggesting he was a sergeant. The armor looked new and unaffected by time, unlike the suit they found days earlier on the trail near the ship wreckage.

"Hey, who are you?" Severine asked. "What's your name?"

The man caught his breath, panting heavily.

"Davenport," he replied between frantic panting. "Marcus Davenport: *Supernova* infantry."

Davenport.

The name sounded familiar.

Marcus Davenport...

The name jumped out at her as a faint memory. Like Brett Ambrose, Davenport was another name she recalled prior to entering hyper-sleep.

Yes, Davenport!

"I remember you. It's me! Corporal Severine Solens."

"Severine?"

"Yes! Maybe you can't remember me very well. Hyper-sleep can do that to you. My memory has been a little scrambled since I got here. I only remember pieces at a time."

"Right. Severine, how long has it been?"

"About three hundred years."

He lifted his head in disbelief, still holding his chest from his heavy run.

"Three hundred years? How can you know that?"

"A logistics bot. He told me from his data logs when the crash happened. He's dead now. I'm not alone out here; there's two others with me. Lieutenant Julius Lexand and Private Brett Ambrose. They're down the river somewhere. We got separated."

"Are they alive?"

"Not sure. We were attacked by the dinosaurs."

"Dinosaurs? Yeah, I've seen them. Big nasty orange ones. They're here in the jungles."

"We've identified the species as Herrerasaurus," she replied. "And yes, they're very nasty. Why were you running? You're out of breath, Sergeant."

He was finally standing on his feet. He was a good-looking man and looked about the same age as she remembered him. Tall and strong, he was a hardened soldier in the infantry, personally commanding her on several occasions. She remembered him as a fearless leader and a quick decision-maker.

"We've got to get away from here! Away from the cliffs – they're coming!"

"Herrerasaurs?"

"No! The human hunters, and they're not far behind me!"

"Shit! How many?"

"Fifty? Maybe fifty…"

Her 90 surely didn't have enough rounds to beleaguer that many.

He looked back uneasily at the quiet wilderness. Severine listened closely but couldn't hear anything coming through the trees.

She wasn't sure what she preferred to face next: the tribe of the wild men or the herrerasaur pack. Both equally horrified her.

"How far?"

"They'll be on us soon if we don't move!" he yelled, ignoring her question.

"Well, we're pretty close to the river here. The drop isn't too steep from the ledge, and the water looks deep enough to survive a fall. We could ride the current downriver…"

Davenport shook his head.

"There's more monsters down there! We need to go back through the woods and take a different trail to evade the tribe."

"Are you sure? The river looks free of any—"

"No! Trust me! We need to go back to the trails."

Davenport was irritatingly insistent on doubling back to the jungle. Severine thought he was being too impatient, and a tad annoying – but he outranked her.

Begrudgingly, she agreed.

What horrors has this man seen that he's so anxious?

"Okay, the 90 still has some juice," Severine said. "Lead the way!"

Davenport darted into the trees. He ran with a speed and athletic prowess that Severine struggled to maintain. He swerved through the paths as if he knew the woods and traveled them often. Behind, the sounds of the rapids gradually faded away as the jungle ambiance returned. After a minute, she found herself disoriented and confused as he bounded up the trampled animal trails.

Suddenly, the path stopped, ending abruptly at the edge of a rocky incline. She paused at the boulders, out of breath and exhausted.

A dead end?

"Now where?" she panted.

BRAAWWWRRRRRRRR!!!!

A tribal horn rang out through the forest, sending more concealed tan reptiles fleeing from their high perches.

Hell no!

"Where are they?"

BRAWWWRRRRRR!!!!

Another horn call – this time from a different direction.

Davenport stopped his reckless sprint and started to look for a better perspective. They were surrounded by thick ferns and plant walls. Visibility vanished more than ten yards out of the clearing.

They could be anywhere.

"I don't know!" Davenport panicked. "They're all around us!"

"They sound close!"

BRAWWWWRR!!!

Severine could feel her hands suffocating her rifle grip.

Running impacts of human feet slowly began to rustle against the leaves that lined the jungle floor. The sound started faintly like soft rain, but quickly escalated into a tumultuous hurricane. The tremors merged with other steps that encircled the clearing. Above the peak of the mountainous summit, more feet clicked down on the stones, sending small pebbles dribbling down the slope before falling to the earth.

Cawwawawwww! Cawwawawwww!

The tan reptiles chirped as they sailed away, avoiding the conflict that would soon commence at the steps of the rocky embankment.

"Don't shoot unless they begin to charge. We don't want to act aggressively!"

Severine nodded.

"Yes, sir," she replied, acknowledging his rank and superiority.

There are hardly any rounds left in here. I might very well turn the weapon on myself before I let these assholes take me down.

Finally, the first warrior brushed through the green. It was a young man painted red with blood and bearing a tall, sharpened pike. Three more forms appeared behind him with similar crude weaponry. They halted as the forerunner picked up a white horn, pressing the end to his lips.

BRAWWWWWWWWWWWRRR!!!

"Sergeant?"

"Hold fire," he replied, picking up a rock to defend himself.

Okay...

Another short call answered on the other side of the foliage.

BRAWWWRRR!

More spear bearers cut through the leaves, extending the chiseled tips towards the colonists. Severine looked up as more indigenous humans emerged atop the rocks with bows pointed down at them. The tribe had them surrounded.

"Sir, they're all over us! Should I fire?" She could feel her sweaty finger massaging the trigger.

"No! They haven't acted yet. They're curious about us..."

The circle of exotic men continued their dramatic approach, while the bowman above perfected their aim. Spaces between the warriors began to thin as they continued to close the gap. Their spears descended outward, forming a deadly arc of spikes.

This is it...

"Sergeant!"

Her gun was shaking in her hands.

"I said wait!" he yelled. "You'll never get them all – there's too many! Let me try to reason with them."

"Sir, you won't be able to talk to them! They don't speak our language. They're murderers! I've seen them kill three of their own just yesterday!"

The pikes continued to push forward. Above, Severine heard the drawing of bowstrings pulling farther back.

We're going to get slaughtered!

"Sir!"

She was sweating now. A couple of blasts from the 90 could kill a few, and maybe scare the rest away. It might even buy some time for an escape. If they stepped within ten feet, Severine knew she would disobey his order and act on her instincts.

"I said hold your fire!" He was furious at her insistent question, growing red in the face. The first spear tip was nearly on her. Severine couldn't take it anymore.

"No! Sir, with all due respect, fu-..."

WHHIAAMMMMMM! CRKKKK!

She felt a terrible pain suddenly smear across her face as the world around her spiraled like a fierce tornado. Her hands sprung open, and she could feel her rifle leave her fingers as it struck against stone.

What the—

She blinked. Her brain throbbed with a chilling pain, pounding her skull and giving way to an impressive headache.

Shit...Davenport...You son of...bitch...hit me with...rock...

"*Hey.*" Her words were reeling as her mind tried to make sense of the situation. "You piece of sh—"

WHAAAMMM! CRRRRRKK!

The mental colors burst beautifully, and she collapsed after Davenport bludgeoned her with the rock again. Her vision faded as the sergeant peered down at her. As she drifted from consciousness, she noticed the wild men hadn't killed Davenport, but instead congregated behind him, watching her slip helplessly away under their predetermined spell.

XXIV

The ground was heavily trampled. Footprints from the wild men left deep impressions in the earth, exposing the soil under the grassy knolls. A large contingent of the tribe had passed through not long before. They had been in a hurry.

Brett knelt to the ground, recovering a discarded spear blade that sat submerged under a muddy puddle.

The wild men were here, he thought, palming the pike tip.

"There was a large group of them," he said as Julius caught up to him.

"Any idea how many or which way they went?"

Brett shook his head. "No. The ground's too screwed up here..."

They were looking for us.

"Let's double back. The others may still be alive."

The colonists began the long walk back several miles into the jungle. Climbing the cliff face had proven difficult the night before. They had to pick different places to climb up a few times – the rocks were too unpredictable and steep. After many futile attempts, they decided to head downstream and find a safer place to ascend, taking them many miles off course. Now it was nearly evening of the following night. They had lost a day.

As they followed the thin trail of worn footprints back upstream, odd, wooden structures began to appear behind the shrubs. They were first spread apart randomly, but soon clustered tightly together as they neared the center of a small plateau. They looked like little scarecrows nestled under the araucaria branches.

"Fire perimeter fences," Julius stated.

She is resourceful, Brett thought, knowing that Severine was the engineer behind the barriers.

The fires had long since burned out. Crumpled, faded pages stuck out from the tips of the wood, and a few had slipped away in the wind. Several of the fences were down, but to Brett's surprise, most of the fortress remained intact.

"Looks like she had herself a regular bonfire," Julius said, brushing past the first perimeter. "The fires must keep the herrerasaurs away – and whatever else lives in these woods..."

Herrerasaurs.

Brett could still feel their savage breath against the hairs of his neck. He was fortunate enough to have escaped again. But the carnivores were still out there somewhere in the jungle, and in a few hours, they might return for a second round. The image of the alpha-male lurking behind the pine trees ingrained itself in his mind. He would never forget the blood-red eyes.

Those cruel, red, reptilian eyes.

He tried to form a picture of what happened the night before, after the ambush. From the impressions along the ground, it appeared that Severine had survived the initial attack, set up a defensive barrier long enough to survive the night, and departed the following morning. At some point, the indigenous people caught her trail and stalked her as she went westward along the gorge.

But did she escape or elude them someh—

"Shit, that's bright!" Brett said, shielding his eyes with his hand.

The sun glimmered off metal and blinded them. The shining object was low to the ground, catching the orange rays through the thick branches.

"Oh, hell," Julius sighed, swallowing hard. "It's him."

Jordy.

Sometime in their absence, the machine's batteries had failed, and the bot lay face down in the dampened dirt. In the turmoil preceding the night before, Brett had forgotten all about the robot and its rapidly depleting battery cell life. From the lack of glowing utility lights, he guessed that the bot finally succumbed to the swamp water.

After they turned the machine over on its back, Brett confirmed his speculation.

Jordy was dead.

The dim panels were cold to the touch, and the inside was quiet, refusing to reboot from the motion detector. From behind the heavy film of mud that clothed the artificial face, the eyelids stared past them, out into the Triassic sky.

"Rest in peace, little guy," Julius said, cradling the head.

"It happened sometime last night," Brett added. "Seems that way, based on his cold temperature."

The water was certainly the cause of death. The bot's armor didn't have any new claw marks from the herrerasaur attack. The lack of wounds told him that Severine's fire fences were successful in scaring off the dinosaurs.

"You think we should leave him here?" Brett asked.

"We don't have a choice," Julius replied. "We don't have the luxury of burying him. We need to find the others."

Others...

Brett nodded gravely.

Paluch and Severine were still missing.

After analyzing the campsite, Brett found little hope that the technician was alive. There were no traces of Francis Paluch around the plateau, except for remnants of his Triassic field manual that Severine repurposed for the fire perimeter. And the only indents on the ground belonged to Severine and Jordy.

"You think he made it?"

"I think we owe it to check. The attack took place just through these trees, right? Maybe a hundred yards in? It's worth a quick look..."

And a quick look was all they needed.

Paluch's eviscerated entrails littered the trail like a gory art masterpiece. They first found the traces in small red pools that the herreras discarded after leaving the area. Then the organs began to appear. Some were hidden below the undergrowth. Others were slung over branches as if thrown forcefully from the body.

The numbing smell of death began to waft through the trees.

"Here he is," Julius said, parting away the leafy fronds.

Francis Paluch was lying face up on the ground. In the day that passed, animals had scourged the remains. The hum of the insects circled the torso where most of the initial feeding had occurred. Paluch's skull looked bashed in and indented from the crushing weight of herrerasaur jaws.

"They got him."

Julius lurched forward and threw up, stepping back from the thick odor that clung like a fungus to the path.

"I was pulling for him," he said, wiping his mouth. "We got off on the wrong foot, him and I. But he was trying hard to redeem himself. If I had known it'd end like this, I'd have forgiven him earlier..."

The flattened skull stared back at them – a testament to the merciless power of the herreras.

"Severine..." Brett managed. "She could still be out there!"

"You think she's still headed for the *Supernova*?"

"If the hunters didn't catch her first!"

Brett knew they would have to make haste. The trek ahead took them all the way back from where they'd come, following the ravine and back again into the forest to a destination unknown.

About two miles from the encampment, they caught up with Severine's footsteps along a beautiful rocky overlook. Behind the brush where her steps turned back into the trees, Brett found another startling confession in the dirt under the diminishing sunlight.

Federation tracks. Another set of them...

"Julius. Have a look here, will you? What does that look like to you?"

The lieutenant leaned in, moving his foot into the impression.

"Another survivor! Infantry, by the looks of it. Hell, it's almost my same boot size!"

"He came out of the trees there, and she saw him coming. She was standing over here, probably with the 90 on him. He fell. He was running from something, probably exhausted. Then it looks like, unless I'm reading the tracks wrong, they both went back into the trees. Shortly after, the tribe passed through here and followed them into the jungle. I'm ashamed I didn't catch this when we first came through here. The tracks were very concealed."

They followed the impressions off the gorge, into the shadowy wilderness.

The trails inside the patch of jungle were random and wild. The plants were thorny and dense, making the tracks a chore to follow. Hardened dinosaur feces packed into the ground along the paths, consumed by the undergrowth, but no new matter had formed. The passage was simply too overgrown to use adequately for transportation, even for the animals.

"Why would they come through here?" Julius asked. "It's hot and crowded!"

"They were in a hurry. Maybe they were being followed."

Brett had been wondering the same question. *Why wouldn't they keep going down the river, where the plateau provided an easy method of travel? Or simply drop down into the river? The water wasn't as chaotic at that point, and not deep enough to drown easily.*

The many unanswered questions deeply troubled him.

She has to be alive. I know it! She's out here...

The thicket suddenly gave way to a small opening.

A clearing opened in the forest, bordered with walls of ferns on the edges and blocked at the far end by a large, rocky precipice. In the shadows that coated the ground, they saw the tracks stop short at the base of the boulders. From the outskirts, many other footprints materialized from the greenery, trapping the two Federation imprints to the center.

"This is where it happened," Brett said, stepping through the opening.

"What? What happened, Ambrose?" Julius asked urgently.

"The attack," he replied. "They ambushed Severine! Hello, what's this?"

Nestled quietly in between two large stones was a heavily worn and scratched XR-90 pulse rifle. The soft light still shined from the grip.

"Lieutenant, I found your weapon," Brett said, pointing down to the rifle.

"Why didn't they take it?"

"I think it's stuck."

The 90 had fallen in a crevice between the rocks, wedged tightly at an odd angle. Any attempt of dislodging the weapon would be challenging.

"She never fired a shot."

"How can you tell?" Julius asked.

"Look at the trees, the rocks. There's no pulse blast residue anywhere."

He scanned the clearing for any trace of dimming glows or charred circular blast marks, but saw nothing. Instead, Brett caught something more sinister on the dirt under their feet. Beside the criss-crossing sudden footsteps and Severine's body impression sat a large rock, stained in drying blood.

No!

He dropped to his knees.

"What? Ambrose!"

A stinging sensation welled up inside Brett's gut. It was a strange, surreal feeling. One that he couldn't remember feeling in recent years. Not since his time spent in space, on the *Supernova*. He couldn't take his eyes off the rock.

"She was struck! With this..."

"What are you saying? She's dead?"

Brett wasn't so sure. The surrounding footprints that lined the trail were very telling. His eyes began to trace their movements. The larger pair suddenly shifted at a certain point, with speed that left a ripple mark in the soil. The blood from the rock was found there too, soaked into the ground in a thick, hardened syrup. The red droplets began in Severine's outline and ended over the rocks where the 90 had fallen.

"He hit her!"

"Our mystery man?"

Brett gave a firm nod.

"It was a blindside! She had no time to defend herself. He led her through that mess of jungle, knowing that it would be impossible to double back, trapping her in the clearing. When he got her here, they held out against these rocks before he made his move. Then he hit her with the rock when she had her gun on the hunters."

"Why would he hit her?" Julius gave a confused smirk. "He's Federation infantry. They might have even served together."

"She knew him – I'm certain of it! Why else would she go into the jungle with him?"

Julius sat down on the rocks, trying to come up with an answer.

"Maybe he just found the suit?"

"What do you mean?"

"Well, after we came out of the hyper-sleep pods, before we linked up with you, we encountered a Federation infantry suit discarded in the jungle, on the outskirts of the crash site. I'm just thinking. Maybe it wasn't a Federation crew member that had been wearing it at all, but maybe one of the hunters, in one of our suits."

"Like a disguise?"

"Exactly."

"You're thinking they found one of the suits and fooled her into walking into a trap?"

"That's what this looks like to me, Ambrose."

The lieutenant's theory made surprising sense. If there were other unused Federation suits lying around, it seemed probable that eventually this mysterious tribe would happen to come across one and figure out how to wear it for their advantage.

"What about the language? They surely can't speak English. How could she not discern the difference between these people and a Federation soldier?"

The lieutenant shrugged. That question had him stumped.

Something still wasn't adding up. Suddenly an obvious fact that previously eluded them slipped into Brett's mind as he studied the ground for answers – a fact that gave him a glimmer of hope.

The body...

"Where's the body?"

Severine's corpse was nowhere in the vicinity.

"It's not here," Julius replied.

"Exactly! Look here. Up that side of the slope – blood drag marks. They didn't leave her here, like they did with the men they slaughtered back at the waterfall! For some reason, they took her with them."

A thin trail of blood danced up the stones and shrank under the darkened leaves. The tribe had knocked her unconscious, but instead of killing her, chose to keep her alive.

They've taken her back to their lair. Wherever that is...

"Let's go! We're losing the light. Lots of miles to catch up on..."

I'm not gonna let her die!

Brett was hopeful again, and knew if they hurried, he may have a chance to rescue her. The years of his exile in the jungle had robbed him of their relationship, and a pack of tribal lunatics wasn't going to extend that timeline any longer.

He started up the hill when he heard the lieutenant's booming voice again.

"Ambrose!" Julius yelled. "Hey, what's this?"

Brett turned down.

In the moss that held tightly to the boulder, a golden rectangle sparkled happily in the orange rays that gleamed down through the canopy. The shape looked pristine and new – clearly of human origin. It was a tiny treasure, no more than two inches in width and less than an inch tall.

Brett scooped up the plaque and focused on the micro printing. The sharp, black lettering was very legible. It was a Federation Infantry identification tag, commonly found attached on armor suits.

Marcus Davenport
Sergeant – Federation Infantry
Supernova
Passenger Account 294

Julius looked at the plaque.

"I think we've found our soldier," he said. "Marcus Davenport. I think I remember him. You have any rope in that pack?"

"Yes, sir."

"Good – give it here. Should be able to get that 90 out of the rocks. Then we're heading into the woods. If we get a fire going, the herrerasaurs shouldn't be an issue anymore. We'll need all night to make up the distance."

Brett smiled, digging out the rope.

Severine was alive. He was sure of it.

And he was determined to save her.

XXV

Severine was awakened by the splashing of footsteps, somewhere close but not in her immediate sight. Her body and arms were covered in scratches from thorns. She had been dragged and carried through the jungle. The Federation armor suit had been removed, and she was left in her original hyper-sleep garments. Her brain throbbed behind her disheveled hair. Itchy, crude bandaging was wrapped over her head and around one eye, reminding her of Paluch after his encounter with the coelophysis.

She struggled to regain her thoughts, retracing the sequence of events that played out back in the wilderness.

Davenport! That son of a bitch!

The sergeant had led her into a trap, revealing himself to be in league with the native hunters. Now she was stuck here in some dark, dank place, awaiting his imminent return.

Where the hell is this place?

She hung by her arms in a standing position, tied to an unseen pillar that supported her from behind. A pair of ropes coiled around her wrists and disappeared above in the absence of light. An identical pair encircled her ankles, scratching into her skin.

A bunker, maybe? Some kind of fallout shelter?

The space was dimly lit by a pair of torches that bordered the open doorway to her front, which led to a corridor that ran in both directions. Her surroundings were muted by the darkness, but she could sense the chamber was experiencing water problems. Mold and fungus clumps formed along the floor and ascended the walls. Above, the ventilation system dripped clouded fluids to the marble tiles below. In the light of the torches, she could see the broken grout seams were filling with water.

She tried to shrug off the noxious fungal fumes.

This wretched cave must be their den.

Splashing continued in the hallway outside the flooding quarters. Shadows began to dance along the walls outside the door. Her head fumed when she heard Davenport's voice coming down the passages.

Severine wished she had her 90. Hell, even the 20 would do. Either would suffice in killing her captors. As the figures loomed through the doorway, she tried to push her hardened soldier feelings of revenge aside and knew it might go easier for her if she camouflaged with a softer side.

You bastard...

Marcus Davenport appeared with two hunters carrying torches and shields. They guarded him tightly from both sides. She saw that his appearance had changed with subtle differences.

Along his forehead sat a strange looking crown of sharpened white tusks. Severine thought they looked like dinosaur teeth. A similar necklace was draped across his throat. His face was smeared with red paint – or blood. He was still wearing the infantry armor.

"You're not worthy enough to wear that suit," Severine said, spitting up blood. "You're disgraceful – a traitor to the Federation and all it stands for."

Davenport turned back to his guards and muttered something in an unknown native tongue. The natives replied with similar sounds and left the chamber immediately, their torch light dissipating into the darkening hall.

"Sorry," he said in her own language. "I had to bring them along to make sure you were still down here. Federation transplants have been tricky in the past. It reassures me to bring guards along when I feel uneasy."

Davenport produced a hidden chair that had been lying in shadow and drew it close to Severine, before taking a seat. She noticed that he had been cautious enough not to place the chair within her reach.

"Why don't you come a little closer?" she taunted, fidgeting angrily in her ropes.

He laughed.

"I've made that mistake before."

Cocky prick...

"Well, it's never too late to try again."

His smirk faded.

"What happened to you?" she asked.

The sergeant looked up, perplexed by the question and struggling to respond. In this dark room, he now seemed older. The crown made him look like a different man, taking on an entirely new persona.

"Severine, I've never *actually* met you before."

Never met me?

"You were a sergeant on *Supernova*. I've seen you! You've commanded my squad before."

The sergeant smiled menacingly. Severine suddenly had doubts of who she was talking to.

This isn't Davenport...

"I've actually heard your words a lot over the years. More often now, we get your kind, coming out from the old pods. Sometimes when we catch them, they'll assume that I'm Marcus Davenport, which I've used as a ruse to lure them here, when in reality, I'm not that man at all. I'm Davenport IV. The original Marcus Davenport, the man whom you knew well, was my ancestor."

As the words came from his mouth, it suddenly seemed obvious. This man was a relative of the sergeant she had served under years ago. Wincing at the sharp pain on her forehead, she cringed as he continued his treacherous folklore.

"My great-great grandfather, the man you knew as Davenport, survived the crash, along with a hundred others. The early times in this world were challenging for our ancestors. There were power struggles and chances to seize power over the colony. In the years preceding the crash, Marcus Davenport led a revolt and claimed leadership over the survivors. He ruled with an iron fist, cutting off the tongues of those who challenged his rule. Over time, our language became forgotten, taught only to me by my father. The others speak another tongue, one that our people created in our time in this forsaken world. Now that more of the original Federation soldiers are waking up from their pods, I've been instructing the guards to seal off various wings of our ship – our home. The home of the Davenport Colony."

The Davenport Colony...

Severine remembered the doors to the command bridge that were sealed from the inside, and the rubble that had been hastily piled against the walls. Since the catastrophe that happened in outer space rendered the door locked from the inside, Davenport's soldiers weren't able to get inside and check on her quadrant, and probably sealed it as a precaution.

They didn't realize my pod was in there all along. They couldn't get through the door, and if we hadn't found Jordy, I probably would've died in there. Shit, this room is somewhere in the Supernova!

"We're in the ship?"

She wondered why her group didn't encounter the tribe after they broke out of the bridge.

"Yes," he smiled. "This is the western wing of the ship! For years, our kind has patrolled these halls, waiting for the remaining pods to open. But it's a big ship. Many of the interior chambers are dark and difficult to access. You can imagine the problems that has caused. I've had many guards get lost in the hull, never to be seen again..."

"So, you've been searching the *Supernova* for years, trying to find and kill all the original crew when their pod batteries finally give out?"

The tyrant nodded.

"We retrieve all the Federation weapons when we find some that still work. Most are useless and drained of power unless they were properly stored in the right compartments. Your rifle would have made a fine addition for my armory if it didn't fall into the rocks. I keep the functional pulse weapons in a guarded armory. Over time, our family taught the others to fear the weapons of the future. If they find any, they are required to surrender it to the armory. Spears and torches are all they wish to use, and it's proven very advantageous for me. As for your original question, we don't kill *all* the survivors."

"No?"

"No. The men are killed outright, just like your two friends will be when we find them."

Brett and Julius! No...

"The males are usually problems that need to be dealt with swiftly. They often kill my hunters – like my second-in-command that your team killed at the waterfall! When we find them, they are exterminated, and their bodies carried to the northern grave by the river as a sacrifice to the water monsters. Over the years, we've managed to catch hundreds of male colonists that come out of the pods. Personally, under my rule, I've caught at least thirty."

She frowned, praying that her friends would survive.

"And the women?"

"The women are given a choice – a very simple one. Succumb to the tribe and assimilate into our culture and way of life. Become a surrogate for our people. Bear our future generations, and my children."

What?

She turned white. The thought of being touched and fondled by these simian Federation descendants made her gag.

"You're joking?"

"I never joke!" he roared. "Those are my demands. Be my queen. Help me carry on the Davenport rule by raising our children."

"You'd be better off killing me," she retorted.

"You may be surprised. I have ways of convincing your kind…"

With a swift dash forward, he was against her, caressing her face with his cold, callused hand. Severine breathed heavily, straining to turn her head away as Davenport's palm fell down her cheek and slid down her neck and shoulder. His breath felt cruel and harsh, hitting her strongly as his face pressed against her.

"And if I refuse?" she mustered.

"What?" Davenport asked, confused.

"If I refuse? To be your queen…"

He frowned angrily, and to her relief, turned away and backed up.

"Your refusal will mean death!" he yelled. "You will be sacrificed to our goddess, the great Gretta. That's why I've come! I'm here for you to make your choice and live forever by my side in glory. With your knowledge of the Federation's past, we'll rule the tribe and forge a new, stronger civilization."

Severine wanted to plead and persuade him otherwise to buy more time, but she knew her attempts would be useless. This culture was horrendous and brutal. She witnessed it first-hand at the waterfall and again in the jungle. Perhaps honesty might grant her a quick death, and she could finally be at peace – be home.

"Sacrifice me!" she yelled in anger. "I won't be your queen!"

"Are you sure?" his brooding voice asked.

She nodded, spitting blood at his feet.

"I'm sure, you bastard. Take me to your god and get it over with."

He was fuming now. In the darkness of the room, she could faintly see his face turning red. "I strongly suggest you reconsider. You don't know the pain that awaits beyond those walls – and you don't want to know…"

She repeated herself.

"I. Will. Never. Be. Your. Queen."

His cold eyes locked with hers – confirming her fate.

Davenport turned and barked a command in the strange tribal language. Responses from the guards returned from down the hall, and a squad of the savages stormed through the door.

The first guard drew a dagger and sliced off her upper and lower ropes, briefly releasing the tension that latched onto her body. Under knife-point, new bounds were coiled around her wrists. Once her fresh bindings were secure, they stepped back, awaiting the command of their leader.

"Follow me!" he said. "I'll give you a beautiful death. The glorious death you and your Federation soldiers dream of."

Go to hell, she thought.

He led them towards the door as his guards urged her onward. Her feeble legs had fallen asleep, which made obeying their commands problematic. They didn't give her a chance to collect herself, but instead prodded her with the pikes.

Torches blinded her as another escort awaited in the hall. With a shove, she was pushed to her left and led down the darkened corridor. The floor was indented from years of falling ceiling rubble. Algae and aquatic plants climbed out from the murky pools that lined the far-left side of the hall, and she recalled that the ship was tilted at a funny angle.

Davenport IV led her past many strange pictographs that had been painted on the walls. The old *Supernova* icons and map information images had been smeared over with gunky residue, depicting ancient scenes of battle and strife. Human icons waged war with one another and at other times hid or even worshiped the orange dinosaurs. The Federation symbols had been painted over with those hideous words.

The Davenport Tribe.

This twisted civilization was right under her nose from the start, while she was suspended in hyper-sleep.

These areas of the ship had no power, much unlike her quadrant where Julius and Jordy were trapped. There were no glowing compartment capsules where the pulse weapons were held. Many of the rooms they passed were dark, lit only by torches and converted to makeshift apartments for the hunters. As she was herded past, many curious eyes watched in excitement. Several of the men even came out and followed her.

Stay the hell away from me!

The beat of nearby drums shifted her focus.

THUM! THUM! THUM!

Davenport led the party down a set of crumbling utility steps that emptied before large, glossy doors. The Federation F logos had been replaced by Davenport's crude artistry. The edges of the doors were smeared with blood. Severine recognized what the entrance used to be.

It's the infantry briefing room!

The room was where the admiral or higher-ranking officers or generals gave their speeches to the infantry. The harsh red smears made her fearful of what awaited behind the doors. The drumming continued behind the barrier.

THUM! THUM! THUM!

As Severine struggled to kick and push away, she was clubbed on the back of her head and saw stars as she was caught from falling forward. She sighed, confused at the sudden pain, but knew she had been hit as a warning. Next time, she would be knocked unconscious.

With a commanding knock, Davenport struck the doors, which quickly swung open by his constituents. The blinding daylight shocked Severine as the Triassic sun filled the room. The guards pushed her into the opening with their spear tips. As her eyes focused, she temporarily forgot where she was.

It used to be the briefing room...

The same ruin that befell the cargo bay had also plagued this area. The walls were collapsing on multiple sides, and the ceiling had crumbled to the ground long ago. The farthest perimeter was sealed off by a large, retractable, wooden door that she guessed Davenport ordered the tribe to construct for defense against the dinosaurs. Ahead was a large balcony area that led to a catwalk, where at one time Federation speakers would address spectators that stood below in the conference area. The horrific sight at the rear of the balcony caught her eye.

Gretta?

Sitting atop a mound of ancient *Supernova* rubble and withered artifacts was a constructed throne made of wood. A bleach white skeleton sat on the throne, looking out forever at the ruined walls of the briefing room and the sky above that baked down on the skull. The idol was surrounded by precious artifacts and shiny Federation treasures, like fuel canisters and metallic Federation currency coins. Over the throne, painted lettering hung on a wooden plank in Severine's native language.

Here sits Davenport I, Ruler and Creator of our laws. The leader of the revolt and the bringer of peace. May he watch over us always. May his authority and wisdom be forever with us in the world of the dinosaurs.

Marcus Davenport.

Her dead comrade sat alone on his perch.

If that's not Gretta...

Hordes of the tribe had already congregated, snickering and leering at her as she was prodded along. She ducked as spear tips were cast carelessly close to her head as her enemies began to chant wickedly. The drums continued to bang and echo through the chamber.

THUM! THUM! THUM!

"Get off me, you shit!" she yelled as one of the grunts approached and took hold of her. She tried to kick him away, but two others rushed and subdued her with more ropes. Suddenly she was on the narrow catwalk and fastened onto a strange medieval wooden device.

Dammit. This can't be good...

She was spun around to face the balcony and the savage army that looked back at her. The cruel drum had stopped, and the arena grew silent.

"My daughter," Davenport began. He took a spot next to his mummified ancestor, at the foot of the shrine. "Do you wish to reject your destiny in this world? Do you choose death over life? Life with our people? Life inside the safety of the Davenport Tribe?"

She spat blood onto the catwalk, struggling to catch a complete view of the army. It was strenuous to stare with one eye covered behind the gauze, but from what she saw, there couldn't have been more than a hundred of them.

This is where it ends...

She was suddenly calm.

"Go to hell!" she yelled. "Kill me! Kill me and live forever in this shit hole, for all I care."

She spat again.

He nodded to the drummer, who set up his instruments on the other side of the idol. With a flick of his fingers, he issued to continue the execution.

WHAT THE HELL?

Suddenly, her body jerked backwards, as the contraption swung her over the catwalk. The ropes ate away at her wrists and arms as she was lowered slowly to the ground far below. Her skin burned and ached, and she could hear herself screaming above the loud pounding of the drums.

Severine could see the horde cheering and raving on the balcony above. She spun backwards, just as the massive wooden door opened, spilling more light into the room. Below, foul smelling organs and porous bone fragments littered the ground among the overgrown, collapsed roofing materials.

What is this place?

A pair of hunters churned away at a wheel on the side of the balcony, cranking open a pulley system that opened the heavy entrance. After the structure was fully opened and the door was resting on the ground, the drumming and primitive cries from the tribe ceased. The contraption above stopped lowering her.

The rope hurt like hell.

Now what?

Then the terrible horns started.

BRAWWWRRRRRRRR!

The cursed sound consumed the room.

BRAWWWWWWLLLRRRRR!!!

Silence followed.

Then a slow grumble began pouring out from the jungle just beyond the doorway. It started as a low reverberation. Severine thought it might be another strange instrument playing outside in the woods. A flash of orange with red stripes bounding behind the outlying ferns quickly changed her mind – the same orange she witnessed in the northern jungle.

SHIT!

The alpha-male herrerasaur exploded through the thicket, racing into the briefing room ruins toward the catwalk.

But it wasn't a male dinosaur at all. It was the Davenport goddess.

Gretta!

#

In the sunny foliage outside the hangar, Brett and Julius viewed in horror as the herrerasaur entered the hangar, watching Severine's body writhe and bend to avoid the dinosaur's snapping jaws. The indigenous crowd snickered and cheered, pounding the catwalk with their spear butts. The soldier known as Davenport watched intently from the center balcony, smiling down at the morbid event.

"How many rounds left?" Brett asked impatiently.

"Six," Julius replied. "Not enough to take down all of them..."

The 90 had a large hole in the back of the grip, where Brett's arrow had pierced it. Tying a rope to the end of the arrow, they pulled the pulse rifle out from the rocks. Julius was relieved to find that the arrow hadn't damaged any of the weapon's firing components.

We don't have much time...

He studied the setting. Around the rubble that surrounded the throne of the tribe's dead king, Brett spotted a series of familiar objects.

Federation refueling cell canisters.

"Aim for those! The cell canisters. Can you hit one from here?"

"As long as none of the humans get in the way..."

Julius raised the 90 and guided the sight over to the orange objects. Severine fought hard and kicked at the herrerasaur as the hunters continued to slowly lower her down. Brett clung to the key-card that hung down from his neck on a lanyard.

There's only one chance to save her.

XXVI

The herrera reached the base of the catwalk, circling several yards below as Severine dangled helplessly over the monster. Gretta snapped her vicious jaws at her feet. She would have to be spry to survive.

Bonded by ropes that continued to wither away at her wrists, she did her best to swing upward and sideways, trying to dance around the deadly smile that awaited underneath. *Supernova's* briefing room had turned into a horrific coliseum: A place where dissenters were sacrificed to the herrerasaurs for entertainment. It was a scene so surreal that, for a moment, she thought it was a dream that her mind had created during hyper-sleep.

"Go away!" she yelled, kicking at the creature's snout that sniffed rabidly at her feet.

Don't panic! Don't panic!

Without her armor suit, the attack would be over quickly if she didn't carefully plan her movements. The animal was ferocious with hunger. It circled and leaped beneath her, roaring before each attack.

SRRRRRR!

With a mighty jump, the carnivore's teeth slashed over her leg, tearing her garments and leaving a burning red slice from her thigh to her calf.

"*Aghh!*"

Severine screamed as the dinosaur's claws tore down her leg.

She bit her lip so hard that it went numb.

Happy vocals from the spectators erupted from the balcony. The hunters waved their spears and torches with sinister fascination at the terrible event unfolding in the arena. Their yelps and war cries made focusing on Gretta even more distracting.

The dinosaur growled and gave another sudden leap upwards.

Her heart stopped.

No!

The claws slashed at her back as she coiled her feet quickly, putting additional strain on her abdomen. Severine felt a small, cold pain nip at her shoulder, but not enough to end the event. As her feet dropped down, she was forced to pull them back up again as Gretta gave a sudden jump.

Another jolt of pain sliced at her shoulder.

Ahhh!

She could feel her teeth grinding together.

Gravity pulled her legs down and she struggled to catch her breath. Lifting her thighs again and pulling herself up was out of the question.

The next jump from the dinosaur would kill her. Her strength had left. The rubbing of the ropes on her flesh burned – she felt as if her hands would fall off. The blood from her thighs had coated the dinosaur's head in red. She felt lightheaded.

Severine looked up to the fractured ship ceiling, preparing for a final blow from the herrera to finish her off. She let out a final sigh, sagging from the rope and looking down at the dinosaur through her sweaty, knotted hair.

Gretta was staring up at her.

The red eyes were locked. The dinosaur craved her flesh, just like it wanted her back in the wilderness.

Severine tried to harness any reserve strength that she had left, but found none.

"Do it," she managed.

The will to live had left her.

She closed her eyes, waiting for teeth to mangle her waist and saliva to saturate her torn flesh.

It didn't come.

Instead, a violent hiss rang out, echoing throughout the chamber.

SSSSSHHHHHHHHOOOOM!

Then the earth shook, and she felt her body dangling violently from the rope.

Severine opened her eyes in time to catch a bright shock wave sailing over her head. The catwalk above exploded, dispersing support fragments in all directions.

The rope snapped, sending her free falling to the arena below.

Severine crashed into the dirt, covering herself in a fetal position. She could hear rubble and fragments from the balcony crashing around her. As the majority of the structure above collapsed, screams from the savages howled through the coliseum. Some sounded as if they were falling too, before landing with loud impacts in the dirt.

When she didn't feel Gretta's wrath tearing into her, she uncurled and was back on defense. In her mind, she tried to understand what had just happened, but kept her eyes on her surroundings. Piecing together her escape would have to wait until later.

Have to find a way out...

She could feel her blood rushing back to her head.

Around her, body parts of the Davenport tribe littered the ground, coating the concrete with a red sauce. Many other hunters had been thrown into the briefing room floor around her, crying in their primitive language. She saw many of their limbs had snapped from the force of the fall. After they realized what had happened, they shrieked as their cruel god pounced.

Gretta wasted no time.

The dinosaur began ripping apart the wounded warriors that had the displeasure of landing in the battle zone. Moving among them, the monster tore them apart swiftly, moving from one helpless human to the next in a vicious, ritualistic killing. The natives put up no fight, refusing to combat their god. But as the jaws clamped down over their heads, their muted screams struggled to escape the monster's deadly grasp.

Above, Severine saw the remaining savages on the catwalk screaming and scrambling for an exit, fleeing out of the briefing room entrance on the balcony. Most of them were heavily wounded from the blast – a few were killed, lying along the remaining support platforms. The shrine in the middle was destroyed and Davenport was nowhere to be seen.

In the chaotic confusion, Severine crawled away, looking for something sharp to cut her bindings. Her hands were still knotted behind the torn rope. The explosion had opened a brief glimmer of an escape, but only for a moment.

Have to hide...

Gretta would soon run out of natives to pick off. Behind her, the awful sounds of the prowling dinosaur commenced, followed by the dying shrieks of her worshiping victims.

In the rocks ahead, a small tribal dagger stuck out from the filth – a way out of the rope knots.

Yes!

Her hands clasped down on the handle. She whipped the blade into the ropes and quickly tore them apart. Her wrists thanked her briefly, but soon began to throb from the scars.

BRMMM! BRMMM! BRMMM!

A series of additionally loud footsteps clattered over the concrete in the arena.

Oh no...

She turned. In the massive wall opening behind Gretta, more herrerasaurs began to spill into the ruined coliseum, drawn in by the demolition of the catwalk blast. She saw more dinosaurs here than when they first encountered the pack in the jungle. The carnivores blocked her escape into the wilderness. She would have to find another way out.

Damn.

The dinos soon found their victims, pouncing on the nearest hunters that landed farther out from the balcony, near the edge of the stadium.

Okay. Calm. Stay calm! Find an exit...

Part of the balcony near the center catwalk had collapsed, and a crooked railing hung down from above like a bent ladder.

That's it!

She had to be quick. The herrerasaurs were running out of targets behind her, and Gretta was still dangerously close. Sprinting to the first railing, she started the long climb back up to the top. Fragments of the structure were ablaze with small fires from the shock wave, forcing her to ascend more cautiously.

Above, she could hear various grunting barks from remaining savages as they fought to put out the fires and reconstruct the Davenport skeletal shrine. On the ground beneath, Gretta had reached the base of the railing, devouring the final wounded hunter that awaited the coming doom. With a quick chomp of the jaws, Gretta latched around the man's waist. Blood flew from his mouth as the jaws crunched down across his abdomen. Severine turned and continued to climb as the sounds of the hunter's mauling faded.

That was almost me, she thought. Gretta surely would have snatched her up next.

Time was still running out. There was enough debris against one of the walls for the herreras to ascend the rubble and arrive on the balcony – and then the rest of the *Supernova*.

Finally! The top...

She tossed a hand over the industrial braces at the summit of the rail ladder, pulling herself up to what remained of the overlook platforms. The floor was hot with the blast residue, forcing her to rise quickly to her feet and avoid the melting rivets.

Much of the balcony was empty and abandoned after the crowds fled from the explosion. Near the ruins of the catwalk, two hunters searched the rubble for the ancient Davenport shrine that was lost in the blast. Fortunately, their spears were on the ground, and their backs were turned.

Getting past them was her ultimate goal. The dinosaurs below would soon make their way onto the balcony. Her only hope was to retreat further into the ship ruins and sneak out through one of the tears in the hull. If the hunters saw her, they would kill her – or worse – toss her back down to Gretta's vicious pack.

She knew these men would have to die. There was no way around it.

Sorry.

Adrenaline flowed through her head and back, fueled by revenge as she regained the will to survive. She felt like a soldier again, but this time, it wasn't a drill or war-time simulation.

This will work!

A broken iron rod sat on the ground ahead. Her fingers closed around it tightly, feeling the weight of the object.

She moved along the platform silently and snuck up behind the first of the natives as the man searched through the debris.

CRACKKKKKKK!

The rod crushed down on the first man's skull from behind, sending him to his knees while he convulsed from a deadly brain hemorrhage. As the dying hunter struck the overlook floor, the second turned in horror, trying to reach for his spear.

CRACKK!

When he turned for the weapon, Severine's rod slammed down on his spine. He yelped in pain, raising his hands in defense as he turned to face her. He pleaded in their foreign language for his life, but when she saw his hand still searching for the weapon, Severine wasn't convinced.

CRACCKKKKK!

The rod swung right across his face, breaking his jaw and rendering him a vegetable. His eyes bulged in terror as his body tumbled over the ledge, down to the herrera feast.

Severine breathed in relief.

The balcony was now empty, and the hallway back to the tribal section of the ship loomed ahead.

How many more savages were waiting for me in there?

There wasn't any time left to wait. Gretta and her pack were leaping onto the balcony fragments and climbing quickly, searching for new sources of nourishment.

Those things don't quit!

She bolted from her position, keeping the iron rod at her front for defense as she ran through the catwalk entrance.

To her surprise, the hallway inside was empty. She quickly pulled the doors to the briefing room shut, but couldn't figure out how to lock them.

That should hold them for a little...

But not for long. She darted into a side hallway that led deeper into the hull of the *Supernova.*

The ship was eerily quiet. The only sound she could hear was the faint crackling of fire back in the coliseum that quickly melted apart as she progressed through the halls.

Still no natives...

She expected one of the crazed humans to jump from their dorms and swing at her, but the rooms she passed were empty. Far away, she heard weeping in one of the parallel hallways. She assumed a large portion of their tribe was injured from the blast and had taken shelter somewhere deeper in the interior of the ship.

What was that blast? The fuel-cells?

She shook off the thought as an approaching shadow approached from the oncoming corner, prompting her to raise the iron rod.

Davenport? Come on you son of a bi –

A native boy appeared, dressed in a dirty loincloth and soaked in someone's blood.

He looked up at Severine as he ran by, taking no interest in her as he shuffled past. His eyes were searching for something in the rooms that lined the corridor.

Probably his parents...

He soon disappeared down the opposite hall that Severine had entered from. His steps in the puddles echoed farther away until they ceased entirely, leaving her alone once again.

She turned and continued her slow, defensive journey, searching for an exit that led out to the jungle. That was her only chance to escape this nightmare.

The hell is this?

She crossed through another set of doors at the end of the passageway and arrived in another Davenport-decorated room.

It was something of a hall of fame art museum.

The room was bright, lit by sunlight that passed through a window covered by green slime high above. She recognized the area as an old *Supernova* access hallway, where crew members could socialize and converse before their shifts began.

This corridor was more sterile than the previous rooms and held a position of importance among the tribe. The marble floors were meticulously clean and scrubbed, although many were crumbling and falling apart. Busts of ancient Davenport heroes and rulers lined the edges of the room on wooden pedestals, chiseled and polished from rock. The statue of the first Davenport, the man Severine knew from three hundred years earlier, was erected at the far end. The sculptor had perfected the intricate details of the Federation suit and subtle skin imperfections. The bust bore a stark similarity to the rest of the Davenport descendants that were erected around him.

To her rear, a native scream rang out in the dark, coming from the direction of the briefing room. Suddenly the bloodcurdling echo was cut short.

Gretta… The herreras are inside the ship!

Ahead, just above the far Davenport statue, a wooden sign hung over an open entrance, leading into a dark room. The words on the plank read:

Davenport Armory

Perfect!

She ran through the shrines, crossing by the glorious Davenport statue, and passed through the archway.

In the dark room, shelves of weaponry materialized under the glow of overhead torches. From what she could see, there were rows of spears, clubs, knives, shields, and torch wood. She knew the room well. At one time, it had been a weapons' depot for the Federation Infantry.

Now, where are those pulse weapons?

A shrouded object flew towards her face.

PHEWWWW!

What!

She fell to her knees as a spear rod passed swiftly over her head. The pike struck a rack of weapons, spilling knives and shields over the floor in a series of loud clangs.

A native guard had been hiding in the room.

Whoa!

Severine crawled backwards as her attacker began to jab and thrust the weapon towards her face. His cruel silhouette stood out against the torchlight from above. The gleam of the spear was dangerously close. Something had to change – fast.

She swung her rod around and blocked an attack, sending the spear out of the hunter's hairy hands. As the weapon fell to the floor, Severine's hands felt a cold device lying on the ground. By the feel of the grip, she identified the object without having to look.

An X2-20!

She didn't wait to check if the pistol was loaded. She pointed the sight at the hunter, who had just recovered his weapon. The trigger squeezed back, and Severine saw the golden pulse beam fly out of the barrel and pass through the man's sweaty scalp. The blast entered between the eyes and disappeared through the ceiling, almost burning through one of the torches.

As the deceased native dropped to the cold marble floor, Severine rose back to her feet and turned around.

There, at the rear of the armory, was a treasure trove of XR-90s, X2-20s, and Federation detonator compartments. They were piled neatly inside preservation canisters that emitted green confirmation lights, indicating that the weapons were in a usable condition.

This is terrific!

She staggered over to the boxes and unlocked a large one at the top, staring down at an active XR-90 pulse rifle, fully charged, with all 90 rounds intact. She quickly shouldered the weapon and opened another box to the side, tossing away the lid.

Detonators lined the insides of the compartment, cushioned with felt padding that neatly separated each grenade. Severine's hands clasped down on a handful, setting the explosives in an old backpack that she found on an adjacent table.

Tired and bruised from Gretta's attacks, she ripped off a tattered cloth from an old tunic that was sitting nearby, and wrapped it over the scars as a temporary bandage. As she tied tight knots around each of the bruises, she regained her defensive stance and planned her next move.

Suddenly, survival seemed more likely, and she smiled.

Whatever would come through those doors was going to get a big surprise.

XXVII

It wasn't long before more horrified screams reverberated through the armory. Severine waited behind a weapon stand, aiming the XR-90 at the narrow entrance. The X2-20 was resting nearby on the counter in case her rifle malfunctioned, and she had to quickly switch weapons.

Outside, the quiet *Supernova* ruins had jumped to life.

As the herrerasaurs continued to navigate the ship, she guessed that more natives were forced out of hiding, prompting Gretta's pack to strike. To her surprise, no one had come through the armory doors.

They must not want the weapons...

From what she saw in the arena, Severine assumed that most of the colony refused to strike their goddess, leaving the dinosaurs running amok and unchecked through the ship, dispatching anyone they stumbled across. The herrera pack had grown significantly from the handful that attacked them in the jungle. From what she saw in the briefing room arena, it had nearly doubled in size.

She stiffened her grip on the 90 as a dinosaur growled far away, followed by distant cries and the running of human feet. Severine knew it wouldn't take long for the tribe to be wiped out. If she waited there long enough, she would just have the carnivores to worry about. She also toyed with the idea of escaping during Gretta's murderous rampage, hoping the dinos would be too preoccupied with the natives to notice her.

I could make it back to the briefing room and slip out through the opening...

CHK! CHK! CHK!

Footsteps were heard in the outer chamber as someone stepped into the room filled with Davenport statues and primitive trophies. It sounded like there may be more than one hunter.

Perhaps three or four of them.

She kept the rifle sight trained to the entrance. It was a clean shot with plenty of cover.

"An armory. Let's check in there?" said one of the intruders.

Severine thought she recognized the voice.

It isn't Davenport, and his army can't speak our language.

Her body relaxed as she saw Brett's handsome face walk through the opening, and she lowered the rifle. Julius was right behind him, watching their rear with the XR-90 that she dropped behind in the jungle when Davenport struck her.

"Hey!" she called out, dropping the weapon and racing to hug them. She hugged Brett first, wrapping her arms tightly around his waist, before doing the same to Julius.

"Shit! Sev, we thought we lost you!" Brett said, hugging her tightly. "That monster almost had your guts for breakfast! We blew up one of the fuel canisters. I'm confident the blast wiped out a good bit of them."

"You two blew up the briefing room?" Severine said. "Why am I not surprised? That blast saved my life."

"Who are they?" Julius asked.

"Marcus Davenport," Severine started, with a hint of revenge. "Remember him?"

Brett nodded. "We found his identification tag in the jungle where they jumped you."

"These people are his descendants – the descendants of *Supernova's* crash survivors. Years after the crash, Davenport led an uprising. After the conflict, he assumed leadership of the crew members. Now, hundreds of years later, his ancestor, the new Marcus Davenport, still rules. His people can't speak our language. I think in the early days, he beat it out of them until they forgot it. Anything he says, they fear – it's his ship now."

"They don't use our weapons?" Julius asked.

"Just spears and torches, really. They're afraid of the pulse firearms. Shit, I'm glad you two showed up when you did! I was almost dinosaur food!"

"We couldn't leave you hanging like that," Julius chuckled, referencing her prior unfortunate predicament in the arena.

"We need to get moving," Brett said. "The herrerasaurs won't stay busy for long! Shit's hitting the fan out there!"

"How do we get out?" Severine asked. "Back to the briefing room?"

"Who said anything about leaving?" he answered. "We're finally back in the ship! This is the closest I've ever been back to the *Supernova* since the *Mudskipper* ejected. My memory's a bit foggy, but I should be able to take us to the mainframe room. This place, it's just so big…hell, it confused me even before we crashed."

Severine nodded.

He's right! We're so close to the mainframe…

"It's changed a lot, Brett," she said. "This side of the ship has been entirely re-fabricated into the tribe's home. Some of the rooms do look familiar, but most are totally different…"

"Well, we're here and we still have the key-card," Julius said. "Right, Ambrose?"

Brett lifted the lanyard victoriously. "Still got it, sir!"

The key-card looked beautiful, spinning underneath the torch light from Brett's fingers.

"Damn! I'm glad to see that," Severine said. "Finding the mainframe room will be difficult. Most of the ship is pretty dark, especially the interior if they haven't set up torch lamps."

"If we can find our way back to the command bridge, we may be able to find another passage that leads right to the emitter…"

"What if we go back to the briefing room, exit the ship, and circle around?" Brett asked. "The ship's pretty big, so it may take a while before we run into the bridge."

"There was a big herd of those dinosaurs out there when we snuck in," Julius replied. "Honestly, I'd rather take my chances in here with the savages. At least we can hide better in the ship!"

"You still think you can get us to the mainframe if we keep to the inside?" Severine asked.

"Should be able to," he answered.

"What are we waiting for?" Julius said. "Let's stock up. I see some weapons cases over here. Sweet – 90s and 20s! And detonators! That's a big plus!" The lieutenant walked over to the Federation section of the armory and began sorting through the weapons cache.

Brett stepped over to Severine, keeping an eye on the armory entrance. The hideous screams continued to echo through the wreckage.

"You all right?" he asked.

"Yeah. Thanks to you guys!"

"Good…"

He slid his hand down her arm softly, his fingertips gliding lovingly down her skin, giving her goosebumps.

His old eyes were gentle and sweet, almost like a caring father figure. Again, the flashbacks from space consumed her. In Brett's younger days, she yearned for him onboard the ship. The damn hyper-sleep still hung to her thoughts, blocking out certain, important pieces. The vision of Brett behind the ice crystal replayed itself: He was banging on the surface, trying to get her attention.

But what did it mean?

She sensed he may be able to fill in some of her gaps when Julius interrupted her memory.

The lieutenant threw Brett an XR-90 and offered him some detonators to store in his backpack. Severine retrieved her X2-20 from the table, holstered it, and joined the others by the armory entrance, tossing aside her romantic thoughts.

"We can't be sure what's waiting for us out there," Julius said. "Stay close. Brett, you're in the lead. Sev and I will be right behind you, watching your back. Move quickly, but quietly. No need to conserve ammunition now, we have full rounds and a ship full of crazies! Any dino or human you see, light em' up, understand?"

"Aye, sir," Brett replied.

"Okay. Let's get to that emitter!"

They slipped through the armory and out through the surreal chamber of Davenport artwork as Brett led them through criss-crossing hallways in the ship's dark interior. Severine could tell by faint directional arrow pictographs on the wall that he was taking them to the command bridge.

Not a minute into the arduous trek, the distant screams commenced again, followed by weeping and labored gasps.

The trio had stumbled upon a dark passage after traveling up a set of stairs. The Davenport depictions on the walls had faded. Severine guessed that they were getting farther away from the tribe's territory in the ship. At the end of the tunnel about twenty paces away, ambient light flooded to the right of the T-intersection as the hall turned sharply in both directions.

"*Aghhhhh!*" called a terrified female voice.

With a shriek, a native woman turned the bend and ran towards them, mumbling prophetic premonitions under her breath. Before she got three steps around the bend, she was sacked from behind by a pursuing young herrerasaur. She collapsed on the corroded marble, face-planting in the moss and fungus as the carnivore bit down from behind. With an abrupt move of the jaws, the dino snapped her neck.

With a flick of her hand, her body froze beneath the hungry monster.

The herrerasaur was surprised by the colonists at the end of the hallway.

"Waste him!" Julius commanded.

A barrage of pulse blasts ripped the beast apart as dissolving body fragments split and blanketed the woman's corpse beneath. The entire event took no more than ten seconds.

"Good hits," Brett confirmed.

SSSHHRRRRR!

"*Whoaaaa!*"

Behind us!

Brett jumped to the right, narrowly avoiding an arrow that sailed past his head.

"To our rear!" Julius yelled. "They're jumping between the doors for cover!"

A company of Davenport followers had been stalking them. Four or five of the archers took cover at the base of the stairwell behind the colonists while a handful of others assumed positions behind rooms that branched off the main passage. Arrows began flying down the hall, embedding swiftly into the marble walls.

The colonists returned fire as they dropped low and hugged the ground. Pulse blasts sailed down the hall, sending two unsuspecting natives splashing into the damp puddles. The savages screeched out commands, reloading their bows and falling back down the stairwell for cover. A fierce conflict for control of the ship had broken out.

"What do you think? Detonators?" Brett asked eagerly with a smirk.

"Sounds good to me!" Severine replied.

"Send them," Julius said.

Good riddance!

Three tiny chrome orbs rolled down the hallway and crashed onto the stairwell. Hissing eruptions spat out sudden glowing shards that indented the walls and hallway. The shock waves were so strong that they brought down the ceiling above the stairs in a deafening avalanche. The native squad failed to avoid the blasts. Severine watched happily as the Davenport hunters were hurled down the stairs. When the sounds of their rolling bodies finished smacking off the stairs, and no further arrows sailed down the passage, Julius suggested they continue.

The interior of the ship was a massively dark maze. The farther they went, the torches on the walls became sparser. As they began to climb another flooding stairwell, the glow from the pistols revealed more fleeing savages climbing the stairs just above.

"They're trying to escape," Brett said. "They're afraid! Should we let them go?"

"And give them a chance to regroup and kill us at the top?" Julius replied. "We need to wipe them out! Bring out the detonators again!"

The footfalls running up the metal stairs picked up their pace at the sounds of the detonators clicking. The savages pushed into each other clumsily, knowing what would soon be tossed up to greet them.

Severine clicked on her detonator.

"All set," she confirmed.

"Good. Kill those bastards, Sev!"

My pleasure!

She tossed up her sphere, making sure it flew high enough that the aftershock wouldn't hit her team far below. Severine took cover with her friends below the doorway to the stairwell as the charge rattled off high above. Cries of grown men careened down the chamber until their figures splattered onto the fractured floor before her eyes.

"Nice hit!" Julius said. "Ambrose, how much farther before we hit the bridge? Or the mainframe, for that matter?"

"We're maybe halfway there," he replied. "Again, everything looks different. I haven't been here in twenty years..."

"Just asking," the lieutenant answered. "Up the stairs?"

"Yeah – all the way to the top! That's the cafeteria on Quadrant C. From there, I think figuring the rest of the way will be a piece of cake!"

Quadrant C. I think I'm starting to remember where we are!

The team scaled the new stairs, cautiously passing over the areas where the pulse goo had formed on the railings and rusted steps. The stairs were cold on Severine's feet. She wished she still had her armor suit, despite how clunky and heavy the damn thing was. Julius pushed one of the native's lifeless forms over the railing as they reached the top, before passing through the floor entrance.

Ahead, a bright room appeared at the end, lit brightly by the natural sunlight above the jungle. A pair of herrerasaurs blocked the entrance, lapping up water near the illuminated opening. At the sound of the colonists' approach, they turned and hissed ferociously.

"I got em'," Severine assured her comrades.

BRRR! BRRR! BRRR!

Severine raised the 90 and dropped the carnivores. The dinosaurs splashed into the water, falling through the large room.

The cafeteria! Shit, what happened?

In an instant, the water flowing through the ship made sense. What she remembered as the cafeteria now sat submerged under a flowing stream, blocked off partially on both sides by crude damns constructed by the Davenport tribe. The runoff water was certainly penetrating the floor vents, meandering throughout the ship and spilling into the lower divisions.

This must be a fairly new problem, probably brought on by the monsoons...

If the small river persisted, the Davenport territory of the ship below would become trapped underwater.

As with the other large rooms they encountered, most of the ceiling was collapsing, leaving piles of wall fragments rising above the flowing current that swept through the room as the water struggled to find an exit. Behind the obstacles on the other side of the cafeteria, Severine saw a pair of eyes watching from behind a fallen ceiling girder – a pair of eyes she identified hatefully.

Davenport!

"Shit, there he is!"

"Who?"

"Davenport!" Severine yelled. "Their leader!"

She raised her pulse rifle, set the firing function to burst, and unloaded furiously on the chieftain's position. Flashes of gold streaked through the room as she dove into the water in an angry pursuit for her enemy. Behind, she could hear Brett and Julius splashing into the river behind her.

"I see him! Behind that structure in the center!" Brett called.

"Take his ass out!" Julius yelled. "Watch out Sev – he's armed!"

A ferocious firefight broke out as Davenport pulled out a 90 and returned fire. A dozen unseen natives emerged from various hiding places, sending a barrage of arrows at the colonists.

They were waiting for us!

"Hit the dirt!" Julius yelled, telling his friends to shield themselves any way that they could.

SHHHHINNGGGG!

A pulse blast from Davenport's 90 zipped by Severine's head. She dropped behind a fallen pillar as more arrows struck her obstacle. To her right, Brett and Julius had dropped down to different positions inside the stream behind similar girders, popping out randomly to return fire. Her enemy was twenty yards away in the water, yelling out orders to his clan as they waded through the brook towards the colonists.

With their single shot bows, they'll be easy to pick off, she thought. *They're pushing forward with no cover...*

She looked down at the rifle, making sure she was still on burst mode, then carefully peered over the girder. Five of the natives were now only yards away, shooting arrows at Brett and Julius.

They had forgotten that Severine had pushed ahead and was dangerously close.

Surprise, assholes!

She popped up and unloaded on the natives, drilling scorching holes into the squad before they sank under the waves and were swept slowly away. The remaining hunters didn't have time to snipe her. Detonators from Brett and Julius splashed below their feet and obliterated their shelters.

With the native forces down, she focused her eyes again on Davenport. She found him near the back of the cafeteria, splashing out of the waves, taking cover behind some ceiling debris. She pointed the 90 at his hiding place and fired her remaining rounds from the 90. The shards struck Davenport's barrier, shifting some of the rubble. With an empty click, she knew her rifle was empty.

Dammit!

She tossed the weapon into the flowing water that swirled around her knees and pulled out her X2-20. Brett and Julius hurried over. With the native detachment defeated, the room grew quiet again.

"He's behind those rocks there!" Severine pointed.

"I'll go around the left side!" Julius said. "You two take the right. We'll surround his position and wipe that sorry son of a bitch off the map!"

They crossed through the center of the flooded former cafeteria and waded towards Davenport's hiding place. Severine guessed that he was out of ammunition since he hadn't jumped out and unloaded on them. Slowly, she turned around the side of the barrier, expecting the wicked ruler to have his pulse weapon aimed at her face. With a quick turn, she was around the corner.

Nothing.

Where is he?

She was furious. Severine wanted nothing more than to put a shard through his skull.

Davenport was gone. Julius appeared on the other side, stepping out from the swampy water and splashing onto the marble floor that formed the shore. At Julius' feet, an open ventilation shaft led downward into the ship, disappearing into the ground below with a sharp turn.

He escaped through a floor vent!

"Shit! He's gone!" Severine lamented. "We have to go after him!"

"Don't worry, Sev," Julius said. "I have a better idea…"

He yanked out a detonator, clicked it on, and dropped the glowing sphere into the duct. A flash hissed out and the vent caved in on itself, sealing the entrance behind the explosion. Severine looked down the hole at the mess of twisted, melting metal. The vent was left in utter ruin. Pulse plasma ate away at the edges, generating sparks and microscopic magma embers.

"That works!" she replied.

He couldn't have survived that!

"Target eliminated. Now where, Ambrose?" Julius asked, as the room was clear of hostiles.

"Down those stairs there," he replied. "We may have to go off the path a little bit, but the command bridge is close! Then the mainframe room shouldn't be too far past that!"

#

From the darkness of the hall behind them, Gretta watched angrily as the three colonists exited the flooded cafeteria and descended through the adjacent corridor.

The herrerasaur was hungry for their flesh. Most of her pack was wiped out or lost in the ship. Her gaze fixated again on the woman, whom the dinosaur treed in the jungle. With a low, guttural growl, the monster emerged from the darkness, resolving to follow the humans and wait for an opportunity to devour them.

Gretta descended into the swampy waters, carefully trying not to generate loud waves as she slipped quietly into the bog, sliding past the sunken bodies of the natives.

XXVIII

"You're certain he's dead?" Severine asked again, as the colonists walked cautiously down the stairwell, presumably toward the obsolete command bridge.

Julius turned and laughed.

"Sev, you saw how tight the duct work was. You saw the metal. Hell, there's no one I know that could survive a detonator blast – certainly not in a tight crevice like that! Even if they did have a Federation armor suit... They build those grenades to destroy everything in their blast radius. You saw what they did to the savages at the waterfall."

"You're right," she replied. "I'm just paranoid."

I should've gone down the vent and found the body, just to make sure.

"You're right to be paranoid," Brett replied. "You've undergone terrible things by these people. If I were you, I'd want to make sure they're all dead!"

She nodded.

"By the looks of it, they might be dead. We haven't seen any in a while. Most of them probably died in the briefing room explosion."

But there could still be a few lurking through these tunnels.

"The rest are probably dead," Julius reassured her. "We've taken down quite a few already. The last batch in the old cafeteria might have been the last of them."

Severine wasn't so sure.

With every passing room, she still felt as if they were being watched.

They passed through another old Federation passage in *Supernova's* ruins, followed by more rooms that fed out into the dim hallway. Severine noticed that these rooms were empty and overgrown by trees and root systems that ballooned out through the wreckage. The disappearance of tribal signs told her she was getting farther away from the Davenport territory of the ship.

"It's a wonder the solar signal emitter has held out all these years," Severine said, trying to pass the time as the colonists proceeded.

"If the conditions outside were right, I could understand how it might still be operational," Julius said. "The crash took the *Supernova* into the swamps, but the roof still faced an upward general direction, with a slight degree of tilt. If the emitter tower wasn't damaged on the roof and remains unblocked by the canopy, it makes sense that it's still been powering various components of the ship, like the mainframe room. The sunlight kept it charged all this time."

"Why do you suppose Davenport didn't break into it and shut it down?"

"It could be a sacred place," Julius suggested. "Like a sacred site. They probably have no idea what it is or how to deactivate it."

Severine nodded.

The notion made sense. Davenport and his wicked colony were descendants of the original colonists, not colonists themselves. They would have no knowledge of how to work the machine or what its purpose was. And thankfully, after years of being buried in the jungle, the emitter was now going to fulfill its purpose: calling for rescue.

We're so close now!

She thought suddenly of her companions through the Triassic jungles that didn't make it.

"We owe it to the others to make it to the mainframe."

Their hazy faces drifted by.

Daddy, the pilot bot. They probably wouldn't have made it past the coelophysis herd without him. Jordy, the Federation logistics bot with a sense of humor. The scientist Francis Paluch was difficult to get along with at first, but proved to be very useful. He identified their time and location, confirming that they were back on Earth. He also adequately described the predators they might encounter during the trek, which (unfortunately for him) proved to be his downfall. And in his final moments, he gave his life to save Severine.

Before that monster, Gretta, tore him apart.

"They won't die in vain," Julius said. "When our people come for us, I'll make sure their names live on."

Well, they better get here fast, she thought, knowing her wish probably wouldn't be the case.

She decided that the primeval time of the Triassic was no place for mankind. The dinosaurs and creatures here were vengeful and rabid, having developed a unique taste for human blood when the *Supernova* crashed. The indigenous tribe was just as ruthless. Years of isolation and revolts had reset the survivors of *Supernova's* crash to the stone age. Severine was grateful she had been trapped in a sleeper pod during the early days of man in the Triassic.

They continued down the stairs, coming into another old atrium area. Severine and her companions recognized it instantly.

It was the old memorial room, dedicated to those who fought and died in the Old War in what was now Earth's bleak future. Plant spores clung to faded, golden plaques that lined the walls. In the center of the room sat a row of benches to observe the memorandum. Several of her relatives' names were among the walls, but the inscriptions were long covered by jungle filth and grime.

"Shit, *Supernova's* Memorial," Julius said. "Ambrose, we have to be getting close! It's all coming back to me now, like a forgotten dream..."

"It's not far," Severine confirmed. "That doorway there should take us right to the command bridge. Western entrance, I believe..."

"That's correct," Brett confirmed. "A few hundred yards! We're close!"

A cracking of glass to their rear made them spin around. The sound wasn't in their immediate room but was within a few corridors away. As the mystery sound dissipated, the ship was quiet once more.

We have company...

Someone – or something – was following them.

"What was that?" Julius asked.

"Footsteps on broken glass," Severine replied. "Something's tailing us..."

"Do we go back and take the fight to them?" Brett suggested.

"We could be walking into a trap. If the bridge isn't too far, then we should be in the mainframe soon. Once we're inside, we can seal the doors. Then they won't be able to do a thing. I say we keep moving forward, but I'll keep an eye on the rear – how's that?"

"Works for me," Severine replied. "Let's just be quick! I can't wait to get out of this place..."

"Agreed," Brett remarked.

They passed through the memorial room, which fed into an overgrown communications bay. Toppled, shredded leather chairs and mossy computer stations lined the sides. Crew member issued headphones and emergency repair tools were draped over the counters, which were swarmed in spiderwebs. The scene painted a picture of a hectic encounter in space before the *Supernova* landed on Earth.

"The crew was trying to fix the computer system," Brett said. "An electrical failure, just like what happened to Daddy in the FATR."

On the other side of the computer tables and various terminal stations was a large sign that read: **Command Bridge**. Underneath the old sign, the access hallway was blocked by many obstacles that fell long ago when the roof collapsed. Through the complexity that filled the narrow hall, Severine could see the bridge. She confirmed the location by spotting the rotting coelophysis carcass slumped across the table.

The little guy's still in there from the other day...

"Dammit!" Julius said. "The bridge is on the other side of the passage!"

"Can we move that shit?" Brett asked. "Let me give it a shot..."

He walked over to the first misplaced support beam that blocked the path and yanked hard on the middle. Some of the small pieces in the pile moved, but his primary pole remained static, locked between the floor and ceiling. Severine joined him and together they managed to shift the pole to the left, moving it from the main passage. The ordeal took more than a minute, and they were both out of breath after it was over.

One down. Fifty to go...

"This isn't practical," Brett said. "Any ideas?"

Severine shook her head.

"Hey, what about that?" Julius yelled.

She looked up.

Another large air duct, just like the one Davenport was killed in.

It was wide enough to fit a body through. The screws were already loose. Brett stepped up and knocked down the vent register cover, exposing a new way to access the bridge.

"Let's take it!" Severine said.

"Here, I'll give you a boost, Sev."

Brett held out his hands, preparing to lift her up into the shaft.

SSSSHHHHHHHH!

"Auugghhh!" Julius screamed. His XR-90 fell to the ground, discharging once and sending the ricochet bouncing wildly through the room before finally burning through a hole to the jungle.

"Damn neolitics!" Julius yelled.

An arrow pierced his left hand and lodged in the palm, spewing blood down his wrist before disappearing under the armor suit sleeve. He fell to the side, hitting into a desk, as more arrows narrowly missed him before striking the wall.

Severine looked back at the savages.

Hell! There's so many...

A large clan of surviving ragtag hunters had entered the room, shooting arrows off before they leaped for cover. The little army was enraged, knowing that their way of life had ended now that Gretta and her pack had destroyed their settlement. It was impossible to count them all as they swarmed the room, but Severine guessed there were over twenty.

"Hit them!" Julius called, crouching behind a desk as he fiddled with the arrow wound.

Brett pushed Severine behind the cover of a small alcove in the room and pressed down on his 90 trigger. A hail of pulse fire rained down on the intruders, making them second-guess their advance and sending a few at the front to swift graves.

Severine popped out from the alcove and fired off two rounds, each carefully planned. The blasts hit a pair of hunters who tried to hug the wall out of Brett's range. He ducked as spears sailed over his head and bounced off a terminal monitor.

"You okay?" he asked.

"Yeah," she replied. "How's Julius?"

She looked past Brett at the wounded lieutenant on the other side of the chamber. Julius broke the arrow off, pulling it painfully through his deformed palm before tossing the remnants to the side. He ripped part of a cloth that was lying on one of the nearby counters and had begun bandaging the wound, giving little indication that he was in pain. Behind him, she could see three more savages trying to flank his perimeter.

"Over there, hit them!"

Severine and Brett unloaded and dropped the group before they could reach the lieutenant.

"Julius, you hanging on over there?"

"I'll tell you Ambrose, I've been better..." He picked up the 90 that was lying at his feet, narrowly avoiding several more arrows as they skirted off the tiled floor. He turned and fired a quick burst of pulse shards, killing a few more men that moved into the center behind an old networking port. Severine saw more savages flooding into the room, chanting shrill war-cries and cheering each other on in their primitive language.

They just keep coming. We're going to die here if this keeps up...

"More are coming through!" Brett confirmed. More arrows shot past, and the colonists returned fire. Severine chose her opponents carefully, only shooting at natives that failed to find cover. Ammunition was running dangerously low.

"Get out!" Julius yelled. "Up the vent! Hurry, before they swarm us. I'll cover!"

"What about you?"

"Don't argue, Ambrose! Just get up the shaft – you too, Sev! Make it to the emitter and send the damn call!"

Shit, Julius...

Severine realized he wouldn't be coming along. The lieutenant's journey would stop here, so close to their final destination.

"You heard the man! Sev, you think you can jump up there while we cover you?"

"Yeah. Just keep the pressure on them, will you?"

"You got it. Go!"

Severine scurried out from the alcove, running behind Brett and emptying her X2 out in the direction of the savages. She thought she heard a few go down, but she was running so fast, it was all a blur. Brett and Julius laid down more fire that struck a few bold hunters who tried to strike her with their bows. The arrows never left the drawstrings before the bowmen went down.

With a running jump, she threw away the useless pistol and flew off the ground, her fingers gripping the right corner of the vent. She scurried up just in time as more arrows flew under her heels. Her scarring from the herrera attack burned as her bruises banged against the ventilation duct.

Shit! That stings.

From the tunnel above she could hear the conflict raging on in the corridor. Eventually, she heard Brett's 90 click off with an empty clip as the sounds of his X2 sidearm began to rattle off. Twangs of bows commenced as darts flew under the shaft opening.

Come on, Brett!

"Ambrose. Get the hell up the shaft!"

"Sir, you won't be coming with us?"

"Look at me? I'm not going anywhere. You two can still make it. Promise you'll send that signal!"

"We promise, sir."

"Good. Now get your ass up there! These guys aren't going to stop and I'm almost out. Make it count!"

She heard more rounds from a 90 echoing through the vent, this time from Julius' position. In a flash, Brett appeared below the opening and jumped up. Severine took hold of his shoulders and pulled him through as he climbed into the duct.

"Do you have anything left?"

"Just a few shots in my X2; that's it. Come on! Let's get to the mainframe. They shouldn't be able to get us in there..."

"What about Julius?"

"He's making sure we get away."

He pushed her down the ventilation shaft towards the bridge. She turned and began crawling down the dark metal framing, trying to stop the tears. They were losing another friend in the quest to escape the Triassic.

Dammit, Julius. I hope they make it quick...

#

Julius tossed the 90 away as the ammunition indicator clicked over to "empty." He turned around just in time to see Brett's scraggly legs shimmying up the vent opening.

Good boy, Ambrose...

He yanked out his X2 quickly, waiting to hear more approaching footsteps against the cold floor.

Come on, boys. I know you're still out there!

A distant shuffling of feet scurried along the floor tile. A similar scuffling answered from the other side.

They're surrounding me...

He rose up from cover and managed to catch two unsuspecting hunters off guard, tagging them squarely in the chest. A silver sheen twinkled at the far corner, and quickly grew towards him with a swift motion blur.

SHHHHHHH!

SSPPLLLLL!

"*Augghhhhh!*"

Another arrow lodged itself in his other hand, sending waves of torment down his forearm. He dropped the gun on the counter and fell back to cover, avoiding another hailstorm from the archers. More footsteps approached his cover cautiously, learning that he was now immobilized and more wounded than before. Julius could hear their spear butts grazing the floor as the sounds drew near.

Go, Sev! Hope you make it!

A trio of hunters closed in around him as he clasped his wound. They disbanded his cover and aimed their weapons at him. Julius could see the pleasure in their eyes as they moved in for the kill, lowering the lances towards his head. Julius waited until he was sure all the savages were in range.

Eight... Eight men... That's all that was left! That's what brought me down...

He couldn't help but smirk at the irony. He had survived the green lizards, the crocodiles, the orange dinos, but not a couple of pricks with sharpened sticks.

The tribal squad leader gave an ominous growl as he prepared to plunge his spear tip through the lieutenant's throat. Julius could feel the other spears and knives closing in, ready to split apart his head from all sides.

"Sorry boys," Julius chuckled between lamented coughs. "A little gift from the Federation infantry."

Their leader paused, grunting an unknown question to his peers.

Clickkkkk!

A lonely chrome sphere rolled out from his bandaged hand, clattering over the floor. Julius looked up with a smile, managing a laugh as he caught their eyes bulging. As the sphere broke apart and a bright warmth enveloped him and disintegrated his face, his last thoughts were of a warm, populous planet far away – a planet he yearned to go to. It was a world he wished to know. He focused on these thoughts as he was enveloped by a white light.

#

As the embers from the blast faded away and fizzled out into wisps that steamed on the charred flooring, Gretta trudged through the hall, sniffing at the ground. The room was black with smoking craters. Much of the furniture and objects had been tossed from the middle, crashing to the sides on top of the shattered terminal computers.

The dinosaur relished in the debris field. The room smelled of death.

At her feet, a slew of deformed bodies coated the floor. One of the colonist's bodies was at the center, charred to a crisp beyond recognition.

The herrerasaur sniffed at the pile of ashes. The snout nudged aside the blackened XR-90 rifle that sat blackened under a mangled chair.

The herrera looked up.

Ahead, the detonator blast had wiped away the debris, leaving the entrance to the command bridge wide open. With a shrill roar, Gretta charged into the opening, knocking over Julius' burned remains and smashing his skull with her massive foot.

She could smell her prey.

They were close.

XXIX

The texture of the vent was gritty and unsanitary.

Severine led the way through the complex maze of duct work. Their progress would've been more tedious if they didn't have the glowing light from Brett's X2 pistol to guide their way.

These could use a good cleaning, she thought, trying not to breathe in the fungal toxins. Her hands tensed as she padded along the cold floor, keeping her head low so she could crawl with ease. The green jungle slime and milky spores dotted the silver surface.

This can't be good for our lungs...

The duct brackets came to life and vibrated under her hands, and a faint *booom* started through the tunnel, originating from somewhere behind her. She knew the sound well – a detonator blast.

Julius!

"Don't stop!" Brett said, close behind her. "They may still be coming after us."

Unlikely, with a D7 blast...

"Look there! I bet that's our ticket out of here!"

As they scurried through the network of tunnels, bounce lighting passed through a cracked register opening just ahead. Ambient jungle noises could be heard below. Severine reached it and tugged on the frame until the grating came off and dropped to the room below with a *clang*.

Severine looked through.

The decomposing coelophysis from days earlier slumped below on the table. There were bite marks in the creature's chest. In their days away from the *Supernova*, other dinosaurs had ravaged the body.

"It's the bridge!" she exclaimed. "We're here!"

The ground below was far down. Severine guessed at least thirty feet – maybe more. The fall would certainly maim them both without anything absorbent to land on.

"Jeez, Sev! That's a pretty big jump!"

"I don't think we'll make it without injury. A broken leg out here would be detrimental."

"Looks like the vent forks to the right up ahead. If I recall, that's the direction of the mainframe. We could probably stay in the vents until we get closer. Once it leads over the hallway, getting back into the ship shouldn't be hard."

"Good call," Severine answered, leading the way around the open grate and through the next series of interwoven ventilation shafts. Brett followed, casting one final glance down at the exotic ruins of the command bridge. Had he waited another few seconds, he would have caught a glimpse of Gretta's formidable form slithering ominously into the room, sniffing intently at the vent ducts above before chomping at the dead coelophysis.

#

The ducts began to ramp downward as the two colonists continued towards the mainframe room. After they made a sharp right turn, the vent came to a dead end, with a final open grating at their feet. Through the thin, rusted slits, Severine could hear a faint *hummmmm* below. This time, the floor was only ten feet down.

"We're close to the emitter!"

"Kick it down, Sev!"

"With pleasure..."

With a strong kick, the grate collapsed to the hall floor, sending a loud *runnnggg* through the corridor. She hopped to the ground. As she rose to her feet, Brett landed beside her.

There it is! We made it!

The pair of titanium security doors greeted them a few feet away. Severine ran to the windows and looked through, cupping her eyes. The shining gears still rotated powerfully inside the emitter console. The access terminal at the base of the machine was still alive, confirmed by a green active light below the screen.

Thank you solar power, she thought.

"Do your magic!" she told him.

"I never thought I'd ever make it this far," Brett said excitedly, rushing over to the access activation panel beside the doors.

"We did it together!" Severine replied.

He smiled. "You bet we did. Here goes nothing!"

"Don't say that! You'll jinx it..."

"Hush, it'll work," he laughed.

He grabbed the lanyard off his neck and swung the card expertly down the narrow groove alongside the keypad. A trio of loading dots appeared on the blue digital monitor before dispersing to the side. After a moment, prompt text dissolved onto the screen.

Mainframe Doors Opening. Please Wait...

Yes!

"We're gold," he said confidently.

Severine couldn't stop smiling.

The green lights on the keypad flickered momentarily, and then an electric sound seeped out from behind the walls. With the screech of metal, the pair of chrome doors slid apart, sending the Federation symbols into the walls and opening the entrance to the mainframe room.

They stepped inside.

Severine shivered with excitement at the coldness that greeted them as they crossed through the metallic threshold.

The mainframe room was without a doubt the most modernized and high-tech room in *Supernova*, both in the old days in space, and now in the Late Triassic. Much of the room was as it appeared during the days of Admiral Perry and the colonist star fleet. Computers and communication ports lined the edges of the room, as well as many other separate workstations that lined the middle. On the walls, various blinking light buttons and notification holograms glitched to life when the doors opened, illuminating the areas around them with flickering brilliance. Several lights above had shattered and were inactive, but the majority of the brownish gold bulbs still made the chamber very visible. As a whole, the mainframe room was comparable in size to the command bridge.

It's right there!

The emitter rose through the floor ahead, humming with artificial brilliance.

It's beautiful!

The translucent spire was erected in the center of the room and shot vertically into the ceiling, supported by a circular support stand accessed by a small set of stairs. Behind the ring of safety rails that surrounded the communications tower, the internal parts spun without error behind the glass. In the central pipe, a cluster of chrome spires awaited on the base, ready to shoot out an emergency call to the fleet, which hopefully still floated nearby in space.

We're finally getting out of here!

"You want to do the honors?" Severine said.

"You sure you don't want to?"

"You're the one with the key-card, and you got us in here! You should be the one that calls for help!"

He smiled. "Okay, let's get the hell off this rock, shall we?"

Brett passed in front of her. As his body crossed her view, a dark box in the corner of the room drew her attention. The shape looked out of place among the chrome bright obstacles that filled the walls. With a closer look, Severine saw that it was an open ventilation duct.

What caused that...

Creakkk...

Something stirred in the room.

Shit! No!

Her heart skipped a beat, before thumping faster and faster as she saw a streak dart through the room. The intruder caught Brett off guard, sticking him in his stomach with a sharp primitive dagger. Her friend fell to the side with a shrill yell, gripping at the wound and knocking over several Federation swivel chairs.

Davenport!

The indigenous chieftain was deformed, barely recognizable. His face was marred with plasma residue from Julius' detonator that deployed in the cafeteria skirmish. Shrapnel from the imploded vent covered his left cheek and descended to his neck until it ran into his bloody Federation armor suit. In his other hand, a partially degraded X2-20 still glowed at the ready. The light on the grip was dim, indicating he only had a few shots left.

Brett coughed on the ground and spat up red bile onto the tile beside his head. With an exhausted breath, he managed to utter a single, urgent sentence.

"Run, Sev!"

Davenport ripped off Brett's lanyard with the key-card and draped it around his swollen neck.

"You!"

His voice had changed with a raspier edge as he turned to Severine.

The detonator blast had modified his vocal ability. "Severine! You ruined it all!"

He swapped out his dagger for his X2 with such speed and precision that it made her tremble. Fortunately, her basic training kicked in with a timely reflex.

Rolling behind a desk, she avoided a blast from the pistol. Multiple pulse shards passed over her head behind cover, scorching into the wall.

VRRRRRRMMMMM!

The detonator screwed up his barrel...

Davenport's corroded pistol was now a mangled shotgun, trading precision for proximity.

She searched frantically for an exit. Running out to the hallway was too risky. The entrance was too far to run, and with the spread of Davenport's pulse shards, she would be impossible to miss. Behind her, she could hear the crazed shaman's infantry boots clicking slowly over the floor tiles. It sounded like he was limping, another beautiful side effect from the lieutenant's detonator blast. Behind him, Brett's breathing was growing harsher.

Shit! He's dying! I have to do something...

VRRRRRRMMMMM!

A second blast struck inches from her head as she looked for cover. He was coming dangerously close. Quickly, she kept low and scooted ahead, diving through a chair opening for another terminal. She entered the next aisle of workstations and silently moved among the obstacles, looking for anything she could use. His porous voice interrupted her flight.

"You took out my home. Wiped out almost all of my tribe. I'm sure the dinosaurs will finish off the rest, if they haven't already."

VRRMMMM!!

Gold lines crossed over her, obliterating a computer that shook from the explosion before the monitor blinked off.

He knows I'm over here...

The aisle ended ahead. She would have to move somewhere else.

"My family has been searching for one of those pretty little level 5 cards for years— there you are!"

No!

VRRRMMMMMMMM!!!

A blast nicked her shoulder.

"Ahhhhhhhh!" The impact felt like an ignited fire poker seared through her, adding further pain to her body that Gretta already inflicted.

He sees me.

She rolled left, behind another division of workstations.

"When I call your people for help, you and your friend will be long gone," he cackled. "I'll barricade myself here. I'll be a hero – admired for generations as the last surviving ancestor of the *Supernova's* crash."

The clatter of his boots was frighteningly close again. She could hear him searching through the various computer ports and utility boxes that lined the corner of the chamber. When he found a section that she wasn't hiding behind, he angrily knocked over the crates in frustration.

"You and your friend will have been martyrs, trying to save me from the vicious clan dwelling at the wreck site. A necessary loss. Don't worry! I'll make sure your names live on."

His laugh was prideful and arrogant.

Asshole.

Time was running out. She could hear Brett coughing as he fought off death at the steps of the emitting platform.

Her shoulder throbbed, making each move along her crawl path exponentially more difficult than the step before. She knew her options were running low. Her only viable thought was to run for Brett's X2 and try to take him down in a firefight. But he had Federation armor, while she was draped in shredded hyper-sleep garments.

VRRRMMMM!

Another computer monitor exploded, sending hot sparks over her back as she scampered by.

Oh! That burns!

The pain didn't stop her. Pausing to check on the wounds would result in her agonizing death.

He must be running low on ammo...that's four rounds already.

She pondered finding a blunt object and whacking him over the head. So far, she found none. Around every desk, she expected to find another conveniently placed iron rod like the one she discovered back in the briefing room. But this room was untouched by time, and thus left in immaculate condition without any perfectly situated weaponry.

THWWAMMM!!

"Uhhhh!"

A hard blow struck her head, causing her to see stars.

Shit. He found me...

She fell forward and turned over on her back, just in time to catch Davenport turning the pistol around from a swinging position into a firing one. The barrel was bent and indented. Deep in the center, she was displeased to see a final round remained as a charge began to radiate. His finger caressed the trigger. Beyond the gun, a sinister smile began to crack across his twisted, scarred face.

"Sorry, Severine. You could've been the queen..."

"Just do it!" she scoffed. "I can't stand to look at your ugly mug any longer."

That did it.

She closed her eyes.

SHRRK!!!

A strange substance dripped from Davenport's firearm. The X2 shook as an internal charge receptor failed, dented from the prior damage to the weapon. In a second, the weapon imploded apart in his hand. Pulse residue leaked from all openings, eating away at his palms as the pistol broke apart.

"*Aughh!*"

Davenport shrieked in pain as his trigger hand was dissolved into nothing from the nasty fluid. Severine spun away as the residue dropped below the gun, seeping onto her prior position on the floor. Billowy smoke began to swirl around where the particles landed. With a swift side kick, she knocked her opponent off his feet by the knees. He fell back, crashing onto a keypad and rolling onto the floor as he looked in horror at his missing appendage.

"Get back here!" he called out angrily. He rose up and reached for her but was too preoccupied with his own pain to give chase, falling back to the floor to soothe his wound.

"Stay there!" Davenport barked as she prepared to flee. "I'll deal with you shortly..."

She rose to her feet and froze, her head barely above the line of computer monitors.

No!

Coming through the amber shades of overhead lights that shone over the mainframe entrance was a massive, orange herrerasaur. The monster sniffed the cold air of the chamber, confused by the brightness of the room and distracted by the spinning sounds of winding machinery. The beast's long tail lashed to the side and knocked over a nearby monitor. As the hardware shattered, the reptilian snout looked down and studied the debris before progressing through the room. Severine recognized the red stripes and moistened jaws.

Gretta!

The dinosaur had been following them.

She dropped and scooted down the aisle before crawling under another workstation, just as the red eyes of the primordial hunter scanned towards her vicinity. She could hear Davenport's whining in the distance as she continued along. As he whimpered and cursed at the wound, she could hear Gretta gradually stepping over towards his position.

She smiled.

He has no idea what's coming...

As long as she moved slowly and carefully, Severine knew Gretta would get the shaman first. She kept an ear open for the dinosaur's terrible grumbling as it moved among the machinery sounds. Pausing momentarily at the corner of a network tower, she shot a quick look over the rows of computers, observing the dreadful scene that was unfolding.

The herrerasaur continued its frightful approach to Davenport's position, who was hidden from view behind the rows of desks and hardware parts. Silhouetted in front of the blinking lights on the wall panels, the monster quickly spotted her target and darted up the aisle. She heard Davenport's whimpering stop as he realized he was about to die. Gretta jumped into the air and shrank behind the workstations. Her tail reared back up and waved wildly as muffled, helpless screams leaked out from the aisle. Severine heard crunching of bone behind the dinosaur's strong teeth, and her arch-enemy was silenced.

That's one problem taken care of...

Brett was lying in between Gretta and Severine's positions behind the obstacles. Any hope of getting to the X2 in time would be a suicide mission.

Her friend wasn't looking so good.

With slow, drawn out breaths that sounded more painful than beneficial, Brett was still alive. In his grim, near catatonic situation, he was fumbling for his X2. Severine wasn't sure if he knew the herrerasaur was in the room or not. In his declining state, he seemed pretty out of it.

Come on, Brett!

To her horror, Gretta's colossal head reared up from the computers, blood and human stringy gobs dripping from the jaws. She spotted Brett and instantly slunk back under the workstation and out of view.

That bitch won't stop until she kills us all!

Severine guessed the dinosaur sensed Brett had access to a pulse weapon and knew how lethal they could be. The dinosaur would try to flank him before he knew what hit him.

Something's gotta be done...

She thought about calling out to him, but quickly lost track of the hererra behind all the industrial machines. For all she knew, Gretta might very well be around the next corner.

Okay, slowly, but quickly...just like before.

Davenport! He had a knife and the key-card.

She started to double back, knowing that the monster was last headed in the opposite direction. The room was unbearably quiet. A few times, she thought she could hear Gretta's claws scraping against the flooring in one of the neighboring aisles.

"Sev, hey, Sev," Brett called.

She could hear the blood gurgling behind his lips before dropping onto the floor.

"Hey, you out there?"

Brett, be quiet! I'm coming!

A workstation collapsed not far away, followed by the quick scratching of dinosaur claws.

"Sev, you back there? Are you wounded? Son-of-a-bitch got me good, huh?"

Looking around another table leg, she made sure the path was safe before continuing. Her body felt overspent and fatigued. Her arm was still hurting from the waterfall incident days before, and the wounds on her thigh and back were quickly become unbearable. Keeping her mind on rescuing Brett and sending the distress call was the only thought that kept her going. The emitter's spinning gears were the only consistent sound in the room.

Under the amber lighting, she arrived at Davenport's mutilated corpse. For the most part, he looked the same, other than his head and neck, which were splattered over the marble like a sloppy stew.

Okay, you piece of shit, what do you have?

She rooted quietly through his armor suit.

I gotta take this bitch out, so you better have something useful for me!

She grabbed the key-card from his neck and was about to snag his dagger when a better, formerly unseen solution decided to present itself.

Underneath one of the desks next to the grisly scene was an inconspicuous box bolted to the underside of the table. An orange circle logo with a skull stenciled in the middle stared back at her, with a glowing green light burning beneath it.

An emergency detonator depot!

These were installed routinely throughout Federation high-profile rooms, like mainframe chambers in case of mutiny. Since the solar signal emitter kept a charge all these years that preserved the room in its original state, the detonator and its deadly contents were still lethal.

And ready to kill...

She popped open the latch, revealing a single pristine detonator sphere.

My last chance...

She grabbed it, careful not to click the activate button. She palmed the device thoughtfully, pondering her next move.

As she looked up to guess the monster's position, she quickly found the target, or rather, the target had found her.

Gretta was feet away, racing towards her from down the aisle.

SHIT!

Severine ducked down, crawled over Davenport's corpse, and rolled under a desk. The dinosaur reached the opening immediately, slashing with her tremendous claws that bore razor sharp marks across the table. The red eyes moved frantically towards her with a voracious appetite. Severine tucked her feet in quickly as the abominable predator threatened to chomp them off.

She fell out the back of the table, crawling at first until she realized her stealth didn't matter anymore, and then running with the detonator in one hand and the key-card in the other. Behind her, her pursuer hadn't giving up. The pounding of massive dinosaur feet shook the room.

"Sev. Jeez, Sev! Watch out! That thing's nearly on you!" Brett's words slurred as he gripped at the X2, his energy returning to him as he realized what was happening. "Hang on-n! I'm trying her-re!"

Severine couldn't hear him over the destructive stampede that was bearing down behind her. She searched for a way out, knowing that if she didn't find one soon, she would be reunited with Davenport and the others.

The damn thing's too close to throw the detonator!

Something struck her leg – a tipped over chair.

She rolled forward, feeling the monster tumble over her before crashing ahead into an operational database structure. The chase resumed instantly, but not before Severine realized that she dropped something of importance.

The key-card! Dammit!

Ahead, under the artificial lighting, a series of plumbing columns formed a prison-like refuge in the corner of the room. The pipes came out of the floor and ran upwards to the ceiling. From the looks of it, it was the only moderately safe spot in the entire room. The herrera would be too fat to fit between the bars.

Click-clack, click-clack!

The claws played their terrible orchestra. Gretta was almost on top of her.

Severine could feel a pounding headache coming on. She was beginning to slip into delirium, brought on by exhaustion and lack of water.

Almost... There...

Free...

Clumsily, her shoulders struck the piping as she wiggled into a crammed space in the middle. As she turned to the opening, Gretta was already waiting there, snapping her fangs furiously in anger that Severine had escaped for a third time. The dinosaur pushed its weight forward, trying to breach through the industrial barrier that wouldn't budge. Several of the support screws turned at the braces, but the structure remained steadfast.

Thank you, Federation industrial engineers...

Only now, the only way out was forward, into the frightening face of the Davenport goddess. Spit and slobbery dinosaur fluids dripped at her face as Gretta convulsed angrily at the opening. Severine slumped back against the rear pipe, unsure of her next move, but grateful for the shelter.

Sticking the detonator in the dinosaur's mouth was the only idea she could devise, but she tossed it aside when she realized the blast would probably kill her too, even from inside the monster's throat. Outside, Gretta could wait her out until Severine died from dehydration.

She began to see spots as she weighed the only two options.

Gretta or the detonator...

WHRRRRRRRRRRRRRR!

A mechanical whirl started at the center of the room. Gretta scooted out of the opening and turned, facing the mainframe room.

Brett had managed to crawl up the emitter stairway and pull himself upright against the access terminal. He yanked the key-card out of the terminal slot and watched as the screen brightened to life. After he pressed through another few options on the keypad, a bright white beam shot out from the base of the glass cylinder and launched through the ceiling as an opening spread apart from above. Many of the internal mechanisms in the shaft moved aside for the rising light source. Above and unseen in the ceiling, the ray triggered the intact communication recorder, relaying an emergency signal out to the endless universe.

Shit! You did it!

Gretta roared in confusion, tilting her ugly head up towards the glowing tube that had whitened the room.

"Hey, Sev. They're coming f-for us..." He fell back on the terminal, sliding off to the side against a support railing. At his feet was a trail of blood he left when he crawled up the stairs. In his free hand was his bloodied X2.

"We're getting out of here!" she called back happily in a fatigued voice.

"It's gonna come for me, Sev. I'm too weak to hit the dinosaur. I know I'll miss. I only have a few shots. You're gonna have to use the detonator."

"What?"

"Toss the damn detonator when it r-reaches me! You can still m-make it..." He spat up more blood, leveling the firearm at Gretta. The dinosaur growled and resumed a challenging stance, calculating how it would avoid the oncoming pulse blasts.

"Brett, no!"

"It's the only way you'll g-get out. The signal is sent. They're coming to get you. No need to protect the room anymore."

An exotic, carnivorous shriek flew out of the herrerasaur as it lifted its head, bellowing through the room. Brett kept the weapon aimed at the dinosaur, but the pistol shook in his hand. Severine knew that none of the rounds would strike the monster.

"Brett, I won't do it!"

"There's n-no time."

"You might still hit the damn thing!" She knew he wouldn't, but refused to accept his fate.

He coughed, wiped his mouth with his trigger hand, and then moved the gun back to a defensive position.

"Sev, m-my mind's been screwed up ever since I came out of hyper-sleep. I'm n-not sure what we were before all this-s, and I'm-m sure you don't remember either... I'll tel-l you, though: Running back into you—oooh—after those l-lonely years... It brough-t some of it back... And-d I'm thankful it-did. I'm not bitter about m-my isolation anymore. You brought me out o-of it... Thank you, Severine..."

It was his impromptu goodbye speech.

Arguing with him was futile. He was near death and had already made up his mind. Her face hurt from the teary eyes that forced her brows down. If she survived this, she would be the last colonist left until the Federation came. If they were still out there somewhere.

For a final, fleeting moment, Severine again experienced the flashback. Brett standing behind the ice – the hyper-sleep pod glass. His reassuring face telling her that they would be united again in another time. She smiled as she finally pieced together the meaning of the memory. A tranquil peace washed over her. She would see him again someday, without the barriers of this life separating them any longer.

"I won't forget you," she managed.

He smiled in acknowledgment, accepting his coming death.

"Just make it a damn good-d-d throw, will-l-l you?"

She nodded. *I'll make it quick...*

Gretta's hideous form surged towards the emitter tower, leaping over a workstation and running full speed at an aisle that led straight for the platform. Brett began to pop off pulse blasts, none of which came close to the dinosaur. The golden beams sparked off the workstations as the herrera snaked past and avoided the sparks.

When the dinosaur arrived at the foot of the emitter stairs, Severine left the piping sanctuary, clicked on the detonator, and hurled the sphere across the room. As the creature hopped up the stairs and landed on the platform in front of Brett, the orb bounced carelessly off the transparent tower and fell directly down on the deck below.

Cliicckkk!

Severine watched as the framing broke apart and a white flash enveloped Brett and tore Gretta apart, sending dinosaur organs somersaulting away from the explosion. The eruption was so powerful that the emitter tower shattered, sending glass and electric volts raining down below. As the shock wave approached and the light beam flickered off, Severine did her best to take cover as the unstoppable aura consumed the mainframe room.

XXX

Below the dense canopy of the Triassic jungle, a group of small, curious tetrapods waded around a pool of river water. Some sloshed around on the shore dunes, while others burrowed underwater in tiny dugouts, kicking up sandy contrails as they vanished into their murky tunnels.

It had been a hot afternoon, and all types of wildlife had arrived at the pond to cool down.

The lagoon had been swelling up for weeks in many areas of the wilderness, especially at the edge of the ruined ship. The monsoons had taken a toll on nearby rivers, creating several offshoots and over-saturated tributaries. Much of the runoff was starting to spill out from numerous orifices and cracks in the hull, creating misty pressure pockets. The young creatures splashed happily under the geysers, eager to frolic in the light mist and escape the unbearable solar rays.

To their surprise, the wall above them suddenly broke apart, sending the amphibians scampering away under the ferns as Severine burst through the opening. Ship fragments around her were sent flying into the creek. Water flew out of the opening, rushing from behind as the wave carried her out into the afternoon jungle.

The force of the water propulsion caught her off guard. She braced herself as she landed with a splash, falling face-first in the shallows. When she resurfaced, smells of dried leaves and grass overtook her, and Severine knew she had finally found a way out of the wreckage.

After the mainframe explosion, she found herself unscathed by the detonator blast, thanks to the impressive stability provided by the piping barrier. To escape the ship, she decided not to retrace her steps, not knowing if there were any savages remaining in the ruins. She found herself descending back down the stairwell to the cargo bay where they discovered the FATR days earlier. When she learned the stairs to the lower levels had collapsed halfway down, she was forced to dart into another corridor. That shortcut led her into a flooded portion of the ship that had amassed much of the runoff caused by the river dam constructed above. The lower floors of the *Supernova* were dark and almost completely submerged. Fortunately, she found an opening from an asteroid impact and was able to break through the fractured gap, which sent her back to the outside world.

And the unforgiving heat that went along with it.

Damn, it's hot out today!

The ultraviolet rays baked into her wounds. Severine craved shade.

She coughed up water as she felt the warm sand grains slipping between her callused fingers. The pounding of the water released from the opening slid over her spine, cleansing her wounds. The pressure felt amazing. She decided to wait there and enjoy the shower, replenishing her fluids by forming a cup with her hands.

Just as long as I'm not drowning...

She rose up wearily and brushed off the sand clumps from her chest. She crawled up the embankment, hiding from the sun under the serene tree ferns. Being a former soldier, she wasn't used to relaxing. But here in the shade, watching the fountain of water spill out of the ship's hull was surprisingly therapeutic.

She tensed up, realizing her adventure in Earth's prehistoric past was far from over.

Now what?

Getting out of the jungle was certainly a top priority. The coelophysis pack was probably roaming nearby.

Severine knew she couldn't go too far out.

The Federation fleet could be days away. Or years.

Maybe even a lifetime…

She shrugged off her dark thoughts. Stressing over it would get her nowhere. There was no way of knowing when rescue would come – or if it would.

Sitting wearily on the mound, she started to envision her future in the Triassic, however long it may be. If there were any herrerasaurs left in the ship, she assumed that they all migrated down as one group from the northern jungle. As far as she knew, the herrerasaurs were the only carnivores in that region, and their absence might make that path the safest route of travel. If the swamps to the east had receded, she might be able to cross through the gap in the hills. She had no intentions of running into the saurosuchus nesting grounds again.

From there, she could cut north to the *Mudskipper* and hold out there until her colony returned.

She shook her head, trying to shake off an annoying buzzing noise.

Her ears were still ringing from the detonator blast that destroyed the emitter tower. The blast that took Brett's life in its welcoming, hellish embrace.

The bright shock wave had made her see spots.

Recalling the conflict in the mainframe room had proven difficult for her. She was still coming out of her exhausted state from water deprivation. On the isolated sandbar, it was all starting to sink in. Severine was forced to confront the obvious, terrible truth.

She was alone, stranded in the thick jungles of the Triassic.

No bots.

And no humans.

Just me…

To her delight, she could feel her hardened soldier instincts starting to resurrect themselves. She knew her infantry training would work overtime to keep her alive.

What's out there? What's my play here? The next move…

Crack!

A snap of a twig made her head swivel.

Beside her, the shrubbery began to slump and bend around a small path that led back into the trees. Low-lying branches and palm fronds began to quiver at the approach of whatever lumbered behind the green. An abrupt snort alerted her that the trespasser wasn't a human. Whatever was coming, it was about to pop through the vegetation, undeterred by her scent.

Coelophysis? Saurosuchus?

Her mind started to reel, recalling all the scientific names that Paluch had ingrained in her. She was surprised her mind had retained them.

Severine rolled over in the coarse sand and searched frantically for a weapon.

Anything will do! Just give me something...

Half buried beneath the coast, a large sturdy log poked out of the grains. With a hard tug, she dislodged the stick and stood up. The sudden dizziness made standing in the infantry defensive stance awkward, causing her to wobble from side to side.

There was no time to run or hide. The mysterious creature was seconds away from breaking through to the sandbar.

The steps grew louder, padding along in the brush.

Severine raised the stick to strike.

It sounds low to the ground...

Then softer, quicker sounds followed just behind.

Shit... There's more than one!

Her heart relaxed and she lowered her weapon as a bumbling exaeretodon wiggled out of the greenery and waded peacefully into the bubbling pool. As the waves surrounded the animal, it shivered at the sudden chill of the water, and took a quick step back.

As the beast began to peck at the surface, several younger ones scuttled through the trail, reuniting with their parent. The adult snorted at Severine, confirming that she wasn't a threat, and continued to drop a bumpy tongue into the lagoon.

"So, we meet again..."

Severine wondered if they were from the same herd that had broken up during the coelophysis attack on the wilderness road.

The dainty juveniles slipped into the pond, wading around the waterfall that was still flowing endlessly out of Severine's indentation. Water splashed off their backs as they tussled with one another while playing innocent, make-believe games.

"I like you. It's the other dinosaurs I'm not too keen on..."

She was relieved to finally see plant-eaters again.

Turning away from the herbivores, she looked into the distance of the bright, confusing jungle that butted up against the *Supernova*. Getting around the ship to the north side would be easy, but after that, the trek through the north jungle to the *Mudskipper* would be a guessing game.

Gambling with her life wasn't something she took pleasure in doing.

It's all a gamble now...

She made a goal for herself. Reach the river to the north by sundown. That meant a lot of ground had to be covered in a short amount of time. If she made it back to the river, she could use the cliffs again as a rear defense when night came. Jumping into the river would be her last resort if she ran into more predatory dinosaurs.

Cawawawaw!

Above, the tan flying creatures cheered as they flew by over the trees.

Looking up to the sky, Severine hoped silently that her fleet wouldn't take too long. She stepped around the fauna, giving the adult a courteous pat on the head while it drank. Using her log as a cane, she walked along the wet dunes until she slipped behind the foliage, knowing her fate would be uncertain until the colonists returned.

Would *they return?*

She didn't know. But she did know that the signal had been sent, and that her mission at the *Supernova* wreck was complete. The cost to send the distress call came at a high price. The lives of all her friends, and now, isolation and exile in the vast unpredictable landscape.

She managed to crack a smile, accepting the challenge.

The new objective was simple.

Survive.

EPILOGUE: 3542 A.D.

In the farthest corners of the universe, a watery green planet emerged from among the starry constellation. The vast oceans and forested regions that dotted the ground were reminiscent of the old depictions of planet Earth. Colossal, puffy clouds rolled over the rim of the quaint, colorful world. An atmospheric, tropical vapor brought refreshing rain showers to the people living below. Faint specs of light shined happily in the planetary surface, emitting out from small, modernized colonies.

The planet was discovered and settled on almost three-hundred years ago by the Federation fleet, headed by Admiral Steven Perry. When the world appeared on *Star Jumper's* radar screen, the admiral quickly sent scientists down to determine the condition of the air. When they returned days later with the good news of a second Earth-like planet with sustainable oxygen levels and a thriving ecosystem, the fleet descended to the surface and begun to construct a new metropolis.

In the aftermath of Earth's demise, a new superior society had taken root.

When the ancestors discovered the new world, they dubbed the planet '*Solis*' due to the planet's proximity to a new sun that provided light and renewable energy. The fiery orb glowed furiously and lit up the skies. Three dimpled rogue moons befriended the planet and hovered nearby in their own orbital paths just above the exosphere.

During the recent decades, long after the death of Admiral Perry, countries had formed, and with them came separate governments and ideas. The Federation was transfigured from a colonization mission to a private communication organization that focused on preserving the human way of life, as well as striving to contact other worlds in the galaxy.

So far, there had been no such contact made.

High above Solis, floating alone in a shadowy place next to one of the moons, was a Federation transmission station.

Music Box.

It was a small, cube-like operations base, with little more than ten rooms, including sleeping quarters, an observation deck, and an escape pod chamber. With thin antenna poles and support wings jutting out through the exterior sides like porcupine quills, it made for an odd-looking command post.

Launched ten years prior by Central Command as a way to communicate with any other forms of life in the universe (if any existed), the small satellite was manned by a crew of two, working periodically in rotating shifts that often overlapped. Their two primary objectives were to maintain communication with Central Command below about events happening in space and keep an eye out for any incoming human contact signals. So far, the crew had encountered many exciting cosmic events and a few meteor scares, but the only human interaction they had maintained was with the planet below.

Often when personnel took shifts working in *Music Box*, they wondered why Central Command was so intrigued at the idea of potential human life outside of Solis.

Are there other worlds containing human life that we don't know about?

Are there more planets like Solis, just waiting to be discovered? With breathable air?

Is Earth still alive?

Are there still people there?

Those questions would soon be answered.

The commanding officer aboard *Music Box* at the time of contact was Adam Ross, a lieutenant in the Federation Watch Force. He was an easy-going Watch officer, not as strict as the others, but well-respected and popular among his peers down on the mainland. He joined the Federation for adventure, after learning that the organization was responsible for colonizing Solis and saving mankind centuries earlier. But so far, the only adventure he found was the fun star ship ride that carried him to and from *Music Box*.

A blurry, gold flash fell over the bed and came gradually into his focus, looping endlessly over Adam's tired eyes that refrained from shutting. It took several minutes for Adam to realize it wasn't an abstract, lucid dream, but a Federation indicator light.

Oh no... What now?

He grumbled and shifted over in his bed, growing more disturbed by the spinning orange glow that blinked relentlessly above his door. It had been pulsating now for a few minutes, lighting up his chamber and the hallway beyond, which led down the access shaft that fed to the control room. It infuriated him that his sleep was being prevented. He cursed quietly that the engineering team hadn't added a terminal port in his bedroom to deactivate the siren. The annoyance would have to be shut off from the control room.

Probably just another message from Solis Central Command. Their timing is impeccable...

"Jade?" he called out, his voice echoing throughout the small base.

No answer.

"Jade. Can you please take care of that? It's too bright, annoying, and it won't go away! Also, it's literally right in my face."

Still no answer.

Jade was a new recruit on the Federation Watch Force and was deployed to *Music Box* to receive protocol instruction from Adam as his newest protege. Their excursion in space was to last five weeks before replacements were to be sent up to relieve them. In those five weeks of instruction, he was to train her about the proper Federation communication techniques: sending out test signals, maintaining a proper work station and sleeping quarters, survival in space under emergency situations, and what to expect in the event of a war.

He hoped that a war would never come.

She must be sleeping, too.

He didn't blame her for it. She was still new to the solitude. Time was lonely up there in the cosmos, and sometimes the dullness made it all but impossible to keep the eyelids open. Yesterday, he found her passed out in the co-pilot chair in the control room, just as orders from the Central Command base were coming through the loudspeakers. Fortunately, he had been passing by the cockpit as the static voice spoke and was able to provide a swift response.

Adam was beginning to find her sleeping ability amusing, but he knew her commanding officers wouldn't be as cheery if they caught her napping on the job. She could risk many demerits for nodding off while on duty in the Watch Force.

The problem was that he found her very beautiful, which made confronting her about potential room for improvement all the more difficult. So he figured, why not let her slide a few times? She'd get the hang of it eventually.

"Hey Jade! *Jaaaaaade...* Dammit."

His echo again returned nothing.

She's so bad about that!

He sluggishly rolled off the comfort of his mattress. His feet paused before hitting the cold floor and he stepped into his warm Federation-issued slippers which sat nearby on a dark mat. The sandals were meant only to be worn when off duty as a civilian novelty item. But he had grown so attached to their comfort that he hardly ever took them off.

I'm bad about that...

Adam chuckled to himself, rising to his feet.

He lumbered out of his small space dorm and went into the hall, shielding his eyes as he passed under the orange emergency lights. He was surprised to see the indicators going off here too, guiding his path down the chrome passage under their demanding rays.

Down the corridor in the dark control room, he could see Jade's tired body looking out onto Solis and the space beyond. Her chest rose and fell with gentle breaths under her Watch suit as distant ships passed by in the distance, leaving behind their gentle contrails. Her body was outlined by several blinking lights on the dashboard panel that played happily like a futuristic piano. Her form was slumped in a goofy pose in her co-pilot seat, just as he had found her the last time. The room was quiet, save for the faint beeping and humming of the console. Over her head, another similar notification light was activated, flooding the room with the same orange hue.

Yep, she's out. How can she not see those light alarms? I should probably at least talk to her about that...

He stepped softly into the room and nudged her shoulder, and Jade began to come out of her catatonic trance.

"Hey," Adam greeted her, as he tried to hide the smirk cracking across his face.

She slowly regained consciousness, sliding back down in her chair before using the armrests to hoist herself back up. She was a young, unmarried woman in her late-twenties who had eagerly joined the Watch Force about two months ago, fresh out of basic training. They had only recently become acquainted. Their relationship so far had been strictly professional, and despite her pleasant charm and their loneliness spent together in the stars, Adam sought to keep it that way.

"Hey, sorry. I did it again, didn't I?"

"Yeah. It's okay. I wouldn't have noticed it if the warning lights hadn't come on in my room."

She looked up as the orange glow waved past her forehead. "Oh, I'm sorry. How long has that been on?"

"Not long. Maybe thirty seconds – a minute at most."

"I've never seen that on before. It's not something bad, is it?" A look of remorse fell across her brow, and Jade suddenly had the face Adam had seen many times before when training the newbies. It was the look that she had just screwed up – and would probably be inheriting a demerit.

But Adam waved it off.

"No, it's nothing. This happens routinely. It just hasn't happened yet since we've been up here together. Normally, someone down at Central Command is just trying to get a hold of us to schedule the next supply drop, and when to send up the carrier drone."

"Oh? And they won't be mad that I missed it?"

Adam shook his head.

As long as they don't catch you...

"I'll just say you were taking your break and I was in the latrine. What's the worst they could say?"

She laughed. "Sorry, I'll do better next time! Promise."

"Happens to everybody. But yeah, just try to keep alert. No biggie. Now let's see what the message is. I'm betting it's the carrier drone request."

Adam sat down in the pilot chair and leaned into the illuminated Federation dashboard, waving off the flickering hologram options that populated at his approach. A *Music Box* logo animation faded onto the viewing monitor, requesting a PIN number that Adam punched into the keys from memory. He would never forget the numbers, having entered the code a thousand times already throughout his mundane Watch career.

1029102.

Then he punched the execute button.

The logo faded and a menu selection populated the screen. He navigated through a series of options and sub-menus before finally arriving on the messages tab. He pressed the screen briskly and the option faded off before arriving at the inbox. When a new notification didn't appear, it took only a moment for Adam to realize that he was staring at an empty folder.

0 unread messages.

Hmm... Odd.

Adam grunted. "Well, that's a new one."

"No new messages from Central Command?"

"Nothing. How the hell are we supposed to shut these lights off if we can't even find the message that activated them? There's probably an outdated alert buried somewhere that we haven't read. Let's check in the deleted. Do you want to take the wheel on this one? It'd be a good test of your knowledge so far."

"Sure!" She smiled. "I think I remember how to get there..."

Jade leaned forward over her adjacent monitor, entered her Federation PIN, and navigated through the network to the deleted folder. Adam was impressed at how fast she had memorized the file paths. Now all she had to do was master how to stay awake at the wheel.

The folder for the erased files flashed open, revealing the same stubborn notification.

0 unread messages.

Damn.

"Well, I'm officially stumped. Do you remember anything about this in training? My instructors sort of glazed over many of the technical issues."

She shook her head. "Could it be a glitch?"

"Yeah, it could be. Although, I've never experienced any glitches up here yet."

"How about the frequency indicator? Should we check that?"

The frequency indicator.

The clunky machine was virtually useless for the Federation to install. It was built to acquire long distance signals in outer space sent from other lifeforms in the universe. The primary goal was to find other potential human colonies or forgotten star ships. So far, the expensive contraption had turned up nothing of interest. For the most part, it sat dusty and neglected.

"I'm out of ideas. Let's give it a shot!"

Adam led the way back to the rear chamber of the small station, down the hall, and past the sleeping quarters. The strange, complex machine greeted them as they walked into the back room. Adam noticed the orange lights were flashing in there as well.

Rising up through the ceiling of the station was a giant antenna-like pillar with a computing station at the base. For such a massive investment, the frequency indicator was surprisingly built simply for easy user-accessibility.

"Well, here goes nothing."

Please work...

Adam entered his PIN into the blinking command prompt.

With a switching noise, the orange indicator lights ceased instantly.

"Wow, that did it! Good idea!" Adam congratulated her, as she returned a rewarding smile.

"Thanks! Lucky guess."

Now let's see what's causing all the commotion...

A microscopic radar map dissolved onto the indicator monitor. At the upper left of the screen, representing billions of kilometers of space travel, a small digital dot blinked on and off. The icon at first glance seemed like a broken pixel behind the screen, but with a closer look, they could see small concentric circles emitting from the speck's glowing core.

What the hell?

They looked down at the data recorder as it spat out analytical data at the base of the screen.

The machine identified the source as a ship emitting tower of some sort, and one that they weren't familiar with. The codes were of Federation origin, but they weren't listed in any of *Music Box's* databases. Adam concluded that it may be a unit no longer in circulation. The processor indicated that the data was being sent from a ship's mainframe computer. After several brief loading screens, the indicator churned out the following data via glitching paragraphs:

Vessel: Supernova
Type: Colonist Transport Ship
Vehicle ID: 20492.12
Clearance ID: 329477

Status: Downed/Damaged (This ship has been listed as MIA – missing in action)
Send damage report: (Y/N)?
Last Seen: Sector 345 – Quadrant 14
Crew: N/A
Responsive: N/A
Keycard ID: 32942-112
Keycard owner: Kale, Derrin
Passenger Access PIN: 185
Name: Ambrose, Brett
Location: N/A – (Possible location: Earth)
Grid coordinates: 2948201-2039-343
Miles: N/A
Last ping: January 27, 3271 A.D.
Current Time: N/A (This file may be corrupt)
Type of Message: Distress signal

The signal was old and very weak. The frequency indicator was struggling to keep the data. Adam doubted the signal was even from this time period. If it was of Earth origin, it may be hundreds of years old.

The Supernova!

The ship the old timers and my grandparents talked about. It disappeared three hundred years ago, just before the discovery of Solis!

Up until now, he thought it was just a ghost story.

"Is this just reaching us now?" Jade asked as her eyes lit up at the discovery.

"Maybe," Adam replied, still mesmerized by the blip on the map. He could hardly believe his eyes. But the proof was there, flashing triumphantly on the console display.

Possible location... Earth? Was Earth still intact?

His jaw descended slowly in awe, unsure of what the signal meant or how they should respond. Or if they could respond.

"I'm going to send a report down to Central Command ASAP," Jade said, hurrying out of the chamber and back down the hall to the control room.

Adam hurriedly snatched out a notepad and pen from his pocket and jotted down the information relayed from the monitor. A second after he finished taking the data, the dot ceased glowing and the readout blinked off, cutting off the signal permanently.

It's still out there! Supernova and her crew are still alive! After all this time...

As Jade's footsteps faded down the corridor to contact Solis about the groundbreaking discovery, Adam gazed up from the terminal, looking through the glossy windows at the endless universe that stretched beyond.

A single, powerful word resonated through his mind.

Life.

END

For more updates on Julian Michael Carver, follow him on social media.
Facebook: @JulianMichaelCarver
Twitter: @JulianMCarve

CHECK OUT OTHER GREAT DINOSAUR THRILLERS

JURASSIC ISLAND
by Viktor Zarkov

Guided by satellite photos and modern technology a ragtag group of survivalists and scientists travel to an uncharted island in the remote South Indian Ocean. Things go to hell in a hurry once the team reaches the island and the massive megalodon that attacked their boats is only the beginning of their desperate fight for survival.

Nothing could have prepared billionaire explorer Joseph Thornton and washed up archaeologist Christopher "Colt" McKinnon for the terrifying prehistoric creatures that wait for them on JURASSIC ISLAND!

K-REX
by L.Z. Hunter

Deep within the Congo jungle, Circuitz Mining employs mercenaries as security for its Coltan mining site. Armed with assault rifles and decades of experience, nothing should go wrong. However, the dangers within the jungle stretch beyond venomous snakes and poisonous spiders. There is more to fear than guerrillas and vicious animals. Undetected, something lurks under the expansive treetop canopy . . .

Something ancient.

Something dangerous.

Kasai Rex!

CHECK OUT OTHER GREAT DINOSAUR THRILLERS

WRITTEN IN STONE
by David Rhodes

Charles Dawson is trapped 100 million years in the past. Trying to survive from day to day in a world of dinosaurs he devises a plan to change his fate. As he begins to write messages in the soft mud of a nearby stream, he can only hope they will be found by someone who can stop his time travel. Professor Ron Fontana and Professor Ray Taggit, scientists with opposing views, each discover the fossilized messages. While attempting to save Charles, Professor Fontana, his daughter Lauren and their friend Danny are forced to join Taggit and his group of mercenaries. Taggit does not intend to rescue Charles Dawson, but to force Dawson to travel back in time to gather samples for Taggit's fame and fortune. As the two groups jump through time they find they must work together to make it back alive as this fast-paced thriller climaxes at the very moment the age of dinosaurs is ending.

HARD TIME
by Alex Laybourne

Rookie officer Peter Malone and his heavily armed team are sent on a deadly mission to extract a dangerous criminal from a classified prison world. A Kruger Correctional facility where only the hardest, most vicious criminals are sent to fend for themselves, never to return.

But when the team come face to face with ancient beasts from a lost world, their mission is changed. The new objective: Survive.

CHECK OUT OTHER GREAT DINOSAUR THRILLERS

SPINOSAURUS
by Hugo Navikov

Brett Russell is a hunter of the rarest game. His targets are cryptids, animals denied by science. But they are well known by those living on the edges of civilization, where monsters attack and devour their animals and children and lay ruin to their shantytowns.

When a shadowy organization sends Brett to the Congo in search of the legendary dinosaur cryptid Kasai Rex, he will face much more than a terrifying monster from the past.

Spinosaurus is a dinosaur thriller packed with intrigue, action and giant prehistoric predators.

LAND OF DEATH
by Eric S Brown & Alex Laybourne

A group of American soldiers, fleeing an organized attack on their base camp in the Middle East, encounter a storm unlike anything they've seen before. When the storm subsides, they wake up to find themselves no longer in the desert and perhaps not even on Earth. The jungle they've been deposited in is a place ruled by prehistoric creatures long extinct. Each day is a struggle to survive as their ammo begins to run low and virtually everything they encounter, in this land they've been hurled into, is a deadly threat.

www.ingramcontent.com/pod-product-compliance
Lightning Source LLC
Chambersburg PA
CBHW031950170626
46807CB00006B/2425